WHO DOES IT HURT?

Paul Robins

PAM !
I'LL NEED A REVIEW
WHEN YOU'RE DONE !
THANKS)
P.Robins 2017

For Helen Robins
who raised four sons
in a home that she filled
with grace and joy.

June, 1953

It's very rude to be loud when someone is dying, so she spoke to her doll in whispers. The other girl's skin was pale compared to her own, and wet with perspiration. She heard snips of adult conversation that were hard to understand.

"She's our only baby," Mama said. "The only one we'll ever have."

"They called again today about Anna, didn't they?" Papa sounded angry.

"God wouldn't take them both, would he? Not both of them…"

"Don't answer the phone anymore."

No, the little girl—just three years old—didn't really understand all that was happening. But she knew to play very quietly while the other girl died.

Paul Robins

Chapter 1

Sacramento, California
Thursday, October 3, 1985

Sid Bigler had only been a private eye for six months and eleven days, but he noticed the guy right away. How could you miss him? He looked like a grown-up version of Danny Partridge, except the nose was all wrong. It was flatter, and the nostrils were double-wide. *Danny Partridge meets Porky Pig.* Yeah, that was it.

Most of the people in the bar didn't give the guy a second glance, but Sid was a people watcher and the face of Porky Partridge was as good as it gets. His eyes were as narrow as his nose was wide—a combination that Sid suspected was not a winner with the ladies—and he had a pretty good scar that ran from one eyebrow down to his jawline. His hair hadn't seen a bottle of shampoo in a while, and the Members Only jacket was way too big for him. The oversized jacket was concealing a large handgun, but Sid wouldn't know that for another thirty seconds.

Somebody to his right—one of the half-dozen attorneys that was sitting at his table—must have cracked a joke, because everyone around him burst out laughing at something. But Sid didn't hear it. He was focused on the

3

guy with the nickel-sized nostrils.

"Hey!"

Porky practically shouted it. The voice was thin and scratchy. Every head in the bar turned and conversations skidded to a halt.

"Hey! Is Thomas Trager here?"

Hmmm. Porky had something on his mind. Sid's creep-o-meter clicked up a notch as he noticed the beads of sweat that had formed on the guy's upper lip and forehead. He recognized the name and knew who Porky was looking for. Hell, anybody who'd lived in Sacramento for more than a few months knew Tom Trager's big grin and cowboy hat from his countless newspaper ads and billboards. He was sitting two tables over. Fifteen feet away.

"Yeah, that's me." Trager raised his Stetson and gave it a little wave in Porky's direction. The famous smile was noticeably absent, and he looked nervous. "What can I do for you?"

And this is the point where Sid, along with everybody else, found out about the gun. Porky reached behind his back and pulled out a big, shiny automatic that must have been tucked in his waistband.

Sid's one previous experience with gunplay had taught him that, when shots are being fired, time simultaneously speeds up and slows down. It's odd. On the one hand, there's no time to react. It's just a flash. But at the same time, the whole world seems to be made of molasses. What occurred over the next few seconds happened in slow motion, and remained vivid in his memory for a long, long time.

He saw the weapon clearly. Saw the arm raising it to eye level, pointing in Trager's direction. He saw Porky's eyes narrow and his nostrils flare even wider. Sid caught himself generating a small list of things that could fit inside that nose. House key. Matchbox car. Maybe a Tootsie Pop. Funny, the things that can race through the mind.

There was a sudden movement to Sid's immediate left. Bertie Jones, was standing and shouting, "Oh, my God, he's got a gun!"

Porky turned his head without firing a shot and looked toward Sid and Bertie, and then the gun was swinging in their direction. The cocktail table in front of him overturned as Sid jumped to his feet, wrapped his arms around Bertie and began pulling her down. They were horizontal, falling through the air, as Sid caught his last glimpse of Porky taking aim. There was a bright flash and a roar, then he hit the ground, his own body now between Bertie and the gunman. The gun roared several more times, accompanied by screams from all directions. Then the sound of footsteps—presumably Porky's—as someone ran from the bar.

The shooting screwed up what had been a very promising night for Sid Bigler. Everything had been going exactly as planned. Thirty minutes earlier, he had made his way through the smoky lounge, inviting admiring glances from every woman in the room. The invitation was universally declined, but he was used to that.

Sid was five foot eight and skinny—all elbows and sharp angles with an adam's apple you could hang your coat on.

His feet were easily two sizes too large for his body, and at thirty-two years old he was still trying to get the hang of maneuvering them through a crowded room. Sid had been a runner in high school and college, and he was still a good one. But he'd learned long ago that being fast and being coordinated are two different things. Sitting atop his head was a nest of red hair, bright and wiry and seldom cooperative. Keep in mind, this was 1985. The hair was big.

The restaurant and bar was called the Ancient Moose. It was a five minute drive from the Capitol and, despite the dumb name, not a bad place for an after-work drink. Before Porky had walked in and screwed everything up, Sid was congratulating himself for looking so casual, so at ease. Everything about the night had appeared unplanned. But it was, in fact, a little scheme he'd hatched with his sister, Gloria, to get himself introduced to a bunch of lawyers. Plenty of private detectives paid most of their bills by doing legwork for attorneys. The night was for schmoozing.

Gloria had caught his attention, waving him toward a table near the bar. She was surrounded by six or seven colleagues, and there might as well have been a neon sign over their heads that read: "Lawyers." Happy hour might have loosened their ties and collars a little, but something about them still oozed 'litigation.' A couple of them looked familiar. Maybe he'd seen them around Gloria's office, or maybe they had a nice photo ad in the Yellow Pages. Sid was known to occasionally flip through the phone book when he was bored.

And, of course, there was one face he knew well. Bertie Jones was the most beautiful woman in the world. The statement is not open for debate. For more than twenty years, Sid was a dog and the sight of Bertie Jones was Pavlov's bell. You'd think a boyhood crush would fade a little after a couple of decades, wouldn't you? But, no. Not this one.

"Sid, you made it." Gloria stood and kissed him on the cheek. "Here, sit down between me and Bertie."

Well, that was going to make things difficult. His goal was to impress a group of potential clients, and now the odds of him saying something stupid just went up about three hundred percent. Sid did not have a good track record of being glib while in the presence of Bertie Jones. It wasn't his fault. It was something chemical.

Just don't look at her eyes, he thought. *Not the eyes.*

Overall, Sid did an admirable job of being charming, especially considering the fact that the cramped accommodations had him bumping knees with Bertie all night long. One of the men in their circle—a guy named Donald who Sid thought bore a strong resemblance to Eddie Murphy—finished a story about some female attorney they all knew that was rumored to have been spotted in Judge Rathman's chambers rummaging around underneath his robe. Then Gloria reported that their firm had just agreed to represent the Hershey chocolate company. Apparently a fellow had snuck away from his tour group at the Oakdale factory and gotten his hand caught in the machine that squirts out the Hershey's Kisses. The guy was now of the opinion that losing his love of chocolate (and two fingers) was worth twelve million dollars.

Eventually—and with only a little coaxing from Sid—the

conversation had turned to Sacramento's newest detective agency, *Bigler Investigations*. The name had a nice ring to it. Upscale and serious.

"Business isn't bad," said Sid. Not exactly a lie, but a very generous description. "For now I'm working out of the office in the back of the deli."

That will sound odd to the uninitiated, but everybody in town knew about *Sid & Eddie's*. The deli was a landmark. An institution. Only a block from the Capitol, the family business had been one of the premier spots in town for a cheap political power lunch since the day it opened in 1947. And the breakfasts were awesome.

"Sid, the Deli Detective," said Donald.

"That's me," said Sid, and he took a swig of his Coke. No ice.

"Tell them about some of the cases you've been working on." Gloria played the proud big sister.

"Oh, nothing very exciting, but it's bread and butter stuff for private investigators. The last two clients were women who suspected their husbands were cheating on them. I just did some checking around. Tailed the guys a few times."

"And…?" It was Bertie.

"Hmm?" Sid cocked his head to his left, avoiding looking directly into the eyes.

"And were they cheating?"

"Oh. Yes and no. One guy was sneaking around with a waitress at the Sambo's on Fair Oaks Boulevard, and one guy was bowling."

"Bowling?" Bertie again, sounding amused. Sid's

knees went a little weak.

"Yeah, Tuesdays and Thursdays. The guy told his wife that he had to work late, but he was bowling. You shoulda seen the wife. You'd have been bowling, too."

That got a laugh from the lawyers, and Sid relaxed a little. And that's when he made a big mistake. At the sound of Bertie's laugh—like honey, like a breeze on a hot day—Sid turned and looked right at her. He couldn't help it. Forgetting the danger, he had looked into her eyes…

It was the summer of 1963. Sid was ten. Bertie had been Sid's big sister's best friend for as long as he could remember. It had not, as yet, occurred to him that she might be beautiful. Such thoughts had never entered his mind. But there comes a time when some mysterious and wonderful gland produces a hormone that renders a boy's frontal lobe completely useless, and strange new thoughts make the world grow foggy. It was the summer of 1963.

Bertie had arrived mid-day and was staying for a sleepover. She and Gloria, both thirteen, had managed to spend the day talking in the living room, talking in the back yard, talking in the bedroom, talking in the bathroom. God, how could they have so much to say? Sid was unable to round up one of his buddies for the day, and so he divided his time between exploring the vacant lot down the street and finding ways to irritate his sister and her friend. He was particularly proficient at the latter.

At the end of the day, long after his parents had tucked the kids safely in bed, Sid decided to mount one final assault on his sister's happiness. He absent-mindedly flipped through some old comic books as he formulated a loose plan, waiting until he was sure the girls were asleep. It had been more than a year since the tragic demise of his Ant Farm colony—perhaps because of neglect, perhaps because of the occasional vigorous shaking it received. Regardless, the Ant Farm's contents of tiny dead insects and crumbly white sand would make an excellent addition to Gloria's bed.

It was just after 1 a.m. when Sid crept down the hallway and into his sister's room. In his hand he clutched a flashlight that was equipped with red and blue filters that made it ideal for nighttime operations. Sid had the filter set to blue. The Ant Farm was tucked under one arm.

A shaft of moonlight poured through the window, clearly showing the outline of two lumps in the bed. Sid went to one side and there was Gloria sound asleep. The early teenage years were not kind to his sister. She was gangly, and she slept with a metal and plastic contraption around her neck that had wires and rubber bands going into her mouth. Perhaps because of the orthodontic torture device, her mouth hung half open in her sleep, and Sid could just make out a little puddle of drool spreading its way across her pillow. There were lots of freckles and a handful of pimples. The soft blue glow of his flashlight did her no favors.

Then Sid made his way quietly around to the other side of the bed, where moonlight framed the sleeping face of Bertie Jones. Long seconds ticked by, and the hand with the flashlight slowly lowered and hung aimlessly at his side. Most guys can't point to the moment when they realized that the difference between boys and girls was going to play a central role in their life—a consuming role both wonderful and terrible. But this was Sid's moment, and it hit him like a freight train. Hit him in a way he'd never forget. He would later wonder just how long he stood there.

Plenty of girls had blonde hair, but not like this. Bertie's was *yellow. To young Sid's eye, it was yellow like lemon pie. Yellow like some flowers his mom had planted in the front yard. It spilled across the pillow in thick waves. And he noticed for the first time that Bertie Jones had a little cleft in her chin. Even in the moonlight it was easy to see, making a soft line that pointed up to her lips.*

A ten-year-old boy stood quietly in the darkness, taking inventory of a sleeping girl's face, and he began to feel something profound that he'd never felt before. It would be a mistake to think that this was merely a sexual awakening. That's certainly part of it, and there would be countless times in the future when Sid's thoughts of Bertie Jones wouldn't be nearly so innocent. Times when he would dwell not on her face, but on other parts below. But on that night, young Sid was defining beauty itself, and coming to understand that vacant lots and comic books were insignificant when compared to something inside of him that was deep and powerful and ancient.

And then Bertie opened her eyes. The green, green eyes.

Sid stopped breathing and his heart pounded in his ears. She was looking right at him. She didn't move a muscle and neither did he. She showed no sign of being startled. Her face wore the same peaceful expression and the lips above the cleft chin remained still. Even as Sid's pulse raced, he could see that Bertie's breathing was slow and steady, her chest rising and falling ever so slightly. She just stared at him, and it took the sum of his ten-year-old courage to stand there, to not turn and run from those green eyes. It was as though her eyes had a light of their own, and the moon itself couldn't compete with them.

Sid had no idea how long the two of them looked at one another. In later years he developed the theory that she wasn't even awake that night. That Bertie Jones had opened her eyes while still sound asleep, like when some people walk or talk in their sleep. Regardless, after a time, the green eyes closed without a word being spoken. Sid returned quietly to his room, following the blue beam of his flashlight and carrying his Ant Farm…

It was pure chaos in the bar. There was screaming and crying, and Sid could hear the bartender on the telephone to 9-1-1. "Yes, there's been a shooting. Yes, there was a guy with a gun. People have been shot!"

From further away, a woman's voice was calling out, "Is there a doctor? We need a doctor! Help!"

Sid realized that he was, for the first time in his life, in a position he'd dreamed of a thousand times in his youth. He was laying next to Bertie Jones, his arms around her. But, of course, in his dreams there was never all this blood. Blood everywhere.

"Bertie? Bertie, are you okay?"

Sid reached up, put a hand on her face and waited for the green eyes to open. And waited.

Chapter 2

Two hours later, Sid and his sister were still in the bar along with everyone else who had been present at the shooting. The only exceptions were Bertie, who was at the UCD Med Center, and Trager, whose body had just been rolled away by two guys from the coroner's office.

Sid caught himself staring at his hands again. As soon as Bertie had been taken away by the paramedics, he'd run to the restroom and washed the blood from his hands. He had to take off his shirt in an effort to rinse out a red stain on the front that was easily the size of a volleyball. But it was his hands that kept bothering him. Like he was some low-budget Pontius Pilate or Lady Macbeth.

"C'mon, man! If you're not gonna let us go, can we at least get a drink?" It was the same jerk who had been complaining loudly from the minute the cops had announced that the bar was closed and that no one could leave until everyone had been interviewed. The rest of the customers and staff—maybe forty people—realized that the shooting was important enough to justify their inconvenience. But there's an ass in every crowd. In fact, consider yourself lucky when there's only one.

In defense of the loudmouthed jerk, the evening was growing long and everyone was anxious to get out of the place. People had spoken in urgent, hushed tones for the first hour or so after the cops had gotten there. Then everyone just seemed to run out of gas. The emotional energy that had been expended in the moments after the

13

shooting had taken its toll, and now people sat quietly in their groups, hollow-eyed, watching and waiting for their turn to be interviewed. It felt a little weird.

Detective Woody Carver made his way across the room toward Sid and Gloria. Picture Stretch Armstrong without the stretch. Now give him a dark suit and a brushy, black crew cut. That's Woody Carver. He slid into a chair next to Sid and his sister.

"Any word on how Bertie's doing?" Gloria asked.

The cop shook his head. "Nothing. She was alive when she got to the hospital, and that's the last we heard. Sorry." Then he turned and looked Sid squarely in the eye. "You okay?"

"Yeah," said Sid, forcing a smile. "Okay."

Sid and Woody were unlikely friends. Sid was born and raised in Sacramento, ran track and cross country in high school and college. Woody grew up in Michigan, all hockey and football. A Chihuahua and a Bulldog. But it was a friendship that ran deep.

"We're just about done getting preliminary statements. We'll have everybody out of here in a little while. Kaminski's just got those last two." Woody indicated one of the other cops chatting with two women who were both wearing little black cocktail dresses and smeared mascara. "The forensics team can finish up after you're all gone."

For the last hour there had been a couple of guys collecting things and putting them in little plastic bags. Empty bullet casings and Q-tips mostly.

"Busy day at the office, Detective?" Sid finally sounded a little like himself.

"Well, it's not every day that two members of the city council get shot during your shift."

Bertie Jones was the youngest member of the Sacramento City Council, and Tom Trager—may he rest in peace—had been the oldest. Sid knew Bertie well, having grown up worshipping her. But Trager was a different story. Oh, everybody knew the public Tom Trager. Trager's Hardware on El Camino Avenue was an institution, and it must be said that it was a wonderful place. Sid's dad had first taken him there when he was very little, and he fell in love with it immediately. Sure, there were hammers and nails, garden hoses and bags of cement. But Trager's Hardware had model airplanes, too. And croquet sets and camping gear and slingshots and mini-bikes. The place was huge, and Sid still loved going there. He'd stopped by the store just a week ago and bought himself a screwdriver set and a Sugar Daddy.

Tom Trager was the smiling face of Trager's Hardware. He'd started it with his brother in 1952. To see his billboards and to walk through his store was to assume that the guy was everybody's favorite uncle. Somebody who knew Santa Claus personally. But the fact was, Trager was a self-serving creep. Just ask any of his wives.

About ten years ago he'd made a run at politics. Given that he'd had his face plastered on newspaper ads and billboards for thirty years, it was no surprise that he cruised onto the city council. People vote for a name they recognize. That's just the way it is.

While the citizens of Sacramento in general maintained the same image of lovable old Tom Trager, those who worked with him on the council came to know a different person. Patronizing, quick-tempered, and always looking out for his own interests. He did favors for friends and nakedly used his position to curry the favor of anyone who might do him some good, whether in business or politics. Sid had known none of this until five years earlier, when he took over the deli after his dad's death. But after he'd spent some time in the business community, he began to hear the stories. You couldn't attend a chamber of commerce event without having two or three people mention that Trager was an asshole. And yet he'd been re-elected twice thanks to the smiling image that peered out from the pages of The Sacramento Bee and looked down from the billboards.

"You guys don't do that chalk outline thing anymore?" Sid asked.

"We figured that photographs and forty-three witnesses would do the trick." Woody leaned forward, elbows on knees. "It's funny. You almost always get some kind of conflicting reports from eyewitnesses. But not this time. Every person we've talked to says the shooter came in looking for Trager."

"Yeah, well, when the only thing the guy says is, 'I'm looking for Tom Trager,' it's a pretty safe conclusion."

"And why do you figure he fired a shot at you and Bertie Jones?"

"Gotta be because Bertie stood up and shouted," said Sid. "She pointed at the guy and she shouted. I guess he got rattled, turned and popped off a shot at her."

"And then he turned back and unloaded on Trager."

"Well, I was on the ground with Bertie and didn't see

him fire the other shots. But since Trager was full of holes, I guess that's a safe bet."

"Woody," said Gloria. "Can you get me out of here? I'm dying to get to the hospital and check on Bertie. And has anybody called her mom?"

"I don't know about the mother. I'll check on that. You should be able to leave soon. But listen…" Woody leaned in closer, and the other two instinctively did the same. He spoke quietly. "This is a big deal for me. Don't get me wrong, it's awful. And I'm really sorry your friend has been hurt. But I was the homicide detective on call tonight. The case is mine for now, and I wanna keep it. This would be huge for me."

"So?" Sid said it, but Gloria had the same questioning look on her face.

"So you guys are connected to this case. This is the most high profile murder in this town in a long time. I want it. But Stokes knows that I know you two."

Aaaah. That made sense. Lieutenant Benjamin Stokes had butted heads with Sid a few years ago—something about a major crime spree and Sid being the prime suspect. It had all worked out fine, but there was no love lost between them. Stokes was now the head of Homicide, and Woody was worried about having the case assigned to someone else.

"So you'd appreciate it if I could keep a low profile during this investigation."

"Yeah. If you could just…"

"Act like we don't know each other and forget about the fact that sometimes you and I work together?"

"We don't *work* together," Woody insisted.

"We don't? I could've sworn you were with me when we staked out that pool hall last month. And I'm pretty sure we were in your car when we tailed that lowlife who was hanging out around the high school. If that's not working together, what do you call it?"

"Charity."

"Oh… Oh, that hurts…"

In the six and a half months since Sid had gotten his Private Investigator's license, he'd had exactly five paying cases. Total fees collected so far: $325. Two of those cases had Sid hanging out in rougher neighborhoods than usual, and he decided that he'd be more comfortable with Woody around. Even out of uniform, Woody Carver had a wonderful, intimidating way about himself. Sid offered to pay him to come along, and Woody had balked at first. But Sid pointed out that plenty of beat cops make extra money on the side by working security at concerts and special events. Why not detectives? "*And besides,*" he'd told him, "*I'm scared and desperate.*" So Woody had helped out on two of his cases, and Sid had paid him $150 for each one. Which means, if you're doing the math, that Sid Bigler was netting an average of five dollars per case after expenses. The business plan needed work.

"Don't be an ass, Sid. You know what I mean."

"If it was charity, I wouldn't be paying you."

"Look, I wasn't breaking any rules when I was helping you. None of those were active cases."

"That's funny. I thought maybe you were breaking a rule when you ran the license plate numbers on that Monte

Carlo we followed. But maybe I don't understand all that stuff."

Woody let out a long breath and ran a hand over his face. "What do I have to say to get you to keep your mouth shut?"

Sid grabbed a handful of nuts off the table and popped a few in his mouth. "How about, '*We really do work together, Sid, and you're a top notch Private Investigator.*' That's what I'd like to hear."

"Do I have to say it right now?"

"Nah. Take a couple of days. Practice in front of a mirror."

It was fifteen minutes later that everyone was told they were free to go. Gloria picked up her purse without saying a word and made a dash for the hospital. Most of the people in the room moved more slowly, gathering their stuff and making their way to the door. It was a little after 9 p.m. Sid enjoyed a brief feeling of relief, but quickly discovered that he didn't know what to do with himself. What do you do after witnessing a murder? Go get a burger? Catch a movie?

When he stepped out of the Ancient Moose and into the parking lot, Sid was surprised by the amount of activity. He shouldn't have been. The press was everywhere. Four TV vans with big, obnoxious logos were parked on the street right in front. Cameras with bright lights were trained on several people he recognized from inside the bar as reporters in rumpled sportcoats held microphones in their faces. Others were being interviewed by guys who were scribbling furiously on notepads. Occasionally a flash bulb went off.

Sid had been the focus of a media frenzy once before, and he wanted no part of it. Good thing he wasn't the first one out the door. He kept his head down, jumped in his car and pointed it in the general direction of his mom's house. After his dad died, Sid had moved back in to help his mother. He'd intended to stay for just a few months, but somehow five years had gone by.

It took less than ten minutes to reach the house in Land Park. He rolled to a stop and set the parking brake. The hula girl on the dash nodded a few times before taking a rest. Sid reached up and turned off the lights, then put his hand on the key. But he didn't turn it. He sat in the dark, engine running, and tried to figure out what he was feeling. His gut was clenched, his breathing was shallow. It was obvious what was bothering him, right? A woman he'd known his entire life—a woman whose image had kept him awake at night through his teenage years and much of his twenties—had just been shot while in his arms. Of course he was upset.

But there was something else. Something that tugged at the back of his mind. A white noise in the background. Something different that he couldn't get at.

Sid crossed his arms, leaned his head back and closed his eyes. He took a deep breath and let it out slowly. And that's when he felt the little hole in his shirt. It was in the right sleeve, up close to his shoulder. He'd dressed very carefully for his meeting with the lawyers, and it definitely wasn't there earlier when he went into the bar. His heart rate doubled.

Sid put the car in gear and pulled away from the curb

and the hula girl began to dance again. Halfway down the street he popped the lights back on.

Chapter 3

Sid awoke in the same position that he'd fallen asleep—flat on his back with his head on Amy's lap. In a dream he'd been playing with his dog. Sid was throwing a little rubber football as far as he could, and Buster was racing after it again and again. God, it was great to throw the ball again for that dog, even if it was only a dream. Buster had been dead for twenty years. It was a shame to wake up.

Sid looked up at Amy who was still sound asleep, her head lolled back against the sofa cushion. Probably not her most flattering angle. Nevertheless, she looked great in the dim morning light. Amy didn't have the paralyzing beauty of Bertie Jones, but the same could be said for every other woman on planet Earth. He lay quietly and studied the face of his sleeping fiancée.

Yes, fiancée. The sum total of Sid's romantic life after thirty-two years was a tale of two women. One he would never have (the one who'd been shot last night, but for the moment a sleepy-eyed Sid had forgotten), and one who was somehow managing to sleep soundly while sitting up, one arm crooked behind her head and one draped across Sid's chest. The tiniest of snores escaped her, somehow still feminine. He took a deep breath and let it out slowly, content to be waking up with Amy.

Sid watched her sleep, allowing his mind to wander, and ended up thinking about a kid who had been his best friend from third grade through the first half of high school. Richie Petigrew—the guy who was accidentally responsible for *Sid's Big Revelation About Women.*

Richie had lived three doors down, and he cared about only one thing in life. Baseball. A lot of kids played and loved the game growing up, Sid included. But Richie was different. He *worshipped* the game. It occupied most of his waking life. In their younger days, Richie would often wear his mitt around even when there was no ball to be played. It wasn't uncommon for him to have the thing on when they were just hanging out, riding their bikes or going to the movies. Most of the year he had that funny tan—all brown except for a pale white left hand.

Richard Petigrew worked his ass off and he got pretty good. He was starting shortstop on the varsity team as a sophomore. But as the years went by it was clear that he didn't have *the gift.* It was something you had to be born with. There was a guy who played for Sac High that went on to have a decent career with the Cardinals. As high school players, the difference between that guy and Richie was day and night. You could see it in the way they walked, the way they held their heads.

Shortly before Richie's family moved away, he and Sid had one of their few serious conversations. Something about goodbyes—like signing yearbooks at the end of a school year—makes philosophers of teenagers. Sid made some joke about maybe seeing Richie one day on TV playing in the World Series, and his friend assured him that was never going to happen. Richie said he'd come to the conclusion that, as much as he loved baseball, it was time to get serious about other stuff.

"It was just a dream, Sid. Regular guys never get to play in

the Big Leagues."

Richie hadn't even seemed sad when he said it. The two stayed in touch through college and for a few years beyond. The last Sid heard, his childhood friend was a civil engineer in San Diego.

Anyway, at the end of that school year—not long after Richie had moved away—fifteen-year-old Sid Bigler was hanging around the house when he had *Sid's Big Revelation About Women*. It was the night of his sister's Senior Prom, 1968. Gloria and Bertie had been upstairs for hours getting ready. The doorbell rang, and Sid's dad let in a couple of guys in rented tuxedos. One looked like Squiggy from *Laverne & Shirley*, and one looked like something from the cover of a romance novel. Sid had never seen the good-looking one before, but it was obvious that this was a college guy. Sideburns and everything. Gloria and Bertie came down the stairs and his sister, looking slightly uncomfortable with her elbow-length gloves and goofy bouffant hairdo, took the arm of Squiggy. Bertie, in a simple white dress and looking like a goddess, took the arm of Mr. Handsome. And as the door closed behind them, the light bulb popped on in Sid's head:

Regular guys never get to play in the Big Leagues.

Bertie Jones was the Majors. She was a dream, like Richie Petigrew's dream of playing for the Giants. Like that game of catch with Buster the dog.

These were the practical, satisfied thoughts of Sid Bigler as he lay on the sofa looking at Amy. Her front teeth, just a little too big for her mouth, peeked out through her slightly parted lips. Marrying Amy Solomon wasn't settling for second best. It was simply growing up. The wedding was two months away.

The room was now noticeably brighter. Sid reached up with one hand and rubbed his eyes. It occurred to him for the first time to wonder why he was waking up at Amy's apartment.

Then the real world came flooding in and the events of last night hit him all at once. The guy with the piggy nose and the silver gun. Holding Bertie in his arms and all the blood. Leaving his mom's house to drive by the hospital, Bertie still in surgery. Driving late to Amy's because he didn't want to be alone. Curling up on the sofa, talking and talking. And now the sun was up.

What was the sun doing up?

"Damn!" Sid sat up with a jerk and startled Amy. "What time is it?"

He hopped up and began patting his pants pockets looking for his keys. Then he turned in a circle in search of his jacket.

"What time is it?"

Amy sat up straighter, running a hand through her hair. She held her watch close to her face and blinked repeatedly. "Uhhh... it's just after 6:30."

"Damn!"

Sid snatched his jacket and headed for the door, then did a u-turn and gave Amy a quick but serious kiss.

"I love you."

"Yep. Love you."

Ten minutes later Sid was running the five blocks from

his favorite parking place to the deli. He could've found a closer spot, but parking was free on P Street. He'd gotten the cheapskate gene from his father. Besides, for an old cross-country guy that still ran forty or fifty miles a week, it was a no-brainer. He generally enjoyed the walk. But this morning he wasn't walking. Sid was late and he was running.

He arrived at Sid & Eddie's Deli at 6:45, almost an hour later than usual. Looking through the window, he could see that Eddie and Joe had the place just about ready to open. Proof once again that the deli really could run without him. He let himself relax a little.

He watched Eddie working—slowly and silently. Childlike, guileless, Eddie was less of an enigma than he once was. Sid had to occasionally remind himself that this handsome black man was almost exactly his own age. A head injury when he was a boy had left Eddie damaged in ways that doctors could never fully explain. He had been robbed of his ability to speak, but there was more to it than that. If he grasped the nuance of social interaction, it never showed. He had a perpetual smile on his face and clear, thoughtful eyes, but the expression never changed. He could follow any simple instruction, but generally wouldn't or couldn't make a decision on his own. Work at the deli seemed to suit him perfectly, and as far as anyone could tell, he was happy there. Sid's father had loved Eddie, and the deli was his place in the world. About six month's after his dad was murdered, Sid changed the name of the place to *Sid & Eddie's*. The old man would've approved.

Joe Diaz' big arms rippled as he scrubbed down the grill

with a wire pad. Joe had been Sid's father's oldest friend. They'd met aboard the USS Texas in the Navy, and after the war they opened the deli together. For thirty-three years, almost every omelet, salad, burger or french fry that had been served at the place came from Joe's hands. Six foot three and barrel-chested, the guy had to be close to seventy years old now, but he was still as strong as a bear.

As Sid pulled the door closed behind him, Joe looked up from the counter and said, "Where the hell have you been?"

Sid stopped in his tracks. He would have been less surprised if that statue of Colonel Sanders at the KFC had spoken to him. The only time Joe talked was when you asked him a question, and you rarely got more than a two-word answer.

"Uh, I overslept. Sorry."

"Your mom and your sister both called. Your mother's worried about you. Said you never came home last night. And Gloria's got some news about a friend of yours that got shot."

Joe went back to work on the grill, a scowl on his face, and Sid stood there silently for a moment. Eddie never even looked up. Feeling like he'd been hit with a two-by-four, Sid headed behind the counter toward the back room to get the money drawer so he could set up the cash register. As he passed by Joe, the big man stopped and looked at him. If Joe had been angry a moment ago, it was gone now.

"You okay?"

"Yeah," Sid said, unsure if it was true.

"You never been late before."

Sid went into the back of the deli and grabbed a clean

shirt out of the top drawer of the old metal filing cabinet. You work in a restaurant, you discover it's a good idea keep a change of clothes. As he unbuttoned the rumpled shirt that he'd slept in, he looked again at what was left of the big stain on the front, now an ugly pinkish-brown color after his attempt to rinse it out. And then he remembered his discovery of the night before. He looked at the right shirt sleeve, and in the light of the back room he saw now that there were actually two little holes side by side. They were a little uneven, less than the diameter of his pinky. One where the bullet went in, one where the bullet went out.

The front door opened at seven and so began a typical, busy workday—maybe busier than usual—and it flew by. It wasn't until about eight o'clock that Sid noticed the headline of the newspaper as somebody at the counter was reading it. "City Council Shooting!" Black block letters ran the width of the front page. Sid looked over his customer's shoulder and scanned the article. Surprisingly, most of the facts looked right as far as he could remember. And he was relieved to not see his name anywhere, at least on the front page.

"Hell of a thing, huh?" The customer had caught him looking.

"Yeah." Sid picked up the guy's empty plate. "Crazy."

The highlight of the morning was the phone call from his sister. Gloria had spent the night at the hospital. Bertie Jones had come out of surgery a little after midnight. The bullet had passed cleanly through her, just below the collar bone on the left side, missing the top of her lung and all the major nerves and blood vessels. Minimal damage, but a lot of blood loss. She was awake this morning and feeling fairly well, considering.

Sid's mom arrived just before the lunch rush as usual, gave him kind of a suspicious look, grabbed an apron and went to work without speaking to him. Sid hid a smile at the time, knowing exactly what this was about and knowing there was a lecture coming. About two in the afternoon—shortly before closing—Rose pulled Sid into the back room like he was a sixth grader.

"So, you spent the night at Amy's last night?"

"Yes, mom."

"You know how I feel about that."

"We fell asleep on the sofa. That's all."

Rose's chin dipped slightly and she raised her left eyebrow. This was the same expression a twelve -year-old Sid would've gotten when he said, "I never even saw those chocolate chips" or "I don't know what happened to the Wilson's cat."

But now Sid was thirty-two, and the confrontation with his mom was a curious mix of annoying and amusing. He learned long ago that it was a mistake to say something when given Rose's 'eyebrow look.' It was best to just keep making eye contact and stay quiet. A few awkward/funny seconds ticked by.

"Hm." Rose may or may not have been satisfied. "I'll talk with Amy. *Her* I can trust."

At that, Sid finally did smile. It was a mistake, but he couldn't help it. His mother's affection for Amy was one of life's wonderful surprises. Sid was three years younger than his fiancée, and for the first couple of years that they dated, his mom was deeply suspicious of the older woman that was after her son. But one day Amy had asked Rose if she could go to church with her, and entirely different alliances were formed from that moment forward. Sid maintained his father's indifference toward church, being dragged along only at Christmas and Easter. But it became a regular thing with Amy and Rose, so now in his mother's eyes, she was the innocent and Sid was the scoundrel.

"I don't like that smile, young man. This is not funny."

"What? Talk to Amy. You'll see."

Rose Bigler, barely five feet tall, raised up on her tip-toes to kiss her son on the cheek, then turned and headed for the door as she pulled off her apron.

"I'll see you tonight?" She said it like it was a question, but it wasn't. It was instructions.

"It's Friday. I might be out late."

"But you're sleeping in your own bed?"

"Yeah, mom. Scout's honor."

The rest of the day was uneventful, particularly when compared to the day before. Sid stopped by the hospital after he locked up the deli, only to be told that Bertie was sleeping. He picked up a Butterfinger candy bar in the hospital gift shop and left it for her. Butterfingers had always been her favorite. Following a late afternoon nap, Sid grabbed dinner with Amy at the Spaghetti Factory. Then she went off to catch a movie with some girlfriends and he went for a ten-mile run. A quick shower and he was in bed by ten. At his mom's house where he belonged.

Chapter 4

Nathan Bomke was a son of a bitch, but he smelled great. Sid was no expert on men's fragrances, but he could recognize Old Spice and Aqua Velva, and Bomke didn't smell like either of those. He smelled expensive.

"Hey, I like what you've done with the place. The big jars of pickles are a very classy touch."

Ten o'clock Saturday morning. The deli was closed on the weekends, but "Bigler Investigations" was open for business. When you work somewhere every day, you become immune to what it looks like. But now Sid sat behind his cheap metal desk in the back of the deli and realized that the place looked like crap. It was, after all, the storage room of a forty-year-old deli in an eighty-year-old building.

"Yeah," said Sid, "I'm gonna be getting a separate office pretty soon. I've only had my license for about six months."

Sid gestured toward the wooden chair that sat across from his desk, inviting his guest to take a seat. But Bomke continued to take his slow, self-guided tour. An ancient black payphone hung by the back door, with countless names, numbers and notes scribbled in pen or pencil on the wall beside it. Since the deli wasn't open on Saturdays, the metal bread racks were empty and the shelves and counters were wiped down. But piles of dishes—mostly clean—sat stacked with no particular order in mind. A mop handle rose from a bucket in the corner that was filled with a liquid that was the color of turd soup, and a small box of artificial

31

sweeteners had been dropped nearby, spilling little pink packets across the floor.

Bomke had very nearly finished his slow circle of the "office" when he peeked into the stainless steel sink and made a little face. Sid couldn't recall what had been left sitting in there, but it couldn't be good. Then, at last, the man who was potentially Sacramento's sleaziest attorney arrived at Sid's desk and took a seat.

"Your Private Investigator's license—you have to pass a test? Fill out a form and pay a five dollar fee? What?"

"There's more to it than that," Sid said. "The state requires at least three years of compensated experience in investigative work, either as a cop or working with a private investigation agency. Then, if you pass the written test, it's a hundred twenty-five bucks for the license."

Nathan Bomke crossed his legs, reached up with one hand and pinched at his lower lip, and a deeply pensive expression crossed his face. Sid had been feeling a little intimidated, but the phony intellectual pose by the lawyer struck him as funny and he relaxed a little. Bomke was more foppish than he remembered.

It had been years since he'd seen the guy. Their one and only meeting had been in a downtown jail cell one summer day when they'd both been arrested. When all was said and done, Sid was found innocent of the charges against him and Bomke, while most certainly guilty of his crimes, was too slippery to get convicted. Interesting that the guy hadn't brought up their first meeting, either on the phone when he called to set up the meeting, or when they exchanged greetings at the deli door just a few minutes ago. *Did he remember?*

The lawyer maintained his stare across the metal desk, apparently studying the deli detective. And in return, Sid began to play the game in his mind that had occupied and entertained him since he was a kid. Everybody looked like somebody—who did this guy look like?

Nathan Bomke was undeniably handsome. The wavy, sandy-colored hair looked familiar, a little too long for most guys in a professional job, but Bomke really pulled it off— strategically blown and sprayed to cross the top of his ears and curl over the collar of his suit. An angular, tanned face. Perfect white teeth. Yeah, he looked like *somebody*. Then Sid got it. *Who was the guy who sang* Sara Smile *and* Rich Girl *and* Kiss On My List? *The one with no moustache—Was it Hall or Oates? Whatever. He looked like* that *guy*.

"How busy are you?"

"Hmm?" Sid snapped out of it.

"How busy are you? You have time for a new case?"

It looked like Mr. Maneater had decided Bigler Investigations was up to the job. Sid resisted the urge to say "yippee".

"Sure. I can make some time for you."

"You can run a deli and do investigations?"

"Not a problem," Sid replied, and he thought it sounded pretty good. Confident. "My staff handles most of the day-to-day here. I haven't had a client complain yet."

"And how many clients have you had?"

Damn lawyers. Sid held his gaze for a few seconds, and Hall (or Oates) gave him a little smirk. Sid figured he'd better say something before it became a problem.

33

"Pick a number between one and twenty."

"Good enough," Bomke said, and he honestly seemed satisfied. He pulled a manila folder from his briefcase and dropped it on the desk. "This will require a small amount of travel."

Sid slid the folder across the desk and opened it. There was a sheet of paper that was clearly a contract of some kind with signatures at the bottom, a few letters and financial statements, and several photographs of a little girl, maybe eight or nine years old. The attorney reached over and pointed at the contract.

"In March of this year, Gerald and Nancy Mercer entered into a legally binding agreement with Li'l Starz Talent Agency of Sacramento to represent their daughter, Mandy."

"Mandy Mercer."

"Well, her legal name is Eunice. Mandy is the stage name. Regardless, certain claims were made regarding representation. Although no specific promises were given, the Mercers were led to believe that Mandy would find employment as a child actress or model."

Sid took a moment to study the photographs of the girl. She looked like a young Gene Hackman with a wig. Sid believed it was important to always be completely honest with clients, so he said the obvious.

"She's ugly."

"Oh, yes. Like a baby 'possum. But Li'l Starz took their money and implied that the girl had 'the look' people wanted. Six months later, the Mercers claimed that nothing had happened. No auditions, no phone calls from prospective employers. The agency responded that not only had they sought employment locally, but they'd taken a trip to Los Angeles specifically to show Mandy's portfolio to some Hollywood casting agents. The Mercers claim no such trip was ever made. After a number of phone calls and letters went unreturned, Mr. Mercer confronted the president of Li'l Starz, it escalated into a shouting match, then violence."

Sid knew enough about Nathan Bomke to see where this was going. Bomke's bread and butter was the easy lawsuit, claiming damages for injuries real or imagined. Or manufactured. And in the universe of accident injury attorneys, Nathan Bomke was one of the brightest stars. You could tell by the suit that he was good at his job.

"So you're suing this sleazy children's talent agency for fraud or false advertising or whatever. And for breaking little Mandy's heart."

Bomke feigned a little shock. "Absolutely not. My client is Li'l Starz. They entered into an agreement in good faith and represented the hideous little girl to the best of their ability, more or less. Look at the photos, Bigler. What work was the child going to get? A commercial for dog food? Pediatric plastic surgery? Li'l Starz did their very best to procure employment for the little girl—I think it's a girl— and what they got in return was an assault."

"An assault?"

"The president of Li'l Starz is Howard Clark, sixty-three years old with a prosthetic left leg. Mr. Clark was confronted and ultimately attacked by Gerald Mercer— father of the ugly girl—on August 16th. The police report is available."

"And I'm guessing that little Mandy's daddy is well to do?"

Nathan Bomke very plainly dropped his façade for a moment and gave Sid a genuine grin. "Loaded."

"Meaning?"

"Five 7-11's, three Straw Hat Pizzas, and the car wash on L Street."

"Not bad. So, what am I supposed to do for you and, uh, the Li'l Starz guy? What's the name again?"

"Howard Clark. Much of this case will simply be one party's word against the other. I'd like you to provide proof that Li'l Starz did, in fact, make a good faith effort to procure modeling or acting work for the Mercer's beautiful little girl. And in particular, prove that Mr. Clark was indeed in Hollywood talking to casting agents on the day he says he was there. Shouldn't be difficult at all, but make it look good. Run up your bill a little. Travel down to L.A. and talk to some people. I'll need the jury to think you really did a hell of a job."

In Sid's limited experience, this was not the typical client-investigator conversation. *Run up the bill a little*? Sid needed the work, but it didn't take a genius to figure that something about this smelled. A very brief, vigorous debate ensued inside his head. Should he take the money, or take the high road?

"I'm a hundred fifty bucks a day." Sid managed to say it without laughing. It was twice what he'd gotten for his first few cases, but what the hell. If he was going to sell his integrity, he was going to get top dollar for it. Besides,

Bomke looked like he could afford it.

"Not a problem," said the lawyer, and he stood up to leave. As easy as that.

"I'll give Li'l Starz a call early next week," said Sid. "And should I contact the girl's father—Mr. Mercer—too?"

"Absolutely not. Under no circumstances."

"Why not? Shouldn't I talk to everybody?"

"Bigler, my job is to paint the ugly kid's daddy as a bully and a liar. I can do that without your help. Your job is specifically to come up with something that can prove that my client is telling the truth."

Sid let that sink in for a moment. Without another word, Nathan Bomke turned and left the office/storage room and headed out through the deli. Sid followed.

"Hey, counselor. What if I don't find any evidence to support your client's story?"

"Oh, I think you'll find something useful," said Nathan Bomke as he swung open the front door. "It's why I'm paying you two hundred dollars a day."

The door closed and Sid found himself standing alone in his deli. He felt an odd mixture of exhilaration and revulsion. Two hundred bucks a day was big. Way more than he thought he could get. On the other hand, it was pretty clear that he had just climbed in bed with a slimeball. The message behind the lawyer's parting sentence was unmistakable: *"Give me what I want—even if you have to be creative—and I'll make it worth your while."* Yuck.

Sid replayed the Bomke meeting in his mind, trying to find a way to feel good about it. And as he negotiated with his conscience, he looked at the framed black and white photos on the wall—the parade of politicos and celebrities who had visited the deli in the days when his father owned it. Ronald Reagan. Ed McMahon. Willie Brown. Spiro Agnew. A woman with huge hair in a swimsuit wearing a sash that said "Miss America 1971". And what was the name of that guy who played Jethro on the Beverly Hillbillies?

The ring of a telephone startled him. Besides the tired old payphone that hung on the back wall of the office, there was a much more modern one—push buttons and everything—that sat by the cash register out front. Sid's dad had cleverly named it, the "Deli-phone," and it rang a lot during the week. It was the number that was in the phone book. The number everybody called to place a to-go order. Plus, it was only one digit off from the phone number of an adult book and video store down on 12th Street, occasionally resulting in an amusing misdial. The ringer was set to full blast so it could be heard over a busy breakfast or lunch crowd. But when the place was empty, the damn thing could really make you jump. It was the Deli-phone that was ringing.

Sid almost picked it up, but changed his mind. "Sorry, closed," he said to the empty room, and he left the phone to ring as he walked past it into the back room. He grabbed a pen off the desk and wrote "Li'l Starz" on the folder that Nathan Bomke had given him and tucked it under his arm. The phone in the deli had stopped ringing by the time Sid flicked off the light to the storage room and headed for the front door. That's when the other phone began to ring. The payphone in back.

That was odd. For years it never rang at all, and nobody even knew the number. Since he started Bigler Investigations, he'd been using the payphone number as his private eye business phone, but business hadn't exactly been brisk. And who would be calling on a Saturday? Sid dropped the Li'l Starz folder on the deli counter and hurried back to the payphone.

"Hello?"

"Sid, it's Gloria." Sid didn't like how his sister sounded. Worried. "I called mom's and she said you were down at the deli. Then I called the main number first. Thanks for picking up in back."

"Sure. What's up, Sis? Everything okay? Is Bertie alright?"

"Oh, yeah. She's doing fine. I just need…" Gloria trailed off. "Can you come by the house? I need to talk to you."

"Now?"

"Yes, if you can."

"Uh, sure, Sis. I got no plans."

"Thank you."

"Can you give me a hint as to what this is about?"

Gloria paused long enough for her brother to wonder if she was still there. He absent mindedly scanned the names, notes and numbers that had been scrawled on the wall over the years. Some of it was in his father's terrible handwriting. Finally his sister answered his question.

"I think I've got a job for you, Sid."

Chapter 5

Sid looked out the kitchen window at his nieces. Nicky was eleven and Nellie had just turned eight. They'd gotten their father's hair—straight and black—but the rest of them was all Bigler. Long necks and skinny arms and legs like their mother had when she was a girl—think of Popeye's girlfriend, Olive Oyl. And all those freckles. But somehow the total package was adorable, and it wasn't just because he was their uncle. How could they have gotten so big?

Nicky and Nellie had an impressive collection of play clothes— mostly grown-up shoes, over-sized dresses and accessories picked up at a Goodwill Store. The endless wardrobe combinations could occupy the girls for hours, and Uncle Sid had even been known to join in. One of the "Little House on the Prairie" dresses, in particular, fit him quite well. But today it was the dog that was modeling a series of outfits. Larry the German Shepherd suffered in silence as the sisters tried a variety of skirts and aprons on him, or squinted as they pulled a blouse over his head.

"That dog looks good in a bonnet," said Sid.

"And did you notice the painted toenails?" Gloria put the finishing touch on four peanut butter and jelly sandwiches and dealt them onto four paper plates. She slid the first one in front of Sid and then headed out the back door with two more and a couple of box juices. "Hey, girls…"

Gloria's husband, Marty, was off at his regular Saturday afternoon golf game, so Sid and his sister had the house to themselves. He hopped up and snooped around the refrigerator. Dr. Pepper or milk. Tough choice. He popped open a soda and took a moment to study the photos stuck to the front of the fridge. Lots of the girls, of course. A dopey shot of Gloria and Marty in Hawaii, both in grass skirts. One of his sister on high school graduation day with their mom and dad. He even saw an action shot of himself in his college cross country uniform. Not a bad stride. A little bow-legged.

And there was a great photo of Gloria and Bertie Jones. It must have been taken recently, and clearly something had cracked them up. They were holding hands and laughing, and both of them looked wonderful.

"That was taken last summer." Gloria was back, PB & J in one hand and a box juice of her own in the other. "Her firm had an open house at the new offices."

"What was so funny?"

"Can't remember. Have you talked to her yet?"

"No. I stopped by the hospital yesterday afternoon, but she was asleep."

"You left the Butterfinger."

"Yeah."

"That was cute. She loved it."

Sid and Gloria took simultaneous bites, and then endured the forced silence that a good peanut butter and jelly sandwich requires as it turns briefly into glue in your mouth. Sid chased it down with swig of Dr. Pepper.

"She's gonna be fine, right?"

"Mmm," Gloria nodded and held up a finger until she could swallow. "I was down there this morning. She's unbelievable. Wants to go home today but they're keeping an eye on her for one more night. She'll be sore and probably a little tired, but that's all. Doctors said she was really lucky."

"Has she talked about Thursday night? Did that guy look familiar? Can she even remember what happened?"

"Oooh, three questions in a row. You must be a private eye." Gloria had a gift for conveying both sarcasm and affection simultaneously.

"Uh-huh. Licensed and everything."

Sid popped the last chunk of sandwich in his mouth, folded his paper plate in half and deposited it in the trashcan under the sink. Gloria pulled some apple juice through the tiny straw in her box drink.

"To answer your questions, little brother, yes, she has talked about the night of the shooting. You must not have read the paper yet today."

Sid shrugged his shoulders and looked intentionally dumb. It was a well-practiced expression.

"Front page article by Jackson Dexter. Nothing you or I don't already know—nobody's giving him much—but he mentions that Bertie was alert and talking to the cops."

"And he doesn't know that you and I were there?"

"Nothing about us in the paper, and I haven't gotten a call. Have you?"

"Nope."

Sid and Gloria knew Jackson Dexter fairly well, and they disliked him a lot less than most people did. He was the Sacramento Bee's most high profile reporter, and he somehow managed to get his damned nose into everything.

They'd met five years ago when Sid had his little run-in with the cops.

"So, how much does Bertie remember about Thursday night?"

Gloria gave him an odd smile and said, "Everything."

The way she said it was curious. Sid couldn't place it. He could tell that more was coming, so he waited. Brother and sister just looked at one another in silence for maybe five seconds. Something about the moment made Sid's pulse pick up a bit, and he wasn't sure why. And then Gloria said it.

"She says you saved her life."

There it was. The six words seemed to hang in the air.

Of course, it had occurred to Sid already. Not right away on the night of the shooting, but later. As he lay with his head on Amy's lap. That's when the thought first struck him that he'd saved the life of Bertie Jones. It wasn't the kind of thing you could say about yourself. Not out loud. It was up to others to declare your heroism. But in the day and a half since the incident, nobody had bothered to point it out.

It does seem pretty obvious, though, doesn't it? What's taken everybody so long? The thought crossed Sid's mind—not for the first time—and immediately felt like a schmuck for it.

"Nah. Who knows? I might've pushed her into the bullet."

Gloria laughed. "No, you're a hero, Sid. You put yourself in harm's way to help somebody else. You're like Ghandi and Sherlock Holmes all rolled into one."

Sid didn't know what to do. He was only just beginning

43

to discover that it's a very uncomfortable thing to be told you're a hero. He decided at that moment that no one would ever hear about the little holes in his shirt.

"Okay, I'm a hero. Back to Thursday night. Did Bertie say anything about the shooter?"

"Just that she'd never seen him before."

"And she got a good look at him?"

"Oh, yeah," Gloria said. "Black jacket, greasy hair, and that crazy wide nose."

"Like a pig-faced Danny Partridge."

Gloria just stared at Sid. *Annoyed Big Sister Look #29.* She'd heard his celebrity look-alike observations for thirty years, and this one seemed more stupid than usual.

"What?" Sid protested. "Tell me I'm wrong."

Gloria sighed, got up and began putting away the sandwich makings, talking as she screwed the lid on the peanut butter and tossed the bag of bread in the freezer.

"Bertie's sure she'd never seen the killer before. Has no idea why somebody'd want to kill Trager. The guy was an ass, you know that, right? But there's never been talk of any member of the city council being in danger. Nobody knew of any threats."

"Trager's business wasn't in trouble? He wasn't up to anything dirty on the council?"

"I don't know, Sid. If he was crooked, he was smart about it. I called my friend at the D.A's office and he said they've never had reason to look into Trager's business or political activities."

"What's Bertie say about him?"

"She says he was really smart and really creepy, and

she's not all that surprised somebody shot him."

Sid thought about that for a minute as Gloria finished tidying up the kitchen. Then she came and sat next to him again at the kitchen table and set down a small stack of Oreo cookies. They each grabbed one. Sid finally spoke up.

"Okay, tell me about the case."

"Hmm?"

"You called me at the deli an hour ago, remember? You've got a job for me?"

"Yeah," said Gloria, a little surprised at the question. "We've been talking about it."

Over the course of their lives, Sid had intentionally given his big sister the '*I don't get it*' look about a million times. It was a crutch. He did it on purpose and it worked for him. Instead of thinking for himself, he'd just give Gloria the bewildered look and she'd lower her expectations, or take care of the situation herself. After all, she was the smart one. The whole thing had become automatic. But the confusion on Sid's face this time was real, and Gloria knew it.

"I want you to look into the shooting," she said.

"Why? What for? The cops are all over this thing. And since when do you care about Tom Trager?"

"I *don't* care about Trager. I'm sorry he's dead, but maybe he deserved what he got. Who knows? I care about Bertie."

"And…?"

"And I'm worried that the cops are only looking at this from one angle. They think somebody wanted Trager dead and that's all."

"Well, Sis, that theory fits the evidence pretty well, wouldn't you say?"

"Of course it does. But what if there's more? There's no doubt that the shooter was after Trager, but he shot Bertie, too."

"Yeah. Because she stood up and said, 'Hey, Porky Partridge! Over here! Shoot me, too!'"

"Maybe, maybe not. How many city council members were in the bar? Two. How many people got shot? Two. What are the odds?"

Gloria didn't really want an answer to the question, so Sid unscrewed another Oreo and waited, unimpressed by his sister's argument and determined to not give her any encouragement.

"Sid, I was there when Woody and another cop came down to the hospital and took Bertie's statement. Every question was about Trager and who would've wanted him dead. It didn't even occur to them that Bertie might have been an intentional target."

"Woody let you sit there and listen while he took Bertie's statement?"

Gloria shrugged. "She said I was her attorney."

"Good one."

"Sid, I can't explain it, but I just have a feeling about this."

"A *feeling*. Well, it's hard to argue with your amazing intuition, Sis. Both times you were pregnant, didn't you have the *feeling* you were having a boy?"

"Funny."

"And weren't you absolutely positive at one point that

you were going to marry the guy from Herman's Hermits?"

"I was fourteen."

"And you had zits. C'mon, Sis, let's just lay low and let the cops do their job."

Gloria's eyebrows came together in a scowl that wrinkled the top of her nose. Based on past experience, the expression was akin to a skunk raising its tail.

"No." The word came out of Gloria's mouth, but it was the voice of their mother. *Weird.* "No, Sid, let's not. Let's not leave it to chance that Bertie is safe. Let's not assume that the overworked, underpaid cops can't make a mistake. Let's not do nothing after my best friend in the world has been shot."

Gloria was a good lawyer.

"And why me, Sis? You've got a couple of very experienced P.I.'s that you use regularly. Why not use one of them?"

"Because you care about Bertie, Sid. That's hardly been a secret. And because—God I hate to say this—you're really good. I never saw it coming, little brother, but you're good."

"If that was a compliment, it was beautifully disguised."

Oh, it was a compliment. No doubt about it. Normal adolescent feuding aside, theirs had been a better brother-sister relationship than most. There was an unspoken warmth beneath every smartass comment. And on the rare occasions when something serious or sentimental was spoken, it was reliably followed by sarcasm. It worked for them.

But Gloria's admission that Sid was good was special. It felt like the culmination of a change in their relationship that had been taking place for several years. Since they were kids, not only was Gloria the smart one, she was also the one who applied herself. Sid, on the other hand, had simply bumped along through school and early adulthood happily letting his sister be the over-achiever. Sid excelled at running and occasionally shooting off his mouth and that was about it. He may even have subconsciously played the dumb card on occasion just to make sure that expectations stayed low. But five years ago, he had run into trouble—serious trouble that landed him in jail. Finding himself the prime suspect in a crime he didn't commit, it was that event that caused Sid, reluctantly, to solve his first case. And the one person who never doubted him was Gloria. She didn't save him—which, to be honest, was what Sid had hoped. Other than bailing him out of jail, she didn't really do anything except believe in him and make it clear that she expected him to save his own ass. He did, and the incident proved to be life-changing. And now, five years later, after hitting the books and working for literally thousands of hours to become a licensed private investigator, Gloria had looked him in the eye and told him what he already knew—He was good. Great moment.

"I'll work for free, Sis, but sometimes it costs a little money to find things out."

"Not a problem. Let me know what you spend."

"Okay," said Sid, and he must have allowed a small look of satisfaction to cross his face. He didn't intend to, but it must have happened.

"Don't let this go to your head or I'll give your fiancée those pictures of you peeing in the bathtub when you were six."

"You've got pictures?"

Chapter 6

"Pizza?"

"No."

"How about Chinese? We haven't done Chinese in weeks."

"Uh-uh."

This was the typical conversation that Sid and Amy had while running. He talked a lot and she gave one-word replies between breaths. Amy was a good runner, but at this pace there wasn't a lot of air left for talking. So Sid carried the load. They'd been going for nearly an hour and twenty minutes, and he'd already filled her in on his meeting with Nathan Bomke and the conversation with his sister. Now, with less than half a mile to go, the conversation had turned to food.

"Burgers at Squeeze Inn."

"No."

"Sizzler salad bar?"

"Yeah. Good."

It was settled. Every Sunday afternoon the two of them did a twelve-miler. They'd drive to the American River Bike Trail near the university, then run to Goethe Park and back, six miles each way. Afterwards, they'd get cleaned up and have a big meal. Eating is running's greatest reward.

Amy picked up the pace the last few hundred yards and Sid let her have a little lead. Pushing harder at the end— when it hurts—another thing he loved about her. He watched her ponytail swing back and forth, and allowed himself some time to admire her round rump. Life's little pleasures. She whacked the trunk of his car with her palm as she stopped. Home base. Then she leaned forward and put her hands on her knees, breathing hard. Sid trotted in and stopped beside her.

"Great run, honey."

"Running, good," Amy puffed between breaths. "Stopping, better."

She wiped her face on her shirt, stood up straight and began walking. Sid fell in alongside her and they silently began a lap around the parking lot. Mandatory ten minute cool down walk. The silence didn't last for long.

"So tell me more about Gloria and Bertie. Does your sister really expect you to find anything? What can you do that the cops aren't already doing?"

"Well, one more guy trying to figure out who Mr. Big Nose is can't hurt. And, according to Gloria, the cops aren't looking for a connection to Bertie Jones at all. So I'll work that angle. I'll check out her list of clients if she'll let me. See if there's anything fishy there."

"Fishy how?"

"I dunno. Won't know 'til I have a look. And I'll see what's been going on with the city council. You never know what might have upset some crazy citizen."

A little breeze had come up, and for the first time that year Sid thought he might be feeling the change of seasons. It'd been fall for almost two weeks, but it really hadn't started to cool down much.

"I only met Bertie that one time at your sister's house, and we really didn't get a chance to talk. Tell me about her."

This was not a conversation Sid was anxious to have. Suddenly the car seemed very far away. What do you tell your fiancée about the woman you've had a crush on for twenty-five years? "What do you wanna know?"

Clever, huh? No need to volunteer more than necessary. For some reason, Amy let out a little sigh.

"Okay, I'll start," she said." Bertie Jones is your big sister's best friend. Since the third grade."

"Second."

"Okay, second grade. And besides being beautiful, she's smart."

"Scary smart," said Sid, "She and Gloria were quite a pair."

"And they went to college and law school together, right?"

"No. Well, yes, you're right, they did room together for three years at U.C. Davis. But then Gloria and Marty got married before their senior year. I think Bertie had her own place the last year of college. Then, once they graduated, Bertie took off for Southern California, went to law school at USC. Gloria stayed around here. Graduated from McGeorge."

"So, who's the better lawyer?"

"I don't know. They're different. Sis does mostly corporate contracts now. Makes sure that David never beats Goliath. Bertie does criminal and civil defense, and she's expensive."

"Yeah?"

"Remember when Dave Evans—the weather guy on Channel 10— got drunk and ran his car into the Der

Wienerschnitzel?"

"No." Amy sounded surprised.

"Yeah. That's because Bertie was his lawyer. She had him out of jail before anybody heard a thing. Cut some kind of deal."

"Really?"

"She has a gift for making bad things go away. If you can afford her. She defended that doctor's son—what's his name, Grasso?"

"Corey Grasso?"

"Yeah, him. College boy charged with sexual assault."

"That was in the news, then I never heard what happened to him."

"Because nothing happened. Bertie's good."

"Good enough to have made some serious enemies?" Amy asked.

Pretty good question. The two of them walked quietly side-by-side for a few moments. Sid was turning things over in his mind, thinking about the shooting of Bertie Jones like it was a real case for the first time. It wasn't impossible that someone—from the courtroom or the council chambers— might want Bertie dead. A couple of years earlier some kook with a gun walked into a city hall somewhere in Minnesota and killed the mayor and two others. And as for killing lawyers, well, Shakespeare wasn't the first guy to think of it.

"So, is your sister gonna pay you?"

"Not a chance. This one's a freebie. If I ask her for money, she'll go back and bill me for the hours she's spent keeping my butt out of jail and dodging lawsuits."

"And besides, you love her, right?"

"She's my sister."

"I don't mean Gloria, Sid." Amy stopped, turned and looked at him. "I mean Bertie."

Sid's entire universe screeched to a halt. He hadn't noticed that his mouth was dry before, but suddenly it felt like he'd eaten a handful of sawdust. A lesser man might have pooped his pants.

"Well, no… I mean, not like… Not like you think I do… I don't, uh…"

This was going badly. Sid had no idea what to say, so he decided to stop trying to say anything. Too late, of course. His mouth remained open for a moment longer—no sound coming out—and then it closed. Amy held his gaze for what seemed like forever, and then she did something wonderful. She laughed. Hard.

"Jeez, that's fantastic." She reached up and patted his cheek, then started walking again and called back over her shoulder. "It's good to know that my future husband is a terrible liar. That'll come in very handy."

Sid stood there like a dope for probably fifteen seconds, then jogged up and began walking next to her again. He wasn't sure what had just happened, but remained committed to keeping his mouth shut until he knew what was going to come out of it. Amy let him suffer a little longer.

"You know I talk to your mom and your sister, right? A lot. If you came to church with us or even joined us for brunch afterwards, you'd know what I know about you."

Not enough information, so Sid walked on in silence

while his mind raced.

"Sid."

Amy said his name quietly, with a combination of amusement and affection. She reached over and took his hand as they walked. Strands of hair that had escaped her ponytail danced as the breeze came up again. Sid waited for her to throw him a lifeline, and she did.

"I love you and you love me. We're getting married in fifty-seven days and it's going to be great and it's going to be forever, okay?"

"Okay."

They stopped walking again. Amy turned to him, looked him in the eyes, and saw that he had no idea what she was saying.

"Sid, other women can have your past. I get your future."

Amy said it comfortably, like it was the most basic fact in the universe, and nothing else needed to be said. Sid wasn't sure she completely grasped the enormous role that Bertie had unwittingly played in his life—the countless, pointless hours that she had occupied his mind. In truth, Sid was embarrassed by what had been his insurmountable infatuation with his sister's friend. How many times had he told himself to just get over it? And here was the woman he loved telling him that it was alright. Amy had opened the door to the closet where he kept every secret thought he'd ever had about Bertie Jones and told him that she didn't care what was in there. The effect of her gesture was huge. Liberating.

"I understand you gave Bertie the cutting board you

made in woodshop in the tenth grade."

"Gloria told you about that?"

"No, your mom. She wanted that cutting board."

As if on cue, they both started walking again.

"Did they tell you I named my rat after Bertie when I was eleven?"

"No."

"They might not have known. I just called him B.J."

"You named a *boy* rat after her."

"Did I mention that I was eleven? That's when I started wearing cologne, too. And she's why I switched to the Davey Jones – Peter Tork hairdo in 1967. Bertie dug the Monkees."

Amy laughed again, and it felt great.

"I've never told anybody this stuff."

"Don't be surprised if Gloria and Bertie know it anyway."

Sid's car was in sight. The only lime green 1970 Dodge Duster in the parking lot. He let go of Amy's hand and put an arm across her shoulders. She reached around his waist and gave him a squeeze.

"I can live with Bertie Jones in your past if you can live with Kenny Bean in mine."

"Kenny Bean?"

"Uh-huh. The cutest boy at Landon High School. He had a Nehru jacket and he played the guitar."

"Oooh. Impressive. I wanna know more about Kenny Bean."

"Sorry. I don't kiss and tell."

"Kiss?"

"C'mon, Sid. It was the Summer of Love."

Chapter 7

"Hey, mom!" Sid called out as he came through the front door. He'd just dropped Amy off at her apartment to get a shower.

"Hello, Siddy!" His mother's voice came from the kitchen. "Have a nice run?"

He found her leaning over a mixing bowl, dropping little balls of dough on waxed paper. She'd recently purchased a small TV to sit on the kitchen counter, and some station was showing *Smokey and the Bandit*. Sid was pretty sure his mom had a crush on Burt Reynolds.

"Yeah, good run. We're going to Sizzler. What're you making?"

"Rum balls. Senior Social tonight at church."

Sid popped one in his mouth. "Wow."

"Good, huh? I think I accidentally doubled the rum."

"Call me later if you need someone to drive you home." He gave her a peck on the cheek. "I'm gonna grab a shower."

"Oh, before you go, Lou called. Said it was important. His number's by the phone."

Sid walked over and picked up a slip of paper next to the fifteen pound black rotary telephone that was probably older than he was. In his mom's perfect handwriting was a phone number and the name 'Lou Martini.'

"When did he call?"

"Maybe an hour ago."

Lou Martini had been something of a father figure in the

years since Sid's own father died. Meeting him was pure luck. Once Sid had gotten it into his head to become a P.I., he discovered that the State of California required 6,000 hours of training or actual experience before you could get a license. Four years ago he opened the phone book to "Private Investigators" and liked the sound of Lou Martini's name. A good, solid Private Eye name. Sid walked into his office and made his best pitch, offered to work for a buck an hour in exchange for on-the-job training, and soon found himself the protégé of a really fine detective. Martini was in his late fifties and, like most P.I.'s, an ex-cop. But, unlike most P.I.'s, he didn't seem like one. He had a friendly, disarming way about himself, and a gift for getting people to talk to him.

"Hello." He picked up on the first ring.

"Lou, it's Sid. What's up?"

They had only talked a few times since Sid got his license and went out on his own. He couldn't remember when their last conversation was.

"Oh, Sid, thanks for calling back. You doing okay?"

"Yeah. Actually got a couple of cases I'm working on."

"That's great. I told you you'd do fine. How's your bride?"

"Calmer than me. You're coming to the wedding, right?"

"Already bought you guys a crock pot and wrapped it up. Listen, I heard about what happened to Roberta Jones. She's a friend of your family's, right?"

Sid had discovered quickly that one of the reasons Lou was good at his job was that he remembered everything. He filed facts away and could always find them somewhere in his head if he needed them. Sid had hardly ever seen him write anything down. Names, numbers, dates—he was like a human Rolodex.

"Yes. She practically grew up with my sister. In fact— and I'd like to keep this quiet if I can—I was in the bar last week when she was shot."

The phone was quiet for several seconds.

"But you're okay?"

"Yeah, Lou. Fine. A lot better than Tom Trager."

"Yeah, I read the paper. Look, Sid, I need to talk to you."

"Okay."

"You free right now?"

"Well, I'm supposed to take Amy to Sizzler, but I could call her and cancel."

"No, don't do that. Wait 'til after you're married to start disappointing her. When are you free tomorrow?"

"Uh, typical Monday. I close the deli up about 2:30. Anytime after that."

"Meet me at Boitano's at four. I'll buy you a Coke."

"Is anything wrong?"

"Meet me at four."

Chapter 8

You can count on Mondays at Sid & Eddie's Deli to get off to a furious start. Credit the Brown Sugar Cinnamon Rolls. Just once a week—on Mondays—Joe Diaz came in two hours early to get the dough started, and the buttery, cinnamony smell was devastating. They had a crunchy crust on top, a doughy, slightly undercooked center, and eating one without using a knife and fork required a minimum of four napkins. The total amount of sugar and fat was unknown, but the things were surely the ticket to an early grave. And they were worth it.

The breakfast rush transitioned into a busy lunch with hardly a break. As usual, Sid's mom showed up in time to work the register and schmooze, Eddie silently delivered food and kept the tables clean, and Joe pounded out one delicious order after another. Sid helped out where he was needed until about 1:30, then had Joe make him a hamburger and snuck back to his desk. He had just taken his first big bite when he heard his mother.

"Siddy!"

He looked up to see Rose's head appear at the door.

"Sid, you need to come out here. I can't talk to that man." Rose said it loud enough to be heard by anyone in the restaurant.

Sid washed down the mouthful of burger with a big swig of Coke and headed out into the deli. He knew who he'd find.

Sitting on one of the stools at the counter was Otis

"Jock" Bell. The man was a genuine local celebrity. He was the proprietor of *Jock's Bail Bonds*, which happened to be headquartered right across the street in *Jock's Pawn Shop*. But to say that he was simply a bail bondsman and pawn broker is to fail to convey just how significant Jock Bell's presence was in Sacramento.

Starting in the early sixties, Bell had tried a series of business ideas that had gotten him a lot of attention, either as huge successes or spectacular failures. But they were always flashy. At one point he had two waterbed stores, a cheesy singles bar and a raft rental company on the American River that were all making him a fortune. It was the profits from those businesses that helped foot the bill for the disasters: The submarine rides for tourists in the murky river out of Old Sacramento. The year-round artificial ski slope. The school for professional wrestlers. And whatever the entrepreneurial endeavors, Jock Bell bought a lot of commercials on late night TV to advertise them. He always appeared in his own commercials—sometimes with scantily clad models whose beauty was open to debate—and over the years he'd become an institution in California's capital.

Most Sacramentans had no idea that the various crackpot businesses and the TV commercials that went with them were really just a hobby. He certainly didn't need the money. Behind the scenes, Jock Bell was easily the most successful real estate developer in town. He'd bought and sold more commercial buildings than anyone else, and he'd never lost money on a deal. He was loaded.

"Jock, nice to see you again."

It was very nearly the truth. There was a time when Sid

shared his mom's contempt for the guy, but times had changed. The two had a unique history together. Maybe not a friendship, but a history.

"I think your mom likes me. She seeing anyone?"

Jock Bell had a bizarrely low voice. He spoke quietly, but the rumble could be heard across the room. Rose shot the man an icy stare.

Sid prudently ignored the comment and said, "Nice pants."

"Thank you. They're custom made."

Jock Bell was somewhere between sixty-five and eighty-five years old. It was tough to tell. Every inch of exposed skin was a maze of deep lines and wrinkles, yet above the darkly tanned face sat an explosion of youthful brown hair that was all his own. Sid had pulled on it once to be sure. But it was Bell's unique fashion sense that was the primary reason Sid had come to enjoy their encounters. Today an impressive gold chain hung outside a burgundy turtle neck sweater that was tucked into his slacks. Orange, bell-bottomed slacks with a big cuff on the bottom. Jock Bell was a visual feast for anyone who sought humor in the appearance of others.

"Custom made. Very nice. What can we do for you?"

"I thought I'd buy lunch for my guys." Bell gestured out the window and across the street with his big James Brown sunglasses. "I take good care of my employees."

The deli and the pawn shop had been across the street from each other for thirty-three years and Bell had never bought anybody lunch. What was he up to?

"Okay. What can we get you?"

"I don't care. Give me three of anything. They'll eat whatever I bring 'em."

"It's nice to see that kind of compassion in an employer."

"Yeah, they're very lucky."

Sid wrote up an order for three B.L.T.'s and three orders of fries, then turned and stuck it on the wheel by the grill.

"Hey Sid," the low voice came from behind him. "I hear you were there when Trager got shot."

Sid turned back and tried not to look surprised.

"Who told you that?"

"I make my money by knowing things most people don't know." Jock Bell gave a little smile and put the sunglasses on. "Hell of a thing, huh?"

"Yeah. It was bad."

"That's a couple of times now you've been around when somebody got plugged."

"Thanks for keeping track."

"He was a dumbass."

"Trager?"

"Dumbass." Jock Bell nodded as he said it a second time. "What about the lady councilman—she gonna be okay?"

"Yeah. She's home already. Probably back to work next week."

"That's good."

From Sid's limited Private Eye experience, good information rarely walks in and sits down on a stool in front of you. He opened an Anchor Steam beer and set it on the counter next to Jock Bell.

"You must've had plenty of experience with Tom Trager over the years in your real estate deals."

"Plying me with alcohol. Good plan, Sid."

"Well…? Don't you need the city council to approve things sometimes or, uh… re-zone stuff?"

Sid heard the sentence leave his mouth and made a mental note to improve his knowledge about the inner workings of the city council. Bell took a surprisingly dainty sip, then put the bottle down and said nothing. Sid waited. Bell took another drink before apparently deciding he had something to say.

"If you were a contributor to his campaign, Councilman Trager could generally be counted on to be helpful."

"And was Councilman Trager helpful to a lot of people?"

A non-committal shrug was the only reply.

"Anything else I might wanna know about the late councilman?"

"Oh, I've probably said too much already, Sid." Jock Bell tipped up the beer for another sip. "I'll let somebody else tell you about the little blonde he kept in a downtown apartment."

"Good looking blonde?"

Another shrug. "Eye of the beholder."

The old man dabbed the corners of his mouth with a paper napkin, then stood up.

"Trager could be bought," said Sid.

"Yeah, but cheap." The voice was lower and quieter. "He didn't think big. He was a dumbass."

"Can I ask why you're telling me this?"

"I like you, Little Sid. And I want you to like me." Jock Bell may have given him a wink behind the big sunglasses, it was hard to tell. "I keep hoping you'll sell me this damn building."

Bell turned and started to leave, and Sid called out, "Hey, what about the B.L.T.'s?"

Jock stopped with a hand on the door.

"Have somebody run 'em across the street if you want. Send me a bill."

Chapter 9

It was 4:15 and Lou Martini was uncharacteristically late. That was fine. It gave Sid a little time to wonder why Jock Bell had bothered to come by the deli, but he still hadn't come up with a good answer. He sat at a small table in Boitano's and doodled on a paper bar napkin, trying to be productive. He'd written down the name "Tom Trager," and below that he'd written "Blonde" with a question mark after it. He wondered if money from the hardware business plus a councilman's salary was enough to pay for a wife *and* a mistress, and suspected that the answer was no. Which meant that Trager found other ways to supplement his income. That made sense.

So maybe Trager disappointed a powerful "contributor." And if someone was willing to bribe a city councilman, then by definition they had no problem breaking the law. Sure, murder was a big step up from bribery, but still. It's just a question of degree.

"You sure I can't get you something?"

It was the third time the waitress had asked. Sid hadn't planned to order anything. He was going over to Amy's for dinner after he met with Martini. This was a big deal. Amy was not a cook at all, and in their five years together had only made him dinner a handful of times.

"A beer or something?"

Sid finally got the message.

"Uh, yeah. I'll just have a Coke. No ice."

The young woman walked off unimpressed.

Sid returned to his napkin and stared at the names. Trager and the blonde. Hmmm. What if Porky Partridge had a blonde girlfriend and he found out who was paying for the apartment? Yeah, that was pretty good. If he could figure out who the mistress was, maybe that would lead him to the shooter. He wrote "Porky" on the bottom of the napkin and stared some more. A minute or two went by and his mind wandered. Then he remembered one of Lou Martini's cardinal rules of the detective business: *"Don't waste your time looking for information that nobody's paying you for."*

Okay, his sister had asked him to make sure that Bertie's shooting was just an accident—that the whole thing had nothing to do with her—so he wrote "Bertie Jones" on the napkin. Now there were four names, and Sid couldn't see why any of them should be connected. Except, of course, that two of them were on the city council. *'What are the odds?'* Gloria had asked him over peanut butter and jelly sandwiches. It'd be good to talk to the blonde, whoever she was. Maybe he could persuade Jock Bell to give him a name.

The waitress returned with his Coke. She set a wet glass down on the napkin he'd been writing on, and the ink began to run immediately.

"Is your name Sid Bigler?"

That caught him by surprise.

"Yeah, that's me."

"There's a phone call for you at the bar."

Sid looked over and saw a telephone, off the hook, laying on the bar with its squiggly cord trailing behind it. Who knew he was there? He stood up, lifted the Coke glass and picked up the damp napkin, folded it once, and managed to slide it into his back pocket without tearing it. Then he started for the phone.

"Hey, this is a dollar," the waitress called from behind him.

Sid turned back and absent mindedly threw two dollars on the table, then went to the phone. Who knew where to find him?

"Hello."

"It's Amy." She didn't sound right. Shaky.

"Yeah, what's up, honey?

"You said you were meeting Lou Martini this afternoon, right?"

"Yes." Sid's stomach twisted into a knot, and he didn't know why.

"Sid, I was just listening to the news on the radio. The police found a body in a car in Fair Oaks this morning. They think it was a robbery or something. Sid, they said it was Lou."

The next couple of hours were an exercise in frustration. Unbelievable, total, goddamn frustration. Someone that Sid cared about—someone he loved—was dead, and nobody would talk to him.

Sid drove to the police station, but he couldn't find out squat from the cops. Woody was off, and nobody else would even come out and talk to him. He gave up after the guy up front told him for the third time that they couldn't release any information "until next-of-kin was notified."

Sid got back in his car and tried to focus. *Next-of-kin.*

Lou had been married once. Where was the ex-wife and what was her name? Diane? Darleen? *Damn*.

It hadn't occurred to him how little he actually knew about Lou Martini. Sid thought back over the countless hours they'd spent together. Lou had been a cop in Vacaville—about halfway between Sacramento and San Francisco—but that was more than twenty years ago. What the hell. Sid drove to a payphone and called the department anyway, but he got nothing.

Then Sid drove to Woody's place. He rang first, then banged on the door with his fist. No answer. He wrote a note on the back of a Burger King receipt he found on the floor of his car and left it on the front door, then went and leaned against the trunk of his Dodge in Woody's driveway and tried to think of something else to do. What next? He squeezed his eyes shut and tried in vain to force an idea into his head. And then, as he often did, he asked himself what Lou would do in this situation.

Lou Martini probably wouldn't have cried. But that's what Sid did.

Chapter 10

Rose Bigler usually showed up at the deli around eleven o'clock. She wasn't a morning person, and at sixty-four years old she wasn't remotely interested in getting up before the sun. But she really loved the hustle and bustle of the place. And, whether she consciously knew it or not, when she was at the deli it made her feel like her late husband was not so far away.

Sid's father—Sid Bigler, Sr.—was a tiny man with a huge personality. Since the day the deli opened its doors a block from the Capitol in 1947, people started coming to the place for more than just Joe's delicious food. They came to see Big Sid. It was impossible to not like the man immediately. He was five feet four inches tall, perpetually full of energy, loud and funny. Every governor since Earl Warren—Republican and Democrat—stopped by regularly for lunch and a chat with Big Sid. Rose used to stop by occasionally in the days before Big Sid died, but he would never have allowed her to work there. Making the money was his job.

He'd been gone for five years now, but when Rose was in the deli, she was somehow closer to her husband. And she decided to come in early on Tuesday morning, October 8th because she knew her son would need her.

Sid, Jr. had shown up right on time to get the place opened for the day, but he was useless. The busy pace of the deli was almost always a great escape for him when he was troubled, but memories and questions about Lou Martini wouldn't leave him alone. So when his mom arrived just before 8:30, Sid took off his apron and headed back to his office. He dropped a dime in the payphone and waited for Woody to pick up.

"Detective Carver." Woody's assertive 'cop voice' jumped out of the phone.

"Woody, it's Sid."

"Oh, hey, Buddy. I'm so sorry about Martini. I didn't see your note 'til I got home really late last night or I would've called."

"You should've. I was awake."

"Yeah, well, I couldn't have told you anything anyway. I didn't hear about Lou's death until I got in this morning."

"So, what can you tell me now?"

"Well, still nothing, Sid. This is an active case."

"Oh, c'mon, Woody."

"You know the rules, Sid. All you get is what the Public Information Officer releases unless you're next-of-kin."

"Don't give me that crap. I'm closer to Lou Martini than his ex-wife. Uh, what's her name?" Sid asked the question casually, like it was on the tip of his tongue.

"Nice try, Sid. I can't give you her name."

"Gimme a break, Woody. Since when do you pay attention to the rules?"

The cop significantly lowered his voice. "Since I'm sitting at a desk right next to three other detectives. You gonna be at class tonight?"

"Oh, I forgot it was Tuesday."

Sid and Woody had been taking martial arts classes together since the day Sid decided he was going to get his Private Investigator license. Fearing for his skinny friend's safety, Woody had insisted.

"Yeah," Sid continued. "I'll be there."

"We'll talk then."

Sid heard the clatter on the other end as Woody hung up, then he put the phone back in its cradle. He stared at Lou's name written among the others on the wall in pencil, with his number below it.

Amy had told him on the phone yesterday that the cops thought it might have been a robbery. Sid watched the news on TV later and saw the story. Lou was found dead in his car. Blows to the head. His wallet had been taken, but police found his name on the registration in the car's glove compartment. Sid had ridden in that black sedan hundreds of times.

"What happened to you, Lou?" Sid said it out loud. "And what was it you were going to talk to me about?"

The only reply was the din of conversation and the clink of plates and glasses that came through the door to the deli.

"Don't waste your time looking for information that nobody's paying you for."

Sid smiled, then went to his desk, sat down, and opened the folder marked 'Li'l Starz.' For the next hour and a half, the deli detective managed to successfully lose himself in the story of little Mandy Mercer and her failed quest for child stardom. He looked—briefly—at the photographs. His favorite was one that featured the little girl wearing excessive make-up and holding a large trophy under a banner that said "Little Miss Pinto Bean." A close examination of the trophy indicated that Mandy had come in third. He placed the photos face down on his desk and moved on to the more tedious paperwork.

Nothing in the contract appeared out of the ordinary. Maybe he'd have Gloria give it a look if she had a moment. There were two pages of scribbled notes that were, frankly, hard to follow. Sid picked out nine different names and four different companies, all with dates and phone numbers next to them. Maybe these were potential employers of child actors. It'd be easy enough to call the numbers and see if they'd ever heard of Li'l Starz. And surely they'd remember if they'd ever seen a photograph of the girl who was almost Little Miss Pinto Bean. It was an image that was hard to forget. There was a monthly credit card statement with a charge from Delta Airlines highlighted in bright yellow and a three-night stay at a Travelodge in West Hollywood. Presumably this was evidence that the guy from Li'l Starz— Mr. Clark—had actually made his promised trip to L.A. to try to land some work for the homely Miss Mercer.

Sid had just grabbed a clean sheet of paper and was beginning a "to do" list when he heard a knocking sound and a throat being cleared. He looked up and for a moment all he could see was yellow hair and white teeth.

"Got a minute?"

Sid's first encounter with Lieutenant Benjamin Stokes had been five years earlier, right here in the deli. From the first moment he saw the guy, all he could think of was a Scandinavian Tony Orlando. Same hair, same moustache, only blonde. And the same gigantic mouth, except the teeth were even bigger. White, perfectly even, and very possibly false.

"Lieutenant Stokes, what can I do for you?"

"You mind talking to me about what happened at the Ancient Moose last week? We got a buttload of witnesses, but you're the only one who had his arms wrapped around one of the victims when she got shot."

"I'll do whatever I can to help."

Yesterday Jock Bell had wandered in and given Sid some useful information. Maybe today it was Stokes' turn.

"I'm impressed that you're here," said Sid. "What's the head of the homicide out doing interviews for? Isn't this Woody Carver's case?"

"Yeah, we can talk about that. But, no offense, you mind if we go someplace else? This place gives me the creeps."

Two minutes later they were in Stokes' sedan driving down J Street. Sid noticed the fast food wrappers on the floor of the car and quickly figured out how the Lieutenant got the stains on his tie and sportcoat. The man was less than meticulous about his wardrobe.

"Funny. Last time we went for a ride together you were in the back seat." Stokes grinned.

"Yeah, funny. What can you tell me about Lou Martini?"

"Oh, I forgot you two knew each other. You were like his helper or apprentice or something, right? Look, I'm really sorry about what happened."

"What exactly did happen, Lieutenant?"

"First officers on the scene were calling it a robbery gone bad—his wallet was missing. But I dunno. Somebody done him up pretty bad. Really worked him over."

The description hit Sid hard, but he wasn't about to let Stokes see it. He clinched his jaw and took a deep breath.

"Any idea who did it?"

"Nah, not really. I've got a couple of guys on the case. I really can't say more about it, you know?"

"Yeah."

A Volkswagen bus pulled out of a driveway right in front of their car. Stokes hit the brakes and leaned on the horn.

"God, I really miss giving tickets to assholes like that. So, give me your version of what happened last Thursday night."

"You haven't read the reports?"

"Humor me."

"Well, I was in the bar with a group of about eight. Bertie was sitting just to my left."

"Bertie?"

"Councilwoman Jones. We've known each other since we were kids."

"Oh, right. I heard that."

For the next forty-five minutes, Sid and Stokes tooled around and talked. Sid didn't hold back on any of the details, except for having a lifelong crush on one of the victims. Sometimes the Lieutenant would interrupt with a question, and Sid did his best to answer accurately. He had nothing to hide, and he wanted to see the bastard get caught as much as anyone.

"You got a pretty good look at the perp?" Stokes asked.

"Yeah, really good."

"When we find who did this, you could pick him out of a line-up?"

Sid almost laughed. "No problem. Danny Partridge

with a piggy nose."

"What the hell does that mean?"

"I'm good with faces. They stick in my head. I think everybody looks like somebody famous, so I kinda make a game out of it."

"Yeah? Okay, who do I look like?"

"Tony Orlando."

"The Mexican singer?"

"I think he's Italian."

"Whatever." Stokes leaned to his right and looked at himself in the rear view mirror. "Tony Orlando. Yeah, maybe."

It was nearly eleven o'clock when Stokes pulled up along the red curb right in front of the deli and put it in park. Sid couldn't help but notice that every question had something to do with Tom Trager, and Stokes never really asked a thing about Bertie Jones. Maybe Gloria was right.

"Well, thank you, Mr. Bigler. You've been very helpful."

"Sure. Now can I ask a couple questions?"

"Shoot." Stokes pulled a pack of Juicy Fruit from his coat pocket and unwrapped a stick.

"Is there any chance that Lou Martini's death is related to what happened in the bar last week?"

"What, when Trager was killed?"

"Yeah."

"Nah. I don't think so. Why would it?" Stokes said it like it was a dumb question, and it very likely was. But it never hurts to ask.

"Okay. Why are you working on Woody Carver's case? You said we'd talk about it later."

"Yeah. Right. And you guys are friends."

"So?"

"So, this is an important investigation. Biggest homicide I can remember. Your pal Carver's a good cop, but, uh, I'm taking this one myself."

"Why?"

"Because up until a couple of years ago, Detective Carver was driving a squad car and running bums off the sidewalk. I've been in Homicide since you two limpdicks were in high school. And this is one investigation we can't afford to screw up."

"Okay, Lieutenant. Just asking."

Stokes had gotten himself a little worked up, which made it a good time for Sid to fish around for some information. He swung open the car door, but paused before getting out.

"Oh, Lieutenant. Back to Tom Trager. I assume you know about the little blonde he had on the side."

"The blonde." Stokes didn't say it like it was a question, but it was.

"Yes. The woman that's not his wife. The one he's been keeping in an apartment downtown for a while."

"Yeah, the blonde. We know about her."

Sid was sure Stokes was lying, and he liked it.

"No, Lieutenant, I don't think you do."

"Well why don't you tell me her name, and I'll tell you if it's the one we know about."

Sid almost laughed. "Are you sure you've been doing this since I was in high school?" He climbed out of the sedan and closed the door behind him.

The car window went down, and a clearly irritated lieutenant Stokes said, "Listen, Bigler! Withholding information from a police investigation is a crime, and I know you've done it before. I find out you know something you're not telling me, I swear to god I'll lock you up."

Sid leaned in the window and looked at Stokes. It was remarkably fun to piss the guy off, but this wasn't the time to let his mouth get in the way of his investigation.

"Here's the truth, Stokes. I don't know her name, either. But I can find out what it is. And when I do, I'll be a good citizen and give you a call, okay? I just want you to keep me in the loop on this case. You keep me informed, and I can help you."

"Oh, that's right. You're a real, live detective now, aren't you?"

"I can get the name."

"Call me."

Chapter 11

If Sid hadn't deflected the blow, he probably would've been out cold. Even so, he was staggered by the kick as it glanced off the side of his head. Now he was down on one knee, seeing stars, and his position was seriously compromised.

That's when the other guy made a mistake. Sid was a sitting duck—didn't even have his hands up. The guy could've stayed back out of range, darting in with a quick elbow or side kick, and Sid would've been toast. Fortunately, the man was big and powerful and over-confident, and he came in close thinking he could just use his strength. But in this instance, his size was his weakness. The man came forward, his weight way out in front of him, and Sid's instincts took over.

He spun around, sweeping a leg underneath the guy and taking him off his feet. The big man fell forward, and all Sid had to do was give gravity a little assist, pulling on his hair as he went down. Sid felt two powerful hands digging into his forearms as the two men tangled together, and that's when Sid Bigler and Woody Carver rolled off the picnic table and landed hard on the grass of Curtis Park. They were hot and sweaty and out of breath, and they were laughing.

"Strong and stupid loses every time, Woody." Stanley Ono stood over them, grinning. "And you looked pretty good, Sid. Except for getting kicked in the head."

Woody and Sid had begun working out together not

long after they met—running and weightlifting. The two men were an odd combination, but it worked and each surprised the other. It turned out that Woody, built like a tree trunk, was a pretty decent runner. And Sid seemed to defy the laws of physics, his skinny arms eventually bench-pressing nearly twice his weight. His muscles never actually got any bigger, at least not so anyone ever noticed, though he was sure that his post-shower posing sessions in front of the bathroom mirror were increasingly impressive.

One afternoon just over four years ago, Woody had called Sid out of the blue and told him they were going to start martial arts lessons. His reasons were two-fold. First, he'd come to the conclusion that young cops going through the academy received only enough self-defense instruction to be dangerous to themselves. They got some basics, but had no idea what street fighting is really like. Once on the job, ninety-nine percent of the people who put up a fight are either drunk or high, and it takes very little skill to get the upper hand. So a young cop starts to think he's street tough, unbeatable. But when that one-in-a-hundred guy comes along that's sober and dangerous, an undertrained, over-confident cop can really get hurt. Or worse.

The other reason Woody signed them up for martial arts classes was that he was worried about his friend. Sid had recently announced his intention to become a private detective, and between his big mouth and his stringy physique, there was something about him that said, *"Beat me up, please."*

Woody had done his homework. There weren't that many options in those days. There was Kang's Institute, which had been around since the sixties, and Bob Lyle teaching out of the YMCA near Land Park. Otherwise, it was mostly ex-military guys who operated "garage schools", teaching what they'd learned overseas out of their homes. But even then, the choices were primarily Karate and Judo, and the fact was, Woody wasn't interested in wisdom or philosophy or discipline or beauty. Woody wanted to know how to beat the hell out of somebody else in a fight. Nothing more. And that's what led him to a sixteen-year-old kid named Stanley Ono and his very informal classes in KajuKenpo.

On one of Woody's last days as a beat cop before stepping up to Homicide, he'd gotten a call to go to Christian Brothers High School where an after-school fight had gotten out of hand. Upon arriving, he found three football players on the ground—two with broken bones and one cradling his nuts with both hands—and a little Asian kid standing over them with a satisfied smile on his face. Young Stanley Ono had recently moved to the area when his dad, an Air Force pilot, had been transferred from Hickam Air Force Base in Hawaii. Sacramento had a couple of bases in the area, and was more of a military town than most people realized. In the Islands, Stanley had learned KajuKenpo— the first martial art form developed in America. It was really a hybrid of techniques borrowed from more traditional martial arts—jiu-jitsu, karate, Chinese boxing, and others. It lacked nobility or pedigree, but clearly excelled at ass-kicking.

Several witnesses at the high school said that the football players had started the fight, and no charges were ever brought. Woody ended up driving Stanley home that day, figuring it might be safest for all parties concerned, and he ended up really liking the funny, laid back kid who could fight like no one he'd ever seen. It was that incident that gave Woody the idea of taking martial arts lessons, and on a lark he stopped by Stanley's house a month later and asked him if he'd like to make some extra money. Now, four years later, Stanley Ono was a freshman at Sacramento City College paying his way through school by offering KajuKenpo classes three days a week. His advanced students met on Tuesdays, and one of his favorite drills was "King of the Picnic Table." It taught balance and strategy. And it was fun.

"Two more minutes! Go hard!"

Stanley barked out the order, and Sid and Woody climbed back up on the table. Both were still breathing hard, and neither was in a hurry to start up again. Sid glanced around at the other three tables and saw that the other students—two girls and four guys—were slowing down a little. "King of the Picnic Table" is an interesting exercise. It teaches you how to fight when your opponent is right in your face, and it teaches you how to stay away, even in close quarters. It's great for timing and balance, and it was one of the most exhausting workouts Sid had ever encountered—as bad as anything the coaches cooked up when he was running cross-country and track in high school and college. When you combine the physical demands of the sport with the ever-present potential that you might get your teeth knocked out, these sparring sessions were completely draining. The two stood for a moment with hands on hips, then Woody held out an open palm, Sid reached out and gave it a slap, and they started again.

It's hard for opponents to circle one another on top of a picnic table, but that's what they did, each occasionally throwing a punch that the other could easily counter. Stanley's attention was focused elsewhere by now, so why not take it easy and coast a little for the last couple of minutes?

"So Stokes said I was a good cop?" Woody asked under his breath.

"Yep. But then he said something about us being limpdicks, so don't let it go to your head."

Sid deflected a weak jab, then stepped forward and brought a big, slow right hand toward his friend's face that should have been easy to block. But Woody tried to spin out of the way, lost his balance, and found himself doing a little tap dance on the edge of the table. Sid reached out an arm to help, and Woody grabbed on to avoid another trip to the grass.

"Thanks."

"Should've blocked that one. If I hadn't pulled the punch you never could've gotten out of the way in time."

"Yeah."

Neither one had said it out loud, but both men knew it. Despite Woody's superior size and strength, Sid had become a much better fighter. Sid quietly suspected that, if they were to ever really try to hurt one another, Woody would come out the loser. And Woody knew it, too.

Their instructor had not yet signaled the end of the day's lesson, so they half-heartedly began again. Sid and Woody locked arms and circled, looking more like two high school kids attempting their first slow dance to *Color My World* than a couple of warriors. Seconds ticked by.

"Time!" Stanley Ono called a merciful end to the day's lesson. The sun was getting low in the sky and everyone was exhausted. "Same time next week."

The other students climbed down and gathered their things. Sid and Woody sat on the edge of their picnic table, elbows on knees, and said nothing as they made little sweat puddles on the bench below.

"Martial arts competition in Oakland on Saturday." Stanley rolled up to them on a rusty, fenderless bicycle with fat tires. "You guys are ready."

"No thanks, Stanley," said Woody. "I'm a man of peace."

"Me, too," said Sid. "Plus, I hate getting punched in the face on the weekends."

"Chickens."

Stanley pushed off and pedaled across the grass. Sid and Woody sat quietly, dripping, as their heart rates and breathing returned to normal.

"So when did Stokes tell you that you were off the case?"

"Middle of the afternoon. You knew before I did."

"Sorry. That sucks."

"Yeah, but I'm not surprised. He and Martinez probably oughta be heading up this investigation. It's a huge case. They've got the most experience, and they understand the politics of City Hall. It's the right call."

Sid turned to his friend to see if he was joking.

"The guy didn't exactly dazzle me with his brilliance earlier today."

"Don't underestimate him, Sid."

"Very magnanimous."

"Thank you."

"So, now that you're off the case, tell me what's happened in the five days since Trager and Bertie were shot."

"Well, we've thrown a lot of resources at it, but we don't have much. We had all those eyewitnesses at the bar, but haven't really collected a lot that's useful since. Got no shooter, got no motive. I had an artist work up a composite sketch over the weekend. I was gonna have you take a look at it."

"Does it look like Porky Pig with a scar on his face?"

Woody thought for a moment. "Yeah, kinda."

"Then it's pretty good."

"I did a lot of background on Tom Trager. Couldn't find anybody who liked him—even his wife—but I couldn't find anybody who'd want to kill him either."

"Not even the wife? I hear Trager had a girlfriend on the side."

"Yeah, Lieutenant Stokes told me you said something about that. A blonde, right? I'm supposed to pry some information out of you without you knowing it. I'm like a spy."

"It may be nothing. It was something Jock Bell told me."

"It's nice that you two have patched things up. He's like your sleazy, mafia grandpa."

"Uh-huh. So if he's right about this other woman—the

blonde—then what about Trager's wife? Some women get pissed off when you cheat on them. Any chance she's involved?"

"Maybe, but probably not. I talked to a few people who said she didn't love her husband, but she loved his money and he gave her plenty of it. No reason to have him whacked. Penny Trager, mid-thirties and seriously hot, was having dinner with three girlfriends—also hot—at Aldo's when her husband was shot. I talked to 'em all."

"Okay, what about Bertie?"

Woody looked at him funny. "Why would Bertie Jones want Trager dead?"

Wow. Gloria was right. It simply would not enter the cops' minds that Bertie might have also been a target that night. Sid didn't really believe it himself, but the damned cops had a responsibility to look at every angle. Protect and serve.

"Jesus, Woody. I don't mean Bertie's a suspect. What if the shooter was trying to kill 'em both? The only victims in a room full of people were both on the city council. That doesn't strike you as odd?"

"Where is this coming from?" Woody actually looked a little hurt. "Nobody that witnessed the shooting—not even you—has said anything other than that the shooter walked into that bar looking specifically for Trager. He called out his name, right? Then Councilwoman Jones stands up and yells something, and the guy fires off *one* random shot in her direction before unloading on Trager. Bertie getting hit was a fluke. It coulda been you that was shot just as easy."

Sid flashed back to discovering the little holes in his

shirt, and his hand subconsciously rubbed his arm.

"Yeah, well I'm surprised you guys haven't even considered the possibility. A good cop has to look at every angle."

Before the words had completely left his mouth, Sid knew he'd said something stupid and he regretted it. It had been Woody's case—a career-maker that he wanted badly—and Sid had just questioned his competence. Woody turned and gave him a cold stare that, if he'd seen it a few minutes earlier when they were sparring, would've scared him.

"My sister asked me to look into it," said Sid, hoping it would sound like an excuse or apology. "She's worried about Bertie."

"Let me ask you something. Do you think the guy came in there trying to kill Bertie Jones?"

Sid thought a moment, then reluctantly said, "No. No, not really."

"Asshole."

Woody got up, grabbed his towel off the grass and headed for his car. Sid sat for a moment wondering what had happened to the legendary Bigler tact, then hopped down from the table and caught up to his friend.

"Sorry."

"Yeah."

Sid racked his brain for something to say that might undo the damage. In a demonstration of restraint that was rare for him, he opted to keep his mouth shut. The sound of birds and passing cars seemed impossibly loud and uncomfortable. It was Woody who broke the tension.

"Is Gloria paying you?"

"Are you kidding?"

Quiet again, then, "Asshole."

This time, the tone was different and the word conveyed an entirely different meaning. This time, it meant '*You're an idiot, but you're still my friend.*'

"Sorry."

"Yeah."

They covered the last twenty yards to their cars in silence. Woody had parked his sedan right next to Sid's green Duster. Both men fished around in their pockets for car keys.

"Hey, did I tell you what case Stokes has me working on now?" Woody said it so casually, Sid had no idea what was coming.

"No."

Two keys went into car doors, two doors unlocked.

"The murder of Lou Martini."

Sid turned to look at Woody, and his friend said, "Buy me some Chinese food."

Chapter 12

The Mandarin on Broadway was Woody's favorite restaurant. It was much too nice for Sid's taste. Chinese restaurants oughta be cheaper and greasier, but it was Woody's choice. The waitress had just dropped off a couple of Tsingtaos and they were waiting for their food.

"I finally talked to Lou's ex-wife this afternoon. They hadn't spoken in a couple of years."

"Diane?"

"Deanne. She's a dead end. Had no idea why anybody'd want to hurt Lou. Actually had very nice things to say about him."

"Why'd they divorce?"

"Didn't ask. Why did Lucy divorce Desi? Why did the Beatles break up?" Woody drank down about half of his beer. "Why do Shriners wear those funny hats?"

"I can answer two out of three of those, but I'll assume they're rhetorical questions. So what happened to Lou Martini?"

"If you watched the news or read the paper, they got it mostly right. Somebody in Fair Oaks called yesterday morning and said there was a man sleeping in a car in front of their house. We sent a unit to check it out figuring they'd find, you know, some guy with no pants sleeping off a weekend bender. But it was Lou."

"What killed him?"

"Blunt object blow to the head. And not just once, Sid. It was bad. Closed casket funeral for sure."

Sid turned and looked out the window, looking at nothing. He pressed his lips together and tried to keep his chin from quivering.

"Sorry. I wasn't trying to be funny."

"It's okay." Sid still not making eye contact.

"Here's the deal. A couple of guys from our office worked the crime scene and filed the initial report. They've got less seniority than me, and to be honest, I think they're a couple of stiffs. They got pulled off to another case when Stokes gave it to me. Stokes was throwing me a bone, Sid, and he knows we're friends."

"What's that mean?"

"It means that if you can keep your mouth shut, I can unofficially give you the details of the case and you can unofficially give me your opinion."

"Stokes knows about this?"

"Unofficially. We figure that you knew Martini better than anyone. Maybe you can help."

The waitress appeared, somehow managing to carry three plates, a bowl, and that chrome basket thing that held the soy sauce and vinegar. Chicken chow fun, broccoli beef, snow peas in black bean sauce and steamed rice was loaded onto plates as Woody picked the conversation back up.

"Coroner got there just after 10 a.m. He figured Lou had been dead about four hours."

Sid was about to take his first bite, but stopped. "Lou Martini had a crappy apartment near his office in midtown—twenty minutes from the crime scene, easy. What's he doing parked in front of somebody's house in Fair Oaks at six in the morning?"

"You tell me. Could be all kinds of reasons. Maybe Lou got caught as he was tailing an unfaithful husband. Or who knows? Maybe he got caught boinking an unfaithful wife."

"I don't think so. Not his style. And the news said it was a robbery."

"Well, his wallet was missing."

Sid could resist the temptation no longer, and took a huge, sloppy bite of the chow fun. He loved the slimy, wide rice noodles and the flavor the searing hot wok gave them. Woody chased down a mouthful with a swig of Tsingtao.

"Was Lou's window up or down?" Sid asked.

"Initial report at the scene says all four windows were down."

"Marks on the arms? Did he put up a fight?"

"Nothing."

"So Lou's parked on the street in some neighborhood in Fair Oaks with his windows down at six in the morning, and he just lets somebody reach in and hit him in the head? With enough force to kill him? I don't buy it."

"Didn't make sense to me, either. And the blows to the head were from in front and behind. I think he was killed outside the car, worked over bad. Then they put him behind the wheel. The coroner's report isn't done, but he thinks so, too."

"So, somebody took the wallet to make it look like a robbery?"

"That would figure. But they left his Rolex."

"Fake Rolex."

"Really?

"He used to joke about it."

The watch prompted some fond, private memory, and Sid's mind wandered for a moment. The two returned to their Chinese food and ate in silence for a while.

"Keys in the ignition?"

"Yep."

"No witnesses, I assume?"

"The first two detectives knocked on every door in the neighborhood, got zip. But I got to thinking, who might have been around at 6 a.m.?"

Sid thought for a few seconds. "Paperboy?"

"Well, he's fifty-seven years old and throws the papers out the window of a '72 Buick Skylark, but, yeah. The paperboy. Willis Frye. I got his name from the Sacramento Bee and woke him up from a nap this afternoon. He was not happy."

"But he saw something?"

"Maybe we got lucky. Willis tells me he remembers a suspicious guy on the same street where Lou was killed."

"Suspicious how?"

"Very tall, overcoat…" Woody paused for dramatic effect. "Baseball bat."

"No."

Woody stuffed an enormous chunk of broccoli in his mouth, then wiped a smear of sauce from his chin. "Why would Willis, the old paperboy, make that up?"

"Any idea who the guy is?"

"Not much to go on. Besides saying that the guy was really tall—way over six feet—Willis says he thinks there was a white or silver Mercedes on the same block that he'd never seen before."

"And that's it."

"That's what I've got so far."

"Nice work, Detective, considering you got the case about four hours ago."

"Thank you."

Woody raised his glass and tipped it toward his friend. Sid returned the gesture, and they each drained their beer.

"Lou Martini was a good guy. He did a lot for me. Thanks for letting me know what's going on."

"Yeah, well, Stokes knows we're talking. And the information comes with three strings attached. First, you keep all this to yourself. We don't want the media to have some of this information."

"I can do that."

"Second, this is my case, not yours. I'll keep you informed, you leave it alone."

"Okay."

"I mean it, Sid. You think of anything that might be useful, you give it to me. But you stay out of it."

"Yeah, cross my heart. What's number three?"

"I need the name of the blonde that Tom Trager was canoodling."

"Oh, that's right. You're a spy."

"It'll be good for both of us if I can give Stokes the name."

"I'll talk to Jock Bell. If there really is a blonde, I'll get her name for you."

The two continued eating, but after a few minutes they were clearly slowing down. The waitress dropped two to-go containers, a couple of fortune cookies and the bill on their table as she passed by without saying a word. Woody pulled a credit card from his wallet.

"I'll get this."

"You're kidding."

"You're an informant. I can turn in the receipt."

Sid laughed. It was strange—and it made him feel a little guilty—but in a way, he was enjoying himself immensely. In the last few days, two men had been murdered and Bertie had been shot, but as a result it felt like he was moving up in the P.I. world. He was being taken seriously for the first time. First, Gloria had told him that he was *'good'*— that she needed his help. Now he was working alongside the police department, and they were asking for his help, too. He was an insider. The first thirty years of his life had been unremarkable. He simply hadn't done much, and his few accomplishments had been things that came easily to him. He'd been a pretty good runner in school, but that was a natural ability. And the success of the deli was a testament to his father's hard work, not his own. He'd never really aspired to anything challenging— anything he thought was important. But as he sat across from Woody at The Mandarin, Sid Bigler began to really think of himself as a private eye for the first time, and he liked how it felt.

"Woody, there's something else you need to know about Lou Martini."

"Okay, what?"

"He called me two nights ago."

"Is that unusual?"

"Yeah. Yeah, we hadn't talked in a while."

"How long?"

"I don't know. Months."

"What did he want?"

"Said he needed to talk to me. Didn't say what it was about, but he wanted to talk right away. I was going out to dinner with Amy that night, so we scheduled for the next day. It would've been yesterday afternoon. I was waiting for him at Boitano's when I heard he'd been killed."

"Jesus, Sid." Woody Carver let the information soak in for a moment. "Any idea what he wanted to talk to you about?"

"I don't know. I've been trying to recall our phone conversation, and all I can remember is small talk. We talked about the wedding coming up—he liked Amy. And he asked how Bertie Jones was doing. Then he said he needed to talk to me and we agreed to meet. I think that was it."

"You think there's any chance Martini's death and the shooting in the bar are related?"

"I asked your boss that very question this morning and he thought I was nuts."

The waitress swooped by and picked up the bill and credit card. Woody began loading the leftovers into the cartons.

"We'll know more tomorrow," Woody said. "I'm getting into Lou's office in the morning to have a look at his records. See what he was working on."

"You got the rabbit's foot?"

"What?"

"Red rabbit's foot on a little chain. He kept the key to his filing cabinet on it."

"Hmm. I dunno. I don't remember a rabbit's foot in the report. He would've had it on him?"

"Always."

"I'll go through his personal effects in the morning before heading to his office. Maybe it's in there."

"Listen, if you do get into the filing cabinet, you might be disappointed."

"Why?"

"I worked with him for a couple of years. From what I gather, he wasn't like a lot of P.I.'s when it came to record keeping and notes. He took the "Private" in "Private Investigator" very seriously. Figured that if someone was coming to him, it might be because they didn't want to go to the police, or they didn't want something to be public knowledge. So he didn't take a lot of notes. And he didn't need 'em. The guy had the most amazing memory I've ever seen. Two out of three cases we worked on he didn't even keep a file."

"I've never heard of such a thing. What about billing records?"

"None that he kept. When a case was over and the client was paid up, he shredded 'em."

"Damn."

"Uh-huh. He said his clients appreciated his discretion. Lou was unique."

The waitress dropped off the credit card slip to be signed and Woody picked up the pen.

"What's ten percent of $19.40?"

"You're kidding, right?"

"I'm not good with math, so what?"

"It's two bucks, but leave her five. She was very efficient."

Woody began scribbling while Sid busted open one of the fortune cookies. The little slip of paper inside was completely blank on both sides. He held it up.

"What's up with this?"

Woody glanced up briefly and grinned. "I don't know, but I like it. You can write down whatever you want." He dropped the pen, pulled off the top copy of the credit card receipt and stood up.

"Hey, do me a favor," said Sid as he dropped his napkin on his plate and got up from the table. "When you go to Lou's office tomorrow, you'll see he had a little turtle in a glass tank. It's only about this big." He held up a thumb and forefinger to indicate the size. "His name's Frampton."

"Okay."

"Unless you think he's important evidence, I'd like to have him."

"I'll drop him off at the deli."

"Thank you."

Chapter 13

Deli owner and private eye is, admittedly, an unlikely combination. But this was one of the times when it really worked for Sid Bigler. He'd fallen asleep Tuesday night with too much Chinese food in his belly and three cases running through his head, each competing for top billing. The faces of Tom Trager, Lou Martini, and homely little Mandy Mercer kept coming back to him in the dark, but once he got to work Wednesday morning, the hustle and bustle of the deli demanded his attention and gave his mind a break from the violence and loss of the past week.

And it was an exceptionally busy day. Wednesday was *Chili Day* at the deli, a brainstorm of Sid's father. For fifty cents, customers could get a big scoop of chili added to any order. It had been a lunchtime phenomenon for years, but they'd recently included breakfast as part of *Chili Day* and it had proven to be surprisingly popular. If you had the stomach for it, Joe's Chili was great over hash browns and a cheese omelet. As the morning wound down and the early lunch crowd was showing up, Sid had been awake for six hours and had hardly thought about Bertie Jones or the cases that had troubled him the night before.

As a side note, one of the first lunch customers of the day ordered chili with chili on top. No one had ever tried this in the fourteen years since *Chili Day* had been instituted. The result was a heated discussion among the regulars over the legitimacy of such an order. A bowl of chili was a buck and a quarter, and this essentially doubled the amount for just another fifty cents. Several patrons felt that topping chili with chili violated the spirit of *Chili Day*. Sid, who knew that a ladle full of chili cost him about nine cents, congratulated the fellow and re-filled his coffee.

Once the controversy died down and the lunch crowd was well under control, Sid disappeared into his office and switched hats. He didn't really give a damn about Nathan Bomke and the homely Miss Mercer, but it was the biggest payday of his fledgling career so he made himself focus on it. He grabbed his jar of dimes off the desk, pulled his chair over to the payphone on the back wall, and spent half an hour trying out the names and numbers he'd found on the scribbled notes that Bomke had given him. As he suspected, he found himself speaking with several people who were in a position to hire actors and models. Two were local companies that produced TV commercials and both recognized Li'l Starz and its assaulted owner, Howard Clark. The first guy claimed to have never heard of Mandy Mercer, but the second guy laughed when he heard the name and said that the girl was "not right for the kind of work that I do."

"What kind of work do you do?" Sid asked.

"The kind that doesn't hire ugly kids."

Six phone calls to the L.A. area produced two no-answers, three take-a-messages, and one ad agency with a vice president that was certain he'd never heard of Li'l Starz. Finally, Sid pulled a business card from the folder, looked for a phone number, and did something that, for some reason, he'd been dreading since he took the case. He dialed the phone, and a young, overly-enthusiastic voice picked up.

"Li'l Starz—Making Big Stars of Little People."

"Yes, could I speak with Howard Clark, please?"

"Speaking."

That was a surprise. The voice just didn't match Sid's preconceived idea of a sixty-three-year-old con man with one leg. Too happy. Too Liberace.

"Mr. Clark, my name is Sid Bigler. I'm a private investigator that's assisting Nathan Bomke with your legal case."

"Oh, yes. Mr. Bomke said you'd be calling. What can I do for you?"

For the next several minutes, Sid asked questions about Howard Clark's efforts to secure work for Mandy Mercer. The guy's story matched the one Nathan Bomke had told him a few days earlier, including the assault by Mandy's father. Sid pressed him for specific details about the special trip he allegedly made to Hollywood on behalf of the girl, and Clark gave him the dates and location for something called *The Prodigy Project*, which sounded like a two-day job fair for child actor wannabes. Sid thumbed through the folder until he found the credit card statement, and saw that the highlighted flights were purchased three days before *The Prodigy Project*, and the stay at the Travelodge coincided exactly with the dates of the event.

"Okay, I think that's all for now, Mr. Clark. Thanks for your help."

"Well, thank you, Mr. Bigler. Call back anytime. Toodle-oo."

Sid hung up the phone and quietly savored the moment. The guy had actually said, '*Toodle-oo.*'

A few minutes after the call with Howard Clark, Woody stopped by for lunch and Sid joined him at a table by the windows. He had a little aquarium with him.

"Hey, Frampton!"

Sid picked up the turtle and placed it in the middle of his palm, then held him up at eye level. "What's going on, dude? You okay?"

"You can pick 'em up?" asked Woody. "They don't bite?"

"No. No, I don't think so."

"I looked around Lou's office for turtle food or something, but didn't see a thing. He's probably hungry."

Sid hopped up and went behind the counter, taking the turtle with him. Joe Diaz gave Frampton a glare as Sid reached down and picked up a lettuce leaf.

"No turtles behind the counter."

Sid waved an apology and returned to the table. Frampton and the lettuce went into the little tank, and the turtle went to work on lunch.

Sid had hoped that Woody would have some new information regarding the Lou Martini case, but at first it looked like the primary reason for his visit was hunger. Eventually, between bites of a pastrami sandwich, he did say that his trip to Martini's office had not been very productive.

"The files are no help at all."

"You found the rabbit's foot?" Sid asked.

"Sort of. I was right, there was nothing about it in the initial report. And I went through the stuff that they found on Lou and in his car when I got to the station this morning. Nothing."

"So how'd you get into the files?"

"Once I got in his office, the key was just sitting there in the lock on the filing cabinet. Little red rabbit's foot dangling down."

"No way."

Woody shrugged and took another bite.

"Woody, Lou wouldn't have done that." Sid was a little louder. "I never saw him leave that thing unlocked. Somebody killed him, took the key and went through his files."

"Okay, maybe you're right, but there's no way to tell. And no way to tell if something's missing. Not by looking at the files, anyway. It was just like you said. Hardly any records, and most of it looked like it was ancient. I'm gonna go through 'em if I have time, but I don't expect to find anything. I don't know how the guy kept track of what he was doing."

"I'm telling you, somebody was in there. They took the key and got into his papers."

"Yeah, well, when you figure out how I can prove that, you let me know."

"Did you check the place for fingerprints?"

"What, like on TV?"

The two friends stared at one another for a moment, Sid looking suddenly irritated, Woody looking suddenly amused.

"Sid, there's no evidence of a break-in at Lou's office. None. I'll ask Stokes if he wants to expend the resources to have an evidence team go down there and go over the place. Don't count on it."

103

Sid looked out the window at nothing in particular, absent-mindedly chewed his lip and tried to make sense of what he'd heard. A minute or two went by, and Woody got tired of the silence.

"I had a little time to work some pretty reliable informants for anything they might know about a tall guy with a light colored Mercedes. Got a bite, but nothing firm."

"So?"

"So I'll tell you if it pans out. It's *my* case, not yours. Remember?"

Woody took another bite of sandwich as Frampton tore off a fresh piece of lettuce, and Sid wondered about Lou Martini's last minutes on earth as the cop and the turtle chewed their food.

Chapter 14

Sid was so occupied with getting Frampton and his tank safely out of his own car that at first he didn't even notice the strange car parked in his mom's driveway—a brand new Lincoln Continental that was still waiting for its license plates. Once he managed to navigate the front door without dropping his fragile cargo, it all made sense. Sitting in the living room next to his mom was Mary Jones. Bertie's mother.

"Hi, mom. Hello, Mrs. Jones."

Rose hopped up and gave her son a kiss. Sid put the aquarium down on the coffee table, then sat in a chair next to the sofa and told the story of how Frampton came to be moving in. Mary Jones had heard about Lou Martini on the news, but had no idea the Biglers knew him.

"I'm so sorry. Such a terrible thing."

Rose and Mary had been casual friends for nearly thirty years. It made sense. They'd met as young moms when their daughters started second grade in the same class. The girls remained best friends over the years, and the two mothers stayed on very good terms, though not particularly close. They'd see each other at events—PTA meetings, back to school night, graduation. And Mary had attended Gloria's wedding when Bertie was maid of honor. But that had really been the extent of the relationship between the two moms until five years ago. Until Sid's father was found slumped over his desk with a suicide note and a gun on the floor.

105

It's a funny thing. When word gets out that someone in your family has killed himself, the phone stops ringing. Oh, you hear from the people who are required to call—pastor, cop, life insurance agent—but friends and neighbors are often silent. It's not that they don't care. They just don't know what to say. So it was a surprise when Sid answered the phone five years ago and heard Mary's voice asking to speak to his mother.

Mary Jones had, herself, been a widow for as long as anyone could remember, and she had never remarried. Her husband, Robert, had died from some kind of cancer in his thirties, just a few years after they moved to Sacramento. Sid knew the name only because Bertie—Roberta—had been named after him. Bertie had been the only kid growing up whose father was dead. In fact, as he sat in the living room with the two ladies, Sid couldn't recall another kid who didn't have a father in the house when he was a boy. It was the fifties and sixties, and every family made an extraordinary effort to appear to be Ozzie and Harriet. The Widow Jones was obviously a devoted mother to her only child, but Sid always had the feeling that some of the other parents kind of kept her at arm's length. Then, years later when Sid's dad died, there came that phone call from Mary Jones and the two widows found for the first time a friendship that was entirely their own, apart from their daughters. Over the years, their relationship had been really good for Rose, and Sid was thankful for it.

"Nice wheels," said Sid as he pointed in the direction of the driveway.

"Oh, thanks. I didn't really want it." Mary Jones tried

106

unsuccessfully to put a frustrated look on her face. "Bertie worries about me. Says she's getting me a new, reliable car every four years no matter what. There was nothing wrong with the last one."

"How is Bertie, Mrs. Jones?"

"Amazing," she beamed. "She insists that she's going back to the office next week. She had somebody drop off a bunch of files and she's already working from home."

"That's great to hear."

Bertie's mother reached over and put a hand on Sid's arm.

"Thank you for what you did."

"What, at the bar? It was nothing."

"No, it wasn't, Sid. Who knows what would have happened if it wasn't for you. Thank you."

Mary Jones smiled, and it wasn't the first time that Sid realized what a looker she was. There wasn't a lot of resemblance between mother and daughter, really. Bertie's mother was a brunette and there was no cleft in the chin. And her eyes were a gray-blue instead of the hypnotizing green. But she was a certified mature hottie, and she looked young for her age. Lee Meriwether in the Barnaby Jones days.

"You're welcome," said Sid. "I'm glad she's doing so well."

For the next few minutes, Sid sat and chatted with the two women. Mary asked how things were going at the deli, and it was Rose who did most of the talking. Sid's mom was a terrific storyteller, and her account of Governor Deukmejian accidentally locking himself in the deli's bathroom was hysterical.

"And how's work for you, Mrs. Jones?" Sid asked. "Things going well at The WAVE?"

W.A.V.E.—Women Against Violence Everywhere. It was a shelter for women and children who were victims of domestic abuse in Sacramento. Mary Jones had started the program by herself more than a decade ago. The WAVE had struggled in the early years, especially when it came to money. But when Bertie started to hit it big as a criminal defense attorney, she became the program's primary benefactor, pumping countless thousands of dollars into the effort over the years and encouraging Sacramento's powerful and wealthy to do the same. Between Bertie's money and her mother's passion for the cause, The WAVE had become a model program, studied by other cities around the country.

"Yes, wonderfully." Mary Jones wore her passion for the cause on her sleeve. "We just celebrated our twelfth anniversary. And I'm flying to Phoenix tomorrow to talk with them about establishing a women's shelter there."

"Mary, how exciting!" Rose obviously hadn't heard the news yet.

"I'm only staying a couple of days. I have an appointment with the mayor, then a few meetings with volunteers."

"That's great, Mrs. Jones. Why Phoenix?"

"Oh, I've always loved Phoenix. I spent some time there years ago. And God knows there's a need for what we do in every city in America."

"Well, have a successful trip. Frampton and I will keep

an eye on mom until you return." Sid hopped up and smooched his mother on the cheek. "I'm gonna go for a run. Nice to see you again, Mrs. Jones."

"Bye, Sid," Mary said with a wave and another warm smile.

Sid went to his room, tossed his clothes on the bed and pulled on a pair of running shorts. He spotted an old white Humboldt State Cross Country t-shirt on the floor, gave it a sniff and slipped it over his head. He had just laced up his Adidas and was heading for the door when he saw the napkin on his dresser. The napkin with the smeared ink that he'd been writing on in the bar when Amy called to tell him that Lou Martini had been killed.

Sid stopped and studied the napkin. Four names, still mostly legible. Tom Trager, the blonde, Porky, and Bertie Jones. Sid shook his head and mentally kicked himself for being such an amateur. He was about to let an opportunity pass him by. He wasn't remotely convinced that there was a case here at all—that there was anyone out there who wanted to intentionally hurt Bertie Jones. But he had told his sister he would do his best, and there was a woman sitting in his living room who might be able to answer some questions.

Chapter 15

Sid ran fairly hard, suburbs to his left and the Sacramento River to his right. It was a little after 5 p.m., and with rush hour traffic, the trail on the top of the levee was a much safer place to be than the city streets. As he clicked off six and a half minute miles, he wondered what he might have done differently. How could he have avoided the disaster he'd just left behind at his mother's house?

Minutes earlier, as Sid was leaving for his run, he had stopped again in the living room and casually asked Mrs. Jones a few questions. He'd tried his damnedest to make it sound like small talk, to not upset Bertie's mom. Now he replayed it all in his mind and tried to figure out how a conversation that was so short could have gone so wrong...

"Oh, hey, Mrs. Jones, before I go... You guys moved here from Ohio, right?"

"Yes, that's right."

"Cleveland? Cincinnati?"

"Canton."

"Oh, Canton. The state capital, just like here."

"No, that's Columbus."

It wasn't particularly clever, but it had seemed like a perfectly innocent way to start a conversation. How do you screw up small talk? It should've gone so smoothly, but from the very first question she seemed uncomfortable, even suspicious.

"Right. Columbus. I used to know all the capitals."

"Sid was very good in school," Rose had chimed in. It wasn't even close to true, but Sid appreciated the effort.

"Uh, Mrs. Jones, does Bertie talk with you very much about the legal cases she's working on, or city council stuff?"

"Almost never about her legal work, but we talk a lot about city politics, why do you ask?"

"Oh, nothing. Just wondering. No special reason."

Why had it gone so badly? Why had the words felt so clumsy? He should've quit while he was behind.

"Is something wrong, Sid?"

"Oh, no. No, Mrs. Jones."

An uncomfortable pause. Would've been a good time to walk out the front door, but he didn't.

"In your conversations with Bertie about city government and the things the council was doing, did she ever sound like she was, uh, I dunno… worried about anything? Or anyone?"

Looking back, that was the point at which Sid had gone too far. The die was cast. The cat was out of the bag. The pooch was officially screwed. Mary Jones hadn't responded. Her jaw dropped slightly and she just stared at him.

"I mean, you don't know of anyone who would've wanted to hurt Bertie, right? I mean, it'd be crazy to think that, right?"

The woman's eyes welled with tears. The clock ticked very loudly. Frampton the turtle turned and looked at Sid.

"I'm sure there's nothing to worry about." Sid made an effort to put the brakes on the conversation, knowing full well it was like pointing a fire extinguisher at the Hindenberg.

"You think it wasn't an accident?" Mary raised a hand to her mouth. *"You think that man shot at my daughter on*

purpose? You... you think..."

And then Bertie's mother had burst into tears. Big time. Rose slid over on the couch, put her arm around her friend and gave Sid a nasty scowl.

"I'm sure everything's fine," he had said. *"I didn't mean to upset you."*

And that had been the end of the conversation. Mrs. Jones sobbed, Rose glared, and Sid stood in awkward silence for a little while before heading out the door.

He had unintentionally picked up his pace over the last mile as he re-lived the agonizing and stupid exchange with Bertie's mom. He was breathing hard now and his sweaty shirt was clinging to him. Maybe he had subconsciously decided to punish himself for being such a schmuck.

Going for a nice, long run by himself had been a source of satisfaction for Sid for a long time. For most of his life it had been an escape. He would hit the road and just space out. A song would get into his brain and his feet would pound out the rhythm as mile after mile went by. But over the last couple of years—since Sid seriously began pursuing the detective business—that had changed a little. Now he'd run and he'd think. It wasn't a formal process. He'd just let the facts of a case bang together in his mind, often accompanied by the Final Jeopardy music. Sometimes he'd have a breakthrough, sometimes not, but he always felt good for having made the effort.

Sid looked around, realized he was several miles from home now and all he'd been doing was reliving the awful scene he'd just left in his mom's living room. Unproductive and uncomfortable.

"Stupid."

Sid said it out loud to himself, then made a conscious effort to think about something else. Anything. He took a moment to appreciate the view. The river was wide and deep. Unnaturally contained very precisely by a levee on each side, it rolled along like a highway made of water. Enormous trees peeked up from beyond the levee on the far side, and Sid knew that beyond them was miles and miles of farmland— fields and orchards and dirt roads spreading across the rich soil of the delta. He backed off the pace a little, and his breathing became deeper and slower. Eventually, he surrendered to the steady rhythm of his stride, and a tune crept quietly into his head. Just like the good old days. A few pleasant miles rolled by before he realized that the song running through his mind was "Wake Me Up Before You Go-Go," that new one by Wham. God, how humiliating. He tried for a few minutes to chase it away, but as long as he was running, George Michael's voice returned again and again.

"You put the boom-boom into my brain..."

Sid came to a dead stop and, mercifully, so did Wham. Blessed silence. Hearing only the sound of his breath and distant traffic, he looked around and tried to figure how far he'd gone. He'd run along this levee countless times, but the scenery doesn't change much and it seldom offers a clue as to where you are. He had to be six or seven miles from home by now. Time to turn around and start back.

Resolving to make the second half of his run more productive than the first, Sid decided to focus on the facts of the case and forget about his disastrous conversation with Mrs. Jones. Bertie's mom had been genuinely blindsided by Sid's question. No doubt about that. It had never occurred to her that anyone would try to hurt her daughter. As far as the investigation goes, Mary Jones was a dead end.

Okay, back to basic questions. If someone had wanted Bertie Jones killed—big "if," and Sid still wasn't buying it—who would they be? There were only two logical answers he could come up with: political enemies and legal enemies.

Unfortunately, Sid didn't know squat about city politics. He could go over the minutes to every City Council meeting for the last couple of years, but that didn't exactly sound like fun and Gloria wasn't paying him for his time. Maybe he'd make a call to Jackson Dexter from the newspaper. Dexter's *Talk of the Town* column featured the city's latest events and juiciest gossip, and whether you liked the guy or not, nobody was more plugged in to what was going on in Sacramento politics. And, to the degree that it was possible for Jackson Dexter to have friends, they were friends. But nobody could completely drop their guard around the guy, for fear of showing up in his column.

If that was Sid's best plan for looking into Bertie's political life, what about legal enemies? Was there someone so unhappy about something Bertie had done in a criminal case that they might want her dead? How would he find that person? Who could help him look at the legal angle? Sid thought about that for a minute or two, listening to the sound of a motor boat going by in the river and the slap of his feet on the trail. When he realized he had been overlooking the one, incredibly obvious resource, he laughed. His sister was the one who asked him to take the case. His sister was Bertie's best friend. And his sister was a lawyer. He almost said "Duh" out loud. Gloria knew Bertie's partners, and must know something about at least some of the cases she had handled. Yeah, that was good. If Gloria wanted Sid to do a proper investigation, she could do some of the legwork herself.

The thought put a little spring in his step. The delta breeze was picking up, and the day was already growing cooler. He trotted along on cruise control and took it all in. He stopped thinking about the case. Stopped thinking about anything at all as miles rolled by. This was the most peaceful moment of the day, and it felt great. And into the vacuum that was Sid Bigler's head, a snippet of conversation returned…

"Oh, Canton. The state capital, just like here."

"No, that's Columbus," Mary had said, not knowing what was coming.

"Right. Columbus. I used to know all the capitals."

For some reason, that stupid chatter about cities in Ohio replayed again and again in his mind. It was supposed to be an icebreaker — something innocuous and friendly before he asked the really probing questions. But looking back, it felt like that was when Mrs. Jones began to lose it. Something about that conversation. Something didn't click.

And then another voice popped into his head. It was something Lou Martini said to him long ago: *"Start at the beginning. Question the things you think you know."*

Sid ran along and the sun began to dip behind the trees across the river. Something wasn't right, and he had no idea

115

what it was. He found himself thinking about playing a hunch. About doing something that would surely be a waste of time. Then again, it would just be a matter of making a phone call.

"Oh, Canton. The state capital, just like here..."

Sid reached the Miller Park Marina, followed a worn path through the grass down from the levee trail, and trotted for home.

Chapter 16

The guy from Kotter's Meats had offered Sid a deal on a case of four-ounce sirloin steaks. Eighty of them in a twenty pound box. Thirty bucks. Sid couldn't say no, and so they were running a special on steak sandwiches and Joe was not happy. He didn't like having his routine broken. It was just past noon, the place was more packed than usual, and the entire grill was covered with cheap little pieces of meat. It ran against Joe's nature to serve anything that wasn't tasty, so he dusted all the steaks with Adolph's Meat Tenderizer and beat them with a wooden mallet before throwing them on the grill. The hot steaks were served on sourdough bread with grilled onions, swiss cheese and a special mayo that had a bunch of smashed garlic in it. Two steaks per sandwich. They were spectacular.

Rose was working the register non-stop—making change, taking to-go orders and keeping anyone who would listen amused. Like her late husband, she proved to have an uncanny knack for remembering the names of customers and making them feel at home. Big Sid would've been proud. Sid Jr. was wishing he had the time to get some P.I. work done in the back, but he found himself out front getting drinks and helping Eddie keep the tables clear. The restaurant's happy lunchtime din seemed louder and happier than usual, occasionally punctuated by a "wham-wham-wham" as Joe brought down his wooden mallet for another order. It was a good day at the deli.

Sid ran a plastic tub full of dirty dishes into the back,

came back out and poured himself a Coke—no ice—and surveyed the room. He happened to be looking in the right direction just as a customer stood up quickly, and inadvertently pushed back his chair in front of Eddie. Eddie swerved, lost his balance for a moment, and several dirty glasses he had been carrying on a tray got away from him. They crashed to the floor, shattering and splashing water, coffee and soda pop onto the pants of a guy who was seated nearby. The sound of the breaking glass was enough to quiet the room, but when the guy shouted "God Dammit!" at the top of his lungs the deli came to a grinding halt. The man stood, looked down at his pants, then looked at Eddie, whose calm, smiling expression remained unchanged.

"Oh, you think this is funny, do you?"

Every eye in the room was on the guy. Forks had stopped in mid-air. Jaws had stopped in mid-chew. Sid moved quickly from behind the counter and headed toward the angry customer. He didn't look familiar, and, of course, if he'd been a regular he'd have known about Eddie.

"Hey!" Sid called out, trying to sound as friendly as possible as he got closer. "Hey, it's okay. Everything's fine."

"The hell it is," said the guy as he reached down and brushed off his pants.

Even in the heat of the moment, Sid couldn't help but notice that the guy looked like Prince Charles. He was clearly bigger and it looked like he spent time in the weight room, but definitely the Prince. Big ears and everything. It required a small effort on Sid's part to not break a smile at the thought of a buff Prince Charlie.

The man was just making a move toward Eddie when Sid stepped in between them, and up close he was not amusing at all. He was pissed and he was big. They weren't standing eye to eye, exactly, as the guy had Sid by at least five or six inches. It was more like eye to chin.

"Look, friend, you don't understand what…

"I understand plenty." The guy glared down at Sid. "Your asshole busboy ruined my pants, and now he thinks it's funny."

"No, he doesn't think it's funny." Sid was sounding calm and conciliatory, like he was trying to soothe an angry dog. "Eddie's a little different, that's all. How about I pay for your pants to be cleaned and lunch is on me?"

Sid snuck a quick glance in Joe's direction. The big, strong cook was watching, but he hadn't moved. Then he looked toward the front door and spotted Lieutenant Benjamin Stokes standing there, arms crossed with a smile on his face. Their eyes locked briefly, and Stokes gave him a little wave.

"Your asshole busboy is still smiling," said Buff Prince Charlie.

Sid turned back to the matter at hand. The guy's eyes were looking just over his head, obviously staring at Eddie. Sid waited a moment, but the man seemed stuck.

"Hey, big fella."

The angry customer made an exaggerated effort to tip his head down and look at Sid. It was a move clearly designed to intimidate, but Sid thought it was kind of funny. Then Sid wondered if finding humor in the face of danger was a sign of confidence or insanity. Time to find out.

"Okay, how about this? How about I pay for your pants to be cleaned, and you go away?"

"You gonna make me?"

"Be pretty embarrassing for a big guy like you if I did, huh?"

The obligatory stare-down only lasted for a few seconds, then things began to happen. The big guy was way too close to try an effective blow, but he proved to be not nearly as smart as the real Prince Charles and tried it anyway. A big hand turned into a fist as it came up toward Sid's head. Sid deflected it easily. The guy ended up off balance as the blow missed, and Sid gave him a little shove in the direction of a table that, fortunately, had just emptied.

The man caught himself and turned to face Sid again. Sid looked in his eyes, saw him give in to complete rage, and knew the guy was toast. Stanley Ono had said it a thousand times. *"An angry fighter is a stupid fighter."* Sid discovered to his delight that he was completely calm.

The guy came at him again, trying some big, dumb roundhouse swing that never came close. Sid blocked that one, too, and stepped out of the way as he went by. Almost like a matador and a bull. He was very tempted to shout "Ole!" Somebody somewhere chuckled. Sid caught Stokes out of the corner of his eye, and got a thumbs up from him.

For the past couple of years, Sid had been sparring with other KajuKempo students—talented students who took fighting seriously. Now, in this scuffle with a complete meathead, he seemed lightning fast by comparison.

Mr. Splatterpants turned around again and approached him slowly this time, still seething. "You little prick," he said as he stopped a few feet away.

"So far it's only the outside of your pants that are dirty. Maybe you oughta quit before you mess up your underwear, too." Now there was an actual smattering of laughter.

As the man began to move closer, he raised his fists like he was the 1927 heavyweight champ. Sid assessed the situation, acknowledged to himself that it'd be fun to beat the guy senseless, but recognized that it might not be good for business.

The guy stopped, planted his feet, and took another swing. This time, Sid deflected the blow with his left forearm, then reached up quickly and slapped the guy hard in the face with his right hand. He didn't want to really hurt the guy, and he figured a good, solid slap might help him avoid a lawsuit. The effect was interesting. Everyone in the room, including the royal doppelganger himself, was stunned. Kind of like a splash of cold water. The man's eyes cleared briefly, then they narrowed and he came again with the big, stupid fist.

Once again, Sid deflected the swing and slapped him hard in the face. Then it happened again. And again. The guy's confidence in his swing was admirable, and it must have worked for him sometime in the past—in grade school or maybe in a bar room brawl somewhere—but it was clearly not working today in the deli.

Sid lost count, but it was probably after the ninth or tenth good, hard slap to the face that the guy just stopped and stared at him, arms at his sides. Sid's hand was throbbing, but he was quite pleased with the bright color on the left side of the man's face.

"Eddie's been with us since he was a kid."

Every head in the place turned and looked toward the cash register at the surprising sound of Rose Bigler's voice.

"We love Eddie here. You go now, or I'll have my son beat the hell out of you."

Several seconds passed. The guy looked once more at Sid, and Sid raised one eyebrow in a very Mr. Spock-like expression. Then the man turned and walked out the door. Everyone in the deli watched as he pushed past Benjamin Stokes, crossed in front of the windows outside and disappeared from view. Then the place erupted in applause.

The hero treatment lasted for several minutes. After a while Sid had to stop shaking hands because it hurt, and eventually the place got back to normal. Sid headed back behind the counter and Rose gave him a kiss on the cheek as he passed by without saying a word. Joe flashed him a very rare smile. He found Eddie in the back room washing dishes in the deep stainless sink.

"Eddie, you're okay, huh?"

A broken clock, so the saying goes, is right twice a day. In the same way, there are times when Eddie's mysterious, changeless smile is exactly the right expression, and this was one of those times. Eddie set down the dishes he was cleaning and extended a wet hand. Sid reached out and shook it. Eddie held on longer than you'd expect, but normal social cues were not his strong suit.

"Hey, maybe now we're even," said Sid. "You saved my life one time, remember?"

Eddie let go of Sid's hand and went back to work, and it

was impossible to tell if he remembered or not. But it was true.

"Nice work, Sugar Ray."

Sid was startled by the voice of Lieutenant Stokes, whose fake but nevertheless magnificent smile had just appeared at his office door. He'd forgotten about Stokes.

"Thanks."

"I mean it. You looked good out there. And that guy deserved a bigger ass-kicking than you gave him."

"Blood on the tables is bad for business."

"Can we talk?"

"Sure."

"Outside."

Sid led the way as they passed behind the counter toward the front door of the deli. He stopped when he heard Stokes' voice say, "Hey, you got Tab."

He turned and saw the cop eyeing his soft drink dispenser.

"Can I have a Tab?"

Sid shrugged and grabbed a big plastic cup.

"I like lots of ice."

Once they were out the door and standing on the sidewalk, Stokes took a big swig of his drink and let out a satisfied "Ahhhh."

"Tab, huh?" Sid found it amusing for some reason.

"What? Something wrong with that?"

"Not at all. I heard John Wayne used to drink Tab."

"Yeah?"

"Clint Eastwood, too."

"Really?"

Sid smiled. "What can I do for you, Lieutenant?"

"Well, it's been exactly a week. You're a detective now, what are your thoughts on the murder of Councilman Trager?"

"My opinion matters?"

"You told me that if I kept you in the loop on this case, you could help. Did you mean it?"

"Absolutely."

"Okay, help. Talk to me. What do you think?"

It was a typical, busy lunch hour in downtown Sacramento. Pedestrians were swerving to avoid the two of them standing there on the sidewalk and Stokes seemed to not even notice.

"Well..." Sid scrambled to collect his thoughts. He'd only been looking at the shooting as it affected Bertie Jones, and Stokes was primarily concerned about the death of Councilman Trager. Still, there was a lot of overlap. "...whoever wanted Trager dead wanted him dead for a reason. Personal, political, or business."

"Okay."

"I don't know anything about his hardware business, except that they're always busy when I'm in there."

"He had the building paid off twenty years ago. Profitable every year since 1955. Zero outstanding bills, zero debts, zero business enemies as far as we know."

The Lieutenant took another big swig of the Tab, and Sid tried to hide his surprise. If he was telling the truth, Stokes was being very generous with his information.

"So let's assume the business is solid," said Stokes, dabbing the golden moustache with the back of his hand.

"What about political enemies?"

"I've looked into that some," said Sid, and he told himself it was mostly true. He'd talked to Jock Bell about Trager, and he was planning on calling Jackson Dexter from the paper to talk about city politics. "As a member of the chamber of commerce, I can tell you that plenty of business owners who have to deal with the city didn't like him. He was only helpful to those who contributed to his campaign, but maybe that comes with the territory. And he played favorites with his buddies, but I don't know that he broke any laws."

Stokes nodded, and appeared to be thinking about what Sid had said.

"But you know of no specific reason to think the shooting was politically motivated?"

"Not right now."

"Hold this for me." Stokes handed Sid his soda and pulled out a pen and a little notebook. It was kind of a trademark of his. He scribbled a few notes that Sid couldn't see.

"Okay, Sid, what about personal motives? How about the name of the little blonde girlfriend you told me about? You got that yet?"

"No. But soon."

"Hmmm. I wish you had the name for me." Stokes took the Tab back from Sid and took another drink. "That would be very helpful. I didn't believe you at first, but a couple of employees at different restaurants that Trager favored have told us he had a hot little blonde as a regular companion. The descriptions matched, but we've got no name."

"I'll get it."

"That'd be good."

"What about the wife?" Sid asked, hoping to move quickly from the subject of the mysterious blonde. No sense dwelling on his failure to produce her name. "If Trager was sneaking around on her, wouldn't she have a motive?"

"Nah, we're thinking the wife had nothing to do with it. But we won't rule her out completely 'til we know who hired the shooter."

"And you're sure the shooter didn't act alone? That he was working for somebody else?"

Stokes just grinned at first, then the lips parted into a smile that revealed the amazing teeth.

"Oh, yeah. We know quite a lot about this guy."

Lieutenant Stokes reached into his coat pocket, pulled out a photograph and held it up. It was a front-on mugshot, and there was no mistaking who it was. Sid stared at the picture, and it almost looked like Porky's narrow little eyes were staring right back at him.

Chapter 17

"That's the guy!" said Sid.

"You think?"

Sid took the photo and studied it.

"Definitely him. C'mon, how many people could look like this? He's one of a kind."

"Yeah." Stokes was oozing confidence. "We've had more than a dozen witnesses from that night positively identify him. It's the guy."

Sid paused, and finally managed to take his eyes off the photo and look at the cop.

"You've got him in custody?"

"No. Just this nice picture. Couple of days ago one of the other detectives recognized him from the composite drawing that Detective Carver had done. I actually had several mug shots to choose from. The guy's got a long rap sheet, although murder is something new for him. Mostly drugs and robberies."

"What's his name?"

Stokes reached out and took the photograph back from Sid and looked at it again, almost fondly.

"I'm afraid that is privileged, police department information, Sid."

Then the cop stuck the picture back in his coat pocket and took another swig of Tab. Sid looked at him and, for some reason, didn't see where this was going.

"For now, the name is not available to the general public. Everyone—Detective Carver in particular—has been instructed to not disclose the name of the suspect at this time. Of course, we could help each other here. I might be able to tell you his name if you were able to get a name for me."

Stokes looked satisfied, and Sid made a great effort to not look as dumb as he felt at the moment.

"You like steak sandwiches?"

"Sure, I guess."

Stokes' answer was tentative. Sid swung open the deli door and gently pushed the lieutenant back inside.

"Hey, mom!" Sid yelled, "Get this gentleman a steak sandwich on me!"

The door closed before Stokes had a chance to object, and Sid turned and jogged across the street. A moment later he was standing in Jock's Pawn Shop.

One of Jock's regular flunkies—a guy named Milo—sat behind the counter reading a worn paperback copy of Jonathan Livingston Seagull. He was a wide, square man, maybe forty, with the thickest head of jet black hair on the planet. It started low, a perfect horizontal line across a wrinkly forehead, and was combed straight back. He looked like a Rottweiler wearing a wig.

"Is Jock here? I need to talk to him. It's important."

Milo thought about it for a moment, then set the book down on the glass counter, momentarily blocking Sid's view of some gaudy jewelry and a pile of baseball cards.

"Stay here," he said in a voice that was so high it was a shock if you weren't expecting it. Teenage girl high. Neil Sedaka high.

The guy disappeared through a doorway into the back

of the building, leaving Sid to browse a little. This was still the only pawn shop he'd ever been in, and he found the place fascinating. He couldn't help but wonder about the stories behind the things that lined the walls and filled the glass cases. Who brought in the stuffed alligator, and how did they get it in the first place? The pearly white drum set, the gold plated tea service, the old AFL football that appeared to have the faded signature of Joe Namath scrawled on it in blue ink. These things meant something to someone once. But at some point, the money that Jock Bell was willing to give for them became more important.

He spotted two silver candlesticks that were actually quite lovely and picked one of them up. It was heavy and cold, and he was cradling it in his hands when he heard that distinctive voice behind him. Like Tony the Tiger with a sore throat.

"You'll have to excuse my appearance. I wasn't expecting guests."

Jock was wearing a powder blue jumpsuit with matching belt, and the initials "J.B." embroidered on the breast in big cursive letters. White t-shirt underneath and white sneakers. Except for the big sunglasses, it had a very Jack LaLanne effect. Nice to see that, even when he was dressed down, Jock Bell maintained his unique fashion sense. And the hair was impeccable.

"These are beautiful." Sid put the candlestick back down next to its twin. "My fiancée would like these."

"Amy, right?"

Sid had no idea how the man knew Amy's name.

"I'm sure the lady would love them. Solid sterling

silver. Gotta weigh a pound each. You can have 'em for what I paid for them." Jock paused and Sid must have looked interested. "Four hundred bucks."

"I'll think about it."

"Whatever you want."

Sid thought about Stokes and hoped he was still waiting across the street.

"Jock, I need a favor."

The old guy didn't react at all. Didn't move a muscle, didn't say a word.

"Remember you told me that Tom Trager kept a woman downtown? A blonde?"

Sid looked for some response from Jock Bell, but again there was nothing. He figured his only options were to wait him out or keep talking, and since he couldn't think of what to say next, he waited. Sid noted for the first time the total absence of any sound in the pawn shop. What business didn't at least have a radio on? There were a number of clocks, but none of them seemed to be working because there wasn't even a tick-tick-tick to be heard.

"You said you needed a favor." The rumble quietly filled the empty room, and Sid had the distinct feeling he might be the fly that had just set foot in a spider's web.

"Yeah. Trager's blonde. I need to know who she is."

Jock Bell nodded his head ever so slightly, and allowed a knowing look to cross his face. The move felt very strategic to Sid.

"Let's sit down."

There were two chairs in Jock's Pawn Shop. They sat side by side in one corner and they looked like Louis XIV on acid. The two men settled into them, and Sid discovered they were as uncomfortable as they were ugly.

"Tell me why you need to know."

Pause. Sid's mind raced. He'd known for days that this conversation was coming, yet he now realized that he hadn't even given it a thought. What a dope. Of course Jock Bell would want to know why he wanted the name. And he'd probably want something in exchange for the information.

"I'm unofficially looking into the shooting." What the hell. In the absence of a good lie, why not try the truth? At least, part of it. "The cops are thinking it was only about Trager, but I don't trust 'em. Councilwoman Jones is a family friend, so I'm just checking it out."

Vague. Essentially true. Not bad

"Tell me why you need to know." Bell said the six words again, exactly like before but slower and even more quietly. It had a very unnerving effect.

"Uh, I wanna talk to anybody who might help me understand what happened. I need to make sure Bertie Jones doesn't have anything to worry about."

Sid sounded a little less confident now and he knew it. Nevertheless, Bell nodded sympathetically, and Sid thought for a moment he was in the clear. But only for a moment.

"Milo tells me that Lieutenant Stokes is over in the deli right now. Said you two were having a talk out on the sidewalk before you came over."

Once, when Sid was fifteen years old, his father had caught him in the garage drinking one of his Pabst Blue Ribbon beers. It was the exact same feeling that rushed over him now. Sid threw himself on the mercy of the court.

131

"Stokes says that if I can find out who Trager's girlfriend is, he'll give me the name of last week's shooter." Sid confessed quickly. He thought very seriously about dropping to one knee and kissing the ring of Jock Bell.

Now the weight of the awful silence grew heavier, and Sid stared down at his hands, awaiting his fate. If he'd been looking at Jock instead, he'd have seen the corners of the man's mouth turn upward ever so slightly.

"Jillian Boyd."

Jock spoke the name, but it didn't register. Sid had momentarily forgotten why he'd even come into the pawn shop.

"Most people call her 'Jilly.'"

Now the light began to dawn, and Sid raised his eyes to meet Jock's.

"That's the name? Trager's blonde?"

Jock Bell reached over and put a hand on Sid's arm. Not as cold as the candlestick, but close.

"I tell you this because we're friends. I don't enjoy talking to the cops myself, but you use the information any way you want."

Newsflash: Jock Bell thinks that he and Sid are friends.

"Jillian Boyd." Sid repeated the name, making sure he got it right.

Jock gave the small nod again. "The apartment is at 10th and P."

Sid had what he came for, and he wanted to take his prize and run back to the deli while Stokes was still there. But at the same time, there were questions he was dying to ask Jock Bell. *Why was he just giving him this information?*

And how did he know things like this?

"I own the building she lives in." Jock answered one of the questions without prompting. "I gave Trager a good deal on the rent. Nice place."

Sid took in the information, paused a moment until it felt appropriate, then stood up very deliberately. "Well, I really appreciate you telling me this, Jock. A lot. Thank you."

Jock didn't make him wait long before he stood, too, and extended his hand.

"Like I said, Sid, we're friends."

"Right. Thanks." Sid shook the hand of Jock Bell, then turned for the door, already thinking about what he'd say to Lieutenant Stokes. He was reaching for the knob when the deep growl of Jock's voice stopped him.

"Oh, Sid..."

"Yes?"

Sid spun back around, and now the men faced each other, perhaps fifteen feet apart. Jock reached up and took off his sunglasses. Sid had looked the man in the eyes on plenty of occasions before, but he was surprised by what he saw this time. Was it warmth? Affection? Maybe they really were friends. It was curious.

"The name, it's a gift. No strings attached."

"Sure."

"But maybe someday you can do something for me."

From where he stood at the door, Sid saw Milo return from the back of the pawn shop, sit back down at his chair behind the counter and pick up his book, apparently oblivious to the scene. He was humming in his high voice.

Sid didn't recognize the tune, but it was not an improvement over the silence.

"This feels a little like a scene from *The Godfather*, doesn't it, Jock?"

"Yes, it does," said Jock Bell. "Doesn't it?"

Sid found Lieutenant Stokes hunched over a plate at the end of the counter with an open stool next to him. The place was still busy, but there was something about the head of Homicide that made people give him a wide berth. Sid sat down.

"Good?"

"Oh, my god, it's the best." There was one bite of sandwich left and two french fries.

"Is everything this good?"

"Sid & Eddie's Deli is a legend. What can I say? Want another one?"

"Still on the house?"

Sid got up and circled behind the counter, filled out an order ticket and slipped it on the wheel by the grill. Joe glanced at it and said, "Only got five left." Sid heard the wham of the wooden mallet, then the sizzle of more meat hitting the grill as he grabbed Stokes' cup and refilled the Tab. By now the plate was empty except for the remnants of a puddle of ketchup wiped nearly clean by the fries. Sid picked it up.

"Jillian Boyd is the name of Trager's blonde."

It felt great to say it. Maybe a conversation like this would seem like old hat someday. Maybe it had been an everyday occurrence for guys like Lou Martini. But deep down, Sid still felt like he was play-acting as a Private Detective. And here he was swapping clues with the cops, sharing some inside information with the head of Homicide. Pretty cool.

"Spell it." Stokes pulled the notebook back out.

"Don't know. I assume it's B-O-Y-D."

"Jillian?"

"That's what I hear. Her friends call her Jilly."

Stokes scribbled for a minute, then looked back up. "Got an address?"

Sid weighed his options for a moment. Should he hold back something, maybe have a card to play the next time he talked to Stokes? Or maybe go have a talk with the woman himself before the cops found her? Then again, he was increasingly of the opinion that he was a lousy liar. Sid flashed back to his terrible and awkward attempt at deception just moments ago in the pawn shop and decided to opt for the truth.

"An apartment at 10th & P. Trager was paying for it. I assume she's still there."

"And you know this how?"

"A reliable source."

"Would that be a reliable source in Jock Bell's Pawn Shop?"

Sid figured Stokes didn't really expect an answer, and he had no intention of giving him one.

"What's the shooter's name?"

"Oh, yeah, we had a deal."

Joe slid a plate in front of Stokes with a fresh steak sandwich and a big pile of fries on it. Sid stared at the food, briefly mesmerized, and realized he hadn't had lunch himself.

"Peter Powell."

Sid glanced up at the cop with a look of surprise. "Porky Partridge is Peter Powell?"

"You know him?"

"No. I just appreciate the alliteration. What do we know about him?"

"Like I said, the guy's just a small time punk. Got a drug problem, picked up a dozen times on minor drug offenses and the stupid things junkies do to pay for their fix. There's no way killing Trager was his idea. Somebody put him up to it."

Stokes picked up half of the sandwich and took a bite. A moment passed with both men clearly thinking through the implications of this new information, wondering if Jilly Boyd could be connected somehow to Peter "Porky" Powell.

"What do you think happened, Lieutenant? Why did somebody want Trager dead?"

"Don't know yet." Stokes washed down a bite with a sip of Tab. "You said earlier it was either personal, political, or business. But from my experience, you wanna know why you pay somebody to kill another person for you?"

"I give up. Why?"

"Because you hate their guts."

Chapter 18

It was 4:30, a few hours since his conversations with Stokes and Jock Bell, and now Sid had been waiting alone in the spectacular office for more than fifteen minutes. He expected the place to be impressive, and it was. Two leather wingback chairs in a deep burgundy color sat in front of a massive desk made of glass and stainless steel. It looked more like a piece of art than a desk where serious work might get done. The thing had to weigh a ton, and it appeared all the more gigantic by virtue of the fact that there was almost nothing sitting on its vast surface. There was a silver pen rising up from a marble holder, a framed photograph of three Dalmatians, and a decanter with some amber liquid and four small, crystal glasses. Nothing else. The desk sat angled in a corner that was all windows, floor to ceiling, and beyond it was easily the best view Sacramento had to offer. At twenty-three stories, the newly completed Renaissance Tower was by far the tallest office building in town.

Sid stood on a thick, royal blue carpet and examined the framed degrees on the wall. The one from UC San Francisco was no surprise, nor the one from Boalt Law School. But he wasn't expecting the impressive looking medical degree.

The door opened and Nathan Bomke glided into the room, still looking like Daryl Hall. Or was it John Oates? He wore a black three-piece suit with a crisp white shirt and a gold tie, and Sid suspected the outfit had cost more than his car.

137

"You're a doctor?" asked Sid, pointing to the framed parchment.

"Yes. The Jamaica School of Medicine. Took me almost a month to earn the degree. I don't actually see patients, but I've been called on to provide expert medical testimony a few times."

"Of course."

Bomke walked casually across the office and didn't stop until he was just a little too far into Sid's personal space. "I hope you weren't waiting long." He placed a hand on Sid's arm, and produced a smile that was more sincere than Sid thought possible. "I hate to keep important people waiting."

The two men held eye contact for several seconds, and there was something profoundly weird about the moment. Sid knew for a fact that the guy was a phony, and yet he found himself being completely charmed. A few more seconds passed, then Nathan Bomke gave Sid's arm a little squeeze before turning and walking to his magnificent glass desk. He held up the decanter with the amber liquid.

"Glenlivit?"

And with that, whatever spell the lawyer had cast was broken. Now that there was some distance between them, Bomke appeared once again to be the pompous ass that he was. But they had shared a moment. Vague and uncomfortable, but definitely a moment.

The lawyer raised the whiskey a tad higher. "Drink, Sid?"

Sid had no idea what Glenlivit was, and so politely declined. Bomke poured himself two fingers worth, then slid into the leather chair behind the desk. He held the glass

to his nose and inhaled, closed his eyes and said,
"Mmmmmm." Then he set the glass down without taking a
sip.

"So, how's the case coming?"

"Well," said Sid, pulling the manila folder from a
naugahyde briefcase that looked anemic in the presence of
the genuine leather chairs, "pretty good so far. I spoke
with…"

"Yes, of course you did." Bomke cut him off, picking the
glass back up and staring at the amber liquid. "I'm sure
you're doing a fine job. Howard Clark at Li'l Starz told me
you'd called, and I presume you checked on the dates of that
seminar or talent show or whatever it was that he attended
in Southern California."

"I did."

"Well, excellent. This one's a slam-dunk."

Nathan Bomke finally took a sip of his Scotch, causing
him to close his eyes tightly for a second, then open them
wide and smile.

"You're sure?" he asked, holding up the decanter again.
Sid shook his head and the lawyer shrugged, then poured
himself a tiny bit more. Nathan Bomke swiveled his chair,
allowing him to cross his legs and lean back, glass in hand,
and look out the office window. Sid figured the lawyer
would have a good view of the Capitol dome from there.

"I'm going to follow up on that event that Mr. Clark
attended in Hollywood," said Sid. "It's called The Prodigy
Project, and I thought…"

"Yes, that's fine. I told you I'd want you to make a trip
down there, right? Take a day or two. Enjoy yourself. Stay

at a nice place. Save the receipts." The lawyer continued to stare out the window.

So far, the meeting was making Sid want to take a shower. If Bomke's two hundred dollars a day was primarily to buy him the privilege of being pompous and dismissive, then Sid was beginning to feel underpaid.

"Why am I here?" Sid allowed himself to sound a little bit irritated.

Bomke continued to gaze off somewhere for a little while, then turned sharply toward Sid. He set his glass down and folded his hands on the desk. When he spoke, he wasn't angry or irritated. He was purely patronizing.

"Sid, I know you're new to all this. Much as it goes against my nature to speak plainly, allow me to tell you how this business works. This is a fairly simple case for an attorney of my experience. We'll end up settling for between two hundred and three hundred thousand dollars, which means there's plenty of money for everyone involved. Right now we're having a very important meeting in my office where we're discussing the details of the case. The time we're spending will be reflected in the bill that I hand my client sometime next month. You're two hundred dollars a day, I'm two hundred dollars an hour, we're both hard at work. It's the American Dream."

Nathan Bomke picked up his glass again and breathed in the vapors while he kept his eyes on Sid.

"You're sure that what I find will support your case?" Sid asked.

"Of course," replied the attorney, stunned, as though he'd been asked if two plus two equaled four. "Clients don't hire me to lose a case, and I don't hire private investigators to find things that aren't helpful. You'll return from Hollywood with proof that my client delivered on his contractual promise and we'll all go to the bank. Look, Sid, I've employed another investigator with more experience and—don't be offended—a little more savvy than you to work up a report on the ugly little girl's father. The guy was convicted of assault twice in the seventies. I've got statements from several people who know him that say he's a hothead. It's almost too easy. You and I aren't doing anything wrong, Sid. When the dust settles and this case is all over, there's going to be a big pile of money and we're each going to get some of it. Okay?"

"So the work you're paying me to do means nothing?"

"Oh, no, you're wrong. Your involvement in this case and the top-notch investigation that you're doing proves to the judge and, if necessary, the jury, that we took this case very seriously. That no expense was spared in getting to the truth."

"But it's all for show."

"Everything's for show, Sid." Nathan Bomke knocked back the rest of his drink and didn't flinch. "Everything's for show."

The lawyer stood and turned and looked out the window again, his hands thrust in his pockets.

"You were here for about fifteen minutes before I arrived, now we've been reviewing the case for…" Bomke looked at his watch "…ten minutes. Let's chat for a few minutes and we'll call it an hour. Hell of a view from here, huh?"

141

Sid didn't respond and Nathan Bomke didn't seem to mind.

A minute or two went by in silence before Sid said, "You don't remember the first time we met, do you?"

"May 21st, 1980." Bomke said it matter-of-factly, still looking out the window. "We spent a lovely hour together in a holding cell at the city jail. It was a Wednesday."

"I'm impressed."

"You and your little deli were being sued by a great big fat fellow, as I recall, blaming you for his enormous girth. I thought that was quite clever." The man finally turned and faced Sid. "How'd that turn out?"

"Nothing happened. They dropped the suit."

A look of distaste crossed Nathan Bomke's face. "Shame. The fat fellow should've called me."

"I guess I'm glad he didn't. Looks like things have improved for you since our days in the slammer."

Bomke smiled, and for the first time it didn't feel like he was posing. He ran a hand through his hair, and it fell back perfectly into place.

"Just took me a little while to find my place in the legal world. Back then I was trying too hard, sometimes stepping too far over the line. I wasn't the ethical fellow I am today."

Sid wondered if this was self-deprecation or self-deception, and the more the lawyer talked, the more he decided it was the latter.

"Yes, I do remember that day, Sid. Our time together in the holding cell was my one and only trip to jail, and a very valuable lesson. I was too close to the action back then — too involved in the cases and spending too much time with low-lifes and hustlers. So I made some mistakes. I think the company I kept in those days was a bad influence on me."

"And you keep better company today?"

"Oh, yes. No need to get down in the gutter when you can pay people to go there for you. That's what private investigators are for."

Bomke reached for the decanter, poured himself some more Glenlivit, and took another one of the small, showy sips.

"I think it's been close enough to an hour," he said. "Have a nice trip to L.A."

Sid was being dismissed. With a more complete understanding of their relationship, he slid the manila folder back into his cheap briefcase and stood up, thinking he had a pretty good idea what a hooker must feel like at the end of a long Friday night. He was headed for the door when something made him stop. Something Bomke had said a moment ago.

"Hey, can I ask you something?"

The lawyer simply waited without expression. It was a long shot—ridiculous really—but as long as they were both on the clock, might as well ask.

"Back when you were in the gutter with the low-lifes and hustlers, did you ever hear of a guy named Peter Powell?"

Nathan Bomke didn't even hesitate. "Big nostrils, right?"

Chapter 19

"He knows him?"

"Yeah. He represented the guy in a lawsuit less than a year ago."

The couple walked hand in hand down Land Park Drive. Sid hadn't really felt like going out, and it was two hours past his bedtime, but he hadn't seen Amy since the weekend. And when she'd offered to pay for the movie, he couldn't resist. "Agnes of God" didn't sound like nearly as much fun as "Commando", starring Arnold Schwarzenegger and that girl from "Who's the Boss", but it was better than Sid expected, and the Tower Theater was just a walk from his mom's house. Over dinner he'd filled her in on his conversations with Stokes and Jock Bell. He'd saved the best for last.

"Peter Porky Powell managed to hurt himself in that Kmart on Howe Avenue in January and Bomke took them to the cleaners."

"How did he get hurt?"

"Tried to steal a bicycle. Apparently he was attempting to ride one of their pre-assembled bikes out of the sporting goods department when the handlebars came off. Powell crashed and his head went through a glass case full of BB guns. That's where he got the big scar."

"Ouch."

"Yeah. But the whole thing worked out for him. The jury awarded him 200 grand. Welcome to America."

Sid and Amy turned left onto 3rd Avenue, now just a

couple of blocks from home.

"You said the cops think somebody paid this Powell guy to shoot Tom Trager," Amy said. "That doesn't make sense if he got all that money just last year."

"Hey, you're thinking like a private eye. I like it." Sid squeezed her hand. "I'm sure Bomke took a big chunk of that money. And whatever was left is gone. Stokes said the guy's got a huge drug problem. Cocaine."

"He has the nose for it."

"Good one."

"So did that lawyer have an address for him?"

"Yes and no. Bomke said that when he was representing him, Porky was living in a dive motel on Auburn Boulevard. I've got the name, and I'll go by there tomorrow, but I can't believe he'd still be there."

"You be careful."

"I will. I'm just gonna stop by the motel office and ask a few questions. I promise."

"And you're telling the police, too, right?"

"Yep."

They walked together in comfortable silence until they arrived at Sid's mom's house, where Amy's car was parked in the driveway. Sid leaned back against the front fender and pulled his fiancée to him.

"How many days 'til we get married?"

"Fifty-three."

They kissed, a long, wonderful kiss that made Sid's head get a little foggy. They'd been together so long—almost six years since they started dating—and their relationship had become so comfortable and easy. But for Sid, this was an unexpectedly intense and passionate moment, leaning against Amy's Honda Civic fifty-three days before their wedding. He squeezed her tightly, then leaned back and looked at her in the light of the streetlamp.

"I love you," he said.

Amy gazed back at him just as intently. Nice moment.

"Sid."

"Yes?"

"I wonder if Jock Bell had anything to do with all this."

Unquestionably one of the great romantic momentum killing quotes of all time.

"Were you thinking about that while we were kissing just now?"

"Yeah, a little."

"I've always had this mysterious power over chicks."

"Sorry. But think about it. Jock Bell knew all about the blonde mistress, even rented Trager their little love nest cheap. Maybe Bell was blackmailing him or something."

"Well, usually it's the blackmail-ee that kills the blackmail-er, not the other way around. So I don't know about that theory."

"Yeah." Amy frowned. Same expression as when she was losing a Scrabble game. "But there's some weird connection there, don't you think?"

"Maybe, maybe not. Jock Bell collects favors. That's how he operates. I'm sure he figured it'd be good for business someday if a city councilman owed him. Besides, Jock was the one who told me about the blonde in the first place. Why would he even bring her up if he had something to cover up?"

"I don't know." The frown deepened. "Maybe I just don't like him."

"Maybe." Sid leaned forward until the tips of their noses were touching. "You think you can kiss me without thinking about creepy old Jock Bell?"

"I can't make any promises."

"Give it your best shot."

Chapter 20

The Motel Capri looked like one of the nicer motels on Auburn Boulevard, but that's like claiming to be one of the taller Munchkins. Not that impressive. By far the most popular area of town for hookers and their pitiful customers to find each other, the stretch of pay-by-the-hour motels and body shops and sub-standard eateries was a blight on the city. A cartoonish palm tree graced the sign out front, leading Sid to conclude that the 'Capri' in the hotel's name probably referred to the island in the Mediterranean and not the ugly little automobile made by Mercury, but you never know.

It was just after 12:30 p.m. Sid had stayed at the deli until his mom arrived and the lunch crowd was under control, then jumped in his Duster. Now it was one of only three cars in the motel parking lot. The swimming pool looked fairly clean, though Sid had to wonder how long it had been since somebody actually swam in it. The regular clientele of The Motel Capri wasn't likely to use the shower, much less go for a dip in the pool. A red neon sign blinked 'Vacancy.'

The office was exactly what he expected — worn linoleum and dusty venetian blinds, faded yellow upholstered chairs. Decor from a 1955 dentist office. The olive green formica counter was chipped along the edges. But the person behind the counter was something of a surprise.

"Hi, can I help you?"

What was Richie Cunningham doing at the Hooker Hotel? The hair was the wrong color and he was a little more handsome than his TV counterpart, but it was still Richie Cunningham all the way. When Sid had walked in, the young man had been looking down, reading something on the counter. As Sid got closer, he could see it was a text book. Next to it was a pencil and a sheet of lined paper covered with calculations.

"I'm Sid." He extended his hand.

"Charlie." The kid had a firm grip and shook with enthusiasm.

"What're you working on, Charlie?"

Charlie tipped the book up so Sid could see the cover. *Dynamics of Structures*.

"It's my last year. Civil Engineering at Sac State."

"Impressive."

"Thanks. How long you need a room for?"

It struck Sid that this was a very odd conversation. Wholesome Charlie was doing his homework and acting like he was checking people into the Mickey Mouse Club.

"I don't need a room, Charlie. Just wanted to ask a few questions."

"You're with the police?" Charlie didn't seem bothered at all.

"I'm a detective," said Sid, repeating the line he'd heard Lou Martini use a hundred times as he flipped open his wallet. Unfortunately, Charlie paid more attention than most people.

"The cops come here fairly often. This isn't what their identification looks like."

"Yeah, I'm a *private* detective."

"Then you're not a cop."

"No."

"Then I can't help you." Charlie remained the picture of wide-eyed innocence, even as he said the next line. "Not for free, anyway."

Sid just looked at him for a moment, then couldn't keep from smiling. The kid played dumb, but he wasn't.

"Hey," Charlie added, "school's expensive. It's forty bucks just to park this semester."

"How about I pay for parking?" Sid asked as he pulled two twenties out and laid them on page 178 of Dynamics of Structure.

"Wow, great! Thanks." Charlie closed the book on the bills and gave Sid his fullest attention.

"You're welcome. How long you been working here?"

"Three weeks."

Oops. Sid laughed at himself for being such an idiot, and made a mental note to always ask that question *before* handing over incentive money in the future. Rookie mistake. His time and his forty bucks were very likely wasted. But still, you gotta try.

"You know a guy named Peter Powell?"

"Sure. Room nineteen."

Sid tried his damndest to show no reaction. *Cool. Stay cool.*

"You're sure? Peter Powell. The guy's got a big nose."

"Like a baboon."

"And he's here?"

"Not lately. I bet I haven't seen him in a week."

"Tell me about him."

"Not much to say. We get two kinds of customers here. Some stay for thirty minutes, some stay for months. Mr. Powell has had room nineteen for a long time, I guess. He never wants the maid to clean his room and he's paid up through the end of the month, so we just leave him alone."

"What kind of guy is he?"

"The customers really don't talk to me very often, unless there's a problem with the room or something."

"You're sure he hasn't been around for a while?"

"Pretty sure. Gotta be at least a week since I've seen him or that beat up old mustang he drives."

"Is it okay if I go knock on the door?"

"Yeah, if you want. Nineteen's on the far side."

"Thanks."

Sid headed out the door and made his way around the corner, his heart beating faster. He thought about what Amy had said last night. She'd told him to be careful, and he had promised to just ask a few questions at the office and then turn things over to the cops. But this was an unexpected turn of events. And, damn, it was exciting!

Before he reached his destination, he saw that the door to number seventeen was wide open, and caught a quick glimpse of a maid picking a blanket up off the floor and beginning to spread it over a bed. Garish wallpaper was peeling up in a few places, and the room made the tacky front office look like something out of *Better Homes & Gardens* magazine. How could anybody possibly sleep here?

Sid stopped in front of number nineteen. The black plastic numeral "1" was missing from the door, but the outline in the badly faded paint made it easy to tell he was at the right room. He listened for a moment and heard nothing, then knocked and waited. No response.

"Mr. Powell? Mr. Powell, are you here?"

Sid knocked again as he said it, a little harder this time, and then caught himself holding his breath as he waited again. Nothing. He leaned his face close to the edge of the door and sniffed, thinking that if Porky Powell had spent the last week lying in there dead for some reason, he might detect an odor. He smelled tired old motel, but he didn't smell death.

Sid was just reaching for the door knob when there was a loud bang to his right, and he looked up to see the maid slamming the door to number seventeen. Sid waved to her, and she gave him a disapproving look. Sid figured she had lots of opportunity to practice that look here at The Motel Capri. The woman disappeared around the corner, and Sid reached up and took hold of the doorknob. Twist left. Twist right. Locked.

Charlie had returned to engineering homework when Sid walked back into the office. The young man looked up with the same smile as before.

"Nobody home," said Sid.

"Yeah, didn't think so."

"Listen, is there any chance I could get a key and look around in there? I won't touch a thing. You could come with me."

"Oh, no, I couldn't do that." Charlie paused, and Sid waited for the second shoe to drop. He didn't have to wait long. "Not for forty bucks, anyway."

"Well, it never hurts to ask. Sorry, Opie. I'll just wait for the real cops to come down and have a look instead."

Sid found a payphone less than half a block away, dropped a coin in, and dialed the number of Lieutenant Benjamin Stokes.

Chapter 21

Sid's Deli was generally locked up and empty long before now, but today there was still one person inside, sitting at the counter with the lights off and waiting for the phone to ring. Sid told himself again that he really should grab his notes for the Bomke/Lil' Starz case and get some work done, but he was still having a hard time getting over the bad taste that was left in his mouth from yesterday's visit to the sleazy lawyer's office. So he was allowing himself a little time to just space out, sipping his Coke with no ice, watching life pass by outside his windows on a Friday afternoon and waiting for the call. At one point, Jock Bell's enormous Cadillac Fleetwood pulled up and stopped across the street. Jock himself emerged from the pawn shop wearing the exact same outfit that Don Johnson had worn on Miami Vice just last week. Exact. Light blue jacket with sleeves pushed up, peach colored t-shirt, white slacks and white loafers. No socks. Jock disappeared into the back seat of the car and it pulled away, and Sid had to admit that the old guy looked pretty good.

What was taking so long? It had been more than three hours since his conversation with Stokes, who was impressed that he had tracked down Porky Powell's most recent address so quickly. Stokes had asked how he did it, and Sid's response was intentionally vague enough to conceal the fact that it was blind luck. The cop had promised him that he'd head right over to The Motel Capri to check it out, then call the deli and let him know what he found. And that's why Sid was sitting and waiting at 4:07 when the phone rang.

"Hello?"

"Hello, Sid?"

Hmm. Definitely not the Lieutenant.

"Bertie, is that you?"

"Sid, how are you?"

To the best of his memory, Sid hadn't spoken to Bertie Jones on the phone since he was in high school and she'd called to talk to his sister. Fifteen years later, her voice still had much the same effect on him.

"Good. I'm good. But I'm not the one who was shot. How are *you*?"

"I'm doing very well, thank you." Bertie didn't laugh, exactly, but Sid could hear the mirth in her voice. "I don't recommend getting in the way of flying bullets, but it hasn't been too bad. The doctor has me wearing a sling to keep my shoulder still, but I don't really need it. I'll be back to work next week."

"Yeah, that's what your mom told me a couple of days ago."

"That's actually why I'm calling, Sid. I just spoke with Mother on the phone. She's in Phoenix right now..."

"Right, I remember."

"Uh-huh, and she's pretty upset about something you said to her. Did you tell her you thought that crazy guy in the bar last week shot me on purpose?"

"Me?" The phone was suddenly sweaty in his hand. "No, no, I never said that. Not exactly."

"Well, can I ask what you did say to her?"

155

Sid's mind raced, desperately trying to come up with some quick answer that wouldn't sound too bad. In his conversation with Bertie's mom, he'd decided to not blame the whole thing on his sister. But now, with the most beautiful woman in the world on the other end of the phone, he decided it might be time to throw Gloria to the sharks.

"Bertie, my sister's just worried about you, that's all."

"I don't understand."

"Gloria asked me to look into the shooting and make sure that the police are considering every possibility. The cops think this was only about Tom Trager."

After a pause, Bertie Jones said, "Well, that's right, isn't it?"

"Yeah, I think that's right. But you know Gloria. She's overly cautious. She wants me to just check around."

"And so you asked my mother if she could think of anybody who might want to kill me?"

"Well, I didn't put it exactly like that, but, uh… yeah, kinda."

There was another pause, but this one was awkward. And when she spoke, she sounded a little less beautiful and a lot more irritated.

"Sid, could you stop by my office sometime next week and talk to me some more about all this?"

"Uh, sure. Pretty much any afternoon is okay for me."

"Then let's do it Monday. How about three o'clock?"

"Yeah, that's fine."

"I'll see you then."

The mirth was gone. Bertie Jones hung up quickly, and Sid was left holding the phone to his ear and wondering how badly he'd screwed up.

It was fifteen minutes and two Cokes later that Stokes called.

"What took so long?" Sid asked

"Sorry if you were inconvenienced. They won't let us just go kicking down doors like the good old days. The kid at the front desk recognized Powell's mug shot right away, but we didn't have a warrant and he wouldn't let us in the room without talking to the owner first."

"Was it a problem?"

"Nah. People who operate places like that don't have any desire to piss off the cops. But we had to track the guy down, and he was out on the golf course."

"So...?"

"Looks like the kid in the office was right. I bet Powell hasn't been there in at least a week. Among the fast food wrappers was a little carton of milk half full, all clumpy and nasty smelling. Sports Illustrated and Penthouse from last month. TV Guide from two weeks ago."

"No clue where he might be now?"

"Not really, but we sure as hell confirmed that this is our guy. Found a notepad that had Trager's name written on it, along with the address of the bar where the shooting happened. Otherwise, no surprises. Some clothes, an envelope with just over two hundred bucks in it, a cute little bag of cocaine."

"You don't leave cash and drugs behind if you're not planning on coming back."

"No, probably not. But maybe something made your boy Porky think it was time to get out of town in a hurry."

157

"Like maybe he never went back there after the shooting."

"Maybe. Oh, you know what else we found in there? Model airplanes. The little plastic kits like I used to do when I was a kid. Had to be a dozen of 'em. There's one sitting on a table half finished right now."

"Model airplanes?"

"Yeah. Go figure. A coke-head with a hobby."

Chapter 22

8:15 a.m. Frosted Flakes and Scooby Doo. At thirty-two years old, Sid didn't feel the tiniest bit guilty about how he chose to spend his Saturday mornings. Life was sure to change once he was married, so he was making the most of his waning days of bachelorhood.

He was scheduled to meet his sister at ten to tell her what he'd found out so far about Bertie Jones and the shooting. It had been a week since Gloria had asked for his help. Since then he'd discovered Porky Partridge's real name and his most recent whereabouts, plus the hot gossip about the late Tom Trager and his blonde girlfriend. Gloria knew none of it. And there was that other information he was waiting for. His hunch. *Shouldn't he have heard by now?* The thought prompted him to glance at the answering machine, and that's when he saw the red light blinking. He set his bowl down on the coffee table next to Frampton the Turtle's little terrarium and hurried over to push the button. Paydirt. He picked up the phone and dialed as fast as he could.

Gloria walked into the Freeport Bakery and found her little brother sitting at a table reading The Sacramento Bee. A cup of cocoa sat next to him along with half of an enormous chocolate éclair.

"How many bowls of cereal did you have this morning?"

Sid glanced up from the paper with a smile. There was a

tiny bit of chocolate at each corner of his mouth.

"Three."

"Very nutritious breakfast." Gloria picked up the éclair as she sat down and took a bite.

"Forty miles a week, Sis. You run enough, you can eat whatever you want."

"Wow, it's delicious." Her mouth was so full it was a little hard to understand.

"Want the rest?"

"Uh-uh." Gloria shook her head and slid the plate across the table away from herself. "I've got a skimpy Halloween costume I need to fit into."

"Skimpy?"

"I'm gonna be Mary Ann from Gilligan's Island. My husband's request."

"Gingham. Very sexy."

"Yeah. Marty's gonna be The Professor. I think it's some fantasy he's always had."

"I don't think I need any more details." Sid folded up the newspaper and dropped it on the floor by his chair. "Ready for an update on the Bertie Jones case?"

"No, not really."

Gloria said it matter-of-factly. At first he thought she was kidding, but it was clear from the look on her face that this was no joke. Sid didn't know what to make of it, so he waited. There would be two times this morning that Gloria would take him completely by surprise, and here was the first of them:

"I'm pulling the plug, Sid. I want you to stop snooping around and leave Bertie and her mom alone."

Sid had arrived at the bakery thoroughly excited about the progress he'd made and looking forward to their conversation. This was supposed to be fun. What had happened?

"You're joking, right?"

"You can't be surprised, Sid. Bertie called me yesterday after she hung up with you. We've been friends forever, and she's never been so mad at me. Her mom just got back from Phoenix and she's still upset. What did you say to that woman?"

"Oh. Yeah, that conversation didn't go well."

"Duh. It wasn't exactly your most clever detective work. Jeez, Sid, I could've called up Bertie's mom myself and asked if she knew if somebody was trying to kill her daughter, but that seemed a little bit stupid and obvious to me."

"Right. I said it didn't go well."

"Well, Bertie has asked me to call you off, and that's what I'm doing. She's assured me that there's nobody out to get her, and she's worried about her mom—I guess Mary has a minor heart condition. She just wants this whole thing to be over and forgotten as fast as possible."

The Bertie Jones Case was just about to go down the drain with a swirl. Damn. Quitting now was out of the question. Not after that phone call this morning.

"And all your concerns about who shot your best friend and whether or not the cops were looking out for her—those are gone? No more worries at all?"

Sid studied his sister and she didn't appear to be budging.

"I know some stuff you don't, Sis." Maybe he was overplaying his hand, but he kept a straight face. "Besides, I've already spent a hundred forty dollars of your money."

"Okay, you can tell me what you've done so far." Gloria had gotten their father's cheapskate gene, too. "But I'm still calling you off."

Sid figured all he needed was a chance to make his case. He pulled a folded sheet of paper from his shirt pocket, smoothed it out on the table and glanced quickly at his notes.

"The name of the guy with the big nose who shot Bertie is Peter Powell..."

And so the Deli Detective began his report to his sister. Over the next fifteen minutes, Gloria got a detailed update on her little brother's busy week. Sid told her about his initial ride in the car with Lieutenant Stokes and the cop's list of questions that were exclusively focused on Tom Trager— "Not a one about Bertie Jones," he pointed out. He tried to make his conversation with Bertie's mom sound a little less disastrous than it actually was, but he did include the awkward exchange about Cleveland, Columbus and Canton, Ohio. As he said it, he watched for some reaction from his sister, and saw nothing except maybe some growing impatience. Sid told her about his impromptu sidewalk meeting with Lieutenant Stokes and his pawn shop conversation with Jock Bell where he got the name of Trager's blonde girlfriend. The way he told it, it sounded like clever detective work that he found out the location of Peter Porky Powell's motel from Nathan Bomke, and he thought the story of his trip to The Motel Capri came off as very exciting and suspenseful.

While still holding onto his trump card, Sid hoped at this point that maybe he'd drawn his sister back into the case, that maybe she wouldn't be so quick to pull the plug. He wrapped up by telling her he thought there still was a possibility—a real possibility—that somebody might be trying to kill Bertie Jones.

"So I've set up a meeting with Jackson Dexter from The Sacramento Bee to talk about any political enemies she might have, and I'm hoping you'll snoop around Bertie's law firm a little and see if she's made anybody mad enough in the courtroom that they'd want revenge."

Sid took a drink of his cocoa and waited.

"That's it?" Gloria asked.

"Yep."

"Look, Sid, it's obvious you've tried really hard, and I appreciate it. You've only been looking into this because I asked you to, and that's very sweet. But everything you've dug up points to Councilman Trager, and that's all. I haven't heard anything that suggests Bertie could've also been a target that night. It's time to drop this, Sid."

"Okay." Sid folded up his notes and put the paper back in his pocket. It was time to give Gloria the morning's big news and see if that changed her mind. "But you'll have to pay me back for the hundred forty bucks I've spent."

Sid waited. Gloria gave him *Big Sister Look #8*, bored and irritated.

"Sid, I was always better than mom and dad at knowing when you were up to something. How about you stop trying to surprise me and just tell me what you know."

Big sisters have to take the fun out of everything.

"I told you I gave that kid at the Motel Capri forty dollars to get him to talk."

"Too much, by the way. I bet college kids will talk for twenty."

"Fine. The other hundred goes to a private investigator in Canton, Ohio."

And now Sid had the satisfaction of seeing a little confusion and surprise on his sister's face. In their entire lives, he could think of very few occasions where he knew something that Gloria didn't. He enjoyed the moment quite a bit.

"What are you talking about?"

It was a shame to not make this last as long as possible, so Sid took another drink of his cocoa before answering.

"I can't put my finger on it, Sis, but there was definitely something about the way Mary Jones reacted when I asked where she and her family lived before moving here. I was just making some small talk, you know? Trying to put her at ease."

"This was before you asked her if there was anybody trying to kill her daughter."

"Yeah. And that's the thing. Mrs. Jones started to act funny *before* I asked the dumb question about Bertie having any enemies. Why would that be? There was something about me simply asking about Ohio that bothered her. I'm sure of it."

"A hunch."

"Sure, if you say so."

"So where did my hundred dollars go?"

"I called information, got a P.I.'s name in Canton, Ohio. Asked him to spend a day checking public records for Robert and Mary Jones and their daughter, Roberta, born 1950."

"You what?"

"You wanted a real investigation, right Sis? One where I checked all the facts?"

Gloria didn't reply. She didn't look happy, but Sid could tell he had her on the hook.

"The guy called back yesterday and left a message. I didn't get it 'til this morning, and I spoke with him about two hours ago. You want the short version of what he found out?"

"Sure."

"No record of Bob and Mary Jones or their baby girl Roberta in Canton, Ohio in the early 1950s. Zero."

Now Gloria couldn't hide her interest, but her eyes narrowed and Sid could see the skeptical attorney taking over.

"How could he know that?"

"Lots of ways. County tax rolls. Billing for services like garbage and electricity. This guy I talked to had a friend at the phone company. Plenty of 'Joneses' in the book back then, but none of them checked out. No phone bill."

"What about the suburbs? What if they didn't live in Canton, but nearby?"

"I hired a pro with your hundred bucks, Sis. Canton area is the heart of Caroll and Stark Counties. Most of the information came from county sources."

Gloria slid the plate with the éclair back over and took a

big bite, then looked out the window, concentrating.

"When there's an honest taxpayer living in an area, there's generally some evidence left behind that's not hard to dig up," said Sid. "Even thirty-five years later."

"You said there was no record of Bertie. She was just three years old when they moved here. What evidence would there be?"

"Easy one. She was born May 26th, 1950, right? Neither county has a recorded birth certificate for a Roberta Jones on or anywhere near that date. There were four major hospitals in the two counties at that time, and none of them had any record of her, either."

"You knew her birthday."

"Give me a break, Sis. I had a crush on her for twenty years. It's burned into my brain. I gave her the cutting board on her birthday, remember?"

Gloria took another bite of the éclair, then they sat in silence. She was clearly thinking through what she'd heard, and Sid was waiting for the verdict.

"There's probably a simple explanation for this," said Gloria.

"Yeah, maybe."

"Why would they lie about where they came from?"

"Great question. I'm gonna find out. And keep in mind, if it's more than just a simple misunderstanding—if somebody's hiding something—Bertie probably wouldn't know. Like you said, she was only three years old when they moved."

"From wherever."

"Right."

Gloria took another absent-minded bite of the éclair, then seemed to realize what she was doing and put what was left of it back on the plate and slid it in Sid's direction again.

"This is crazy," she said. "Even if there's something odd about Mary Jones' past, this couldn't have anything to do with the shooting."

"Yeah, probably. But how can you be sure?"

"Because... I don't know. But it just doesn't make sense."

Sid watched the tug-o-war go on in Gloria's mind for several seconds, felt the momentum shifting in his direction.

"What do you want me to do?"

"I promised Bertie I'd tell you to quit," Gloria said.

"Uh-huh."

He pushed what was left of the éclair back across the table to his sister. Gloria reached down and scooped up a little bit of the custard filling with her finger. Before she put it in her mouth, she stunned him for the second time. He really didn't see it coming.

"You're fired, Sid. Leave it alone."

Chapter 23

"So it's all over?"

"Hell, no, it's not over. It's just not an official case anymore. Now it's… I don't know what it is. A hobby."

An hour after Gloria gave him his pink slip, Sid was sitting with Woody Carver in an off-white interrogation room—a metal table, two chairs, four block walls and a mirror.

"You sure it's okay we're in here? I don't like it. What's the smell?"

"Lysol or something. Look, you wanted a private place to talk, this is the best the police department has to offer. You wanna sit out there by my desk and let all the other nice detectives listen in?"

"No."

"Then relax. Kick off your shoes. The place grows on you."

"Yeah. Like a dentist office." Sid stood and began walking the perimeter of the room, pacing slowly. "So why do you think Bertie's mom would to lie to me about where they came from?"

"C'mon, Sid. You paid a P.I. to spend one day snooping around, right? You've got a long way to go before you know for sure that she's lying."

"What's that mean?"

"It means there could be other explanations why their names didn't turn up in… where was it, Canton? Maybe your investigator did a half-assed job. Maybe Bertie's father was a flake, and they never stayed in one place long enough to leave a trail. Maybe some dimwit county clerk misfiled the records. Think about it, Sid. You've got no solid evidence, right?"

"Like what?"

"Like any one of those things your Ohio private eye *didn't* find. Phone bills or school records or birth certificates. Whatever. You wanna prove that they weren't in Canton, you have to prove that they *were* somewhere else. That's proof."

Sid stopped walking. He was standing right in front of the room's one mirror, and in its reflection he saw his friend tip his chair back on two legs and lean against the wall. Woody was right and they both knew it.

"I'm telling you, there was something wrong with the way Mrs. Jones reacted when I asked where they moved from. She came unglued, Woody. I think she lied."

"Prove it."

Sid glanced back and forth between the image of Woody and his own reflection in the mirror.

"I will."

"Okay. You want to tell me how?"

"No. I don't think so." Sid got close to the mirror, then tilted his head back and flared his nostrils. "How come the hair on my head is red, but the hair inside my nose is black?"

"Mmm. One of life's great mysteries. By the way, I can't guarantee that there's nobody watching on the other side of that mirror."

Sid stopped examining his nose hair and looked up, trying to see through the glass. He squinted. Nothing.

Then he stuck his tongue out. Woody leaned forward, putting his chair back down on all four feet, and rested his elbows on the bare metal table.

"Very nice. If you're all done, I've got some news for you."

"Yeah?" Sid turned and leaned back against the mirror.

"Yeah. I think I know who murdered Lou Martini."

It wasn't even noon, and here was the day's next big surprise. Sid pulled out the chair across from his friend and sat down.

"Tell me."

"I said a few days ago that I had a couple of informants I thought might know something, remember? I gave them the only description we have—tall guy, light Mercedes—and I told them this guy killed somebody with a baseball bat. Well, both of them acted funny. One of 'em said he had no idea who it could be, but it wasn't right. He was real nervous. The other one—a reliable guy—I could tell he recognized the description, but all he'd say was that he would ask around for me, and I didn't want to push it."

"Okay."

"So I looked them both up again last night, and this time I pushed a little bit."

"Meaning what?"

"Well, these guys are, uh, entrepreneurs. They don't exactly work out of an office, but they're businessmen, and their business goes better when the police are happy with them. Is that enough information?"

Sid just smiled and Woody continued.

"So the first guy looked very uncomfortable, and tells

me he doesn't want to have anything to do with the German."

"Is that supposed to mean something to me?"

"Meant nothing to me, but that's all the guy would say. *The German*. So I find my other guy, and he's a little more talkative this time. But he makes me absolutely swear that I won't tell anybody where I got my information. He's jumpy."

"I'm pretty sure I saw this episode of *Starsky & Hutch*."

"Do you want to hear this?"

"Sorry."

"So guy number two tells me there's a man with an accent that's shown up maybe three times in the last couple of years. White guy, blonde, very tall, drives a Mercedes, and whenever he's around somebody ends up dead."

"Damn, Woody. Cue the spooky music. Nobody knows a name?"

"That's all I could get. What do you figure is going on?"

Sid didn't have to think long.

"The tall guy—the German—is hired muscle from out of town."

Woody grinned.

"Took fifteen minutes. Fresno P.D. had a small file on a Mr. Dieter Hoffmann. Six foot five, German born, suspect in several violent crimes, but never enough to prosecute. Once I had the name, I called the FBI and their file was a little fatter. He's known to have killed two in L.A. for sure— witnesses in a fairly high profile organized crime case. They're confident he was behind at least a dozen other hits, but the guy is hard to pin down. Never kills people the same way twice. Very clever."

"And this guy came to Sacramento to kill Lou Martini?"

"Don't know for sure. But it's the best thing I've got right now."

Sid drummed his fingers on the table, and Woody tilted the chair back again.

"Where's Dieter's home base?"

"Guys like this don't have an address. Looks like he's in Fresno a lot for some reason, and the rest of the time it's Southern California."

"How do we find him?"

Pause.

"We?"

"*You.* I meant *you.* How do you find him?"

"Well, my plan is to get lucky. Past history says once he does a job, he gets out of town and doesn't come back for a while. FBI knows I'm looking, and I've already contacted the agencies in Fresno, San Diego, L.A. Maybe he'll turn up somewhere else."

"So we just sit and do nothing?"

"Oh, I'll keep working it here, because maybe Dieter isn't our guy. Fresno's sending me a photo, and I'll show it around. Of course, my only possible witness right now is a fifty-seven-year-old paperboy. But if this German killed Lou, there's not a lot more I can do, buddy. Gotta wait for him to make a mistake."

"In the four years we were together, Lou never had any case that was worth getting killed for. Nothing that would've gotten the attention of serious bad guys or hired killers. What was he working on?"

"If he kept records worth a damn I'd tell you."

"No guesses?"

"Hard to say," Woody shrugged. "Some kind of organized crime thing is a good guess. This German guy, he doesn't have an ad in the phone book. If this was a professional hit, it eliminates a whole lot of suspects. You know, typical scorned lovers and angry next door neighbors just don't know who to call when they want somebody killed, and they'd never find a guy like Dieter Hoffmann. Whoever wanted Lou dead was someone with access to serious professional muscle."

Sid stood again, jammed his hands into his pockets, and resumed his pacing. He racked his brain, but couldn't see any way this new information fit in with what he already knew. It was frustrating. As a competitive runner in high school and college, he discovered that he always had another "gear"—that when he really needed it, he could dig deeper, push harder. It hurt like hell, but he could will himself to do it. In a weird way, he came to enjoy the pain, because his ability to handle it was what made him better than other runners. The pain made him focus. It made him stronger. But that couldn't help him now. There wasn't a way to simply *think harder*. No amount of desire and no physical effort could force an answer into his head. He wouldn't mind if it hurt—in fact, he might have preferred it. The pain would be better than the frustration.

"Shit."

Sid smacked the wall with his hand. Just moments earlier he'd felt a certain excitement at being so close to a developing murder investigation. It had almost been fun.

173

But now it hit him anew that one of the reasons he was in this room talking to Woody was that Lou Martini was dead. Beaten to death with a baseball bat.

"Listen, Sid, when I first got this case, you said you'd leave it alone if I kept you in the loop. You promised me."

"Yeah."

"Well, I've told you everything I know. You stay away from it. This German's seriously bad."

"Scout's honor."

"Okay. This isn't my only case, buddy." Woody stood up and took a step toward the door. "Gotta go serve and protect."

"Hang on." Sid held up a hand. "When Lou Martini got killed, you and I both asked the same question, remember? Both of us wondered if his death could somehow be related to the shooting of Tom Trager."

"Uh-huh."

"I know there's nothing obvious that links them together, but think about it. Two people killed just a few days apart, and it looks like both of them were hit jobs."

"You don't know that. The guy who killed Trager— Powell, right?—he's just some street punk with a big nose and a drug habit. Nothing like our German friend. It wasn't exactly the quiet, professional job you'd expect."

"No, but still, it wasn't a crime of passion. Porky walked into the bar looking for Trager and shot him. No evidence that he and Trager knew each other, no reason to kill him. It's a pretty safe bet that somebody else put the shooter up to it. Your boss, Lieutenant Stokes, thinks so, too. Told me so two days ago."

"Okay, maybe." Woody clearly wasn't convinced. "So what?"

"So how could the two be connected? C'mon, think this through with me. Call it an intellectual exercise."

The two friends stared at one another. They'd known each other a long time, and it was clear to both of them that the following two things were true: Woody didn't want to do this, and Sid wasn't going to let it go.

"Uhhh, how about this?" Woody sounded as intentionally unenthusiastic as possible. "Trager and Lou were both screwing the wife of some famous mobster."

"Couldn't possibly be true, but thanks for playing along. What else?"

"The *daughter* of a famous mobster?"

"Okay, let's suppose screwing had nothing to do with it. What ties two people together that gets them both killed?"

"You know the answer to that one, Sid." Now Woody didn't sound like he was joking at all. "If it's not a woman, there's only one other possibility. Money."

"Hey, that's good."

"It's not exactly an original thought. They didn't teach you this in 'Detective 101?'"

"How about this? Lou had a client that was being blackmailed by Trager. The client finally decides he's had enough, has Trager killed, then decides Lou has to die because he's the only one who knows he was being blackmailed."

"If there was a shred of evidence that any of that was true, you might have something."

"What if there was some big issue before the city

175

council. Somebody was bribing Trager to get his vote, and Lou found out about it."

"Well, that doesn't sound quite as desperate, but if Trager was playing along, I don't know why that would get him killed. And why would Lou know about it?"

"I don't know."

"And again, you've got no evidence. Look, if you're just gonna pull stuff out of your ass, how about this—Maybe Trager found an old pirate map that led to a buried treasure chest. Somebody hired Lou to steal the map, then had them both killed so he could keep all the treasure for himself."

` Another pause as the two men had a brief staring contest. Sid threw in the towel, sullen and pissed off.

"Okay, Woody. You don't have to help if you don't want to."

"I want to help, Sid. But I don't want to waste my time. Dammit, we just don't have enough evidence to link these two murders together, so whatever we come up with is just wild speculation. Let's wait and see what turns up, and I'll keep an open mind, okay?"

"Like I said, you don't have to help."

Woody had offered an olive branch, and Sid clearly had no intention of taking it. The cop opened the door, and made one final observation before stepping out of the interrogation room.

"I'll tell you one thing that the murders of Tom Trager and Lou Martini have in common. You shouldn't be screwing around with either one of them. One case is mine, and your sister just fired you from the other one."

Sid pushed past him without a word and silently walked

through the collection of desks that made up Sac Homicide. As he approached the double doors that led to the outer hallway, Woody came up alongside him.

"Hey."

Sid stopped, turned to his friend and waited.

"Don't pout, Sid. It's unprofessional."

Chapter 24

Sunday night, eight o'clock. Overcast skies with a chance of rain before morning. Above the clouds there was no moon at all, so it was exceptionally dark. A perfect night for Sid's first break-in.

Despite Woody's advice the previous day, Sid had spent quite a bit of his weekend pouting. There are times when a little runaway self-pity can be very satisfying. Sometimes he dwelled on his big sister's lack of confidence in him. Sometimes on what a jerk Woody had been. The more he thought about how badly they'd treated him, the more he convinced himself that he was right—that there really was something odd and mysterious about Mary and Bertie Jones' past. In turn, the more he dwelled on the case, the more he wanted to prove Gloria and Woody wrong. It was a cycle that fed on itself, and Sid savored his misery. Amy had called early Sunday morning to cancel their weekly run— some emergency had come up at work—which put him into an even deeper funk. And then when his mom told him that she was going out to a movie that night with Mary Jones, Sid knew exactly what he was going to do.

The Land Park neighborhood was one of Sacramento's oldest and most elegant. Huge elm trees rose from the ground on thick trunks and disappeared into the darkness. Quaint old lampposts cast pools of light here and there, and windows glowed from the brick tudors or wooden bungalows on both sides of the street. Still, it was dark enough that a five-foot-seven guy with a navy blue hooded sweatshirt pulled over his red hair was very hard to notice as he walked casually down the sidewalk.

Mary Jones' home was on Vallejo Street, just five or six blocks from Sid's mom's place. How many times had Sid gone out of his way to walk or ride his bike past Bertie's house when he was a kid? Or later, after he got his license, tooled by in his car? Always dreaming of the green-eyed girl inside with the yellow hair and the little cleft in her chin. He'd never actually been inside the place, but that was about to change.

Sid made a conscious effort to notice his own breathing and heart rate as he was approaching the house. Nice and calm. You never know how you'll react to something like this, and he was pleased with how relaxed and aware he felt. Mary Jones had left the porch light on, but the rest of the house looked like it was dark and empty. Sid remembered Lou Martini telling him the most important thing about being some place you're not supposed to be— "*Just act like you're supposed to be there.*" So he didn't sneak or dash or do anything out of the ordinary. He simply turned up the driveway, let himself through the gate and into the side yard. He even thought about whistling, but decided that might be overkill. The gate closed behind him, and then he heard the dog.

First it was the jingle of an oncoming collar and tags, then a deep, loud "Woof! Woof!" Sid spun in the darkness and saw nothing. He put his arms out to block whatever was coming and braced himself for the impact. And that's when the dog collided with the chain link fence. The familiar, metallic rattle of the fence was followed by a yelp, and then the dog—it must have been a black dog because he still couldn't see a thing—began growling and barking wildly from the neighbor's yard.

A light popped on next door, and some guy stuck his head out and shouted, "Jennifer, shut up!" Sid dropped to the ground and wondered who the hell would name a dog *Jennifer*. The heart rate that he had been so proud of a moment earlier skyrocketed, and he had a very strong urge to run back through the gate and sprint for his mother's house. But he didn't. He stayed low, scurried the length of the side of the house and rounded the corner, with Jennifer the dog paralleling him the whole way, barking wildly on the other side of the fence.

Sid made his way across some fairly wet grass before finding himself crawling across a small expanse of concrete—probably the back patio. His suspicions were confirmed at the moment his head made solid contact with the wall of the house. He leaned back against the bricks, breathing hard, and waited for Jennifer to shut up. *First lesson of the evening: check for dogs before going into somebody's back yard next time.* Stupid.

It seemed like a long time before the dog gave up. Sid sat quietly for another couple of minutes, just to make sure the coast was clear. No hurry. He had checked the movie show times in the newspaper, and "Remo Williams" starring Fred Ward had only been on for about thirty minutes. His mom and Mary Jones wouldn't even be half-way through their tub of popcorn yet. His eyes had adjusted a little to the absence of the streetlights, and he discovered he could just barely make out the back of the house. There was a window directly over his head. Guessing by its size and height, probably a kitchen window above a sink. A few feet to his right was a door, with other windows beyond that.

Sid slowly stood, and felt the big front pocket of his sweatshirt to make sure his tools were still there. His handy cat burglar kit contained a total of two things: a flashlight that he planned to use as little as possible, and a screwdriver that he hoped to not use at all. Sid had locked himself out of his own house on at least a half dozen occasions through the years, and most of the time he discovered a door or window that had been inadvertently left unlocked. Time to find out if Mary Jones was just as careless.

The window he'd been sitting under and the rear door were both locked tight. On his way to check the other windows he kicked some metal patio furniture, and Jennifer barked twice, but apparently didn't think it was worth investigating. After removing screens and confirming that the remaining windows on the back of the house were solidly locked, he made his way carefully around to the far side—the one opposite the dog—and he hit the jackpot. The first window he tried slid easily, and without a second thought he let himself into Mary Jones' house.

Sid slid off his damp shoes, not wanting to leave tracks in the house. It was darker inside than it was outside, and he deliberated whether he should use the flashlight or simply flip the switch. If a neighbor happened to be looking, the flashlight might seem very suspicious. He decided to stick with the "act like you're supposed to be there" philosophy and flipped on the lights to discover that he was, without a doubt, in Bertie's old bedroom. A twin bed was almost completely covered with frilly pillows in bright pinks and yellows and greens. Curtains in the same colors framed the window he'd just crawled through. Sid's first impression was that it had been decorated at a time when "Laugh-In" was the number one show on TV. On a mirrored dressing table was a framed photo of Bertie at age twelve or thirteen, posing arm in arm with Mary. A big, fat teddy bear sat in a chair wearing a t-shirt that said, "McClatchy High School, Class of '68". It was identical to one his sister had, though he hadn't seen it in years.

The light from Bertie's room spilled down a short hallway, providing a little bit of illumination to what Sid presumed to be the living room. There was one other door in the hallway that opened onto a bathroom. He took in as much of the layout as he could see, then flicked off Bertie's light and closed the door behind him. There was a tiny nightlight in the bathroom, and Sid was struck with the sudden urge to take a pee, but figured that would be a very unprofessional thing to do, so he pressed on. He could see pretty well in the living room. The porch light shone through the front window, the parted drapes glowing a bronze color. There was a long sofa in front of the window, with the obligatory coffee table in front of it and a pretty good sized television on the opposite wall. Sid kept moving, confident that what he was looking for would either be in the kitchen or in Mary's bedroom.

The kitchen was off to his right, at the rear of the house and really dark. Sid decided it was worth flipping on the light, but he didn't have it on for long. There was no kitchen desk area that might be used for paying bills, no little nook with a filing cabinet, no place that looked like you'd keep important papers. He turned the light off.

The master bedroom was on the front corner of the house, with a door just off the living room. With its exposure to the street, Sid had no intention of using his flashlight. Besides, this was the side of the house closest to Jennifer the dog, so he felt his way through the room with the help of the very little ambient light from the windows. This room was clearly more lived in. Magazines and books were piled on a nightstand. Sid came across a pair of shoes and some article of clothing on the floor next to the bed. At one point a car drove by, providing a little extra illumination. Just enough to see the desk with wide drawers in the corner.

In his hurry to get to the desk, Sid caught a little toe on the leg of a table and came very close to crying out in pain. He hopped up and down on the other foot for a moment, biting his lip. Then he got down on hands and knees and crawled the rest of the way. The big desk drawer slid out easily, and he reached in and felt file folders.

This was the most 007 moment of Sid's young detective career. A grin crossed his face in the darkness as he took out his flashlight. He thought about the one he'd had as a kid— the one with the red and blue filters—and wished that he had it now. He cupped a hand over the end of the flashlight to block most of the light, and flicked it on, making his fingers glow red. With one free hand, he began thumbing through the papers in the drawer. There were tabs on the top of the files with impeccably printed labels that said things like "Life Insurance" and "Mortgage" and "DMV."

And the one that caught his eye said "Bertie."

Sid pulled the thick file from the drawer, moved a chair that was in his way, and he crawled under the desk. In his little cave, he allowed the full beam of the flashlight to shine on the papers in Bertie's file. What would he have given to have had a look at this stuff when he was younger? There were report cards full of A's, and class photos going back to elementary school. Sid caught himself taking a moment to look at the images of the girl through the years, and had to make himself move on. There were immunization records and some drawings that Bertie must have done when she was younger. And there was a tiny little white tooth in a plastic sandwich bag which, for some reason, made Sid feel for the first time like he might be doing something wrong— like maybe he shouldn't be there. He flipped quickly through the rest of the file, and didn't find what he was looking for.

The file marked "Bertie" was slid back into place, and Sid scanned the ones that remained. There was one that said "Misc.," so he pulled that file and crawled back under the desk. This one certainly lived up to its title. There was a receipt for a Kenmore refrigerator from 1972 and an owner's manual for a Panasonic clock radio and a lot of other things that most likely would never serve a useful purpose. Sid stopped when he saw the words "Death Certificate", and took a minute to discover that Robert Pearson Jones died of liver cancer at Sutter General Hospital in Sacramento on July 15th, 1956. He was just thirty-four-years-old. Sad, but nothing out of the ordinary.

He shined the light on his watch. Remo Williams had

been on for an hour. Still no need to hurry, but Sid was
beginning to think that his break-in was going to be a waste
of time. There were some Disneyland ticket books that had
all the "D" and "E" tickets missing, and a pamphlet full of
recipes that had been put together by some PTA in the 1960s.

Only a few items were left in the folder and Sid was
getting ready to put it away when he saw what he came for.
He had really begun to give up on the idea that he'd find
Bertie Jones' birth certificate, but there it was in the back of
the "Misc." file. Most of the information was exactly what
he expected. She was born at 7:49 a.m. on May 26th, 1950.
She weighed six pounds, nine ounces. Mary Jones was her
mother and Robert Jones was her father.

But the beam of Sid's flashlight revealed one bit of
information that might be especially interesting to Woody
Carver and Sid's skeptical sister, Gloria. Bertie Jones was
born at Miami-Dade Hospital in Dade County, Florida.

Florida.

Sid stared at the paper for at least a minute. Should he
put it back or take it with him? It was incredibly unlikely
that its absence would be missed. To steal it or to leave it
was a simple enough decision, but for some reason it was
paralyzing. He held onto the birth certificate for the moment
while he closed the folder and slid out from underneath the
desk. With his hand once again blocking most of the light
from his flashlight, he put the "Misc." file back where he
found it, then he examined the birth certificate one more
time in the red glow that escaped his fingers.

He decided that the risk of being discovered, however
small, was too great, and was reaching in to slide the

certificate back when the room suddenly filled with light, and then began to dim. It took a brief, panicky moment for Sid to realize that car headlights were illuminating the bedroom as someone had turned off Vallejo Street and pulled into the driveway. He quickly flicked off the flashlight and crawled over to the window just as the lights outside went out, and he faintly heard an engine turn off and a car door open. He raised up and looked through the sheer curtains, fully expecting to see two cops emerging from a squad car with guns drawn. But it was a brand new Lincoln Continental, and the light inside the car revealed Mary Jones as she climbed out. Either he'd gotten the movie showtimes wrong, or Remo Williams sucked.

Sid turned away from the window, and the bedroom seemed darker than ever. He fumbled back toward the desk and closed the drawer, then crawled around the bed and made his way to the door. His desire to go fast battled with his desire to be quiet, and it felt like an agonizingly long time before he was entering the living room again. Out the front window, the porch light brightly illuminated Mary Jones as she approached the front door, keys in hand, and Sid realized he wasn't going to make it. The key rattled into the lock as Sid slid across the hardwood floor on hands and knees in his stocking feet. The deadbolt turned, and a shaft of light from the porch entered the room as Sid dropped down to his belly. And as Mary entered her living room and flipped on the light, Sid just finished crawling behind her couch that sat in front of the big picture window. He heard the door close and the deadbolt thrown back again, and he tried to not make a sound.

Chapter 25

Sid had no idea what time it was. In fact, it had taken him a moment or two to even remember *where* he was. It was cold and dark when he woke up laying behind the sofa in Mary Jones' living room, and he was pretty sure there was a cat on his head.

The earlier events of the evening came back to him. Somewhere around 8:30 Mary had come home unexpectedly. She had disappeared into the kitchen briefly—Sid could see her feet from his hiding place—then she'd returned to the living room, flipped on the TV, and sat down on the sofa above him.

Sid had never seen *Murder, She Wrote*. It was about half over when Mary Jones turned it on, but he picked up the story pretty quickly and enjoyed it very much. Pretty impressive, considering that from his place on the floor behind the sofa he could only see the bottom third of the television screen. When the show was over, Mary got up and walked over to the TV, and Sid held his breath, hoping that she'd turn it off and go to bed, allowing him to make his escape. But after she fiddled around for a minute, it became apparent that she'd popped a copy of *The Sound of Music* into the VCR. Sid's heart sank, in part because he was desperate to escape, but mostly because he hated the film. And then, to his horror, he discovered that Mary liked to sing along with the movie. She couldn't carry a tune, but she knew every lyric and she sang with enthusiasm. Mercifully, he fell asleep before "*Climb Every Mountain*" was turned into an agonizing duet.

Now it was dark and quiet, and there was unquestionably something warm and furry curled up on the side of his face, emitting a slight purr. Very slowly, Sid raised his one free arm and gave the cat a gentle push. It resisted briefly, meowed once, then disappeared into the darkness. Sid was pretty sure that Mary's feet were not on the floor in front of the sofa, which meant that she'd either gone to bed, or was asleep just above him. With the patience of someone disarming a bomb, Sid slowly slid himself out from behind the couch. He raised his head enough to see that there was no one on the sofa, then got to his feet and walked quietly across the room and down the hallway past the bathroom with the nightlight. Now he *really* had to pee, but it was out of the question. The door to Bertie's room creaked as he closed it behind him, and he noticed it was suddenly colder than the rest of the house because of the open window. As soon as his feet touched the damp grass outside, Sid realized he'd left his shoes on the bedroom floor. He climbed back in, grabbed his sneakers, went back out the window and slid it shut.

He was still moving slowly and deliberately as he rounded the corner from the back yard when Jennifer began to bark. Within seconds, the gate had closed behind him and Sid Bigler was running down Vallejo Street at 2 a.m. in wet socks—shoes in one hand and a birth certificate in the other.

Chapter 26

3:10 p.m. Sid felt remarkably good as he sat in the waiting room. Knowing a secret always made him feel good. He'd managed to get a couple more hours of sleep in his own bed before heading down to the deli. The Brown Sugar Cinnamon Rolls had attracted their usual, rabid Monday crowd of customers, and the place stayed busy right through lunchtime. Throughout the day, Sid's thoughts had occasionally drifted to the intrigue of the night before, and the piece of paper that was now concealed at the bottom of his underwear drawer.

Bertie Jones' offices were at least as impressive as Nathan Bomke's, but in a different way. Bomke's office had been flashy and expensive and pretentious. The offices of Bertie Jones and her partners didn't try so hard. They quietly oozed power, and an assurance that the people who worked there were deservedly well paid. The receptionist was a man with graying temples in a perfectly tailored suit, and after taking Sid's name and asking him to wait, the guy hadn't even glanced in his direction. That had been fifteen minutes ago, and now Sid was thumbing through the current Architectural Digest for the third time.

"Sid! There you are! How are you?"

She said it like she'd been searching for a dear friend and finally found him. Sid looked up from his magazine to see Bertie Jones in a dark blue pants suit and silver blouse, her blonde hair pulled back. All business, but perfect and stunning. And there was no trace of the irritation he'd heard

189

in her voice when she called him to make this appointment three days ago.

"I'm good. Just catching up on my architecture."

Sid dropped the magazine on the coffee table with the leather top and stood up. Bertie's smile grew a tiny bit, and her emerald eyes drew him in as she reached out her hand. Sid took it, intending to give it a good, professional shake, but that was not her intention. She held onto his hand and began leading him through the waiting room and past the receptionist.

"Come back to my office with me."

'Professional Sid' had walked into the waiting room wearing a coat and tie and thinking about his strategy for this meeting. But now, 'Giddy Schoolboy Sid' was trying to take over as he walked down the hallway with butterflies in his stomach, holding hands with Bertie Jones. Professional Sid fought valiantly to stay in control of the situation, but it looked like a losing battle.

She led him into a spacious office that was covered in rich wood paneling—even the ceiling. An elegant oak desk and two chairs for guests stood by the windows, but Bertie walked past the desk and didn't let go of his hand until they were standing by a small leather sofa in the corner. "Wait here just a second," she said, and she crossed the room and closed the door. Sid's knees grew a little weak.

It was in this fragile state that Sid Bigler was about to have a life-changing encounter with Déjà Vu. If he'd known it was coming, he could have braced himself. But he was unprepared. Unsuspecting.

Bertie removed her jacket and hung it on a coat rack in

the corner. Then she walked casually across the room, stopping so close to him their bodies were almost touching. "I hope you weren't waiting long," she said and she placed a hand on Sid's arm. Then came the dazzling smile, and she added, "I hate to keep important people waiting."

The green eyes were only inches away, and Sid stared into them for several seconds before Bertie gave his arm a little squeeze, then turned and walked to her desk. She held up a little green bottle.

"Perrier?"

Epiphany.

It was a moment that Sid would never forget. Lightning flashed and bells rang and curtains fell and heavenly choirs sang. Bertie couldn't possibly have realized what she had done. Sid gave no outward cue that anything had happened. But in his head—and in his heart—everything had changed. Everything.

"Sid?"

"Hmm?"

"Perrier?"

"Oh. Sure."

Bertie began pouring the bubbly water into a couple of glasses, and Sid replayed the moment just to be sure. She had said, *"I hope you weren't waiting long,"* then put a hand on his arm. *"I hate to keep important people waiting."* They had stood close together for another few seconds before she gave his arm a gentle squeeze, then walked to her desk and offered him a drink. And it was a carbon copy—not just the words but every movement, every nuance—of what Nathan Bomke had done last week when Sid was at his office. Oh, the beverage choice was different, and the curves of her silver blouse made her much more pleasant to look at. But the substance was the same.

Bertie Jones was Nathan Bomke with boobs and green eyes, and he'd just seen it for the first time.

Growing up, one of the extraordinary things about Bertie Jones was that, even though she was the most beautiful woman in the world, she never acted like it. Never tried to take advantage of it. As the years went by, Sid would see plenty of pretty girls use their looks to manipulate helpless, stupid guys (present company included). It was an unfair battle if ever there was one. Yet Bertie had always seemed unaware of her devastating, unparalleled beauty. It was a quality that made her even more extraordinary. Even more desirable. But in an instant, it had all come undone.

The realization was painful. All his life, he had really only been around Bertie Jones in the presence of his sister. To put it bluntly, Gloria was never a rival to Bertie's beauty. Not even close. No need for Bertie to ever appear vain or petty. It was no contest. And as for Sid, well, none of the Biglers had a future in modeling. He had been a goofy looking kid and now he was not a handsome man. He had known Bertie Jones his entire life, and she'd never shown him the slightest interest. He realized now it was because she'd never needed anything from him. But today, because for some reason she wanted to influence him—to manipulate him—she had turned on the charm. *And she had held his hand.* If he had been alone, he might have cried.

"...and it's just not good for her to get worked up. You understand, don't you?"

Bertie was seated next to him on the couch now, and while his twenty-year fantasy had been crumbling, she had been talking about her mom's heart condition and why Sid should leave her alone and just forget about the shooting.

"Yes. Yes, of course," he said, and he noticed that Bertie's hand was draped casually across his knee. He looked into the green eyes, and felt nothing. Nothing at all.

"Please tell her I'm sorry I upset her," he said.

"Oh, I'm sure she'll be fine."

Bertie stood up, her mission accomplished, sending the subtle clue that she really didn't have anything else on her agenda. Sid, on the other hand, picked up his Perrier, took a sip, then leaned back on the couch. His world had been rocked, but he was recovering fast, and now that he was free from the burden of his infatuation, he was surprised to discover that he liked how it felt. The bondage of Bertie's beauty was broken, and his liberation brought with it some new possibilities. This was definitely not the time to end their conversation. The Case of the Shooting of Bertie Jones was unquestionably open again.

"Hey, there's something I've always wanted to ask you."

"Yes?" Bertie said it with a smile, then walked over, leaned against her desk and crossed her legs.

"Your mom started the shelter for abused women. The WAVE. Now she's establishing one in Phoenix, too. They're places for women and kids who have been hurt by creeps."

"Yeah, you could put it that way."

"So does it bother you that it's your job to keep creeps from going to jail?"

Sid hit a nerve. It wasn't a big change, but it was there.

193

The jaw tightened. The head tilted slightly.

"I don't defend abusers and child molesters."

"Yeah, but the principle applies, right? Because of what you do, terrible people end up on the streets."

If Sid's initial question caught Bertie off guard for a moment, she quickly regrouped. She circled her desk and sat behind it. The smile looked genuine.

"I think maybe you're watching too much TV, Sid. Criminal defense attorneys are the good guys, not the bad guys. The government holds all the cards, has all the resources. They collect all the evidence and they decide who they'll prosecute. People like me protect the public from all that power."

"Very noble. And how nice for you that it's also very profitable."

"Think what you like." Now the smile looked strained. "But I believe in what I do. Even my *pro bono* work is defending people that you wouldn't approve of from the power of the state. Without people like me, there's no real justice."

"And bank robbers and tax cheats—and guys who beat up women—they never get away with it?"

"It's not my fault if the prosecution fails to make a case."

"So when some novice junior D.A. goes up against a talented defense attorney like you, no matter what happens, justice is done?"

"They don't send novice junior D.A.'s against me."

"So justice is always done."

Bertie Jones sighed. Clearly, the conversation had grown wearisome, and she was tired of making the effort

194

that courtesy required. Just what Sid wanted.

"Sid, the court system recognizes that the government always has the advantage. That's why they need twelve jurors and I only need one. They've got the power. All I have is creativity and reasonable doubt."

"Okay." Sid stood up, Perrier in hand, and walked over to Bertie's desk. "And when a jury gets it wrong, it's for the greater good. Better that a few creeps walk away than an innocent man goes to prison."

"That's right."

"Yeah, I guess I get that." Sid set his glass down on Bertie's desk. "But I still think it's kinda funny that your mom spends her time protecting women from bad guys, and you spend your time sending them back on the streets."

Bertie stood and said, "I have another meeting in a few minutes," and she walked to her office door with the clear implication that Sid should follow. He noted that she didn't want to hold hands this time. She waited for him to leave, but he paused for another irritating moment before moving. Here was his chance.

"Yeah, I've gotta get going, too." He headed for the door. "Hey, your mom said the other day that you guys were from Canton, Ohio. I thought it was Columbus."

"No, Canton." A short answer, even a little snotty. "I was born there."

Sid smiled and reached out his hand. Bertie gave it a quick, professional shake.

"Good-bye," she said.

"Thank you," he said.

It took just over four minutes for Sid to ride down the elevator, pass through the lobby and walk to his car. Along the way he laughed out loud on three occasions, and he wasn't exactly sure why. He had an overwhelming sense of freedom. A lifelong obsession with a woman he always knew he could never have had just come to an end. The spell had been broken. Toto had pulled back the curtain, and he'd seen the real Bertie Jones.

And now, for some reason, he really wanted to be with Amy.

Chapter 27

It's hard to run and laugh at the same time, but Amy Solomon was doing a pretty good job of it. She had a wonderful laugh.

"What?" Sid asked. "You think Sherlock Holmes never hid behind an old lady's couch?"

It was one of their regular 'Dinner and Run' dates. They'd grabbed a bite to eat after Amy got off work, quickly changed into running clothes, and now they were on their second lap around Land Park. The sun had just gone down, car headlights were coming on, and Sid was beginning to think that the enchiladas at Luis's on Alhambra Boulevard might have been a mistake.

"So how long were you under there?"

"Three or four hours, I guess.

"Were you scared?"

"Only when Bertie's mom started singing '*Do-Re-Mi*'."

Sid had deliberated all through dinner whether or not to tell his fiancée what he'd done the night before. He certainly couldn't tell Woody or Gloria about his break-in. Not yet, anyway, but that day was coming. In the meantime, he was dying to tell someone, and ultimately decided that it was a good time to find out how Amy would react to the occasionally dangerous nature of his new profession. He hadn't expected laughter.

"Well, if you'd gotten caught, I would have come and picked you up from jail again."

"I know, honey. It's one of the things I looked for in a

girlfriend."

When Stokes had locked him up years ago, it was Amy that had been there to give him a ride when he made bail.

"So now you're convinced there's some big mystery in Bertie's past."

"You're not?"

"I don't know. Maybe."

"C'mon, the woman lied to me this afternoon."

"Only if that birth certificate you stole is legit, and only if her mom hasn't hidden the truth from her. Maybe she doesn't know."

"You sound like my sister and Woody. Why is it that all the people I care about are second guessing me?"

"Maybe it's because we care about you, too."

"Nah, that couldn't be it."

The two trotted along Freeport Boulevard single file for a couple of blocks without talking, and Sid was increasingly confident that running and Mexican food didn't go together.

"Hang on," he said. "I need to walk a little. The enchiladas are making trouble."

"Really? That's funny, I would've thought that the two Cokes and all the guacamole would have helped settle everything down."

"Thanks for the sympathy."

Sid and Amy walked together in the grass, and after a minute she took his hand.

"You okay?"

"Better."

"So, after your little run-in this afternoon, do I take Bertie Jones off the wedding invitation list?"

"Well, after today, I don't think she'll come. But leave her on the list anyway. Maybe we'll get a good wedding gift."

"I wasn't worried about her you know."

"I know."

"Speaking of invitations, I'm going over to your sister's Saturday afternoon to get them all addressed. You want to help us?"

"I don't have pretty, loopy handwriting."

"No, you don't. But you can stuff and lick envelopes."

"Yummy."

Amy gave Sid's hand a squeeze and said, "C'mon, tough guy." Then she let go and started jogging slowly. Sid stayed right next to her as they took a shortcut straight across the open grass of Land Park. Sid hated shortcuts, but wasn't going to complain tonight.

"If you're right about Bertie," Amy said, "why would she lie about where she was born?"

"Ahhh. So you're coming around."

"No, this is hypothetical."

"Well, hypothetically, I've thought about it and I can't come up with a single reason that makes any sense."

"So is it a dead end?"

"More like a road block. Dead ends are dead ends, but you can always get around a road block."

"And does that involve breaking into more houses?"

"Probably not, but you never know."

Chapter 28

On Tuesday morning, customers at the deli were talking about the Jets big win on Monday Night Football (they retired Joe Namath's jersey at halftime) and that day's launch of the Space Shuttle Columbia. Sid was busy taking orders and making change, and for the time being had forgotten that he was a private eye. But then Lieutenant Benjamin Stokes walked in.

"So you guys are closed on the weekends."

It was an odd way to start a conversation, but that's what Stokes said as he slid onto an open stool at the counter. Blue jacket, brown pants, green tie. Rumpled.

"Yep," Sid replied. "Every weekend since 1947."

"I stopped by on Saturday."

"Something wrong?"

"No, I was hungry. I can't stop thinking about those steak sandwiches I had last week."

"Good, huh?"

"The best. I got divorced a couple of years ago, and I can't cook worth a damn."

It was Sid's first personal glimpse at the man behind the big teeth.

"You like corned beef hash?"

"Love it."

"Why don't you go grab that table over there. It's on me."

"Great," said Stokes. "I like bacon, too."

Sid put the order on Joe's wheel, poured two cups of

coffee, then joined Stokes at a small table near the window and said, "I assume it's a little early for a Tab?"

"No, actually, but this will do. Thanks."

"So, any luck tracking down Peter Powell?"

"None. The little turd shot Trager, and then just disappeared."

"It's surprising. He doesn't seem like the resourceful type."

"No."

"Any other leads? Did you ever talk to Trager's girlfriend, Jilly Boyd?"

"Yes I did."

"And?"

"Well, this is supposed to be a reciprocal relationship, Sid. We're supposed to help each other. How about you go first?"

Damn. Sid had lots to tell, but not to the head of Homicide. Not yet. His initial hunch about Mary and Bertie Jones and their past had only grown stronger, and he was trying very hard to talk himself into believing that it was no coincidence that Porky had shot at both Trager and Bertie almost two weeks ago. But he had failed to convince Gloria, Woody or Amy that he was onto something. And he didn't want to say anything to Stokes until he had some more solid evidence. He flashed back to their last conversation, and opted for the truth.

"I've got nothing specific I can tell you right now. I'll be honest, Lieutenant, you and I are looking for the same guy, but from two different angles. You're after Trager's killer, and I'm after the guy who shot Bertie Jones. I've come across some interesting stuff—and it might lead us to Porky Powell—but it's personal, and it's got nothing to do with Trager."

"So you want me to tell you what I've got, but I get nothing in return."

"Except free breakfast."

Stokes took a sip of his coffee and studied Sid for a moment without saying a word.

"I get bacon?"

"Eight slices."

The lieutenant set down his coffee, pulled out his famous notebook and started thumbing through pages.

"I stopped by the woman's apartment four or five times over the past few days, finally found Jilly Boyd at home yesterday afternoon. She's not as good looking as Trager's wife, but she's younger and stupider, so I guess that was the attraction."

"Was she helpful?"

"Well, Miss Boyd doesn't like the police very much. No surprise there. She was picked up for prostitution twice in 1982 and 1983."

"So she didn't want to talk to you."

"Not at first. But once a hooker, always a hooker. C'mon, that was all she was for Trager, right? He paid for the apartment and clothes and nice dinners, and she screwed him whenever he wanted. Same deal. So I let her know that if she didn't wanna talk, I'd have her charged with a long-term solicitation arrangement with the late Councilman."

"You can't do that, can you?"

"No, of course not. But as I mentioned before, Miss

Boyd is stupid." Stokes had finally found the page he was looking for, and laid his notebook down on the table in front of him. "Let's see… They first met in the lounge at John Q's on top of the Holiday Inn about two years ago. She recognized him from the billboards and TV commercials, he recognized her obvious assets, and they got the apartment a week later. Trager almost never spent the night, but he would visit her there four or five times a week. I guess she provides a very entertaining lunch."

Stokes stopped talking when Eddie approached the table, and he eyed the corned beef hash and double side of bacon that was set in front of him.

"Hey, could you bring me some Tabasco, too?"

Eddie didn't say anything, of course, but headed off to get it immediately.

"Taste it first," Sid said. "Tabasco's already in there, and some other secret ingredient that Joe won't tell me."

Stokes took a bite. He looked like a kid who had just seen his new puppy on Christmas morning.

"Oh my God."

"Yeah, it's good."

"Oh my God."

"Uh-huh."

Eddie returned to drop off a little bottle of Tabasco and refill both coffee cups.

"Thanks, Eddie," Sid said.

Stokes stuck another forkful of hash in his mouth, closed his eyes, and said, "Oh my God."

"Glad you like it."

It was looking as though the lieutenant was going to be

unable to speak for a few minutes, which was just as well because Sid heard his name called from across the room and turned to see Joe pointing to the cash register. One customer was waiting to pay, and it looked like a couple others had to-go orders.

"I'll be right back."

By the time Sid returned, the corned beef hash was mostly gone. Stokes was snapping one of his last two slices of bacon in half, staring at it in wonder.

"It's tender, but it's crunchy."

"Yep. I don't know how Joe does it. So tell me more about Jilly Boyd."

The initial shock of the food must have worn off, because Stokes was able to get back on track. But he did talk with his mouth full for most of the rest of their conversation.

"Okay, here's the most interesting part," Stokes said, returning to his notes. "I asked the girl if she ever met any of Trager's acquaintances or business partners, or ever saw anything unusual. She told me that Trager only brought somebody else to the apartment on a couple of occasions. Two times he had a man join him for dinner there at Jilly's apartment. Both times, he had a big, fancy meal catered. Both times he told Jilly to beat it for a few hours so he could be alone with this guest."

"Yeah, that's odd. Like he didn't want to be seen with the guy."

"Uh-huh. The girl said she'd never seen him before, but Trager introduced him as his friend 'Donny.'"

Stokes said the name like it was important, then popped the last chunk of bacon into his mouth.

"Osmond?"

"Probably not. All Jilly Boyd knew was Donny, but it's a safe bet it was Donald Kakavetsis."

"Is that name supposed to mean something to me?"

"Donald Kakavetsis." Stokes said it with a tad of incredulity. As though Sid had never heard of Abe Lincoln or George Jetson. Then he continued, talking to Sid like he was a toddler.

"He's the head of ABC Enterprises. You've heard of ABC, right?"

"ABC, like Channel 13? Love Boat? Laverne &Shirley? *That* ABC?"

"Jesus, Sid. Not the TV network. ABC Enterprises is a shell corporation. They've got some apartment buildings in the Bay Area and that big casino as soon as you cross over the border into Nevada on I-80. Kakavetsis has a zillion acres of land just north of town that's gonna be covered with houses one day, and he produces low-budget pornographic movies. And there's a lot more. Basically, ABC Enterprises and Donald Kakavetsis specialize in business ventures that are generally but not always legal, and almost never admirable. Get the picture?"

"Not the kind of guy a city councilman likes to be seen with."

"Very good. So they meet at the little love nest."

"And you tied them together just because Jilly Boyd said the name '*Donny*?'"

"No, that's just what confirmed it. I've been squeezing this whole damn town trying to find any motivation for somebody wanting Trager dead. I've talked to everybody from the mayor down to punks on the street. ABC came up a couple of times from completely different sources. It was already starting to look like our favorite hardware man was getting caught up with a very rotten crowd. But Jilly Boyd was the icing on the cake. Thanks for finding her for us."

"My pleasure."

Stokes wiped his mouth with his napkin and stood up.

"Listen, Bigler. I don't know what else you're working on. Whatever it is, I wanna know if you turn something up, okay?"

"Sure. I promise."

"And listen to me. Donald Kakavetsis is serious bad. You stay away from him."

"I will."

"I hope you do. Thanks for breakfast."

Stokes turned and walked out the door and Sid watched him go. It struck him that this was an odd turn of events. The people that had always been his biggest supporters—his sister, Woody, and even Amy to a certain extent—hadn't been showing a lot of confidence in him lately. But this cop who had once charged him with attempted murder was now his buddy.

Benjamin Stokes was already halfway down the block when Sid hurried out the front door and called his name. The sidewalk was getting crowded as people were making their way to the office on this Tuesday morning. The lieutenant stopped and Sid caught up with him.

"Hey, can I get a little advice?"

"Sure."

"I said earlier that I'm working on something that might

lead us to Trager's shooter. I feel like I'm close, but, uh…
I'm not sure what to do next."

"And you can't tell me what it is."

"No."

"And you want some advice."

That was exactly the situation, and Sid realized now
how dumb it sounded. There was nothing else to say, so he
just shrugged.

"You know, for a long time I really didn't like you,
Bigler. But for some reason I'm starting to think you might
be a smart little bastard, so I don't know what I can tell you.
As long as you're not doing something stupid or dangerous,
go with your gut. You already know the secret for finding
people."

"I do?"

A bus had stopped right next to them, and now the
doors opened and a clump of passengers emerged, making
their way around Sid and the cop like they were a couple of
boulders in the middle of a stream. Stokes had to raise his
voice to be heard over the crowd.

"You find people by talking to people."

Then he turned and walked off, and Sid stood alone on
the sidewalk. That was the moment he decided to make a
trip to Miami.

Chapter 29

The morning encounter with Stokes haunted Sid for hours. He kept thinking of the last thing the cop had said. *You find people by talking to people.* Yes, it was something Sid already knew, but he'd never heard it put so simply. A complete course in private investigation boiled down to one sentence. Seven words.

Who had he talked to so far? Who should he talk to next? The questions made him realize he'd been doing a fairly unprofessional job with the case so far. He had never really opened a proper file—just scribbled some notes on a bar napkin and a sheet of lined paper at his mom's house. And even if this investigation was a freebie, he should be keeping track of his hours and expenses. Pretty lame.

The thought made Sid want to get away from the customers and get some real work done, but by the time his mom arrived to help out at lunch, the place was even more packed than usual. He ended up taking orders, clearing plates and working the cash register until the last customers paid up and he locked the door behind them. He flipped the open/closed sign around and turned the lights out in the front of the deli. And finally, just after 3 p.m., Sid sat down at his desk in the back room.

He started by getting a fresh manila folder and writing "Bertie Jones" on it with a black marker. Then he grabbed a spiral notebook and went to work. For the next few hours he wrote page after page, one name after another, each followed by the details of his conversations: Gloria's initial

request for help as they sat at her kitchen table; His brief
telephone call with Lou Martini the night before he was
killed; Jock Bell's curious appearance at the deli—he'd called
Trager a 'dumbass' and said there was a blonde in the
picture; The first ride with Lieutenant Stokes after he took
over the case; His disastrous chat with Mary Jones in his
mom's living room; Getting Porky's real name from Stokes
and giving him Jilly Boyd's name in return; The details of his
conversation with Charlie, the kid at the Motel Capri, and
Stokes' recap of what was found there; The largest entry was
his record of what the private eye from Canton had told him
on the phone—all the evidence that he *didn't* find; Gloria's
and Woody's objections and criticisms; his memorable
exchange with Bertie Jones at her office.

But he wrote nothing about the break-in. Nothing
about the birth certificate. There are some things that need
to stay hidden. Lou Martini had taught him that.

Sid thumbed through the notes and allowed himself a
moment to appreciate how much he had accomplished so
far. He had no idea how close he was to finding Peter Porky
Powell, but he'd clearly been doing the main thing that
Stokes' little proverb required. He had talked to people.

Feeling a little satisfaction, Sid stood up and stretched
his legs. He wandered out into the deli itself and was
surprised to see that the sun had just gone down. The clock
above the grill said it was 6:45. The occasional pedestrian
passed by the window, but the sidewalks were already
thinning out at the end of the workday. Sid grabbed a
plastic cup and poured himself a big Coke, no ice, then
flipped on the radio on the counter. He rolled the dial down

to KZAP and caught Blue Oyster Cult halfway through *Burnin' For You*. Then he wandered back to his desk, turned to a fresh sheet in his notebook and, across the top of the page, wrote the words, "Who do I talk to next?"

The first name he wrote was "Jackson Dexter"— the Sacramento Bee writer would be his best resource for knowing what was happening with the city council. That meeting was already set for early next week. Below Dexter's name he wrote "Trager's Wife." Sid couldn't recall her name, but he figured it couldn't hurt to pay her a visit. *You find people by talking to people*. Then he added "Jilly Boyd" to the list, followed by "Donny the ABC Guy." He'd probably never really go talk to Donald Kakavetsis, but it felt good to make the list a little longer.

And there was one last name he needed to write down. It was someone he definitely needed to talk to if he was going to find answers to all of his questions. Unfortunately, he had no idea who that person was, so he just wrote: "Somebody in Florida."

Behind Blue Eyes came on the radio. Sid laid down his pen, leaned back in his chair, closed his eyes and listened. It was one of his very favorite songs. Roger Daltrey's voice floated through the doorway from the other room, sounding distant and even more melancholy than usual.

No one knows what it's like to be the bad man. To be the sad man…

If he'd not been listening so intently, he might not have heard the front door quietly open and close. But he did. No doubt about it. Hmmm. He was sure that he'd locked it earlier.

Sid slipped from his seat, walked to the doorway and took one step into the deli. It was slightly darker than it had been just a few minutes ago, but enough light made its way through the blinds for him to clearly see the man standing on the other side of the counter. It was a genuinely weird moment—two men, motionless, less than ten feet apart, staring at each other in the half light. And *The Who* providing the soundtrack to what would be the most terrifying encounter of Sid Bigler's life.

Sid's first impression was not that the guy was huge, though certainly he was. His first impression was that he was powerful. The man's presence didn't make him feel small. It made him feel weak. The light, coming mostly from behind the man, revealed the angular features of his face, but his eyes were deep in shadow. Other than the slightest rise and fall of his chest, the guy hadn't moved a muscle.

Sid began to wonder just how long they could stand there before one of them talked. Despite the very menacing nature of the situation, it was the awkwardness that was getting to him. Somebody was going to have to say something sooner or later. Sid was just opening his mouth to speak when the man moved.

Slowly—really slowly—the intruder turned and circled around the end of the counter, gradually closing the distance between them while blocking Sid's path to the front door. He lifted his hands and held them up, empty and relaxed. He rotated his wrists, still in slow motion, showing open palms. Sid had no idea what the gesture meant, but something told him it was not good. The space between

211

them grew smaller until the man stopped, maybe three feet away, and the light from the back room illuminated him for the first time. He was a foot taller than Sid, maybe thirty years old, blonde and strikingly handsome. Sid thought he would've made a hell of a J.C. Penney catalogue model. The eyes that had been hidden were a bright, clear blue, but the face showed no expression as they stood, facing one another behind the counter of Sid's Deli. Roger Daltrey was on the second verse now.

But my dreams, they aren't as empty as my conscience seems to be…

Sid wished that some other song was on the radio. Whatever was about to happen, the lyrics just felt way too creepy now—like the music itself was rooting for the other guy. The whole scene would've felt a lot different if they were listening to something by Abba. Or maybe *Uptown Girl* by Billy Joel, but unfortunately that one wasn't on KZAP's playlist. Sid decided he'd had enough of the drama, and finally spoke.

"Is there something I can do for y…"

Sid didn't even see the guy move. All he knew was that incredibly powerful arms had him by the shoulders and he was flying backwards through the doorway and into the storage room. Instinct took over. He brought his hands up through the guy's arms and planted his palms firmly under the man's chin. Then he pushed with all his might, digging his fingers into his opponent's face while simultaneously sweeping a leg underneath him. The two of them hit hard on the linoleum floor, Sid on his back and taking most of the weight. Sid used the big guy's momentum against him, pushing even harder as they started to roll. For an instant, it was the much smaller man who had the advantage of leverage, and Sid had used the advantage well. His opponent recognized the change in momentum instantly and let go. It was in that moment—before either had a chance to find his balance or plan the next move—that both men knew that the other could fight.

There was a crashing sound, and as Sid regained his feet he saw that the blonde guy had knocked over the bread racks as he rolled to a stop. The man stood up as a few loaves of sourdough hit the ground, and now they faced each other again. There wasn't a lot of open space in the storage room/office. The men now stood in an area between the desk and the stainless steel sink. Between the old metal filing cabinet and the door to the walk-in refrigerator. An area slightly larger than the top of a picnic table in Curtis Park.

For the first time, the blank expression left the stranger's face. He gave a very slight smile and nodded his head, as if to recognize Sid's accomplishment in surviving his assault. Sid flashed back to the Prince Charles look-alike that he'd slapped around in the deli last week, and the way the dufus had completely lost his composure. *"An angry fighter is a stupid fighter."* But the big blonde man that he faced now wasn't angry at all. He looked amused.

Taking the initiative a moment ago hadn't paid off very well for Sid, so he waited. After a little while, the man gave a little shrug that seemed to acknowledge that it was his turn, took a step forward and threw one lightning fast jab. Sid blocked it. Pause. Next came two quick jabs with his left, a big, powerful swing with his right, and then a hard elbow toward Sid's ribs. Sid managed to deflect every blow, just like he was sparring with Woody, but with one big exception. This wasn't practice. This guy was built like a rock and he was coming at him with full strength, and even a successful deflection hurt like hell. Sid's wrists and the backs of his forearms throbbed, and it made him a little mad. Stanley Ono never warned him about that.

The blonde guy took a couple of steps back, and Sid responded by stepping forward and taking a couple of jabs himself, both brushed aside by his opponent. It wasn't all Sid had, but it was a good test. He began to back away, even dropping his hands for a second, then, as fast as he could, turned and planted his right foot and directed a side kick at the big man's mid-section. The man caught Sid's foot—actually caught it and held onto it with his vice-like hands for a moment—then pushed Sid away with it and let go. Sid lost his balance pretty badly and had to catch himself on his desk, but stayed on his feet.

"Not too bad. I had no idea you could fight."

The man's words hit Sid harder than any blow. They actually made him lean back and sit on the edge of the desk. He really should have been expecting it, but he wasn't. The words themselves weren't what caught Sid off guard. It was the way the man said them. It was the German accent.

Sid got back solidly on his feet, and recognized now that he was the one at risk of giving in to his anger. There could be little doubt that he was looking at the man who had killed Lou Martini. He fought to stay cool, reminding himself again of Stanley Ono's advice. He even thought about making a run for it, but calculated that the odds were not good. He probably couldn't get back out through the front of the deli without being caught, and the German was standing between him and the door to the back alley.

"It's not like on TV," Stanley Ono had once told his students. *"Real fights are over quick. Find an advantage and win fast."*

Sid glanced around the room, saw what he was looking for, and came up with a plan. He stepped away from the desk and raised his hands in front of him, then began to circle slowly to his right. He needed to get to the sink. The other man obliged by circling, too, as his expression returned to neutral. It was all business for the German now. The big man feigned a step forward, and Sid stepped back in response.

The sink was just a few feet away now. Sid glanced over briefly just to get his bearings, and that was when his opponent made his move. Sid didn't even see the first strike, and surprisingly didn't really feel it either. It was a short jab that caught him squarely on the right eye socket. He saw a bright light, but there wasn't any pain associated with it. Not yet. He managed to keep his hands up and protect himself from the next couple of blows that came his way, but then the German landed a shot to his ribs and Sid gave into the natural reaction. He leaned forward and allowed his arms to come down to protect his midsection.

The man's palm-strike was picture perfect. Sid had to admire it, and he had a hell of a view. As the big hand was approaching his face, Sid noted how the thumb was pressed tightly against the side of the open palm, the end joints of the other fingers curled closed. He only had a fraction of a second to study it, but it was perfect.

The hand connected with the side of Sid's face just above the jaw, and a couple of upper teeth popped free. Sid couldn't identify the little hard, white objects that were suddenly loose in his mouth, and let them escape as his head snapped back. He fell backwards against something solid—against the front of the stainless steel sink—and tried to cover his face. He heard the two little objects clatter to the floor and still didn't know what they were. With his hands out of the way, the German went to work on Sid's gut, delivering five or six punches to the ribs in rapid succession that were blindingly painful. Sid was very close to vomiting. Just as Stanley Ono had promised, it was happening quickly.

But then the man stopped. Maybe he was taking a moment to admire his handiwork. Whatever the reason, the man stopped and Sid felt the pain, and the pain did for him what it had always done. It focused him. It was his reminder that he had a job to do. And it reminded him of why he wanted to get to the sink.

In the back of a many restaurants there's a magnetic strip on the wall. It's generally near the food preparation area, and it only has one purpose. It holds knives. Since Sid first started working part-time at the deli when he was a kid and his father was running the place, how many times had he washed the big knives, dried them off, and stuck them to the magnetic strip next to the sink?

For the first time, Sid took his hands away from his face and looked up. He could tell that his right eye was already swelling badly. The small smile had returned to the German's face, and Sid felt a powerful hand grab his shirt and pull him up straight. Pain radiated from his ribs. The man leaned forward, down toward Sid's face, and Sid leaned back over the sink in response. The German looked like he was going to say something, and Sid decided this would be his best opportunity to reach up and take hold of the white plastic handle of a knife. Before the man could speak, Sid brought his arm down with all the force he could manage, and felt another little wave of nausea return as the blade sank into something fairly soft before stopping abruptly, like a hatchet stuck in a tree stump.

The German let out a roar and stumbled backwards, and Sid saw the knife sticking out of the man's leg just above his knee. Sid dashed straight for the back door that led to the alley, threw back the deadbolt and lunged for freedom, confident that no German with a knife in his leg could ever catch the three-time MVP of the McClatchy High School Cross Country Team. But to his surprise, he felt a hand grabbing him from behind, and Sid fell onto the uneven pavement of the alley that ran behind the deli.

Instantly the German was above him, grabbing him by the throat, lifting him from the ground and slamming him against the brick wall of the building on the other side of the alley. His strength and speed were unimaginable—something Sid hadn't seen before—and Sid understood that that the man had only been toying with him. The German increased the pressure on Sid's neck, and with just the one hand, began to slide him up the wall. Sid choked, felt his feet leave the ground, and fully embraced the thought that this was the time and place his life was going to end. He saw the trash dumpsters and the gas pipes and electrical wires and the sign painted right onto the bricks on the back of his father's deli that said, "No Parking This Side of Alley."

Sid could no longer breathe at all. The man had him pinned by the throat so that he was just about eye-level, and his face was contorted in either pain or rage. He leaned in very close to Sid and mumbled something in German. Then, in English, said, "You stupid little shit. I was only supposed to scare you. But now maybe you die." The man held up his free hand, and there was the kitchen knife smeared with blood.

Sid's urge to find a way to get air into his lungs was becoming uncontrollable and violent, and he twisted and fought against the man. But the German was like a statue, motionless, and after a moment Sid began to grow weaker.

His eyes rolled upward, and he realized he could just see the top of the spire of the Cathedral of the Blessed Sacrament. He'd never noticed that you could see it from the alley. Suddenly it was very quiet. The view was beautiful, and he found himself regretting not going to church with Amy these last few years. It wasn't a religious conversion or anything, just the thought that it would have been nice to sit next to her, to hold her hand and listen to the music on Sunday mornings.

That was the last thought that went through Sid's mind as he slipped from consciousness. He didn't feel the knife blade press against his throat.

Chapter 30

Sid had his tonsils taken out when he was four and a half years old. Twenty eight years later, for the second time in his life he was waking up in a hospital with a sore throat. Bright light pushed past thin drapes on the window. Machines were beeping all around him, and Amy was sound asleep in a chair by his bed.

He lay there thinking something looked funny about her, and eventually came to the conclusion it was because his right eye was very nearly swollen shut. He reached up and put a hand on it, and the effort hurt his ribs. A quick inventory revealed that much of his torso was wrapped like a mummy with wide bandages, and there was a strip of tape running across the front of his neck. Both hands appeared to be working just fine, though they were scraped up, and the right one in particular had some very tender knuckles. He drew his knees up, wiggled toes on both feet, and decided he was just fine from the waist down. Then he stuck his tongue in the space where two teeth used to be. He started to laugh, but it sent a jolt of pain through his ribs and neck and suddenly it wasn't funny anymore.

In his head, he worked backwards, retracing the steps that had led him to Room 503 at Sutter General. He could remember Amy kissing his face in the emergency room last night and crying, saying he was going to be fine. Before that there was the ambulance ride and somebody giving him a shot and telling him it would help him rest. And before that, he was laying in the alley behind the deli, the world coming back into focus, a flashlight shining in his eyes.

A beat cop had found him unconscious on the ground and recognized him immediately. The deli was just a few blocks from the police station, and Woody Carver actually got to the scene before the paramedics.

"You look like crap, pal."

The two sat cross-legged in the alley, an ambulance siren sounding faintly in the distance. Woody studied the line that ran across the front of his friend's neck. More than a scratch, but not a bad cut. The blood was already turning from red to brown as it dried.

"You sure it was the German?"

"I could smell the sauerkraut." Sid's voice was just a hoarse whisper.

"Why aren't you dead?"

"He said he was only supposed to scare me."

"What's that mean?"

Sid made no effort to answer. He closed his eyes and breathed deeply as the ambulance made the turn into the alley. The siren had grown quite loud, but now it stopped abruptly. The flashing emergency lights continued to throw eerie shadows.

"Why would somebody like the German give a damn about you, Sid? I don't get it."

Sid swallowed and it hurt like hell. "You still think Trager's shooting and the murder of Lou Martini aren't tied together somehow?"

"I don't know. It doesn't make sense. There's no link between them."

"Yes there is." Sid heard the slamming of car doors, and

a couple of paramedics began heading toward them. "I'm the link, Woody. It's me."

Woody had said something else after that, but Sid couldn't remember what it was.

"How are you doing?" Amy was awake, and looked like she'd spent the night sitting in a chair worried about someone she loved.

"I should probably get a peek in the mirror before I answer that."

Now Amy smiled, and Sid's condition immediately improved. Her amusement came, in part, from the fact that the voice coming out of his mouth was someone else's. Raspy and low, like he'd had a cold for ten years.

"You sound like Barry White."

"Yeah. Sexy. What time is it?"

"Just after eight." Amy leaned forward, took his hand and gave it a kiss, then pressed it against her face.

"I'm still a little fuzzy on last night," said Sid. "Do I remember somebody in a white coat saying something about a broken rib?"

"Just one. And you're missing two teeth."

"Yeah, but they're on the side. I don't think it'll show in the wedding photos. How many days?"

"Forty-seven. Doctor says your eye will look all better by then, too." She moved the I.V. line out of the way and sat down on the edge of the bed.

"I love you." Sid had been the first one to say it, over five years ago. It was more true now than ever.

"I love you, too."

Amy leaned down and kissed him on the mouth, then swung her legs up onto the bed and laid down next to him, her head on his shoulder. They were quiet for several minutes, each awake, each wondering if the other had fallen asleep. It was nice, but it didn't last long.

At the sound of the knock at the doorway, Amy jumped off the bed as if her parents had just caught her on the sofa with a high school boyfriend.

"Hey, is there room for one more in here?"

Lieutenant Benjamin Stokes breezed into the room showing the full complement of dazzling teeth and walked right to the side of the bed.

"How you doing, Sid? Tell me you feel better than you look."

"Except for this eye and the broken rib, I'm one hundred percent."

"And the missing teeth," Amy added, and she settled back into her chair.

"Missing teeth." Stokes seemed genuinely impressed. "Nice."

"Thanks. It was nothing."

"What's the bandage on your neck?"

"Just a scratch."

"Yeah, right. You know who you sound like?"

"Barry White."

"No. You sound like Jock Bell. Like you're his baby brother or something."

"Maybe I'll get a wig."

"Listen, I hate the smell of hospitals, and I'm sure you need to rest or take a sponge bath or whatever, so how about

I ask you some questions and then I get out of here?"

"I'm all yours, Lieutenant."

Stokes turned to Amy. "This is official police business, Miss Solomon. Can I ask you to give us a few minutes alone?"

Sid was pretty sure the two of them had only met once before, and it had been years. Impressive that Stokes remembered her name.

"Sure." Amy said it with a smile as she stood and picked up her purse. She was half-way to the door when Sid spoke up.

"Can she stay?"

Sid wasn't even sure why he'd said it. Perhaps he thought she had the right to know the kind of trouble her soon-to-be-husband had gotten himself into, but that was, at most, only a part of it. There was more. Something about how it felt to have her near. Something about her confidence in him. He had discovered fourteen hours earlier that, at the moment his life was slipping away, his last thought had been of her, and now he simply didn't want her to leave.

"Maybe she can help. I went to Amy's right after the shooting two weeks ago, and ever since then I've told her everything about the case. She might remember some things that I don't."

"It's okay with me if it's okay with you, Miss Solomon."

"Sure."

"Okay then..." Stokes pulled out the notebook. "Talk to me."

It took about fifteen minutes for Sid to croak out the story of his encounter with the German from the previous night. Stokes only interrupted a couple of times with questions, and Amy was silent. It was the first time she'd heard the details of what had happened.

"So why is it…" Stokes paused briefly, tapping his chin with his pen. "Why is it that a genuine badass hit man almost killed you last night? Don't take this the wrong way, Sid, but I can't figure why you're important enough for that."

Sid gave him an *I-don't-know* shrug.

"And why didn't he finish the job? Why didn't he give your throat a real good slash and turn out the lights? The doc tells me it's not much worse than a bad scratch on your neck."

There was no logical answer to the question, so it just hung awkwardly in the air for a few seconds.

"Your pal, Detective Carver, spent the rest of last night trying to find a silver Mercedes or anybody who might have seen the big kraut, but it's like he just vanished."

"Woody says he's the same guy that killed Lou Martini," said Sid.

"Yeah, so he tells me. I don't get that one, either. But the German's disappeared, so right now, you're my best lead in this case."

Sid's one good eye opened a little wider.

"You're working on the murder of Tom Trager."

"Right. And I'm thinking that maybe it's somehow related to what happened to you and Martini."

"Gee, officer, which one of us was the first to suggest that idea more than a week ago?" Sid asked, and he smiled broadly.

"Hey, you really are missing a couple of teeth."

Sid had given up on vanity long ago. A squirrely looking guy like him didn't have a lot of options. Still, he was suddenly self-conscious about the missing teeth, and as his smile vanished he discovered that the side of his upper lip got hung up on a tooth where the freshly made gap was. It stuck there in a half-smile until he actually reached up with his fingers and pulled it free. Amy laughed.

"So," Stokes got back to work, "if there is some connection between the murders of Lou Martini and Councilman Trager, you're the guy in the middle of it all. You said yesterday morning at breakfast that you were working on something having to do with Roberta Jones, but you didn't wanna tell me what it was. Maybe now it's time."

Sid pushed the button to make the back of his bed sit up a little.

"It's just a hunch, really. Something that doesn't feel right."

"Understood. What's the hunch?"

"I think there's something odd about Bertie Jones' past." Sid glanced at Amy, then back at Stokes. "Or at least, *her mother's* past. She's covering something up."

"Like what?"

"I'm not sure."

"I'm assuming there's more to the story."

"Bertie moved here with her family from Ohio when she was three. That's what they've always said. But I don't think it's true."

"And this matters why?"

"I don't know. But Mrs. Jones—her mother—went to pieces when I brought it up, and when I pushed a little, Bertie insisted that I drop it."

"And that's it?"

It did sound pretty thin, even to Sid himself. Benjamin Stokes flipped his notebook closed and put the pen in his shirt pocket.

"I hope you won't be offended if I'm not real impressed."

"I said it was a hunch."

Stokes turned to Amy. "Did the doctors say anything about brain damage?"

"No, but they're still waiting on some tests." Amy gave the cop a charming smile. "Sid's usually right about things like this, Lieutenant. He can prove they're not from Ohio. He has Bertie's birth certificate from Miami, Florida."

"Yeah?"

The cop returned his attention to Sid, who was suddenly looking very sheepish.

"Uh-huh."

"Where'd you get that from?"

Seconds went by, and either the beeping noise from the machines actually got louder, or it just seemed that way. Sid honestly had no idea what to say, so it was Amy who answered the question.

"Somebody stole it from Mrs. Jones' house."

"Really? And Sid ended up with it?"

Stokes turned back to Sid, who did his best to give him a 'Who, me?' expression, but with his smashed up eye he wasn't sure it worked.

"Well, I'll be damned." The look on the cop's face was somewhere between surprised and pleased. "Y'know, carrying the badge really sucks sometimes. It's you private detectives that get to have all the fun."

"Do me a favor, Lieutenant. Don't tell Woody about this."

Stokes laughed. "You confess your little break-in to the head of Homicide, but you don't want one of my men to know?"

"I didn't confess. But, yes, I don't want Woody to know.

"Alright. It's our secret. Besides, I don't think your birth certificate mystery is gonna have anything to do with anything. So knock yourself out."

"Thanks."

"Get better, Sid." Stokes gave him a pat on the leg and headed for the door. "Let the cops worry about the actual bad guys. You stick with old ladies and birth certificates. Nice to see you again, Miss Solomon." And then he was gone, leaving Sid and Amy alone once again.

Amy got up without saying a word and pushed the button to flatten out Sid's hospital bed, pulled back the white sheet, then climbed up next to him again. This time she turned her back and nestled into him, he rolled onto his side and put his free arm around her, and they spooned together facing the window in Room 503, Sid's back to the door. The position hurt his ribs, but it provided a comfort that medication could not. He breathed in the scent of her hair and gave her a gentle squeeze.

"Know what?" Sid spoke in barely more than a whisper, making his voice even lower.

"What?"

"I'm pretty sure that the back of this hospital gown is wide open, and anyone walking by can get a free look at the Bigler butt."

Amy giggled. "Want me to pull up the sheet?"

"Nah. Let's give the nurse a thrill."

"Your nurse's name is Cliff."

Sid might have giggled, too, if it wasn't for the bandages around his ribs. The two laid quietly, returning to the comforting stillness that Stokes had interrupted earlier. His hand slid across her flat tummy, and as he pulled her even closer, Sid began to have thoughts that were completely inappropriate for someone in his place and condition.

"I've gotta go pretty soon," Amy said. "There's a ten o'clock meeting at work I can't get out of, and I have to get cleaned up and changed first."

Sid continued to hold her tightly, feeling the warmth of her body, as a minute passed by. Then another.

"What day is this?" he asked. "Is it Wednesday?"

"Uh-huh."

"Can you do me a favor?"

"Sure."

"I need you to book a flight for me."

Amy didn't respond right away, and Sid found himself wishing he could see her face. He waited for what felt like a long time.

"I'll book your flight for you, but make me a promise."

"Sure."

Amy turned, raised up on one elbow and looked him squarely in the eyes. "Promise me that nothing like this ever happens again."

Chapter 31

The morning after you've been beaten up is fairly unpleasant. But the second morning, that's the really bad one.

Sid awoke in his room at his mom's house a little after 7 a.m., and just the thought of moving hurt. His right eye that had seemed to improve the day before was almost completely shut again. His teeth—or, in the interest of accuracy, his gums—were killing him. But mostly it was his ribs. If he tried to take a deep breath, it was almost like getting punched again.

Somewhere around thirty minutes into his shower, the hot water started to run out. Sid quickly soaped up and shampooed his hair, and discovered that his moving parts were starting to work a little better. By the time he was shaved, dressed and blow-dried, the eye was about half-way open and his spirits had substantially improved. The doctor had warned him that the prescription pain killers might make him drowsy, so he popped five Excedrin tablets instead and put the rest of the bottle in his jacket pocket.

The house was empty and quiet, and the sound in his head as he crunched the Frosted Flakes was bizarrely loud at first, but diminished as they got soggy. Funny how quickly you adjust to chewing on just one side after somebody knocks out a couple of your teeth. Amy had said she couldn't miss work today, so he told her he could drive himself to the airport. Rose would be down at the deli already. She'd insisted that he take a couple of days off—

"That face would scare the customers" —and Sid hadn't put up a fight. His mom had left some of her make-up on the kitchen counter as she promised, so he spent about half an hour in front of the mirror in the living room using something called Maybelline Concealer (beige #2) and a fleshy-colored powder. The goal was to make his eye look a little less punched, but when he eventually stopped he wasn't really sure that it looked any better for the effort.

Sid was just turning away from the mirror when he stopped and looked at the thin, straight line across the front of his neck. He'd taken the bandage off before jumping in the shower. It didn't really hurt much, and he figured it wasn't bad enough to put on another bandage. Compared to the black eye and the missing teeth, it was no big deal. Except for the message that it sent. A little reminder from the German.

I was only supposed to scare you. But now maybe you die.

A little shiver went up Sid's spine. Dieter Hoffmann was only following orders. Who had sent him? And why would they want Sid to be scared, but not dead like Lou Martini?

He lingered for a moment in front of the mirror, and reached up with his finger to trace the path that the knife had taken. What did it mean?

Sid threw some clothes in a small canvas duffel bag that had been his father's, grabbed one of the manila folders he had picked up at the deli on the way home from the hospital, and was headed for the front door when the phone rang.

"Hello?" It was the first time he'd spoken that morning,

and his voice still sounded like gravel.

"Sid, is that you?" It was the last person he expected, but there was no mistaking the voice on the other end. To the best of Sid's knowledge, the guy had never, ever called the Bigler house before.

"Jock?"

"You sound terrible, kid."

"Somebody told me I sound just like you."

Jock paused, considering it. "Yeah, you do sort of. But with me it sounds good."

"Well, the doc says I'll be sounding like me in another day or two. Listen, Jock, I was just about to take off. Is there something I can do for you?"

"Nah, I just heard about what happened a couple nights ago. Wanted to make sure you were okay."

Hmmm. The rumor that Sid and Jock were friends gets another boost.

"I'm feeling pretty good, considering. I'm gonna take the next couple of days off, then I'll be back at the deli on Monday."

"Good. That's good."

There was a long pause, and Sid had a moment to consider what was one of the stranger phone calls he'd had in a while. He was actually growing to like the old guy, but the suspicion that Bell was up to something was unavoidable. Sid checked his watch and realized he was running late for his meeting. He was just about to say something—anything to move the conversation along— when the other man spoke first.

"Listen, this guy who almost killed you... he had an

accent." Jock Bell said it matter-of-factly. A statement, not a question. Sid couldn't think of how to respond, so he remained silent until Jock continued. "In certain circles, he's rather famous. Any idea why someone like him was interested in you?"

"Not really. I'm a pretty harmless guy."

"The name I gave you—the blonde, Trager's girlfriend— did you talk to her?"

"No, why?"

"Just trying to figure how you got on somebody's radar screen. People like the German are expensive."

"I'm not following you."

"Somebody doesn't like you, Sid. They've got connections and resources, and they don't like you. Might be nice to know who they are."

Jock's voice was a soft rumble, like far away thunder. Sid pressed the receiver harder into his ear in an effort to hear him clearly.

"Do you know who it is?" Sid asked.

"I'll ask around. Take care of yourself, Sid."

The phone went dead. Sid dropped it back in its cradle and headed out the door at 8:55.

Chapter 32

Sid Bigler was not what you would call an experienced traveler. In fact, he'd only been on an airplane twice before. Once when he was thirteen and his folks took Gloria and him to Hawaii on vacation, and once just after college when he and two buddies flew down to Acapulco for a week that was forever fuzzy in his memory. Now he looked out the window at thirty-two thousand feet, seeing nothing but clouds and feeling bad that he'd just lied to his only paying client.

Right after his odd phone conversation with Jock Bell, he'd hurried downtown and bought a turtleneck at Macy's to hide the knife wound. He figured it'd make him appear a little more professional and a little less mugged. Sid arrived ten minutes late for his meeting with Nathan Bomke, who was looking even more Hall-and-Oatsy than usual. Bomke's first words to him were a fine example of just how sensitive and caring a lawyer can be.

"You've been punched in the eye."

"Yes, I'm sorry about that."

"I don't know. It kind of gives you character."

Bomke's primary concern was, of course, with his wallet. The attorney for Gerald Mercer—father of the homely little girl who was very nearly Little Miss Pinto Bean—had called and was apparently interested in a settlement. Now Nathan Bomke was in a hurry to put the finishing touches on his legal extortion, and wanted to know how Sid's trip to Los Angeles had gone. When Sid informed him that he'd not yet traveled to Southern California on behalf of the Mercers, the guy hit the roof. And it was in his effort to calm down the raging attorney that Sid had told the lie. Sort of.

"I'll be on a plane later today."

It seemed to placate Nathan Bomke, and technically, it was the truth. If the man wanted to jump to the conclusion that Sid was flying from Sacramento to Los Angeles, that was his choice. Sid only said that he'd be on a plane. And so he was. After a two-hour drive to San Francisco International Airport, he was on a plane, wrestling with his guilt, bound non-stop for Miami.

Sid flipped down the tray in the seatback in front of him and got out the folder marked "Bertie Jones." It had only been two days since he'd written her name there, but it seemed like a lot longer. He stared at the folder for a moment, no thought in particular, and realized he was hurting. For much of the morning he'd actually forgotten that he had been beaten up, but now it was early afternoon, and a general achiness settled over him, punctuated by a throbbing in his mouth and ribs. It had been over five hours since he took the Excedrin, so he found the bottle and chased down five more pills with the 7-Up the stewardess had brought him.

"Bertie Jones."

Sid had been thankful for the open seat next to him, and hadn't paid much attention to the woman sitting by the aisle. She hadn't spoken a word until now, and Sid gave her a good look for the first time. At least seventy, gray hair that was big and swoopy like something from the Lawrence Welk Show, and an underbite like a bulldog. Odd, but somehow friendly looking.

"Hmm?"

"Bertie Jones." The woman pointed to the folder in Sid's lap. "Is that you?"

"No." Sid smiled. "It's short for Roberta."

"Oh. Is it your girlfriend?"

"No."

Sid took a sip of the 7-Up and turned to look out the window, hoping the woman would take the hint, but she apparently found his lack of eye contact encouraging.

"Who is she?"

"She's a client."

"Oh, I see. So, are you a salesperson?"

"No."

"Lawyer? Accountant? Travel Agent?"

"No."

Sid didn't say it rudely, but it was a tad louder, and he did his best to send a 'leave me alone' vibe. For a moment he thought it worked. The bulldog woman looked forward for a little while and didn't say a word. Then she tried again.

"Male Escort?"

Sid couldn't help but laugh, which hurt quite a bit, but it was worth it.

"Good guess. But it's hard to get that kind of work with this eye." He winced a little as he turned and reached with his right hand. "My name's Sid."

"I'm Vivian." The woman shook firmly, and that hurt, too. "Very nice to meet you. So what *do* you do?"

"I'm a private investigator."

Mistake. Over the next hour and a half, Sid learned a very valuable lesson. For the rest of his life, he would never answer that question the same way again when posed by a stranger. Vivian, it turns out, had read hundreds of mysteries and her son-in-law once worked as a cameraman on the TV show Mannix. She was just full of questions for a real life private eye. On six or seven occasions, Sid tried his very best to sound like he was all out of answers, but Vivian was relentless. Eventually, he simply told her that he had to get some work done, so he'd have to stop talking. The woman was very understanding, and asked if he'd answer just one last question.

"Did you get that black eye doing one of your investigations?"

"Uh-huh. And got two teeth knocked out." He opened his mouth to give her a look.

"Oh, how exciting!"

Vivian sounded like she meant it, but it mustn't have been that exciting. Within a couple of minutes she was passed out, snoring, wearing one of those blackout eye masks.

Sid finally opened his folder and started to look over his notes on the Bertie Jones case. He glanced at his watch. Still more than two hours before the plane would be landing in Miami. It would be almost eleven o'clock at night when he arrived, leaving him only tomorrow—Friday—to see what he could find out.

Sid stared at the pages in front of him, his thoughts fairly unfocused. There were a lot of names and dates written there, but one jumped out at him. Lou Martini. He hadn't taken the time to think it through since the fight with the German, but there was really only one solid connection in anything that had happened over the last two weeks, and it appeared to have nothing to do with Bertie: The same guy that had killed Lou Martini had tried to kill him. What the hell was that about? Sid and Lou hadn't spoken in months, and hadn't worked together in over a year. Maybe Lou had gotten mixed up with something really bad—something related to an old case they'd worked on together. Maybe that's what Lou was calling about the night before he was killed, wanting to warn him. It was possible, and it certainly made more sense than any scenario that involved Bertie Jones.

Sid's eyes fell on Jock Bell's name, then Jilly Boyd's, and he flashed back to the strange, brief phone call early that morning. Jock had specifically asked if he'd spoken with Jilly, Trager's blonde girlfriend. *"Just trying to figure how you got on somebody's radar screen"* was what he'd said. What did that mean?

He took out a fresh sheet of paper and wrote *"Who would want to hurt Bertie?"* across the top of the page. From his first conversation about the case with his sister, that had been the primary question, right? *"Who would want to hurt Bertie?"* Then something completely surprising happened. He put the tip of his pen on the paper, fully expecting to write something, and nothing happened. Absolutely nothing came to him, and it was thoroughly unexpected. He'd been looking into the shooting for two weeks now, and off the top of his head, couldn't think of a single person with a motive for hurting Bertie Jones. How could that be? He'd made progress, right? He'd talked to a lot of people, even broken into Mrs. Jones' house. Where had it gotten him? Why could he think of nothing to write?

Sid read through every name he'd written in the file so far—Martini, Bell, Trager, Stokes, Bertie's mom, Jilly Boyd, Charlie at the Motel Capri, Gloria, Woody... It all added up to nothing. Trager and Martini were dead, of course, and everyone else on the list lacked motive or opportunity or both. He looked at each name once again, making sure not to skip one, and asked himself what the connection was between that person and Bertie Jones. And when he was done, he had exactly nothing. No connections, no solid link between Bertie and anything suspicious. Zip.

He started to feel a little nauseous. Maybe it was the flight, and maybe it was too many Excedrin. Or maybe it was the sudden and reasonable fear that he was wasting two days and the 389 dollars he'd put on Amy's credit card. He was betting his time and money on some stupid hunch based on Bertie's mother's reaction to a casual question. What could he possibly find out on this ridiculous trip to Florida? Bertie was adopted? Bertie's parents weren't married? Bertie was born with two heads? So what? What mystery about her birth could possibly have anything to do with what was happening today? What the hell was he doing on this plane?

Sid's stomach felt worse, and he was beginning to sweat. He closed his eyes and put his head back, aware once again of the throbbing where his teeth used to be. He resolved to keep his eyes shut until he started to feel better, and he didn't wake up until the wheels chirped on the runway at

Miami-Dade Airport.

Chapter 33

Friday morning in Miami. Sid had never heard of a
"Motel 5," and now he knew why. Suffice it to say that the
sink was not firmly attached to the wall, and there was
something vaguely sticky about the crushed shag carpet.
Inflation had worked its magic, and so the bill at Motel 5
was $17, which Sid paid in cash and then headed to his
Chevy Cavalier rental car. Even with the driver's door lock
broken and cigarette burns on the passenger seat, it seemed
luxurious compared to his accommodations.

He took inventory as he drove aimlessly down the
street, sporting yesterday's turtleneck once again. On a scale
of one to ten, Sid's achiness was a six and a half, which was a
great improvement. It was really only his ribs that hurt
significantly. The place where his teeth used to be was
tender when he poked around with his tongue, and the eye
was a more impressive color than yesterday, but less
swollen. In general, he was in a much better mood than the
funk that had overtaken him on the flight from San
Francisco. The facts were still the facts, but this sunny
Florida Friday morning saw the return of Sid's usual
optimism, and a perhaps unjustified confidence that there
was something about Bertie's past—something about
Miami—that was important.

It only took four tries to find a telephone booth that
actually had a phone book attached, and three tries to find a
gas station where somebody knew how to get to the Dade
County Administrative Offices on West Flagler Street. After

a drive-through McDonald's breakfast, it was just before 9:30 a.m. when Sid arrived at the building where his plan was to find a friendly and talkative county recorder. Were it not for a huge stroke of luck, the plan would have been a complete failure.

Carrying his folder marked "Bertie Jones" and, because he didn't want to leave it in a car he couldn't lock, his father's duffel, Sid asked a receptionist in the lobby where he could find birth records and other information dating back to the 1950s. After a brief conversation he was told he would "have to talk to Vic." Up the stairs and down the hallway, Sid found a plaque by an open door that read: "Victor Meyers, Recorder." He knocked lightly on the wall and stuck his head in.

"Hello?"

Vic was not in. A portable radio on the desk was on, and Andy Williams or Perry Como was singing. Everything about the office sent the mixed message of cluttered efficiency. Filing cabinets lined the walls, and atop each one sat stacks of additional file folders. Shelves on the wall filled the space above the cabinets with three-ring binders and more files. Everything seemed deliberate in its placement, but there wasn't a square inch of space that wasn't filled. The effect was claustrophobic. A door behind the desk was open onto another room that appeared to be equally jammed with records.

Sid dropped his duffel bag and folder on the one open chair by the door and perused the headings on the file cabinet drawers, hoping one of them would say "Bertie Jones Info Here", but discovered most of them simply had numbers on them. No telling what might be in the drawer marked 158.997 – 159.255. He wandered behind the desk and was peeking into the next room when Vic walked in behind him.

"Looking for something, young man?"

The Dade County Recorder was slightly shorter than Sid, and Sid was not a tall man. He was somewhere around twice Sid's age, thickly built, but in decent shape for a guy in his sixties. He was dressed in a white short sleeve shirt, gray slacks and a black tie, and Sid got the impression that this was probably the extent of his wardrobe. Like it was his uniform. One tanned forearm bore a faded tattoo that couldn't be made out. Victor Meyers wore a gray flat top and brushy gray moustache like he'd been born with them. Two parts Milburn Drysdale, one part Sgt. Carter.

"Are you the county recorder?"

"I am."

Sid's first impression was that the guy was all business. Schmooze-proof. It didn't bode well for his chances. Vic circled around behind his desk, and Sid circled to the front, where he belonged.

"Mr. Meyers, I've flown in from California looking for some information going back to the early 1950s. They said downstairs that you'd been here a long time."

"I started January 15, 1948. County population at the time was just under half a million. 8,178 births that year, 6,341 deaths."

"Yeah, they said you were good with numbers, too."

"And names. I have an excellent memory."

"Impressive."

Vic Meyers sat at his desk and neatly added the files he'd brought with him to the top of an existing stack. He squared up the edges.

"How can I help you?"

"I'm trying to track down information about a Robert and Mary Jones. I'm sure they were here in 1950, because they had a daughter that year at Miami-Dade Hospital. I'm guessing they lived in the area for a few years before moving away, but I don't know exactly when."

"Bob and Mary Jones," said Vic and he made no effort to begin looking for records.

"Yes."

"A lot of people named Jones."

"Really? Exactly how many?"

Sid regretted his words immediately, but sometimes the smartass in him didn't ask for permission before speaking.

"A lot." Vic failed to see the humor. "You're an immediate family member?"

"No, but I'm only asking for public records."

"And what's your interest in the Jones family?"

"I'm a private investigator."

"I see." Something about the way Vic Meyers said it made Sid feel fairly certain that he'd flushed his $389 for airfare down the toilet. Vic pulled out his top desk drawer, licked a finger and produced a sheet of paper. "Well, we have a 'Request for Public Information' form here. If you'll fill this out, including names and specific dates, I should be able to get back to you within a few weeks."

When smartass meets bureaucrat, bureaucrat always wins.

"I'm sorry, Mr. Meyers, but I'm only in town for the day." Sid actually sounded more desperate than sorry. He didn't reach out and take the form. Didn't want to admit defeat. "Is there any way you can help me?"

Surely there had to be some way to get the information today. Sid himself had been with Lou Martini on several occasions when they'd walked right into county offices back home and gotten what they needed. And it had only taken a couple of days for the P.I. in Canton to go through the records there. Maybe it paid to have established some relationships with people like this. Or maybe this old guy didn't like out-of-towners.

"I'm happy to help you, young man, but we do have rules and procedures for these things." Sid still hadn't taken the form, so Vic set it down on the edge of his desk. "You can leave the form with me, or drop it at the desk in the lobby on the way out."

With that, the man was clearly all done with Sid. He grabbed a file, flipped it open, and began scribbling notes with his head down. Sid had an excellent view of the top of the flat-top. He reluctantly picked up the 'Request for Public Information' form and headed for the door, trying to think of Plan B. He grabbed his duffel and folder from the chair on his way out, and was several steps down the hallway when he heard Vic Meyers' voice calling.

"Hey, wait a minute!"

Sid didn't really expect that the man was talking to him, but he stopped and turned back toward the office door anyway. The crew cut and moustache appeared a moment later.

"Where did you get that bag?"

Sid looked down at the duffel, then back at the man. He raised his arm up.

"This?"

Vic emerged from his office with an enthusiasm he'd not shown before. He took the duffel in his hands and turned the side toward Sid. The words, "U.S.S. Texas" were stenciled there, faded black and barely legible against the worn green canvas.

"Where did you get this?" Vic asked again.

"It was my dad's."

"What's your name?"

"Sid Bigler."

Until that moment, Sid had no reason to notice that Vic Meyers had not yet smiled. But now the man's face lit up, and he displayed a substantial gap between his front teeth. It must have been generally hidden behind the moustache, but when he smiled it became the central feature of his face. The reason for the smile became clear with the next words he said.

"Junior, right? You must be Sid, *Junior*."

"Yes."

At that, Vic Meyers let out a laugh and said, "I'll be damned!" Then he turned and walked back into his office, still carrying the duffel bag, still staring at what was written on the side of it. With a renewed sense of optimism mixed with curiosity, Sid followed.

"You're taller than your old man." Vic was half sitting, leaning against the front of his desk, the green canvas bag on his lap. "And better looking, but not by much."

Now Sid smiled for the first time, too. "You were on the Texas."

"Best damn ship in the United States Navy. North Africa, Europe, and the Pacific, only lost one man."

"I heard Pop say that a thousand times."

"Judging by that black eye, you're a lot like him. I bet I saw him with shiners like that once every six months during the war. The Germans and the Japs never got to him, but his mouth got him into plenty of trouble with guys on our side." Vic smiled the big, gap-toothed smile again.

"Yeah, so I hear."

"How is your father?"

There's no other way to say it, so with very little hesitation, Sid replied, "He's dead. Dad was murdered five years ago."

"Oh, my god. I'm so sorry."

"It's okay. He had a good life."

"I'm sure he did."

For the next half hour, Vic Meyers got caught up on the life of one of his old shipmates after the war. He also remembered Joe Diaz, the big, quiet cook from the galley, and laughed hard when Sid told him that Joe and his dad had opened a deli together. In return, Vic told Sid several stories about his father from back in his Navy days. Sid hadn't heard any of them, and most were ones that he couldn't repeat to his mother.

"I'm surprised you remember my dad so well. There were a lot of guys on that ship."

"795," said Vic. "I was in charge of the manifest and all non-military shipboard supplies." Then, almost apologetically, "I'm good with names and numbers."

"So I hear. Listen, Mr. Meyers, I'm sure you're busy. I'll get this form filled out and hopefully you can get back to me pretty soon about the Jones'."

Sid stood and extended his hand to shake, but Vic walked past him and closed the office door.

"No need to wait, son. I can tell you about Robert and Mary Jones right now. Daughter Roberta, am I right?"

Sid must have looked dumbfounded. "How... how can you possibly remember?"

"That one's hard to forget. There was quite a bit about it in the papers at the time." Vic circled back around his desk and sat down. "Plus, I saw the name written on your folder there. I might make a decent private eye myself."

Vic smiled again, but it looked like it required an effort. The lips stayed pressed together, no friendly gap in the teeth to be seen.

"The girl was born in the middle of 1950 as I recall. Nothing special about that, and I would have had no reason to remember recording her birth. We were in a different building then, over on the other side of the expressway. Anyway, a few years later—in 1953—Robert and Mary Jones took another little girl into their home—part of a foster program. You know what that is, right? A kid from difficult circumstances gets placed by the county with a good, normal family until things can get worked out at home. Sometimes things never get worked out at the foster kid's real home, you know? And the foster parents end up adopting the kid."

Sid nodded, and Vic continued.

"So Robert and Mary take in this little girl. The child's name was Anna, as I recall. The girl's biological mother was just a teenager, unmarried—had an alcohol problem or something and the county took the daughter away. The little girl was just about the same age as Roberta. Beautiful girl."

The man with the moustache paused. He was looking straight ahead, at some place beyond Sid. Beyond the second floor of the Dade County Administrative Offices. Some place thirty-two years ago.

"It was June of 1953 when Mr. or Mrs. Jones called the hospital to report that the foster child, Anna, had died suddenly. She'd had a high fever. They'd taken her to the doctor just the day before and were told she'd be fine. But she wasn't. It was meningitis, and she was gone in less than twenty-four hours. I recorded her death myself. You usually don't forget the little kids."

Vic stopped again, as though he caught himself staring at the past and it embarrassed him. He made brief eye contact with Sid, then looked down at his hands folded on his desk. Sid gave him a moment, but didn't wait for long.

"You said there was something about this in the newspaper."

"Yeah. Yeah, that's right. The little girl's biological mother wasn't told what had happened until after the funeral. Maybe four or five days after. Missed her own daughter's funeral. She was terribly upset, of course, and it ended up being a pretty big story in the local news. You can understand how she felt. Nobody wants to believe their child is dead."

Sid had a heavy, sinking feeling in his chest. An ache that had nothing to do with the broken rib. It didn't take a genius to see where this was going.

"Was it true?" Sid asked. "Was it really the foster child that died?"

"I honestly don't know. Somebody from Child Welfare stopped by the Jones' house a week after the funeral and they were gone. Left most of their stuff behind. A reporter from the paper talked to friends and neighbors who said the couple was so distraught by what had happened that they had to get away—just took Roberta and left the area. And they talked to other people who thought the same thing you're thinking right now. That their own little girl died that day, and they ran off with little Anna instead."

"And nobody tracked them down to find out? The cops or the F.B.I. didn't go after them?"

"It was 1953, son. Tracking people wasn't so easy as it is today. And to be honest, back then there wasn't hardly anybody who thought it was a good idea for a child to be raised by an unwed nineteen-year-old girl instead of a married couple. You understand? So, no. Nobody tried very hard to find them."

"What do you think really happened, Vic?"

"Like I said, I honestly don't know. Whatever happened, it was for the best. The little girl's mother— Anna's biological mother—died a couple of years later, homeless on the street. Drugs."

"Jesus."

"Amen."

The two men sat without speaking. Sid felt a deep

sadness, and more than a little anger at the complacency of people more than thirty years ago. It had happened the year he was born on the other side of the country, but for the moment that didn't seem to matter. Whatever had happened, people had simply looked the other way.

Dinah Shore or Doris Day sang from the little radio on the desk.

"Can I assume you know the whereabouts of Roberta Jones today?" Vic Meyers asked.

"She's a family friend."

"Did things turn out well for her?"

"Yeah. She's a lawyer. On the city council. Very successful."

"So the story has a happy ending." Vic seemed to really mean it.

"Yeah. Happy." Sid stood and picked up his dad's old duffel bag again. "Thanks very much for your time and the information. I really do appreciate it."

For the second time that morning, Sid tried to leave the County Recorder's Office, and for the second time, Vic Meyers stopped him.

"One more thing, young Mr. Bigler..."

Sid turned back to the desk.

"You're not the first person to ask about Roberta Jones this year."

The return flight to San Francisco took off at 7:22 p.m. Sid had booked the late flight not knowing how much time he'd need in Miami, so he ended up killing part of the afternoon watching a matinee showing of a movie called Re-Animator. It was exactly how Sid liked his horror films—gory and funny. Finally, after doing crossword puzzles in the airport for over three hours, he boarded the plane to discover that there was an abundance of empty seats on the flight, and ended up with a whole row all to himself. Sid was stretched out with a blanket over him as soon as the fasten seatbelt light went off.

He drifted in and out of sleep for much of the flight. At some point, he had a fairly vivid dream about two little girls—twins—both with blonde hair and green eyes and clefts in their chins. In the dream, some person that Sid couldn't see was calling out a name again and again, but he couldn't make out exactly what they were saying. Each time the mystery voice called, both girls would turn and look at the same time, their heads turning in perfect unison. He tried talking to them, but it was like they didn't even know he was there.

By the time Sid landed in San Francisco and drove the two hours to his mom's house in Sacramento, it was almost three o'clock in the morning. He crawled into his own bed and fell asleep, trying to think of what he was going to say to his sister in the morning.

Chapter 34

10:08 a.m., Saturday, Freeport Bakery. Same time, same place, exactly a week since Gloria had fired him. This time she was the first to arrive, because Sid was running late. After the long day of travel, he would've still been sleeping if his alarm hadn't woken him. He'd thrown on a rumpled McClatchy High sweatshirt and jeans and dashed out the door without even looking in the mirror. On the left side of his head he had a hair bump roughly the size and shape of a large hamster. Add the big black eye, and he was looking pretty smooth.

"Sorry I'm late, Sis."

"No problem. Marty's got the girls over at the zoo, and I'm enjoying the peace and quiet. Boy, that eye looks worse than I thought it would."

"It's improving with age."

"How's the neck?"

"No big deal."

Gloria took a sip of coffee, and Sid noticed the half eaten chocolate éclair for the first time.

"Is that on your Halloween diet?"

"No, but I'm thinking about switching from Mary Ann to Mrs. Howell instead." She took a bite, then slid the plate toward Sid. "I stopped by the house on Thursday to check on you once I knew you were out of the hospital, but you weren't home."

"Right. I was on a little trip."

"Yeah, that's what mom told me. Said she didn't know

where you went, and didn't know when you were getting back."

"Uh-huh. My plane didn't land until really late last night."

"Plane?"

"Yeah." Sid took a bite of the éclair, buying himself one more moment to think of what to say, and perhaps subconsciously postponing just a tiny bit longer the coming storm. "When I called you yesterday and asked you to meet me here, I was at the airport in Miami."

Gloria didn't react for a second, then her eyes narrowed a little, followed by a too familiar knitting of the brows. Sid had been marginally successful at sneaking things past their parents as they were growing up, but his sister had always seen right through him. Always.

"I figured if we met in a public place, you might not yell at me."

"Sid, what have you done?"

"I didn't give up on the Bertie Jones case."

Sid watched Gloria switch from big sister mode to lawyer mode, taking in this first piece of evidence and analyzing it. She leaned back in her chair, crossed her arms, and said, "Tell me."

"Last week you asked me to stop bothering Bertie and her mom. And, by the way, Woody also told me the whole thing was a waste of time. Then Bertie had me come down to her office and she asked me to stop snooping around, too."

"So you couldn't help yourself." Arms still crossed.

"Not when all three of you were so insistent. Sis, I

found proof that she was born in Florida."

There was the tiniest change in Gloria's expression. She was still making an effort to look disapproving, but there was a little softening. She was little less skeptical.

"Bertie?"

"Florida."

"What proof?"

Sid considered telling the truth, but only briefly. It was much too soon to tell her about the break-in.

"Trust me," he said.

"When has *that* ever worked out in the past?"

Sid scooted his chair forward and began the story of his trip to Miami, which turned into the story of his chance encounter with their father's old shipmate, which turned into the story of Robert and Mary Jones and two little girls in 1953. He probably talked for fifteen minutes, and Gloria didn't interrupt a single time. As Sid finished, one big tear rolled down his sister's cheek.

"Oh, my god. Poor Bertie."

"If she *is* Bertie."

Sid had seldom seen Gloria cry. She was a wonderful person and he loved her dearly, but she didn't show a soft side very often, even when they were young. Funny sometimes. Warm. But hardly ever soft. At Sid's last comment, the tender Gloria vanished and the strong one returned.

"Don't talk like that. She's Bertie Jones no matter what you or that man in Florida says. And no matter what happened. If it was something bad—something criminal—it was over thirty years ago and it wasn't her choice. You can't possibly blame Bertie."

"No, of course not. But what about her mother? Can I blame her?"

Gloria didn't have a quick answer.

"I'm gonna get a cocoa. Want a coffee refill?"

She didn't respond. Sid stood up, grabbed her coffee mug anyway and headed for the counter, leaving his sister to wrestle with the same dilemma that had been troubling him since he left Vic Meyers' office. When he returned, coffee and cocoa in hand, Gloria was on the offensive.

"What evidence is there that a crime was committed? Or that anything at all happened? The man in Miami... what's his name?"

"Vic Meyers."

"Mr. Meyers—he said nobody really knows which little girl died, right? And authorities didn't investigate. So no one knows for sure, and there's no hard evidence that Bertie's parents weren't telling the truth, right?"

"I never realized you were such an 'ends-justify-the-means' girl."

"Oh, shut up, Sid. I'm not saying Mary and her husband didn't do anything wrong. I'm just saying we don't know beyond a reasonable doubt."

"Well, you're the lawyer, Sis. I don't know what's 'reasonable' and what's not, or what would hold up in court. But how about 'fishy?' Is that a legal term? Can we say the whole thing looks pretty damn fishy?"

Gloria's eyes were watery once again, and she looked away. Sid gave her some space and focused on his cocoa for a minute. He had very little experience in holding his own in a disagreement with his sister, and he took no pleasure in upsetting her.

"Do we keep this a secret?" She was still looking out the window somewhere as she asked the million dollar question. "What would be the point of it all, really?"

"Believe me, I understand, Sis. If the other little girl—Anna—if she was the one who died, it doesn't help anyone to raise a bunch of old questions. And if it was Mary's biological daughter who died—if it was the real Bertie Jones—what good does it do to bring it all up now?"

"Right."

She picked up her napkin from the table and wiped her face. Sid had the sense that she had given her emotions more leash than she intended, and now the practical Gloria was once again taking charge.

"Nothing you've found about Bertie's past or her current associations links her in any way to the shooting of Councilman Trager, right? You may or may not have uncovered a big, dark secret from thirty years ago, but that's a fluke. You've got nothing that suggests the shooting was anything more than an accident."

Sid had already thought it through a hundred times and didn't hesitate to answer.

"Yeah, that's right."

Gloria looked at Sid, and he recognized that this was her closing argument.

"So who does it hurt if we don't say anything?" she asked. "Bertie and her mom have a good life. Both of them. Who does it hurt if we keep quiet?"

"Nobody, I guess."

She was right. That's what his head told him. But Sid had the sense that neither one of them felt very good about the decision. Gloria sipped at her coffee and Sid finished off the chocolate éclair, and both of them told themselves that the truth—at least in this instance—was not the most important thing. In the back of his mind, Sid heard Vic Meyers say, *"So the story has a happy ending."*

"Hey," said Sid. "Can I tell you something else that was kinda weird?"

Gloria actually wanted to say 'no,' because she'd had enough big news for one day. But 'no' didn't seem like a reasonable option, so she said, "What?"

"The guy in Miami told me that somebody else had asked about Robert and Mary Jones, maybe ten months ago."

Again the eyes narrowed and the brow knitted.

"Did he say who?"

"Nope. He didn't know. He said he got a phone call somewhere around the first of the year from someone asking what records were available for a Robert and Mary Jones and their daughter, Roberta. Whoever it was had the right birth date and everything."

"So what happened?"

"Vic gave 'em the same line he gave me. Told them they had to fill out an official 'Request for Information' thing and he'd get back to them. The person said thanks and hung up, and he never heard back from them."

"What do you figure that's about, Mr. Private Eye?"

"No idea. I was hoping my lawyer could figure it out."

Sid walked with Gloria down Freeport Boulevard toward Land Park and the Zoo where they'd find Marty and the girls, and it was really nice to just be walking along with his sister. They'd talked enough, and the silence felt good. She took his arm at one point as they crossed 13th Avenue, and then held onto it as they reached the park and started off across the grass.

"Hey, I'm gonna see you this afternoon," said Sid.

"You are?"

"Uh-huh. Amy wants me to help you guys with the wedding invitations."

"You have horrible handwriting."

"Yeah. I'm in charge of licking and stamping."

"Lucky you."

They could just see Fairytale Town through the trees as they crossed one of the little roads that cut through the park, and beyond that, the entrance to the zoo. The opportunity for a private conversation was slipping away, and something still gnawed at the back of Sid's mind. He wasn't exactly sure what it was, but it prompted him to say, "So we're not telling anyone about any of this, is that right?"

"That's right," Gloria replied.

"No reason to even bring it up, because nobody really knows what happened for sure."

"That's right."

"If you were Bertie, would you want to know this stuff?"

"I don't know."

"Me, either."

They reached the crosswalk at Land Park Drive that led

right to the entrance of the Sacramento Zoo and waited for a break in traffic. Sid put his arm around Gloria's shoulder, and she leaned against him.

"She's your friend," said Sid. "I'll let you decide."

He glanced over at his sister, and once again her eyes were wet and shiny.

Chapter 35

Sid Bigler woke up Sunday morning feeling pretty damn good. It was his first decent night's sleep since the fight and he had the whole house to himself. He was still sore, but each day got a little better, and he didn't even think about the multi-colored eye until he looked in the mirror. Rose was off at church with Gloria's family and Amy, so it was just Sid and Frampton watching football together. One of them enjoyed two bowls of Frosted Flakes sitting on the sofa in his underwear while the other munched on wilted lettuce in his little glass aquarium. Sid spotted a dead fly on the window sill and dropped that in Frampton's tank, too, but he didn't seem interested. Sid had no idea if turtles ate flies.

His mom got home around noon, and by two o'clock he and Amy were off on their weekly twelve-miler on the American River bike trail. And that's when a good day started to go bad.

He hadn't tried running since the German broke one of his ribs, and he discovered with the first step that it hurt like hell. He tried to tough it out, but after a couple of miles he had to give up, and they turned around and walked back to the car. The walk gave Sid an opportunity to catch Amy up on his trip to Miami and his conversation with Gloria. Yes, he'd promised his sister to keep Bertie Jones' past a secret, but surely that didn't apply to fiancées, right?

As they got back to his car, Amy told him she had to skip out on their usual post-run meal because she and her mom were getting together to finalize some wedding plans.

"Forty-three more days," she said. "Invitations are done, but we've still got lots to do for the reception." Sid smiled, but he didn't like it and he didn't want to spend the rest of the day alone.

After dropping Amy off at her apartment, he stopped at Togo's by the college and ate a pastrami sandwich all by himself, growing grumpier and more restless with each bite. He wanted to run and he wanted to be with Amy and he couldn't do either one, and for the moment it was sort of satisfying to sit and feel sorry for himself.

Sid's life had simply come to a grinding halt. For weeks he'd been consumed with the Bertie Jones case. But it looked like he'd followed it as far as he could, and he and Gloria had come to the mutual decision that it was time to let it go. The deaths of Tom Trager and Lou Martini remained a mystery, but it was up to the cops to handle those investigations. He didn't want to admit it, but he was scared. Scared of what could happen if he kept sticking his nose in where it didn't belong. His association with Lou had resulted in the visit by the German, who had taught him the lesson that private eyes getting into fights with bad guys was only cool on television. In real life, it's awful and potentially fatal, and scared was a reasonable thing to be.

So his afternoon loomed empty before him. He was in too lousy a mood to do anything fun, so he decided to work, and the only case left to work on was Nathan Bomke's. There was nothing about the slick, pretty lawyer that he liked, but it was the only thing currently bringing money into Bigler Investigations and hopefully it wasn't too late to save the job. He had, after all, slightly misled his client a few days ago, and Bomke would be expecting a report from the trip to L.A. that he never took. For a moment he actually entertained the idea of jumping in the Duster and driving down to Southern California right then. He could snoop around tomorrow, ask a few questions, and only miss one more day at the deli. But then he pictured Nathan Bomke's smug, tanned face, and decided that he wasn't going to let the guy yank his chain any more. After all, the case was, in Bomke's own words, *'a slam dunk.'* Sid was a trained, licensed private investigator, and it was his professional opinion that he could easily accomplish what he needed to do without wasting his time on a trip to Los Angeles.

If he'd been in a better mood, Sid would never have made the decision to flat out ignore a client's instructions. But he was grouchy and Bomke was a dick, so he drove himself home, spread out the contents of the Li'l Starz folder on the kitchen table, kissed his mom and asked her to leave him alone for a few hours.

It had been over a week since he'd looked at the stuff, but it all came back to him: The sad photos of little Mandy Mercer, over-dressed and under-beautiful; the pages of notes with phone numbers that the guy from Li'l Starz, Howard Clark, had called trying to find work for the homely kid; the credit card statement with the bright yellow highlighter marks indicating the airline tickets and the West Hollywood Travelodge expenses, allegedly proving that Mr. Clark had been down in L.A. at the time of *The Prodigy Project*.

Just to double check, Sid grabbed his mom's calendar off the kitchen wall. Nicky and Nellie had given it to their grandma for Christmas last year, and each month featured a different photo of Burt Reynolds. Sid flipped back to July (where Burt was wearing a red, white, and blue vest with no shirt underneath) just to look at the dates Howard Clark had given him for *The Prodigy Project* and saw that the 20th and 21st were a Saturday and Sunday, the third weekend of the month. He noted payment was made for three nights at the Travelodge on Monday the 22nd, which made sense. Clark must have stayed Sunday night after the seminar and flown home the next day.

Sid picked up the heavy black phone, dialed long distance information, then called the Anaheim Convention Center, where Clark had said *The Prodigy Project* was held. To his surprise, even though it was a Sunday, a nice woman at the information desk was able to look at the events calendar and confirm that *The Prodigy Project* was held in Meeting Room AR1 on the 20th and 21st of July.

"Do you have any information about who attended the event?" Sid asked.

"I'm sorry sir. The Convention Center just provided the facility. You'll have to talk to the event organizer about that."

Sid expected that, but it never hurts to ask. Just trying to be thorough. He thanked the nice lady and hung up the phone. It looked like Bomke was right. A slam dunk.

He was just about to close the folder and take a Mountain Dew break when something on the credit card statement caught his eye. Lou Martini would've seen it right away, but for some reason Sid hadn't noticed it until just now. In between the two highlighted expenses for the airfare and the Travelodge, there were two other charges.

One was for an Avis Car Rental at the Los Angeles International Airport location, and the other was for the Stardust Hotel and Casino in Las Vegas.

Sid's lousy afternoon was just beginning to improve. He figured the first call would be easy, and he was right.

"Travelodge."

"Hello," said Sid. For some reason, he was doing a little southern accent, but it sounded pretty good. "This is Detective Peter Bone with the Los Angeles Police Department. Who am I speaking to?"

"Carl Bisagno." The kid who answered the phone sounded like he was about fourteen years old.

"Carl, I'm working on a murder investigation and I need you to check your guest register for me, can you do that?"

"Uh, yes, sir."

Now the kid sounded nervous. *Good.* Sid told Carl it was very important that the police confirm the dates that a Mr. Howard Clark stayed at their motel, and Carl was very helpful. After putting Sid on hold for a couple of minutes, he came back and told him that Clark had, indeed, checked into the West Hollywood Travelodge.

"He checked in on Sunday night, July 21st, pretty late. Almost midnight. And he checked out the next morning."

"Well that's funny, Carl, because the suspect told us that he spent three nights at your motel."

"No, sir. He had reservations for Friday and Saturday, and he didn't show up and he didn't cancel within twenty-four hours, so he had to pay for all three nights. But he didn't check in 'til Sunday night. I'm lookin' at his signature right now."

"Well, thank you, Carl. You've just helped us put a killer behind bars. We may ask you to testify in court."

"Yes, sir."

Sid hung up, smacked the counter with his hand and laughed out loud. Howard Clark had paid for three nights, alright. But he'd slept somewhere else. Sid grabbed a Mountain Dew from the fridge and took a big swig. Ahhhhh.

The people at the hotel in Vegas wouldn't be so gullible. He thought for a minute, then picked up the telephone again. When he got through to the Stardust, he asked for the billing department.

"Hello, can I help you?"

Professional. Impersonal. It was a woman's voice, no telling how old she was. Sid took a deep breath.

"Yeah, hi, my name is Howard Clark. I stayed at the Stardust back in July, and I was just going over my credit card statement. Sorry it's taken me so long to call, but I think there's been a mistake."

"What seems to be the problem?"

"Well, I was charged, uh…" Sid looked at the bill. "…$584 on my credit card, but my wife says that the room wasn't that expensive."

"Can you hold a moment?"

"I sure can."

Sid listened to *Mack the Knife* on hold, and the woman was back in less than a minute.

"Mr. Clark, as a Platinum Club member, you do receive discounted rates here at the Stardust. Our records show that you stayed Friday and Saturday, July 19th and 20th, and your room rate was just $169 a night. But you did charge three meals to your room, plus one room service charge, and a $93 purchase at our gift shop. With taxes, the charge on your credit card is correct. Five hundred forty eight dollars."

"Well, Miss, I'm sorry to have bothered you."

"No problem, can I help you with anything else?"

"Oh, I don't think so. You've already been very, very helpful."

Sid hung up, smiled, and finished off the Mountain Dew. It was the best moment so far in the history of Bigler Investigations. Howard Clark had flown to Los Angeles, claimed to have spent the weekend trying to find a place in show business for Mandy Mercer (a.k.a. the second runner-up to the Little Miss Pinto Bean crown), but instead he was doing god-knows-what for two days, running up a bill in Sin City. He drove to Vegas and back, spent one night in the Travelodge, and then flew home. *A slam dunk.* And Sid didn't have to go to L.A. to figure it out. Pretty impressive.

Nathan Bomke was going to be very upset, of course, and would probably never pay him a dime. But so what? Nathan Bomke was a weenie.

The only other event of interest that Sunday was a phone conversation with Lieutenant Benjamin Stokes. After his uplifting phone calls to L.A. and Las Vegas, Sid had decided to try riding his bike instead of running, and discovered that it hardly hurt his rib at all. He rode hard for a couple of hours, got home and announced he was taking his mom to Zelda's for pizza after he got a shower. Rose said she loved the idea (Zelda's was right up there with Burt

Reynolds as far as she was concerned), and told him that Stokes had called while he was gone. Before jumping in the shower, Sid dialed the number written on the note pad in the kitchen.

"Stokes."

"Lieutenant, it's Sid Bigler."

"Oh, Bigler, thanks for calling back. Sorry to bother you on the weekend."

"No sweat. What's up?"

"Nothing. And I mean *nothing*. I've brought in a couple more of my guys trying to find that little son of a bitch who shot Tom Trager, and we keep coming up with nothing. It's like he vanished."

"Sorry, Lieutenant. I wish I could help."

"Yeah, well that's why I called. Just checking to see if you came up with anything else. Your little fishing trip about the birth certificate turn up anything at all?"

"Nope," said Sid. "Not a thing." And he had no idea if he was telling the truth or not.

Chapter 36

The wound on Sid's neck was much less noticeable by Monday morning, but he must have been asked thirty times about his black eye during the breakfast rush. The deli was packed, of course, as Joe's legendary Brown Sugar Cinnamon Rolls brought in the usual mob. After a while, Sid decided he might as well have a little fun with it, so each time someone asked what happened to his eye he changed the story. It was blamed on several different household objects (doorknob, coffee table, rolling pin), attacks by random animals (dog, very large cat, ostrich), encounters with angry women (Amy, his mother, meter maid), and a number of other explanations with various degrees of believability (car wreck, shopping cart, cannibals). Some of the regulars asked him more than once just to see what he'd say. It was nice to be back to work.

His mom took the day off after all the extra hours she'd put in last week, so Sid never really had a chance to catch his breath right through lunchtime. Now Eddie was wiping down tables and putting away silverware. Joe was stretching plastic wrap over square metal pans filled with pickles or mayo or sliced tomatoes and putting them in the fridge below the counter. It was just past two o'clock and there was only one customer left when Jackson Dexter walked in. *Damn*. How could he have forgotten about Dexter?

He was the man in Sacramento that everybody loved to hate. Almost everyone read his *Talk of the Town* column in the newspaper, and almost no one wanted to be mentioned in it. He could occasionally be very eloquent and gracious, especially when writing about distinguished senior citizens or little kids. But if you were anywhere in between, it was generally bad news when your name appeared anywhere beneath his byline.

"Are we still on?"

Jackson Dexter smiled and dropped a notebook and pen on the counter as he slid onto a stool. Sid was on the other side, just like the first day they'd met five years ago. And for all he knew, the guy was wearing the same clothes from five years ago, too, but how can you tell when all somebody owns is Hawaiian shirts? He was also sporting the same two-day stubble and light sheen of perspiration that seemed to accompany him year 'round.

"Of course we're on. How could I forget?" Sid asked, and Dexter had no idea how serious the question was. "Can I get you something to eat?"

"Love your cheeseburgers."

"Grilled onions."

"You remembered."

Sid scribbled the order on a ticket and gave it to Joe Diaz, who had already dropped the burger on the grill. Then he poured the reporter a Coke and set it down on the counter in front of him.

"You know I've been dying to talk to you about that attack last week," said Dexter. "But since we already had our little meeting scheduled today I figured I'd leave you alone for a few days."

"Very nice of you."

"That's a hell of a shiner you got, Sid. Does it hurt?"

"Not much. I've kinda forgotten about it."

"So, what is it, open season on private investigators?"

"Hmm?"

"Well, last week somebody attacks you right here in your restaurant. A couple of weeks ago some local P.I. named Martini got killed. Seems like a bad time to be a private eye. Did you know him?"

"Yeah. Yeah, we'd met."

"Honestly, that's a hell of a shiner." Jackson Dexter said it again, then drank down about half of his soda. "You know, it's been about six months since I've written anything about you. Maybe it's time for a piece called 'A Private Black Eye.' Private Eye. Black Eye. Get it?"

"It's genius."

Six months earlier, Dexter had written one of his rare columns that actually portrayed someone in a positive light, and Sid had been the fortunate subject. It started with the sentence, *'From slinging hash to professional sleuth—who does something like that?'* and that article was the source of the nickname that had kind of caught on: *'The Deli Detective.'* Dexter had also referred to him as a *'Gumbo Gumshoe'* and the *'Pastrami on Rye Spy,'* but thankfully those titles never seemed to stick. Overall, there was surprisingly little sarcasm in the story about the young proprietor of one of Sacramento's legendary eateries becoming a part-time detective, and Sid had appreciated it.

"So, I haven't gotten a wedding invitation."

"I didn't think you even knew I was getting married."

"Please," Dexter rolled his eyes. "I know everything.

What is it, a couple of months 'til you give up your freedom?"

Sid thought for a second. "Forty-two more days."

"That's very cute."

Joe Diaz slid a plate covered with fries and a picture perfect cheeseburger in front of Jackson Dexter, who appeared to briefly go into a trance.

"Look at that," he said. "Best burger in town. You know I wrote that in the paper."

"Yes, I know. Thank you."

The reporter picked up the burger, and just before taking a huge bite he said, "So, what are we talking about?"

"What do you mean?"

A shiny, two-inch strand of grilled onion flopped down onto Dexter's chin, and he struggled to close his mouth around the quantity of food he'd shoved into it. Twenty or thirty seconds went by before he'd worked it into a manageable wad and stuffed it into one cheek.

"You called me, remember? So what did you want to talk about?"

If Sid had enough time, he wasn't bad at coming up with a believable lie. However, his track record for spur of the moment prevarication was not good, and he needed a first class fib right now. At the time Sid had called last week to set up this meeting, he was trying to dig up whatever he could about Bertie Jones. But now he wanted to keep her past buried, and Jackson Dexter was the last person on earth he wanted to talk to.

For a moment he couldn't remember specifically why he wanted to talk to the reporter in the first place, but then it hit him. Sid had been wondering if Bertie had any political enemies, and Dexter knew more about personal lives and local politics than anyone else.

"Sid?"

"Oh, I didn't have anything in particular to talk about. I just hadn't seen you in a while. Figured I never thanked you properly for the nice article a few months ago."

"Yeah?"

"Yeah."

It was a simple little lie, but Dexter actually looked touched, and Sid wondered if maybe everybody the guy knew kept him at arm's length for fear of being publicly humiliated in his column. Then Dexter took another gigantic, sloppy bite, and Sid thought maybe people avoided him simply because of his table manners. Either way, Sid allowed himself to relax a little as Jackson Dexter—his mouth still crammed with hamburger—leaned forward and sucked down some more Coke through a straw, then packed his cheek again with food so he could talk.

"So, how's Bertie Jones doing?" Dexter asked.

Oh, crap. Just when Sid thought he had everything under control.

"Why do you ask?" He tried his best to appear nonchalant, but couldn't think of anything to do with his hands. Out of desperation, he grabbed a stack of the plastic coated menus and started wiping them down with a damp towel.

"She's your sister's best friend, right?"

"Yeah, that's right." Wipe. Wipe. Wipe.

"Well, she got shot, remember?" There was a little of the

famous Dexter sarcasm. "So I thought maybe you'd know how she was doing."

"Oh, *that*. Uh, I think she's doing fine."

Jackson Dexter put down his cheeseburger, rested his elbows on the counter, and just looked at Sid for a moment. Maybe looked *through* Sid.

"Have you actually talked to her since the shooting?"

"Oh, yeah. Twice."

"Why don't I believe you?"

Sid suddenly found himself feeling a little bit defensive, because that part, at least, was the truth, and he didn't like being doubted.

"I don't know, Dexter. But it's true. In fact, I went by the hospital the day after it happened, but she was asleep. Then we talked once on the phone, and I stopped by her office last week. Like I said, we've spoken two times since we were in the bar that night."

There was a long pause, and the reporter smiled very slightly. Sid didn't realize what he'd said.

"You were in the bar the night Tom Trager was murdered?"

Sid stopped wiping the menus and looked Dexter in the eye. Then he told the truth, and it felt like he was stepping in front of a moving bus.

"Yes. I was sitting right next to Bertie."

The one remaining customer got up and walked to the cash register, and Sid was thankful for the timing. He walked down and rang the guy up, made change and closed the register drawer. Then he looked at the other end of the counter, where Jackson Dexter sat scribbling in his notebook.

He hadn't taken another bite of his food. That had to be a bad sign.

"So you were there when the hot lead was flying at the Ancient Moose."

Dexter said it without looking up and without taking a break from his writing. Sid wandered back down to his end of the counter.

"Yes I was."

"God, I can't believe I didn't know that. How about Gloria? Was your sister there?"

"Uh-huh."

"Beautiful."

There was a whooshing sound as Joe poured some water on the hot grill and steam erupted from the surface. Sid felt the heat behind him. Next was the familiar metal against metal noise as Joe scraped the grill clean at the end of his day.

"So tell me about the shooting." Dexter stopped writing and looked up from his notebook. "What were you doing there? What happened? How did Councilwoman Jones end up getting hit, too?"

"I can't talk to you, Dexter." Sid discovered that, now that he had nothing to hide, he wasn't the least bit nervous.

"Sure you can. Give me the details and I'll keep you completely anonymous."

"Nope. Write what you want, but you get no quotes from me. I'm a witness. The cops have asked me to not talk to the press."

"Oh, c'mon, Sid. Nobody really expects you to keep your mouth shut. You've gotta give me something."

"I just gave you a cheeseburger."

It looked like Jackson Dexter had forgotten about the food until Sid reminded him. He set his notebook aside and went back to work on the burger, talking and eating at the same time.

"Okay, how about this: I break the news that you and your sister were present at the shooting of Tom Trager and Bertie Jones, but I don't make up any quotes or anything."

"You make up quotes?"

"Duh. I do it all the time. Anyway, I make sure you guys look good for now, and then, whenever this is all settled—if they ever find the guy who did it—you and your sister give me an exclusive interview."

Dexter was going to write whatever he wanted, so there was no sense in trying to strike a better deal, whatever a *better deal* might be. Besides, it couldn't hurt business to get his name back in the paper. Sid's Deli and Bigler Investigations could both stand a little free press.

"Yeah, that's a deal."

"Great." The burger was gone and the fries were disappearing fast. "And just to confirm, you've talked to Bertie Jones twice and she's doing well."

Sid realized he'd been giving an interview all along, and wondered what else he'd said that might make the paper.

"That's right."

"I'm glad to hear it. Jones is my favorite councilperson."

Dexter's comment was a surprise. Especially after Bertie's recent fall from her lifelong pedestal when she and Sid met in her office last week.

"Your favorite," said Sid. "Really? Why is that?"

"Well, she's young, for one thing. And she's smoking hot, too. Maybe you noticed."

"Bertie? Yeah, I guess." It was a fine piece of acting by Sid Bigler. "I suppose she's kind of attractive."

"And as somebody who observes local politics, I think she's just been a breath of fresh air. She paid for her own campaign, she came in with no agenda other than what she thought was best for the city, and she didn't give a damn about stepping on toes. Of course she's changed a little over time. Politics does that to everybody. You gotta play the game if you want to get anything done."

"What's that mean?"

"Nothing. It's just real life, that's all. Politics— especially local politics—is the art of compromise. You want another councilperson's vote for your pet project, you've gotta give them what they want sometimes. She figured it out. Occasionally she'll go along with some big project that the pro-growth members wanted—guys like Trager and Mickelman. But then those guys will end up voting for some new homeless program she wants, or maybe something for that women's shelter her mom runs. Bertie Jones has been smart and she does a good job. I just like her, that's all."

"Don't you call her *'City Council Barbie'* in your column?

"Sure, but that's just to sell papers. C'mon, you don't think I believe everything I write, do you? People read my column expecting me to be an ass, and who am I to let them down?"

"Just doing your job."

"Exactly right. Wait 'til you see what I write about that

black eye." Dexter wiped his mouth with a paper napkin, missing a small ketchup smear on his cheek, then gave Sid a big grin. "Got any ice cream?"

Chapter 37

As it turned out, the meeting with Jackson Dexter at the deli wasn't Sid's most memorable conversation of the day. Not by a long shot.

From the chair next to the sofa, he looked out the front window of Mary Jones' living room and saw the street lamps pop on. A striped orange cat rubbed up against his legs, presumably the same one that tried to take a nap on the side of his head as he hid behind the couch just over a week ago. Now his sister gave him a strained smile as she sat on that very couch, her back to the window and her fingers silently drumming on a pillow. Neither one spoke as they waited for Mary to return from the kitchen with coffee. It was definitely weird to be sitting there.

Earlier in the afternoon, just as he was locking up the deli, the phone had rung.

"Sid, I've been talking to mom."

"Okay, Sis."

"The other night you said you'd let me decide about talking to Bertie, remember?"

"Sure." Sid had no idea where this was going, but she had his fullest attention.

"Well I couldn't stop thinking about what you said. I was so useless at the office today I went home at lunchtime. Do you think we can really just forget about what happened and do nothing?"

"I don't know."

"Well I don't think we can. So I talked to mom and she suggested we talk to Mrs. Jones about it. Maybe Bertie's mom can

279

explain everything."

"You're kidding."

"No. She's the only person who knows what really happened. There's no reason to upset Bertie if Mrs. Jones can clear everything up."

"I don't know, Gloria. I'm not sure I like the idea."

"Well mom just got off the phone with Bertie's mother, and she's expecting us at her house tonight at seven."

So the decision had been made, and now Sid and Gloria sat in Mrs. Jones' living room as the woman rounded the corner from the kitchen with three cups of coffee. She looked stunning in a simple blue dress and a small string of pearls.

"Taffy, get away!" She waved a hand at the cat, but the cat apparently either misunderstood or, more likely, ignored the gesture as it remained firmly attached to Sid's leg.

"It's okay, Mrs. Jones. We're old buddies."

Sid thought back to his last conversation with Bertie's mother, the disastrous one about Canton and Columbus and Cleveland, when he had looked for some resemblance between mother and daughter. He searched her face again, wanting to see it. Maybe he did. Maybe.

Mary set the cups down on three saucers she'd already set out, each next to a perfectly folded cloth napkin on the coffee table. The little group of dishes surrounded a stack of *Ladies Home Journals.* Mrs. Jones sat on the sofa by Gloria and folded her hands in her lap.

"Isn't this nice?" she asked, though Sid thought *'awkward'* might have been a better choice of words. "I'll admit I was a little surprised when your mother called and said you wanted to come over. What can I do for you two?"

Mary glanced back and forth between Sid and his sister, and it was at that moment that he realized they hadn't talked about what they were going to say to this woman. Hadn't even considered it. How do you casually bring up something like this? If their suspicions were correct, they were here to undo the happy life that Mary Jones had been living for over thirty years.

"Well, Mrs. Jones," said Gloria, "There's something we wanted to ask you about."

Thank god it was Gloria that started talking. Sid realized he'd been holding his breath, and let it out slowly.

Then Gloria said, "Go ahead, Sid."

Bertie's mother and Bertie's best friend sat side-by-side on the sofa and looked at him expectantly. Gloria shot him a quick look of apology. Hoping that the desperation he was feeling on the inside wasn't too obvious on the outside, Sid opened his mouth, unsure of what was going to come out, and started talking.

"Uh, Mrs. Jones… I happened to be in Florida last week, and I happened to meet someone who, uh, happened to be in charge of public records in the 1950s…"

Gloria rolled her eyes and he wanted to crawl behind the sofa again. Why was it that every conversation with Mary Jones was a train wreck? He had used the word *'happened'* three times in the first sentence. Unbelievable. His mind raced to think of something else to say. Something that would sound natural and clever. Maybe even funny. Something that would put the brakes on and let him ease back into the subject.

"Mrs. Jones, I…" Sid started but stopped short, and understood that he wouldn't have to say another word.

The first thing he noticed was her hands, clasped together in her lap and gripping so tightly that her knuckles were turning white. He followed a slight tremor up her arms to a blood vessel that throbbed at the base of her neck. Her mouth still managed a strained smile, but her face had grown colorless. And her eyes were fixed on him, staring intently at him, brimming with tears that shimmered and jiggled, but somehow refused to fall. The general impression was one of a lovely statue, ancient and fragile, that was just about to crumble.

Sid's sister, however, didn't have the advantage of his perspective, and so didn't see what was surely the beginning of the end of a charade that Mary Jones had been living for decades. She turned to the woman sitting beside her and said, "Mrs. Jones, what Sid is trying to say is that…"

And then she saw it, too.

Slow, agonizing seconds ticked by. Gloria reached out a hand and laid it gently on the woman's lap, but she seemed not to notice. Her eyes were still locked on Sid's.

"You know."

Mary's voice was a whisper, so low he wouldn't have heard it if the room hadn't been so deathly quiet. Gravity won its battle and one lonely tear broke free, starting a path down her cheek that others were soon to follow.

Sid felt a profound helplessness. Sitting and watching Bertie's mom at that moment hurt as much as anything that the German had done to him almost a week ago. It was a different kind of pain, to be sure, but just as real.

Mary Jones took a deep breath, halting and ragged, then let it out. And then she said it again, louder this time.

"You know."

Both cheeks were streaked now and her nose had begun to run, but Bertie's mother remained motionless, staring back at Sid until he finally nodded. That seemed to be her cue, and the statue came back to life. Mary took a napkin from the table and wiped her face with it, then stood and began a slow walk across the room. Gloria and Sid could only watch and wait. She stopped in front of a grouping of five framed photographs on the wall. Five school portraits of Bertie through the years.

"There were complications when Bertie was born."

Sid couldn't see her face, but her voice sounded surprisingly clear and strong. She looked at the pictures as she spoke.

"I couldn't have any more children. Bob and I wanted a large family, but that wasn't going to happen. So we agreed to be foster parents, and it was just a week or two later that someone from the county brought us another little girl, almost the same age. Beautiful. A miracle."

"Anna," Sid said.

"Yes. Anna." Mary Jones said it like it was a fond memory. "We had Anna for nine months. Fell in love with her like she was our own. Her mother was an awful thing. Just a teenager. We had to let her visit occasionally, but she didn't love the child. Didn't know what to do with her. Anna called us 'Mama' and 'Papa,' and she called Bertie 'Sissy.' But she was frightened of her real mother." Mary still hadn't turned around, and must have gotten lost in one of the pictures on the wall, because the story stopped there momentarily.

"What happened to Anna, Mrs. Jones?" It was Gloria who asked the question.

"The people at the county were idiots." Mary turned around and the tears were gone. "The girl's mother had them convinced that she was getting her life together. That she might be capable of caring for Bertie."

Sid and Gloria exchanged glances. The woman clearly had no idea she'd made the mistake.

"You mean '*Anna*,'" said Sid.

"Hmm?" She looked confused, but only for a moment. "Yes, of course. *Anna*. There were more frequent visits by the mother, and our case worker told us that she anticipated a successful reunification. What kind of word is that for tearing a family apart? '*Reunification*.'"

It looked like the word tasted bitter in her mouth. Sid didn't want to make her tell every detail—to live the story all over again—but this was the time to eliminate any doubt.

"Was that when your daughter, Roberta, got sick?"

The moment of truth came and went in, literally, a moment as Mary nodded without hesitation.

"Got a fever Monday afternoon. Bob said I should take her to the doctor right away, but I waited 'til Wednesday. They said it was the flu and sent us back home. She died on Thursday. So fast. So fast."

Mary Jones pulled out the piano bench and sat on the end, and the cat jumped up in her lap. She stroked its head and it leaned into her.

"Just to be very, very clear," Sid could hear the lawyer

in his sister's voice, "your biological daughter, Roberta, was the child who died. You and your husband left Miami with the foster child, Anna, and have raised her as your biological daughter ever since."

"Yes."

"Does Bertie know?" Sid asked.

Mary Jones took the cat up into her arms and held it close to her face, closing her eyes and rubbing her cheek against the soft fur for a moment.

"I don't know. I don't know."

Tears pushed their way through Mary's closed eyelids, then she buried her face into the side of the cat and sobbed loudly. Taffy seemed oblivious to her owner's anguish.

Sid and Gloria sat, feeling almost alone in the room. This entire conversation had been his sister's idea, and he wondered what they had accomplished. Because now that they knew the truth, they faced a question he had no idea how to answer: What next?

They waited in painful silence for more than a minute as the sobs grew quieter and then stopped. Mary set the cat down on the floor and wiped her face with her hands, then walked back to the sofa to sit down again by Gloria. Her eyes were puffy and red but she was remarkably composed.

"My daughter was only three years old. She couldn't possibly have understood what was happening, and we never talked about it." She picked her napkin back up and wiped her nose. "We just started calling her 'Bertie,' and that was that. I know this must sound terrible to you, but it wasn't. Really."

"She was someone else's child," Gloria said.

"No. She was ours. She loved us and we loved her. And we were providing for her. The woman who gave birth to her couldn't do that. She was just a teenager for God's sake. I'm sure that girl had a better life without the responsibility of a child to care for."

"She died on the street a couple of years after you moved away," said Sid.

A brief look of concern crossed Mary's face, but only for a moment. "Well then it's certainly better that Bertie was with us, don't you see?"

Mary looked back and forth between Sid and Gloria, seeking approval maybe. Or forgiveness. But apparently she didn't see what she was looking for.

"Don't think that I was a bad person. You weren't there."

"No, we weren't," said Sid.

And then Mary Jones asked a very hard question. "Will you tell her?"

Brother and sister looked at each other, another moment where each hoped the other would do the talking. But neither one did, and the room fell silent once again until Mary spoke.

"I want to tell you something else. You may think it has nothing to do with what happened, but it does. And I want you to know."

"Okay."

"My husband…" Mary stopped, and Sid wondered if she'd changed her mind about whatever it was she wanted to say. She twisted the cloth napkin with her fingers for a few seconds. And then she began again. "My husband was a violent man. He was often angry, emotionally abusive. Occasionally, when he'd been drinking, he was physically abusive, too. It's hard to believe, but it didn't seem like a big deal at the time. He treated me the same way my father treated my mother. It was the early fifties, I loved my husband, and I made excuses.

"Then our daughter died and Bob blamed me. Maybe he was right. Maybe there was something else I could have done. Bob got drunk and beat me up pretty badly. It had never been like that before. Then it happened again right after the funeral. The county was already talking like they were going to take the other little girl, too, and I was terrified. She was the one good thing in my life. So I kept it quiet, and I begged Bob to take us away from there, and he did. We loaded up what we could in our station wagon and we left. And this is where we stopped running."

"Why here?" Sid asked.

"No reason, except we thought Bertie was ready. We drove for almost four months, stopping overnight in some places, up to a week in others. We bounced around. We didn't want to stay in one place too long because we didn't know if people were looking for us. And we wanted to stay on the road long enough that the little girl was completely used to being called 'Bertie.'

"Your husband," said Gloria, "He remained violent?"

"Yes. Bertie never saw it, but yes. There was nowhere to turn to for help back then. Nobody to help Bob stop what he was doing, either."

"So years later you started The WAVE, first here in Sacramento and now in Phoenix," said Sid.

"Yes."

"Penance?"

"It was the right thing to do. And so was bringing my daughter to a place where she could have a chance at a decent life. Look at who Bertie is today and tell me I didn't do the right thing."

Once again, Sid and Gloria had no response for the woman.

"Please don't tell her. What good would it do? Please don't."

Chapter 38

He was breathing hard, circling the track at Hughes Stadium for the sixteenth time, barely able to see in the half moonlight. But it didn't matter. His feet could find their way around that track even if he was blindfolded. How many thousands of laps had he run here? He reached the end of the final straightaway drenched in sweat, then slowed to a walk.

Sid Bigler was a lot of things. Fiancé. Deli owner. Turtle custodian. Above average martial artist. Newly minted private eye. But if you had to pick just one identity, Sid was a runner. Starting from the time he was in junior high school when he was good at nothing else, he was good at running. In high school and college, coaches all over the country knew his name. Easily good enough for a scholarship, and almost good enough to go to the Olympic trials (he had checked the mailbox every day in the months leading up to the trials for the '76 games, not really expecting an invitation, but hoping.) Nevertheless, some of the best in the country were surprised a few times to find the kid from Sacramento with the funny stride right next to them on the final lap. For so much of his life, it was exclusively what defined him, and at thirty-two years old he still loved to run. Sometimes needed to run. And this was one of those times.

Gloria had picked him up and driven to the meeting with Mary Jones that had been both successful and terrible. Just after 8 p.m. they returned to his mom's house, where he went straight to his room and put on shorts and running shoes and his favorite old Humboldt State Cross Country t-shirt. His sister and mother were seated at the dining room table, Gloria recounting every word of their conversation with Mary, and Sid didn't even stop to say good-bye. He was out the front door less than three minutes after they got home. Stepping onto the street, he relaxed for the first time in hours and rolled into a nice jog. That's when he remembered his broken rib. It was just yesterday afternoon that he'd quit after two miles on the bike trail with Amy, and it didn't feel a lot better now. But he went on, pushing pretty hard pretty quickly. It hurt to go faster, which was okay. The run was to clear his head. To forget about Mary Jones and her stolen child and everything else that had happened over the last few weeks. The pain in his side gave him something else to think about. So he ran and he hurt, and it felt good.

The lights at Hughes Stadium had clicked off at nine o'clock, so Sid finished his four mile track workout in the dark. And despite the hard pace, he felt more rested than he had in days. Between the jog to the college and the sixteen laps, he'd been focused on running for nearly forty-five minutes, and now he felt great as he started the two-mile walk back home.

But the feeling didn't last. He tried not to think about anything, but that's a gift that comes and goes. Snippets of the conversation with Mary Jones flashed through his head, or sometimes just the image of a woman crying, sobbing into the soft fur of Taffy the cat.

He tried unsuccessfully to imagine any scenario for

Mary and Bertie that could possibly be described as a happy ending, and a sadness settled over him. Like rings radiating out from a pebble dropped into a pond, the sadness spread, swallowing up the other lives that had intersected with his over the last two weeks. Tom Trager was dead, and the punk who shot him had disappeared without a trace. Lou Martini had been murdered, too, the reason for his death still a mystery. And whoever wanted Lou dead must have sent the German after him. So many questions, and absolutely zero answers.

He was only a few blocks from his mom's house when he stopped and stood on the sidewalk, hands on his hips. He shivered. He'd been walking for quite a while, and the sweaty t-shirt was cold against his skin. A low cloud cover was moving in, gradually swallowing up the stars. Sid had to be up at five, and he really should have gone home, had his bowl of cereal and crawled in bed. But he didn't. He turned around and started jogging in the direction of Amy's apartment, and that's where his Monday came to an end.

Chapter 39

Sid had no intention of going to KajuKempo class the following night. Just the thought of taking a punch in the ribs made him wince, and his hands and forearms were still bruised, though not quite as colorful as his eye, which had recently added some nice greens and yellows. Besides, why pay for a lesson when the German had given him such a good one for free last week? But then Woody had called the deli in the early afternoon and told him there had been a little break in the search for Porky Powell, and he had some interesting news about the Lou Martini case— "*Really* interesting," he said.

So Sid was sitting in the grass, watching the class in McKinley Park and thoroughly enjoying himself. Since Sid wasn't available to be his partner, Woody was sparring with Stanley Ono, and it was hilarious. The cop was bigger and his face was a mask of tortured concentration. In contrast, their nineteen-year-old instructor was half his size and relaxed, chatting with Sid while he completely kicked Woody's ass.

"It's an awesome black eye, Sid. Really cool."

"Thanks, Stanley. But you'd think with a teacher as good as you, this wouldn't have happened to me."

" Teacher only as good as student." The kid slipped into his best Charlie Chan voice.

"That some ancient Asian wisdom?"

"Maybe. I think I heard Arnold say it on *Happy Days*."

Sid laughed and the kid turned and gave him a grin.

Woody must have thought that was his opportunity, because he tried a back leg round kick. Stanley saw it coming, blocked the kick, then gave the cop a gentle push while he was off balance on one leg, and Woody found himself flat on his back in the grass.

"Not a bad idea, Woody," said Stanley. "Probably would've worked on Sid."

"If I was blindfolded," said Sid.

Woody made several more trips to the turf before that drill ended and the class moved on. Stanley wrapped a thick pad around a big, sturdy oak tree and they punched and kicked it until everyone was exhausted. Then the students had to find sticks or broken branches, and Stanley taught them some techniques for disarming an opponent. Their inscrutable teenage instructor finally called it quits, and Sid and Woody walked toward their cars together.

"Hey, where'd you go last week?" asked Woody.

"Hmmm?"

"I stopped by your mom's house to see how you were doing, and she said you'd left town."

"Oh. Yeah."

"Where'd you go?"

"Uh, the coast. Went to Bodega Bay just to rest for a couple of days." Nothing like lying to your friends. Time to change the subject. "So you said you had some news for me," said Sid. "Porky Powell and Lou Martini."

"Yeah. Buy me dinner and I'll tell you."

"Okay, but I pick the place."

Sitting at the cleanest available table—clean being a

relative term at this particular Stockton Boulevard Burger King—Woody held up his soda and said, "This is such a rip-off."

"Yeah?"

"You know what I heard? I heard it only costs them like a nickel for a large Coke. They could give free refills and still come out way ahead."

"Right," said Sid. "Free refills. Like that's ever gonna happen. So what's the news you've got for me?" Sid was tearing and squeezing little packets to make a pile of ketchup on the paper next to his burger.

"Okay, I've got kinda big news, and I have *huge* news. What do you want first?"

"Save the best for last. End huge." Sid dipped an onion ring in the ketchup and popped it in his mouth.

"Okay, kinda big: We finally got a little break in the search for Peter Powell."

"Porky? The guy who shot Trager? Where is he?"

"Well, it's a *little* break. We got a copy of Powell's mug shot out to every police agency in Northern California as soon as we ID'd the guy. I don't know if the Chico PD had their heads up their butts or what, but we got a call today from Chico, and they just started showing it around this weekend. So far they've had two different people tell 'em they saw the guy, maybe a week and a half ago."

"They're sure?"

"As sure as they can be. Your boy Porky is unique looking."

"So they think he was there not long after the shooting. But nothing since then?"

"Nothing yet. They know this is important. They're gonna get another couple of guys out on the street with Powell's photo tomorrow, and we're alerting departments further north, beyond Chico, in case he was just passing through."

"Well, at least that's something. Nice to know the guy didn't vanish into thin air."

"Yeah."

"How about the German? Any idea where he is?"

"Nope. The guy's a pro. He's disappeared again."

The conversation had to defer for a moment to their appetites, and each guy made about half of their Whopper disappear, followed by a big chug of the sodas that allegedly only cost Burger King a nickel.

"So with no leads to follow on your German friend, Stokes has me helping him on the Trager investigation."

Sid raised an eyebrow. "Teacher's pet?"

"He thinks I do good work."

"Can I assume this is leading up to the huge news?

Woody stuffed at least eight french fries in his mouth, sucked on his straw until the cup made that empty, gurgling noise, then leaned back.

"So... I'm working on the Trager case. Stokes has had other guys going through all his professional records, right? Things like the financial statements for the hardware store and his datebook to see who he's had meetings with over the last few months. Talking to city council staff. Stuff like that."

"Sure."

"Well Stokes asks me to go to Trager's house and look

over all his personal papers again. He had somebody else do it a couple of days after the murder, but now we're pulling our hair out trying to find a break, and he wants me to go do it again."

"Wait. This story doesn't end with the hot widow Trager walking into the room wearing a see-through negligee, does it?"

"Better."

"What could be better?"

"I'm going through bank statements for the last two years. Month by month, line by line. Turns out, less than a year ago, Trager wrote a very interesting check for a thousand bucks."

He paused, and something told Sid that Woody wasn't kidding when he said it was big news. His friend waited just long enough to be irritating, then he dropped the bomb.

"January 14th. The check was made out to 'L. Martini.'"

Sid heard him clearly, but it didn't register for a second. Even when it did, he had a hard time connecting the dots.

"Lou Martini was doing some kind of investigation work for Tom Trager?" Sid asked.

"Pretty good bet. Signature on the back was "Louis Martini." And there was one more check a couple months later for five hundred."

"When was that one written?"

"Late March. Same signature."

"Holy cow."

"Uh-huh."

Sid sat motionless as Woody powered down the rest of his value meal. So many thoughts raced through his mind—

random, unproductive. He didn't notice when Woody reached over and polished off his Coke, too.

"What do you figure it means, buddy?" Woody started working on Sid's onion rings.

"I... I don't know. Does this officially connect the murders of Trager and Lou Martini?"

"Yeah, that's the conclusion everybody in the department wants to jump to. And maybe it's right, but there's no guarantee. Life's full of coincidences. The cancelled checks are the only evidence we've got, and according to them Lou stopped working for Trager more than eight months before either one of them was killed."

"Yeah. That's right."

Sid said it, but he didn't believe it. He was still having a hard time focusing. Perhaps because the moment Woody had told him that there was a solid connection between Trager and Lou Martini, a strange little shiver had run down his spine. Because the first conclusion leads quickly to a second one. A scary one. One that Sid was realizing had somehow been in the back of his mind all along.

"But what if Lou *was* killed because of some job he was doing for Trager?" Sid asked. "What if the murders *are* related?"

"I know where you're going. Thanks to the German, we know there's some connection between the Martini murder and you. If Martini's also related to the Trager shooting, then maybe you're somehow connected to Trager, too."

Woody was close, but that wasn't exactly it. That connection was pretty obvious, and Sid could put two and two together as well as anybody. No, the thought that had messed with his head and briefly robbed him of the ability to consider anything else was this:

What if the shot that hit Bertie Jones was intended for someone else? Someone standing right next to her?

Subconsciously, his hand reached up and touched the place on his arm where the bullet had torn though his shirt almost three weeks ago. Sid had almost forgotten.

Chapter 40

Sid's mother had breakfast at Denny's every Wednesday morning with a group of ladies from Westminster Presbyterian Church. Officially, it was the weekly meeting of the Hospitality Committee, but unofficially, it was all about gossip and the $1.95 Seniors Breakfast. As a result, it was tough to persuade her to work another breakfast shift at the deli, but her son had assured her it was terribly important. So at 7:45 a.m., Rose Bigler was busy taking orders, making change and joking with customers, and Sid was standing at the door to Jilly Boyd's apartment.

He knocked non-stop for just over two minutes, gradually increasing in volume. At one point, he had to change hands when his wrist and knuckles began to run out of gas. Eventually, the door opened.

"Mike, you asshole! I told you not to..."

A blonde stood at the door, barefoot and sleepy-eyed, wearing white boxer shorts and a baby blue bra with little pink lady bugs on it. She stopped in mid-sentence when she saw Sid standing there.

"Expecting someone else?"

The woman, presumably Jilly, turned and disappeared into her apartment, neglecting to close the door behind her. So Sid walked right in.

"Helloooo! Miss Boyd?"

A door closed rather loudly somewhere down the hallway, and Sid took a moment to peruse the place. Jock Bell had said it was nice, and he was right. There was a big marble fireplace in the living room, and a gorgeous, gourmet kitchen littered with dirty dishes and old Chinese food cartons. He saw a pile of mail on a bookshelf and was just starting to leaf through some envelopes all addressed to Jillian Boyd when the woman came storming back into the room wearing jeans and a white t-shirt.

"Whoever you are, get the hell out or I'll call the cops!"

"Oh, Jilly, I don't think you want to do that."

She looked like she lost a little momentum when the strange man knew her name, but she still made her way across the living room and picked up the phone and began pushing buttons.

"Jilly, haven't you talked to the police enough lately?"

The woman stopped dialing.

"Who are you?"

"I'm a friend of your landlord," said Sid, as he sat down on a comfy looking La-Z-Boy and crossed his legs. "And I'm a guy who'll give you fifty bucks and then go away if you'll just answer some questions for me."

Jilly Boyd hung up the phone. She looked him over.

"Let me see the money."

With a confident flourish, Sid took his wallet from a back pocket and pulled out some cash. He leafed through the bills.

"Uh, okay, I've only got forty-three dollars, but it's yours."

"Jesus." Jilly Boyd rolled her eyes, walked over and took the money, then flopped down on a futon next to Sid and lit a cigarette. "Okay, mister. You got five minutes."

"Forty three bucks for five minutes. That's a hell of an

hourly wage."

The woman took a deep drag and blew out a cloud of smoke. "I provide a quality service."

"Yes, I understand that you do."

Jilly gave him a *'screw you'* smile. "You've got four minutes and forty seconds left."

It was a conversation Sid had thought would never happen. After all, the decision had been made to leave Bertie's past buried, and the investigations into the murders of Tom Trager and Lou Martini were officially police business. He had washed his hands of everything and he liked it that way. But Woody's news from last night had changed everything. Suddenly, everything was deeply personal. Now he was undeniably part of something bigger, and somehow connected to two people who were both recently murdered. He was determined not to join them. After all, he had to be in a wedding in forty days. No more waiting for someone else to figure out what was going on.

"Okay, I won't waste time. I'm not a cop, but I'm friends with cops. I know Tom Trager paid your bills here for a couple of years and occasionally stopped by for sex. Any idea why somebody would want Councilman Trager dead?"

"No." Jilly Boyd answered with the same mixture of boredom and superiority a parent gets from a smug teenager. "We never talked about business or politics or nothing."

"What did you talk about?"

"I don't know. We watched a lot of TV. I guess we talked about that. Sometimes Tommy would tell me about some of the places he travelled to."

"What places?"

"Oh, Las Vegas. Dallas. The Grand Canyon."

"Wow, your boyfriend was quite the *bon vivant*."

"I took French in high school, mister."

"Wonderful. Did he ever bring anybody else here with him?"

"No, I don't think so."

Sid didn't think she was lying intentionally, but she clearly wasn't putting much thought into her answers.

"The name Donald Kakavetsis doesn't ring a bell?"

"Oh, is that Donny's last name?"

"So he *did* bring someone here."

"Well, yeah. Donny. He's a bald guy with big, bushy eyebrows, but I never really talked to him. Trager said I had to leave them alone when Donny was here."

"And he never mentioned anybody else or brought anybody else here?"

"I don't think so."

Sid thought for a moment, then he stood up and looked at his watch.

"Okay, Miss Boyd. Thank you very much. I only used four of my five minutes. Do I get any money back?"

Jilly took a long, intentional drag from her cigarette again, staying planted on the futon.

"No refunds."

Sid stopped half way to the door.

"So who's Mike?"

"Huh?"

"When you came to the door, it sounded like you were

expecting someone named Mike."

"Oh, he's just a guy who comes by sometimes."

"Does he help pay the bills?"

Jilly Boyd smiled again, more genuine this time, and for the first time Sid thought she might be pretty.

"Your time's up."

Chapter 41

Milo wore a black leather jacket that came down to his knees, his hands jammed into the side pockets and his eyes darting back and forth under the wrinkly forehead as he slowly paced back and forth in the park at 9th and J Streets. Downtown workers affectionately and accurately called it "Wino Park," and for that reason, generally avoided it. So on this splendid October day, many of the lower end of Sacramento's social strata gathered to fill the park with coarse laughter and empty bottles, but they generally kept a wide berth between themselves and the beefy bodyguard in the black jacket, and his boss who sat nearby on a bench next to Sid Bigler.

"Nice day," said Jock Bell.

"Yeah. Beautiful. "

Bell wore a mint green three-piece suit that was the pinnacle of 1980s polyester technology. Protruding from his satiny yellow shirt, open at the collar, was a robust patch of white chest hair that almost looked like it was trying to escape. Quite a contrast to the unnaturally brown, unnaturally large hairdo that sat atop his head, catching the sunlight and sparkling in a way that is generally only seen in shampoo commercials.

"See that statue over there?" Jock gestured with a finger at a bronze figure atop a granite column. "Do you know who that is?"

Sid turned and looked at the statue that he must have passed hundreds of times over the years. From where he sat, it could've been anybody. George Washington. Carol Burnett.

"It's A.J. Stevens," Jock continued. "Nobody has any idea who he was anymore. The man didn't go to college, ended up being a master mechanic for the Central and Southern Pacific Railroads. Designed and built the largest locomotive in the world. Died in 1888."

Sid wondered for a moment why he was being told the story, and was unable to come up with an answer. So he went for the easy joke.

"You ever meet him, Jock?"

"That's real funny." Hard to tell if the guy was amused or irritated. "Okay, Sid. This little meeting was your idea. What do you want?"

"You called me at home last week," Sid began. "We talked about the German who tried to kill me, and you said that I must have gotten on somebody's radar screen or something like that. You ever figure out who sent him?"

"I'm still working on it."

"Any guesses?"

"Guessing is no good when it's something important. You either know or you don't. If you don't, you keep your mouth shut."

"Still, I think your guess might be better than mine."

Jock Bell shrugged, and gave no sign that he had more to say.

"What do you know about Donald Kakavetsis?"

Bell continued looking casually out across the park without making eye contact—the picture of detached cool. But at the sound of the name, Sid saw a little change. He didn't appear to be afraid. Fear wouldn't look right on Jock's face. It was surprise maybe, and apprehension.

"I know he's somebody you should leave alone."

"Yeah, people keep telling me that."

Jock finally turned and the two held eye contact in silence for several seconds. Sid couldn't tell if the old guy had more to say on the subject, so he waited.

"I'm like a matchmaker." Jock finally said, then paused for a moment like it was profound. "Everything I do—it's all matchmaking. Like, at the pawn shop, maybe there's some guy that needs money and he's got a… I dunno, he's got a tuba. Well, somewhere there's somebody with money that wants a tuba. And I'm the guy in the middle that gets them together. I might have to hold on to the god damn tuba for six years, but eventually I put those two guys together. That's what every business deal is, Sid. It's just making a match. I know a lot of people, and I'm good at it."

"So what kind of a match did you make for Kakavetsis?"

Jock nodded a small approval. "Ordinarily I steer clear of men like him. We're both businessmen, but he's different. Cold. Hurts people and doesn't care. He's not nice like me."

Sid wasn't sure if that was a joke or not, but he suspected it was completely sincere. Jock looked away, once again scanning the park as he spoke.

"What I tell you now doesn't get back to your friend Lieutenant Stokes or any of his people."

"I promise."

"Okay. Donny came to me with a request a couple of years ago. Seemed pretty harmless at the time. He had a substantial amount of land north of town, between the airport and that stupid basketball arena they just built. He needed a little help with some zoning problems and development fees, and was looking for a sympathetic ear on the city council."

"And it just so happened that you had recently set up Councilman Tom Trager in a lovely apartment with a cute young blonde."

"I don't know what those two talked about, or what Trager did or didn't do for Donny Kakavetsis. I just made the match. I got paid for the introduction and I walked away."

"And that's the end of the story."

"For me, yeah. Until the German almost killed you."

"I don't get the connection."

"The German—his name is Hoffman—he's self-employed, so you can't be sure. But I know he's done some work for Donny Kakavetsis in the past."

Sid wasn't surprised to hear it, but it made his head spin a little anyway. Suddenly there were so many pieces that fit together, but no clear picture. The names ran through his mind. Kakavetsis and Trager had some kind of relationship. Trager hired Lou Martini to do something for him. Martini was killed by the German. The German worked for Kakavetsis. The names ran together in a circle, and it was too much at once. He tried to focus, tried to separate the players and then find the thread that pulled them all together, but it eluded him.

"You're a nice kid, Sid." Jock interrupted his thoughts. "Donny Kakavetsis is not somebody you want to mess with. Stay away from him."

Jock Bell leaned forward, elbows on knees. Sid leaned back, arms crossed. And the two men sat silently side by side on the bench in Wino Park, both facing forward, watching lunchtime life go by. Neither face gave a hint at the thoughts behind it. Jock, of course, was a puzzle and seldom showed emotion anyway. And for the moment, Sid allowed himself to slip into neutral. Sometimes he still had the blessed, almost exclusively male ability to simply think about nothing at all. People walked by, Milo hovered a few yards away, and Sid's mind was blank. Idling at a stop light. It was in this inner quiet that a new thought occurred to him. A probably unrelated question, but a good one.

"Why the change?"

"Hmmm?" Jock sounded like he'd been in limbo, too.

"You just said I was a nice kid. And last week you said we were friends."

"Yeah."

"Why the change?"

It wasn't necessary to say more. It had been a long time since the two of them had a fist fight in the street right in front of the pawn shop. And once, as Sid was being taken away in the back of a police car, Jock had given him a smile and the finger.

"Your father was a stubborn old bastard. That deli business should've dried up and blown away in 1950, but it didn't." Bell's voice was deep and low. If this was an answer to Sid's question, it was hard to see where it was going. "We didn't like each other much, but I saw Big Sid bust his ass over there. Him and that big cook ran that place all by themselves. Showed up in the dark every morning, cleaned up and closed at the end of every day. Hardly took a vacation. Hell, if it needed painting, your old man was in there painting it on the weekend. So when he died, I figured that was it. Your generation doesn't know how to work. I saw you trying to keep the place going and thought you'd last a couple of months before you gave up and sold me the building."

Jock stood up and buttoned his minty green polyester jacket, still looking out across the park. One hand reached up and smoothed out the back of his hair.

"It turns out you're like your old man."

That was the only explanation Sid would get, but there was no doubt it was intended as a great compliment. Milo fell in behind his boss and the two of them headed off in the direction of the pawn shop.

Chapter 42

Sid stood in the magazine aisle of Tower Books with the current *Guns & Ammo* in his hands. He'd never really liked guns, and had decided long ago that it was possible to be a private investigator without owning one. But recent events had him rethinking that position.

"Guns & Ammo?"

He looked up to discover Amy standing beside him.

"Yeah. I don't know. I'm just looking."

"Might be a good idea."

She took the magazine from his hands, added it to the November issue of *Modern Bride* she was holding and started toward the register. Sid stood and watched her walk away. It's not just any girlfriend that'll buy you a copy of Guns & Ammo.

After his curious lunchtime meeting in the park with Jock Bell, he'd gone back to the deli and worked the rest of the afternoon. Then his mom had invited Amy to dinner that night, and the three of them had shared a can of Del Monte green beans and a lovely chicken dish with crushed Fritos on top. Rose was the queen of casseroles. Afterwards, he and Amy had walked over to the bookstore.

He joined her at the register while she finished paying, then they headed out the door and back toward Rose's house.

"Any plans to shoot somebody any time soon?"

"Nope. I'm not really serious about a gun. I don't even know why I'm looking."

"Well it's okay with me if you think you need one." She reached over to take his hand and laced her fingers with his. "Maybe I'll get you one for a wedding gift."

"That is so romantic."

Sid said it to be funny, but at some deep level it was true. He'd first been attracted to Amy because she was a really good runner for a girl, and because she was cute. But he'd fallen in love with her for better reasons. Because she was wonderful and confident, and complete on her own. She didn't need Sid to make her happy, but she was happier when she was with him. And vice versa.

"I really admire Bertie's mother," Amy said, and to Sid it came out of the clear blue— a pin that popped his bubble of thoughts about guns and girlfriends and love.

"Yeah?"

"Yeah, I do. Your mom said at dinner that she drove Mrs. Jones to the airport today to fly back to Phoenix again and help with that new women's shelter. I know what she did in the past was wrong, but she's trying so hard to help people today. To do the right thing."

"Maybe."

"What's that mean?"

"It means that it's nice she does all that work for abused women. But is she doing it because it's the right thing to do, or is it all about guilt?"

"Does it matter?

"Not to me, and not to the women at The WAVE or any other shelter. But it matters for Mrs. Jones. If she's doing it because it's the right thing to do, that's fine. But if it's just out of guilt, I don't know. I don't think you can *earn* your own forgiveness."

Sid Bigler was not given to profound thoughts, but that one was pretty good. Both of them walked the rest of the way to Rose's house without saying anything.

Chapter 43

"I'm sorry, Mr. Kakavetsis doesn't see anyone without an appointment."

It was Thursday afternoon and that's what the receptionist had said at first. It may have been true, but Sid had insisted she let the man know that *'someone named Sid Bigler'* was waiting to see him. The woman had disappeared through a doorway, then returned shortly and said that Mr. Kakavetsis would be available in a few minutes.

It was a good ploy. If Donny Kakavetsis really had nothing to do with anything that had happened in the last few weeks, he probably would've just had the receptionist get rid of him. But that hadn't happened. Sid's name apparently meant something to the president of ABC Enterprises, and he would soon find out why. Stokes and Jock Bell had both warned him to stay away from the man, but here he was anyway.

Sid paced around the waiting room wearing what he was sure was a very sharp private detective ensemble. The turtleneck was back, topped by a Levi's jacket. The offices of ABC Enterprises were on Del Paso Boulevard. Not one of Sacramento's exclusive neighborhoods and not at all what Sid expected. Everything he'd heard about Kakavetsis had produced an expectation of wealth and power. Especially power. But the building he worked out of was, frankly, a dump. The businesses on each side were a used RV dealership and a very tired looking donut shop. Assuming the two cars out front belonged to Kakavetsis and his receptionist, it was hard to tell which was which. Did Donny drive the '79 Ford Fairmont or the slightly newer VW Rabbit?

Sid was staring out the front window watching a grubby looking guy push a shopping cart that surely contained all of his worldly possessions when the phone on the receptionist's desk rang. She picked it up, listened, then said, "You can go in now."

At first glimpse, Donny Kakavetsis was far from imposing. Sid decided right away he was the spitting image of Captain Kangaroo. Yes, Donny was bald on top, just like Jilly Boyd had said, and the eyebrows were a little out of control. But he was Captain Kangaroo all the way. Give him the fake military outfit and a wig and they'd be twins.

"Mr. Bigler, what can I do for you?"

The man sat behind a desk as modest as his offices. The corners of his mouth went up and some very nice teeth became visible, but no warmth was conveyed.

"Mind if I have a seat?"

"Please." Kakavetsis indicated a chair across from him.

"Thanks." Sid sat and tried to find a way to ease into a conversation. "Nice place."

The pseudo-smile didn't move, and Sid quietly kicked himself for a stupid opening line. Not even that bum with the shopping cart out front would have been impressed by the offices of ABC Enterprises. Kakavetsis waited, and each passing second made *"nice place"* feel increasingly lame.

"I'm a private investigator," said Sid. He didn't know where he was going with this, but he desperately needed to say something that might rescue his credibility. "I'd like to ask you a few questions."

Donny gave him a little half-shrug half-nod that implied, 'go ahead,' but still said nothing.

"Did you know Tom Trager?"

"The city councilman."

"Yes."

"I knew him."

Well, assuming Jock had told him the truth the day before, so far Kakavetsis was telling the truth, too, though he certainly wasn't volunteering anything. It struck Sid that the guy was very much like his offices—plain, unimpressive, a little boring. Sid had been warned several times to stay clear of him, but what was the big deal? Kakavetsis was, at best, bland.

"I was there in the bar with some friends a few weeks ago," said Sid. "The night Mr. Trager was shot."

"Must have been scary." Captain Kangaroo on Quaaludes.

"Do you have any idea who shot the councilman or why?"

"What are you saying? That I was somehow involved?"

Still zero emotion attached to Kakavetsis' words. No surprise. No affront. No fear. Sid unexpectedly began to feel the needle move on his creep-o-meter for the first time.

"No. Just asking if you know anything about it."

"I don't."

"You know anybody who might know anything?"

"I don't."

Sid didn't have anywhere else to go from here. He'd hoped to get some bit of information—even just a reaction—

that might lead him to other questions. But Donny Kakavetsis was like a statue. They stared at one another, and Sid's meter clicked up another couple of notches. Then it was the president of ABC Enterprises turn to ask a question, and his words came out so softly that Sid barely heard him.

"What happened to your eye?"

The same expression that was not quite a smile returned to Kakavetsis' face, and he waited for an answer. The room was quiet, and suddenly uncomfortably warm. Sid shifted in his chair

"It… it was an accident." He struggled a bit to get the words out.

"Looks like it hurts." Calm. Void of concern.

Sid could think of no response, so he said nothing. He waited. His breathing grew shallow and he could hear his own heartbeat pounding in his ears.

"And what happened to your neck?"

Sid subconsciously reached up to touch the line that the German's knife had made. And when his hand felt the fabric of his turtleneck, he understood everything. Kakavetsis couldn't see the wound, but he knew it was there. Sid made no attempt to hide his fear. His eyes grew wide and his jaw went slack, and in his mind he thought he could hear the message that Donny Kakavetsis was sending: *'I did that to you. I could do it again.'*

Sid had seen the devil, and he looked like Captain Kangaroo.

His hands were shaking as he drove. He had no

destination in mind. The only thing that mattered was that he was no longer in that office. No longer in that man's presence. He tried hard to convince himself that the encounter with Donny Kakavetsis was not what it seemed to be. Hell, plenty of people knew about his fight with the German, right? Word had gotten around. Kakavetsis must have heard about the wound on Sid's neck, right? And just because he knew it was there didn't mean he was responsible for it, right?

Right?

He thought about the last words Kakavetsis said to him before he left the creepy, boring office.

"You and I will never speak again, so let me give you some advice before you go." His voice still flat, almost disinterested. *"Someone like you has no business talking to someone like me. You understand?"*

Sid hadn't really understood at the time, but he nodded anyway.

"Good. I suspect that you know enough to know that I had an arrangement—a professional relationship—with Councilman Trager. And I hope you know enough about me to tell no one else about this conversation."

Sid had nodded again.

"Good. Here is all you need to know. I had no reason to hurt Trager. I paid him for a service, and he delivered what I asked. I was getting what I wanted from him. Why would I want him eliminated?"

Sid would think about that later, and it would make sense. But for the moment, all that mattered was his foot on the gas, his hands on the wheel, and each passing mile that put him further away from Donny Kakavetsis.

Chapter 44

Rose Bigler laughed out loud again, but her son didn't crack a smile as he sat next to her on the couch. It had been a long time since Sid had hung out with his mom on a Thursday night and watched her favorite shows with her. He usually really enjoyed the evening, but tonight Cliff Huxtable and Alex P. Keaton couldn't get him out of his funk. For nearly an hour he had been staring in the general direction of the television, dutifully keeping his mother company, while his mind was elsewhere.

No doubt about it, the meeting with Kakavetsis had him rattled. He told himself that he wasn't really scared anymore. Just distracted. Just preoccupied with the case. But he knew deep down that wasn't it. Hell, what was *'the case,'* anyway? The Trager murder? Martini and the German? Bertie Jones' secret identity? No. There was no case. Except for Nathan Bomke, nobody was paying him to do anything.

Meredith Baxter-Birney, the TV mother, said something Sid didn't hear, and his real-life mother laughed again on the sofa next to him.

In the absence of hard evidence, Sid was forced to play the *'What if?'* game. He hated *'What if?'* What if Donny Kakavetsis was telling the truth earlier? What if he really had nothing to do with the murder of Tom Trager? Did that mean he also had nothing to do with the murder of Lou Martini a few days later? Not necessarily. Yes, Trager and Martini were somehow connected by those checks that

Woody had found, but maybe it was nothing. What if the killings of Tom Trager and Lou Martini were completely unrelated. What would that mean?

On the television, the girl who played Mallory was saying something about having a higher I.Q. than Alex, and Sid actually managed to pay attention for a moment. He'd always thought she looked a little like Amy. She was younger and her hair was longer, but pretty close. He glanced over at his mom, who sat completely entranced by the show, and he envied her. He would have loved to escape—to spend a happy half-hour with the Keaton family—but the thoughts that raced through his head wouldn't leave him alone.

What if Donny Kakavetsis really *was* responsible for the death of Lou Martini? Kakavetsis was known to use the German's services, but what would have been the reason? Why have Lou killed? And if he had sent the German to kill Lou Martini, had he also sent him to visit Sid at the deli that night, too? Kakavetsis had certainly sent that vibe, hadn't he? What if? What if?

Sid's thoughts hit a familiar and frustrating dead end, and he balled his hands tightly into fists and fought the urge to shout out loud. *Dammit!* How many times had he thought this through, always ending up at one dead end or another?

Rose got up from the couch and headed for the kitchen. The show must have ended, because now Brooke Shields was on the television talking about Calvin Klein jeans. After her came a commercial for the all new, completely ugly Ford Escort EXP.

"I'm having a dish of ice cream," Sid's mother called from the doorway. "Want one?"

"No, mom. Thanks."

Sid thought again about the night the German had very nearly killed him. What was it he had said? *I was only supposed to scare you, but now I think maybe you die.* Sid had almost forgotten about that. Someone had sent the German, not to kill him, but to frighten him. What did that mean?

Rose returned to the living room with two dishes of ice cream and handed one to her son. Cherry vanilla. He took it from her and smiled for the first time that evening.

"Thanks."

"Mothers know when their sons need ice cream."

They sat side by side, bowls and spoons in hand, and the cherry vanilla began to work its magic. When *Cheers* came on, Sid finally managed to allow his mind to let go of the meeting he'd had with Donny Kakavetsis. He sat next to Rose and he ate his ice cream, and eventually, Sam and Norm and the gang began to carry him away to a bar in Boston where everybody knows your name. To that vast sitcom wasteland where American brains go to rest. And atrophy.

It's a cliché, but it's occasionally true. Sometimes you find what you're looking for when you stop looking for it. The show was about half over—Cliff Clavin was convinced he'd grown a potato that looked just like Richard Nixon—when a new thought floated into Sid's head. He wasn't looking for it. It just appeared without fanfare.

He left his empty ice cream bowl on the coffee table, walked to the kitchen and picked up the phone. Woody answered on the fourth ring.

"Hello."

"Woody, it's me."

"Hey, what's up?"

"Anything new on the search for Porky Powell?"

"Oh, I see. This is a *professional* call. I thought maybe this was my friend Sid inviting me to a poker game or a movie."

"Maybe later. Anything new on Porky?"

"A little, yeah. Chico PD found a few more people that say they saw your boy around town a couple of weeks ago, probably not long after he shot Trager. But that's it. No trail leading anywhere else."

"Can you do me a favor?"

"What?"

"Porky's been in the system before. Stokes told me he'd been arrested several times over the years. Some of those went to trial, right?"

"Yeah, I think so."

"Can you go look at his criminal history for me?"

"Sid, I'm sure somebody from the department's been all through that stuff."

"I'm sure they have, too. But I want you to do it again. Pull the files from whenever he's actually been in court and see what you find."

"And what would I be looking for?"

Sid paused to think about what he was doing for the first time. He couldn't really put his finger on what had given rise to his suspicions. He just knew that there was something there.

"You're looking for names. Any interesting names you find that might be attached to one of the cases Porky was involved in. Maybe familiar names."

"C'mon, stop with the secret agent crap. If you want me to do this, what name am I looking for?"

Sid hesitated. He almost said 'Donald Kakavetsis,' but he didn't. He wasn't positive that's where his search would lead him. Besides, in the back of his mind, he could still hear the man's warning— *"...I hope you know enough about me to tell no one else about this conversation."*

"I'm not sure, Woody. But you'll know it when you see it."

Chapter 45

Sid & Eddie's Deli and The Sutter Club are both about two blocks from the beautiful California State Capitol building. They're close together in proximity, but miles apart in style. They're Beer and Champagne. Pretzels and Foie Gras. Buddy Hackett and Audrey Hepburn.

The Sutter Club was born in the nineteenth century when Sacramento was primarily a city of dirt streets populated by countless souls whose hearts had been broken by a Gold Rush that made tycoons of only a handful of people. But the fortunate few who found wealth in Northern California banded together and formed what would ultimately become one of the oldest and most exclusive private clubs in the state—a place where the city's very successful could confirm their place in society by the simple fact that they were members. The club's permanent home—a gorgeous, mission style building at Ninth and Capitol—was finished in 1930, and it reeked of the wealth and power that had walked its corridors for more than fifty years. Of the many proofs of its significance, perhaps this is the simplest and best one: Every single governor of California had been a member.

Sid looked around the dining room and couldn't help but be impressed. The ceiling looked like it was as high as his old high school gym, but this one was covered with rich, dark wood panels and beams. Gigantic paintings on the walls—mostly of the English fox hunt variety—were roughly the size of drive-in movie screens. The terra cotta floor was covered by a plush floral carpet that somehow looked like it had never had food dropped on it. White-jacketed waiters hovered over white-tableclothed tables while members spoke quietly to one another, making deals and telling stories of conquest on a Friday afternoon.

It was in this hushed atmosphere of old money and muscle that Nathan Bomke suddenly threw his napkin on the table and loudly shouted, "You stupid shithead!"

Every head in the Sutter Club turned and looked in their direction, stared for a moment, then returned to the business of business with a slight look of distaste on their faces. Surely this wasn't the first time Bomke had been an embarrassment to them, and Sid wondered how these pillars of Sacramento society had come to let the ambulance chaser into their club. Oh well. Everybody makes mistakes.

Nathan Bomke's outburst notwithstanding, Sid was really enjoying himself. The lawyer had called earlier in the day and asked if Sid could join him there for a lunch meeting to go over the results of Sid's trip to Los Angeles. The one he never took. So he'd left Rose and Joe at the deli and driven home to get his one and only sport coat. Considering what he had to say to Bomke, it was good that they were meeting in a public place. Sid figured the guy would be a lot less likely to go ballistic or take a swing at him.

It occurred to Sid that the conversation leading up to Bomke's outburst had been the precise opposite of yesterday's meeting with Donny Kakavetsis. He'd gone from a dingy, low rent office to an opulent dining room. From a plain looking man who terrified him to a slick and handsome man who was increasingly a joke. Yesterday's meeting was intimidating, but this one was fun. It was Sid Liberation Day. Sid had listened for a while as Bomke postured, or watched as he occasionally got up to go say hello to a member at another table. But by the time their food had arrived, Sid had begun to drop the bomb.

"I'm sure you're good at your business, Bomke," Sid had told him. *"But I'm good at mine, and I don't like to be told how to do it."*

It was the lawyer's first exposure to a Sid Bigler with a backbone, and he wasn't sure how to react.

"You told me what information you needed," Sid had continued. *"It was my job to figure out the best way to find it. I decided there was no need to fly down to Los Angeles to get the answers you wanted. It would've been a waste of my time and your client's money."*

It had felt great to tell the guy to his face that he was all done being bought. As Sid began to recount the story of his phone calls—first to the Anaheim Convention Center, then the Travelodge in West Hollywood, then the Stardust Hotel & Casino in Vegas—he could plainly see the concern and then contempt on the face of Nathan Bomke. Again, the opposite of Donny Kakavetsis.

Sid had actually practiced his closing lines in advance, and when the moment came he had delivered them pretty well.

"Your client, the president of Li'l Starz, is a liar, MrBomke. He lied to the little girl and her parents. He lied to you and me. And he'll lie on the witness stand if you put him there."

And that was the point where the lawyer had thrown

the napkin and screamed at him. As the dining room recovered from his outburst, Bomke just stared at Sid and worked his jaw muscles, fuming. Finally he leaned forward and spoke again in a quiet, even tone.

"You think I didn't know?"

Sid just looked back at him and gave no reaction.

"Are you that god damned stupid, Bigler? You think I'm in business to make the world a better place? I knew about Vegas and I don't give a shit. My client got on a plane and went to Los Angeles to find acting or modeling work for the ugliest kid on earth. He paid for the plane ride and he paid for a hotel in L.A. I gave you the proof, and I didn't hire you to tell me something else!"

As the guy got wound up, he had allowed his volume to creep back up again, and once again a few nearby tables cast glances in their direction. Sid noticed, but Bomke didn't.

"Then you hired the wrong guy," said Sid. "I quit."

Nathan Bomke gave him the nasty glare a little longer, then pushed back his chair and stood up. Apparently he didn't intend to finish his Cobb salad.

"Since you haven't been doing this very long, I'll remind you that anything you learned about my client while you were working for me is privileged information. You understand?"

Sid didn't give him the satisfaction of a response.

"God, you're a moron, Bigler. This could've been easy money for you. My client was here in Sacramento, and he went to L.A. That's the whole story." Bomke buttoned his jacket, then reached down and picked a piece of bacon off his salad and popped it in his mouth. He was getting his swagger back. "In this world, all that matters is where you end up. Nobody needs to know what happens along the way."

A lovely bit of Nathan Bomke philosophy. The way he lived his life and the way he practiced his profession demanded that he elevate his 'ends justifies the means' lifestyle to the status of virtue.

"Thanks for lunch," said Sid.

Nathan Bomke turned and walked out of the Sutter Club. Sid wondered how much it cost to join the place. The food was pretty good.

Chapter 46

There were now only five weekends of bachelorhood remaining, and Sid Bigler was more reluctant than ever to give up his traditional Saturday morning cereal and cartoons. He was increasingly of the suspicion that Danger Mouse and Inspector Gadget would not be a part of married life. But he woke up Saturday with too many thoughts in his head, and decided that a quick run might clear things out. Five or six miles, and the box of Frosted Flakes would still be there when he got back.

It was a great decision. When was the last time he felt this good out on the road? Hardly a hint of pain in his ribs, and that went away after the first few hundred yards. Within a mile he had slipped into that elusive zone where he simply forgot about the elements of the sport—pace and stride and breathing. It wasn't an effort, it was a ride. He would occasionally catch a glimpse of the tips of his shoes out of the corner of his eye as they gobbled up the road below him, and that was the only thing that reminded him that he was running. In those rare moments, it's hard to not say, "Wheeee!"

Mile after mile clicked by. Sid ran up 15th Street and circled Capitol Park four times, passing within a block of the deli with each lap. Then it was over to Old Sac and down along the levee trail until he could cut back over to Land Park Drive and head for home. He backed off as he made the turn onto 3rd Avenue, coasting toward his mom's house. And then he came to a complete stop about a hundred yards short of the driveway. There was a black and white police car in front of the house with its rooftop lights flashing.

The young officer turned out to be very nice, but wasn't able to tell Sid anything useful. All the guy knew was that the head of Homicide wanted Sid at the police station by nine o'clock. He pulled on some sweatpants, swiped on a little Right Guard, grabbed a fresh t-shirt and jumped in the car. It was a short ride downtown, and although the lights and siren were turned off, the young cop hauled ass pretty good. Sid had no watch on, but the anxiety that comes with being late to something important filled the squad car. They stopped at the red curb in front of the station and hurried through the front doors. A clock above the desk said 9:08.

"Sid! This way!"

He turned and saw Woody Carver in jeans and a sweatshirt coming toward him down the hallway. Saturday morning wardrobe at Sac PD. Sid fell in alongside him as they made their way back toward Homicide.

"What's going on?" Sid asked.

"I just got here, too, so I don't know much. But they found Peter Powell," said Woody. "They found your boy Porky."

The two men walked through the double doors to find five detectives sitting at their desks and Lieutenant Stokes standing at the front of the room, studying the familiar notepad in his hands. Nobody was smiling. It looked like a scene from Barney Miller. Minus the jokes.

"Carver. Mr. Bigler." Stokes gave them an empty smile. "Glad you could make it."

Woody took a comfortable seat on the edge of his desk,

but Sid had no idea where to go. He folded his arms and stood near his friend. Casual cool. He only recognized two of the other detectives. Martinez was probably fifty, essentially the second in command, and there was Kaminski, who had worked with Woody the night of the shooting.

"Gentlemen, this is Sid Bigler, he's a private investigator that was looking into the murder of Councilman Trager. He's done some pretty good work and I wanted him here in case he had any thoughts. Sid, you understand this is a confidential police matter."

Sid nodded and tried to look smooth and slightly disinterested. In fact, he was thrilled. Stokes was including him in some serious behind-the-scenes stuff, like he was a heavyweight. He may have looked the same on the outside, but inside he was suddenly Magnum, P.I.

"To varying degrees, you are the people who have been working on the Trager Case. For those that haven't heard, Chico PD called this morning about 6 a.m. They found Peter Powell."

"Is he talking?" It was Sid, the heavyweight private eye, that spoke up.

"Not much," Stokes replied. "They figure he's been dead for at least two weeks."

That got a little chuckle from the boys behind the desks. Sid stuffed his hands in his pockets and decided to keep his mouth shut unless he was asked a question. Stokes continued.

"I'll tell you guys what we know at this point, then I'm open to opinions. But unless somebody's got some information I don't know about, we're probably looking at '*case closed*' for now." The lieutenant picked his notebook back up. "Chico PD got a report yesterday of a smell coming from a house several miles outside of town. It's on Taffee Avenue, out somewhere past the airport. Anybody know the area?"

No hands went up.

"They tell me it's farmland. Not uncommon to find unoccupied houses out there. Nobody's surprised that it took awhile for someone to report something. A couple of officers entered the residence yesterday afternoon about 1 p.m. and found a body in pretty advanced stages of decomposition."

"They're sure it's Powell?" It was one of the younger detectives that asked.

"Yeah. They fished a wallet out of his jeans with I.D., and there was a '74 Mustang parked out front with his name on an expired registration."

"Pricks." Martinez jumped in with an opinion. "They find him early yesterday afternoon, and we don't get a call 'til this morning."

"Go figure," said Stokes. "Anyway, I woke up the Butte County Coroner, and he's confident it's our guy. They haven't done an autopsy or checked dental records yet, but he tells me that, even dead for a couple of weeks, you can tell the guy had a big ol' nose."

"How about cause of death?" Woody asked the question.

"Well, like I said, the coroner doesn't have anything official. But the officers that found him said there was enough heroin and coke in the house for a three-week party.

Some dirty syringes laying around, and a dozen brand new ones he never got a chance to use."

"No surprise," said Martinez. "This guy's been an overdose waiting to happen. Twelve arrests, four convictions. Always drugs."

"Any cash laying around the house?" Sid took a chance with a question he hoped was not as stupid as his first. He had been convinced from the moment he saw Porky in the bar that he was just some poor stooge that was being paid to pull the trigger.

"Yeah, good question." Stokes threw him a bone. "They found twenty-five hundred bucks in an envelope inside a box of Special K."

"Nice that he was taking good care of himself," said another detective, and another laugh worked its way around the room. As it settled down, Stokes took the lead again.

"We got no weapons in the house, no sign of a struggle, no evidence of forced entry. We got a dead junkie and enough drugs nearby to kill him ten more times. And we got newspapers and TV stations and the mayor breathing down our necks wondering why we haven't found the guy who killed a city councilman in plain view of more than forty witnesses. So..." Stokes paused, glanced around at the faces in the room. "Have we got enough to say this investigation is over?"

Sid immediately thought of four or five reasons why they couldn't close the books on this one yet, but ten or fifteen seconds passed in silence and no one said a word. Was that how things worked around here? Stokes had pointed out that they were under pressure to get this murder investigation resolved, and with Porky Powell dead, their job was done. It was all so simple. But surely they knew there were way too many loose ends, right?

"What about a murder weapon?" Woody finally spoke up. At least one of the obvious questions was going to be asked.

"What do you mean?" asked Martinez. "The Lieutenant already said he died of a drug overdose." Either the guy was stupid, or he was just trying to make sure Stokes only heard what he wanted to hear.

"He means the gun that Powell used to kill Trager in the bar," said Sid. "Where is it? You don't have a murder weapon."

"Oh," said Martinez. "I dunno. He threw it in the trash. He sold it to buy drugs. C'mon, we got a ton of people who saw him pull the trigger."

"What else?" asked Lieutenant Stokes, apparently satisfied with the answer.

Once again, Sid was beginning to worry that nobody was going to say anything, but eventually the cop named Kaminski spoke up.

"Doesn't the whole thing seem kind of out of character for this guy to just walk into a bar and kill somebody? He was a loser, but he was small time. Had he ever done anything like this before?"

"Maybe he was high when he did it." Martinez the lap dog again. "He was out of his mind on drugs and he didn't know what he was doing."

"Yeah, that makes sense," said another detective that Sid didn't recognize.

"Oh, come on!" Sid couldn't stand it anymore. "I was in the room when Trager was killed. I looked right at the shooter. He might have been a little strung out, but he knew what he was doing. Jesus, you guys, he yelled, '*Hey! Is Thomas Trager here*?' before he killed him. Is there anybody in this room who doesn't think that Powell was put up to this? That he wasn't paid to kill Tom Trager?"

It was a convincing little speech, and nobody felt the need to answer him. Sid let the question hang in the air for a moment, then wrapped it up for those who hadn't figured it out.

"Woody pointed out that you've got no murder weapon. And if this wasn't a paid hit, then you've got no motive, either. Yeah, you've got your shooter. But there's somebody else out there—a bigger fish—and you don't have him."

A phone rang on one of the empty desks. Nobody made a move to answer it, and after six or seven rings, whoever it was gave up. Sac Homicide fell quiet, and most of the faces in the room looked appropriately concerned. Pensive. Martinez didn't appear to be very happy, and clearly would've have preferred to not have Sid at their little meeting. But Stokes was smiling. It was a surprisingly genuine smile.

"Bigler's right," he said, and began to pace a little at the front of the room, tapping his pen on the note pad. "I have no doubt that somebody paid Powell to kill Councilman Trager. Powell did the job, got his money, and fled to Chico. That explains the twenty-five hundred bucks in the cereal box—a lot of cash for a junkie who hasn't held down a job since who-knows-when. So he got his big payday, then he scored some coke and heroin, but he partied too hard, right? One too many speedballs, and our suspect saves us the trouble of taking him to trial and locking him up for the rest of his life. That's what I think happened. Is that what you think, Sid?"

"Yes," said Sid.

"And so we're left with a question," Stokes continued. "Who paid this low-life to kill our city councilman, right? That's what's missing, isn't it? Okay, everybody, give me your ideas."

It felt like a classroom after a teacher asked, *"Who threw that spitwad?"* No one said a word, and everyone wished that someone else would do the talking. Sid felt a familiar wave of frustration wash over him. Stokes had essentially just asked the question that he'd been wrestling with for over three weeks, and he had to confront the fact once again that he had no idea what the answer was. Who the hell wanted Trager dead—and maybe Bertie, too? Or Sid himself? And what was their motive? Sid looked around the room at the puzzled faces, but took no comfort in the fact that he was not alone in his frustration.

Then he saw Stokes, still looking at him with a knowing smile, and for the first time he put himself in the shoes of the head of Sacramento Homicide. The realization hit him hard. Stokes must have wanted to put all the pieces together at least as much as Sid did. Probably more. He'd been working this case 24 hours a day, had called or stopped by to talk to Sid about it in the evenings and on the weekends, too. *"I got divorced a couple of years ago, and I can't cook worth a damn"* he had said one morning at the deli. His job was his life, and this was the biggest case he'd ever have. And right now it was pretty hard to feel like a hero.

"What about you, Sid?" Stokes broke the silence, and something in his voice confirmed what Sid had been thinking about the man and his life. "Who's the bad guy that's behind all this? Do you know?"

"No," said Sid without hesitation, and the admission was painful. But it was the truth. He could play the *'what if'* game with these guys if he wanted to, but he already knew that it didn't ultimately lead to any solid answers. He thought for a moment about bringing up Donny Kakavetsis just to see if anybody else could figure out a connection, but something kept him from opening his mouth. The thought of the guy sent a shiver down his spine.

"What about Lou Martini?" Woody spoke up, and Sid was thankful for his friend who was not ready to give up. Not afraid to keep trying. "He's the private investigator that was killed three days after Trager. I found that check that indicates he'd been working for the councilman. Does that mean anything to anybody?"

Apparently it didn't. No surprise. Stokes let the group stew for a few seconds, then took the lead again.

"Unless one of you guys has something else, let's wrap this up." He paused but only briefly. The lieutenant was all done taking input. "We know who murdered Trager and we've got him. Everybody in town has been waiting for this department to deliver the little bastard, and nobody's gonna be sorry that he arrives in a box. Martinez will write up the report, I'll call the Mayor and then we'll make a statement to the press as soon as we're ready. It is officially *'case closed'* for the murder of Councilman Thomas Trager. But listen to me…"

Stokes glanced around the room, carefully making eye contact with every one of his men. Then he looked very deliberately at Sid, and finished his thought without blinking.

"This doesn't mean our job is done. We're doing what we've gotta do, but we're not stupid and I won't be satisfied if this is where the story ends. Anybody in this room figures out what really happened, come talk to me."

Chapter 47

The first time they played was several years ago, and Sid never paid attention to the score again after that. He was clearly a much faster runner, but when it came to mini golf, Amy was a mini-Jack Nicklaus. Fortunately, the suffering was almost over. She had an eleven stroke lead as they approached the final hole of the night.

The day that had begun with news of the pitiful conclusion to Porky Powell's life was ending much more pleasantly. It was late October, but the weather was surprisingly warm and Amy wanted to humiliate Sid one last time under the lights at the miniature golf course before they were man and wife. She smoothly drew back her putter, and with an easy stroke the bright yellow ball rolled straight from the tee into the 18th hole like it was caught in one of those Tractor Beams on *Star Trek*.

"This can't possibly be fun for you, can it?" he asked.

Amy began intently recording her score on the little card using a stubby green pencil, her brow furrowed in concentration. Sid wondered how long it takes to write a 'one'.

"*Really* fun," she said.

"C'mon, it's pitiful. It's embarrassing what you're doing to me. "

"Nope. Fun." Amy tucked the tiny pencil behind her ear. "Your shot."

Sid placed his ball on the ribbed rubber mat, closed one eye and began lining up the first of what would eventually be five strokes.

"So what do you do next?" Amy asked. "Can you really just forget about the Trager shooting and move on?"

Sid had been filling her in on the morning's events while they played.

"Yeah, I guess. Looks like I'm semi-retired for now."

"Hmm?"

"Well, Nathan Bomke fired me yesterday, and today they closed the Trager Case. I'm back to being just Sid the Deli-man."

"I love Sid the Deli-man." She gave him a quick kiss between puts two and three. "Besides, I've got the feeling some big case is gonna walk through your front door any day. Maybe a lost cat. Or some old lady will ask you to help her find her purse."

"Or a supermodel will need a bodyguard while she's in town for a bikini convention."

Sid didn't quite let the ball come to a complete stop before making his two final putts and it clunked into the cup.

"This isn't hockey," Amy said.

They turned in their putters, got a couple of Cokes and a bag of Peanut M&M's, and settled at one of the outdoor tables. He watched Amy as she watched other couples enjoying the night together, or the occasional group of noisy kids as they ran by. The whack of aluminum bats rang out from the nearby batting cages. A light breeze came up, lifting a lock of her hair a little and then gently setting it back down.

"What are you thinking?"

Amy didn't answer quickly, and Sid was just beginning to wonder if she'd heard him at all when she spoke.

"Just watching the people. These kids."

There was something about the way she looked—maybe it was the tilt of her head or the slow, deep way she was breathing—that told Sid there was more to it than that. He waited for her, and he was right.

"You think we'll have kids?" she asked.

The question was a surprise. They'd talked about kids before on a number of occasions and she already knew the answer.

"Yeah. Definitely kids," he said.

"If you're a private investigator, will our kids grow up knowing you? Can you promise us that nothing will happen?"

Wow. Someone walking by and seeing the two of them sitting there would have had no idea that Sid had just been run over by a truck. It wasn't exactly a glimpse of the future, but it's fair to say that in that moment, he had an eye-opening, life-changing insight that a marriage ceremony was more than just an excuse for a party, and that when Amy went from girlfriend to wife, her expectations would change. Were already changing. He understood clearly for the first time that his life would not be exclusively his own, and he found the thought simultaneously wonderful and frightening. A moment both clarifying and confusing.

On the one hand, Amy's question was an admission that his life was desperately important to her, and it melted a part of him. Made him want to put his arms around her and make promises about a perfect future that he knew he couldn't guarantee. But at the same time, something inside him felt an urge to reach for the emergency brake. To accept someone else's deep need of you is to relinquish your freedom, and Sid confronted for the first time the decision to let it go. It's a hard thing to do.

"I don't know what to say."

"It's okay." She said it, but it didn't sound okay.

"What's the matter?"

Amy looked at him, and he could see her searching for words. She reached up and gently touched his eye with her fingers. It had been a week and a half since the German had punched him. There was now just a smear of deep, eggplant purple beneath his lower lid, surrounded by some fading shades of greenish yellow.

"That man who did this. Who sent him? Why did they want him to hurt you?"

Sid hadn't told Amy or anyone else about his meeting with Donny Kakavetsis. He thought about telling her now, but didn't. He couldn't prove that Kakavetsis had sent the German, and he wasn't sure that knowing about him would do anything to ease Amy's mind. Ultimately, the only answer he had for her was the truth.

"I don't know."

He didn't want to say it, and it wasn't what she wanted to hear. But there it was. The happy sights and sounds of the mini-golf course went on around them, and the two sat in their private silence for quite awhile.

"You want me to give up being a private investigator?"

"No."

She said it tenderly, with a little sadness. But it sounded

like she meant it.

Chapter 48

The ride back to Amy's apartment to drop her off was a quiet one. It wasn't awkward. There was no sense that something was wrong. It was just quiet. Their kiss at her door was long and somehow important, then Sid drove to his mom's house and sat alone on the porch for a little while before going in.

He closed his eyes, and pieces of the day that was just ending drifted through his mind. Amy had said, *'Can you promise us that nothing will happen?'* Us. As in, *'me and the kids.'* Like the future was already here. The woman who wasn't yet his wife was already trying to protect their children who weren't yet born.

'Who sent him? Why did they want him to hurt you?' Sid's hand subconsciously reached up and touched his eye, just as Amy had done. The pain was gone, but not the threat. To his surprise, he began to feel a twinge of guilt, and it took him a minute to figure out why. Self-examination had never been one of Sid's strengths, but it occurred to him that Amy's question—the one about the kids—had stirred in him his first feelings of responsibility to his family of the future. And now he was feeling like he'd been reckless. Irresponsible. Had he done everything he could to figure out who had sent the German to find him? And whoever it was, had Sid heard the last of him?

Those questions led him back to the conversation he'd had after the meeting at Homicide that morning. Woody had given him a ride home after Lieutenant Stokes had closed the Trager case, and they had a chance to talk through what had happened.

'Case Closed doesn't have to mean Case Solved,' Woody had said.

'Meaning what?'

'Meaning nobody in the department believes we've answered all the questions. Somebody put Porky up to shooting Trager. Which means there's a bad guy that's still out there, right? But what the hell. We're all out of leads, and maybe whoever ordered the hit is satisfied now that Trager's dead. Maybe he'll be a model citizen from here on out.'

'You believe that?'

'Not even a little.'

The weight of the things Sid didn't know was beginning to feel very, very heavy. He didn't know who had paid Porky to kill Trager. He didn't know for certain who had sent the German to kill Lou Martini and to attack him that night at the deli. And he didn't know how it all tied together.

Sid stood up, and something between a sigh and a groan came out of his mouth. He recognized it right away as the sound his father used to make at the end of a long day, but couldn't remember ever making the sound himself before. It sucks to be thirty-two.

As he headed into the house, he decided that he'd done enough thinking for the day. It was exhausting, and all the good brain cells were ready to call it a night. Maybe some of the puzzle pieces would magically fall into place tomorrow. Rose must've already gone to bed, as the place was dark and quiet. Time to rummage around the fridge and then see if there was a good movie on TV. Or even a lousy movie. Whatever. As long as he could space out a little.

On the way to the kitchen, he spotted the note on the dining room table. Big, curvy cursive handwriting that didn't look familiar. Feminine handwriting. He picked it up and read it. It was short and to the point—only three sentences—but it was enough to ruin his plans for the rest of the evening.

Chapter 49

Dear Sid,

Would you please stop by my house tomorrow afternoon at 2PM?
We need to talk. Your mother will be there, too.
Sincerely,

Mary Jones

———————

The note was still sitting on the dining room table back home, but Sid had read it enough times last night that he had it memorized. He wondered again what it meant as he took a seat in Mary Jones' living room. What the hell was this about?

It was his third trip to the house this month, and the first two visits had been extremely memorable. Memorable like a yeast infection. Exactly two weeks ago he'd snuck in the bedroom window and ended up on the floor behind the couch with his heart pounding and a cat on his face. And the last time he sat in this room—Mary's tearful confession of child abduction—was one of the most uncomfortable moments of his life.

So it was with a mix of fear and curiosity that he sat in the familiar chair next to the sofa and looked at the other faces in the room with him.

Sid had woken up that morning with the same question running through his head that had caused him to lay in bed and stare at the ceiling until almost 2 a.m.—*What did Mary Jones want?* She was the one who had pleaded with him and Gloria to keep her secret hidden. You'd think the woman would've been happy to never lay eyes on him again. Out of sight, out of mind. And the weirdness of it was magnified by the timing. Just as the cops were ready to close the books on the shooting of Councilman Tom Trager, the mother of Councilwoman Roberta Jones wanted to talk again. Surely a coincidence, but it gnawed at him.

Rose had already left for church by the time Sid got up, so he and Frampton had watched the Bears trash the Vikings while they waited for her to return. The note had said his mom was invited to the meeting at Mary Jones' house, and he assumed they'd ride there together. But Rose had called a little before noon to say she was having lunch with some friends from church, and would meet him at Mary's.

"What's this about, mom?" he had asked her. *"What does she want?"*

"I'll see you at two," she had said.

So Sid had arrived alone, expecting to see only his mother and Mary Jones. But when he walked in the door, the mystery took another turn. One that would've kept him awake even later last night if he'd known. His sister and Bertie were waiting for him, too. It was like a surprise party. A crappy one with no cake and no presents.

It also felt a little like a trap. He was clearly outnumbered, and it wasn't just that it was four women and one man. The others in the room had something else in common. It was unspoken, but it was obvious. They all knew what this meeting was about, and he didn't.

348

After some of the phoniest and most perfunctory small talk in world history, the five of them were now seated in the living room. By the way the room was arranged, it was clear that somebody had a plan. Sid sat in the middle in the same upholstered chair he was in the day of Mary's confession. To his right were Gloria and Bertie on a couple of dining room chairs that had been brought in and set across from the coffee table. To his left were his mother and Mrs. Jones seated on the sofa. It was a nice setup for a conversation, but nobody was talking.

"Well, here we are," said Sid, feeling the need to fill the silence. "Mothers on the left, daughters on the right."

Not actually funny, but it broke the ice and the ladies all smiled and took a breath. He almost added, *'Widows on the left, lawyers on the right,'* but decided that he'd done enough. Time to wait and see what happens.

"Thank you for coming, Sid," Mary Jones began, and it sounded rehearsed. "I really appreciate it."

"Sure."

"You must be wondering what this is about." The woman had a gift for understatement. "The four of us met here together yesterday afternoon and had a long talk. We said things that should have been said a long time ago. It was a really good conversation, and it never would have happened if it wasn't for you."

Mary paused and looked at the other women in the room, each of whom was looking back at her. Hopeful. Reassuring. Bertie didn't move, but Gloria gave her friend's mom an encouraging nod. Rose reached over and put a hand on Mary's lap. It seemed obvious where this was

349

going, but Sid wasn't about to open his mouth until somebody else said it.

"I told her," said Mary. "I told Bertie the whole story."

She offered Sid a fragile smile, and as if on cue, the other three women in the room turned and looked at him and waited. Apparently it was his turn.

Sid, however, had no idea what part they expected him to play in this drama, and didn't know what to say. He looked at their faces, one by one, left to right, until he came to the one with the green eyes and the tiny cleft in the chin. How do you react when you find out your parents are not your parents? That you are not you? This was the first time he'd seen her since their meeting in her office when her spell had been broken, and she didn't look like the same woman. Jeans and a Bruce Springsteen t-shirt. Her hair was loose around her shoulders, and she wasn't wearing any make-up. The last time he'd seen her without make-up she was selling Girl Scout cookies with his sister.

He expected to feel nothing at all, but he discovered to his surprise that he had overestimated the degree to which he was *over* Bertie Jones.

For only a moment, it was the summer of 1963 again and he was looking at the face that had stirred in him something that, once awakened, could never go back to sleep. The manipulative and powerful attorney and politician was gone, and she was once again as pure and simple as the girl who had opened her eyes in the moonlight, laying in his sister's bed when he was ten years old. Then, like a video on fast forward, moments of his secret life with Bertie Jones began to flash by. He was twelve and Bertie was laying out

350

in their back yard with his sister wearing a red bathing suit. He was fifteen, finding and studying every photo of Bertie in their high school yearbook. He was eighteen, visiting his sister's college dorm room when Bertie walked out of the bathroom wearing only a towel. He was alone in his room, somewhere in his twenties, thinking about Bertie Jones in the dark...

"Sid, she knows everything."

It was his sister's voice that startled him, pulling him from the past and back to the present. He had a brief moment of panic. *She knows everything.* Of course Gloria meant that Bertie knew everything about her own past now, but for a second, Sid misunderstood. For just a moment he thought Bertie knew everything he'd ever thought and felt about her, and his face flushed red and he looked away.

"It was Mary's idea, Sid," his mother said. "And she wanted you to know that everything's okay now. Everything's fine."

"Is it?" Sid looked first at the two older women seated on the sofa, then once again at Bertie Jones. "Is everything fine now, Bertie?"

Everyone in the room had spoken except for the person whose life had just been turned inside out. He saw that the famous green eyes were a little puffy. Bertie had done some crying in the last day, but she was composed now. Her answer was calm and deliberate.

"Yes and no. I'm glad to know the truth. Believe it or not, I think the truth is really important." She smiled, and he knew the words were just for him. An apology, perhaps, for the way she'd treated him in her office the last time they were together. "I'm glad my mom doesn't have to hide anymore. Doesn't have to live her life afraid that somebody will learn her secret."

"What about *your* life? It's your secret, too."

"I don't know. It feels like it's somebody else's life, really. I remember that dad was violent." Bertie looked at her mother. "It was terrible, but it was just the way things were. Mom and I never talked about it, even after he died." She turned back to Sid. "But the things that happened when I was little—when I was in Florida—I don't remember any of it. When mom told me, it was like she was talking about another little girl. Somebody else's little girl. Not me. I'm sorry for what my mother went through, but I don't know... I feel like it doesn't change who I am."

At that point, Mary began to sob—the first tears of the afternoon—and Rose put an arm around her. Bertie got up and squeezed next to her mom on the sofa. Sid watched them for a little while, then turned to his sister. Gloria met his gaze. In the clear, unspoken language of brothers and sisters, his expression said, *'What do I do?'* Gloria offered no help.

Mary's sobs faded. She pulled a Kleenex from a dispenser on the coffee table and wiped her eyes and nose.

"So, what happens next?" Sid asked.

"Well, that's why I invited you here," said Mary, still sniffing and wiping. "What happens next is entirely up to you."

Sid must have looked more confused than usual.

"Besides the four of us," said Gloria, "you're the only other person who knows the story. We've talked about it, and we don't think there's any reason anyone else needs to know. If it was up to us, we'd like to keep this whole thing a secret. But that'll only happen if you agree to keep the secret, too."

And so the reason for the note—the reason for the meeting—became clear.

This was a conversation that Sid and Gloria had already had. That morning a week ago in the bakery, when they were first suspicious of Bertie's past. *"So who does it hurt if we don't say anything?"* Gloria had asked. *"Bertie and her mom have a good life. Both of them. Who does it hurt if we keep quiet?"* The question hadn't changed now that Bertie knew the truth.

The four women in the room looked at him, waiting for his permission to bury the past and get on with their happy lives. Why is it that so many people in world history have sought power over the lives of others above all else? For Sid, it was an awful thing. A terrible burden that he had no desire to carry.

"I won't tell anyone."

Mary began to cry again and embraced her daughter. Rose inexplicably got up and gave Sid a big proud hug, as though her son had done something noble. She had it all wrong. He had, in fact, done the *easy* thing, unsure if it was the *right* thing or not. But there was comfort in the thought that Mary Jones might now find some of the peace that must have eluded her for more than thirty years. To have carried that secret alone for so long, waking every morning and not knowing if the truth would find her that day and snatch her child away. Even today, as she worked to establish another WAVE women's shelter in Phoenix, knowing all the time that her past might undo everything. Sid couldn't imagine.

Bertie looked at him, with her mother's face buried in her shoulder, and said, "Thank you."

"Before I go," Sid said, "can I ask a question of the attorneys?"

The mere mention of the word 'attorney' is often enough to suck the joy out of a room, and it had that effect now. Rose sat back down on the sofa. Bertie and her mom untangled themselves. Gloria looked at him with concern.

"If we know what we know and we don't tell anyone, are we breaking the law?"

Awkward pause.

Sid's mom looked at him with the same look he used to get when he was a kid and he burped at the dinner table. "Don't be ridiculous," she said, then turned to her daughter for help. "Gloria, tell him that's ridiculous."

Awkward pause number two.

"Bertie's the criminal defense attorney," Gloria said, and all eyes turned to the woman whose name had once been Anna.

Bertie looked at Mary, then reached up and gently pushed a loose strand of hair away from her mother's face.

"Kidnapping and transporting a child across state lines. It's a federal crime and there's no statute of limitations." She said it tenderly, almost apologetically. "And to withhold knowledge of a crime like that from the police… that's a felony, too."

"But it was all so long ago," protested Sid's mother. "Surely nothing would happen today."

"I don't know," said Bertie. Then she looked at Sid.

"You told my mom that the woman who gave birth to me is dead."

Sid nodded.

"That might make a difference," Bertie continued. "And they'd look at mom's life, the work she's done with women's shelters. I don't think they'd prosecute."

"Fine," said Sid. "But back to my question. Just to be clear, I asked if we—all of us—were breaking the law with our silence, and it sounds like the answer is 'yes.'"

"Yes," said Bertie.

"But no one will ever know," added Gloria.

"Right," said Sid.

And that was the conclusion of the mysterious meeting at Mary Jones' house. A thirty-two-year-old secret would remain hidden. Assuming everyone could keep their mouths shut, it was the end of the story.

Chapter 50

Except it wasn't. Not for Sid. Something inside him knew it wasn't the end.

He struggled to focus. Fragments of thoughts, clues that were just beyond his grasp, faint impressions of people and places popped uninvited into his mind as he drove home from Mary's. He had to clear his head.

He parked in front of his mom's house, hurried in and threw on some running clothes. He noticed the hole was getting bigger where the big toe on his left foot rubbed the inside of his Adidas. Same spot as always. On the way out he saw the light flashing on the answering machine and very nearly chose to ignore it, but curiosity got the better of him.

"Sid, it's Amy. Wanna grab dinner tonight? I'm craving some Jimboy's Tacos. Love you. Call me." Click.

He was smiling as he took off down the street. Amy sounded good. Whatever had happened at the mini golf course last night, everything was fine today. He ran at a quick but comfortable pace until he got to the levee, and then it was time to crank it up. He picked out a tree about two hundred yards ahead and sprinted until he reached it, then coasted along, filling his lungs with air and blowing it out for thirty seconds or so. Before he had completely recovered, he picked another tree farther down the trail and took off again. He repeated the pattern exactly twenty times, counting them until he was drenched with sweat and his lungs and legs were burning. Then Sid laid down flat on his back on the trail, looked up at the late afternoon sky and waited to feel good again. As always, it was an almost out-of-body experience. In small or large doses, the euphoria that followed the pain was his addiction. Too bad there was no other way to get the feeling.

After a few minutes, Sid got up and started back down the trail at an easy jog. His mind was clear, and he slowly began to think in an organized way about what had transpired at Mary Jones' house just a little while earlier. The room was full of happy tears and hugs as he left, but something hadn't seemed right. What was it?

Part of it was simply the lack of justice. Yes, Sid had agreed that it was best for everyone—especially Mary—to leave the past alone. What would be accomplished by going public with the story now, other than the destruction of a fine woman's life and work? But still, something terrible, something unforgivable was done in Miami in 1953, and no one would ever answer for stealing a three-year-old child away from her real mother. It was a depressing truth, but probably not the primary thing that troubled him. He could set that thought aside.

What else? Gloria had said something during the meeting at Mary's that had bothered him. What was it? Right about the time they were asking him if he would keep their secret, his sister had said, *'Besides the four of us, you're the only other person who knows the story.'* Yeah, that was it. The four women were welcome to think they were the only keepers of the secret, but Sid was skeptical. First of all, there was Vic Meyers, the Dade County Recorder. Vic wasn't positive that Bob and Mary Jones had switched the little girls, but he clearly had his suspicions. Then again, who was

Vic going to tell?

That was the question that caused Sid to suddenly stop running and stand on the levee trail, his arms hanging at his sides and his eyes wide open. How could he be such an idiot? How could he have forgotten?

'You're not the first person to ask about Roberta Jones this year,' Vic had told him. Somebody else had called him, looking for information about Bertie. Somebody who knew her date of birth and knew where to go for answers.

Sid rolled back into a jog, but his entire body felt heavy. Maybe it was the weight of the sudden, sure knowledge that Mary and Bertie's happy ending wasn't going to last. No doubt about it.

He picked up the pace a little and went back to asking questions. Who else would have been looking into Bertie's past? Who had a motive to do it? Who had the skills to trace the Jones family back to Miami in 1950?

Sid stopped in his tracks again. *Son of a bitch.* He was no longer running, but his heart was hammering in his chest. How could he not have seen it before? A cub scout would've figured this out by now. Vic Meyers had told him that someone else had called asking about Bertie's past early in the year. *'Maybe ten months ago.'* And Woody Carver had told him that Lou Martini had been working for Tom Trager. It was about ten months ago that Lou had cashed that first check. It had to have been Lou who had tracked Mary and Bertie Jones back to Florida.

Sid heard the gravel crunching underneath his feet, and discovered that he had started walking. He couldn't remember making the decision to get moving again, but no matter. Maybe it was just hard to stand still while his mind was racing.

If he was right about Lou being the person who had been snooping around in Florida, it meant that before Councilman Tom Trager was murdered, he had hired a private investigator to discover the secret past of Bertie Jones.

Okay. So what? What did Sid know about Trager? He was a philanderer and an asshole. Everybody knew that. He played hardball in business and in politics. And it wouldn't be at all surprising if he made an effort to dig up some dirt on everyone who stood in his way. It wouldn't be the first time that a powerful, unscrupulous creep paid for information he could use to leverage his enemies. Hmmm. That was an interesting thought.

Sid took a deep breath and realized that, if he was right, he had figured out something that no one else on earth knew. At least, no one who was alive. Tom Trager and Lou Martini would have known, of course. But they were both dead. Spooky.

His stomach growled, and he remembered Amy's voicemail. Tacos sounded good, and he took off running again. He found a nice stride and relaxed a little.

Sid allowed his mind to wander. Names and faces of suspects and victims floated randomly through his head. He thought about Porky Powell lying dead on the floor of a farmhouse in Chico for two weeks while cops all over Northern California looked for him. He flashed on Donny Kakavetsis' face and wondered for just a moment if he was somehow tangled up in all this. He pictured tall, handsome

Nathan Bomke and short, ugly Mandy Mercer standing side by side before a judge and almost laughed.

Then he thought about Amy and the wedding, now thirty-six days away, and he picked up his pace to make sure he got back in time to join her for dinner. She loved him enough to be worried about his future, because his future and hers were the same now. He thought about what she'd said last night as she reached up and touched his eye. *'That man who did this. Who sent him? Why did they want him to hurt you?'*

Sid felt again that twin stab of responsibility and guilt. And then another piece fell into place.

The German. The German. The German.

He didn't stop this time, but he subconsciously slowed down as it hit him, shaking his head at what a lousy detective he was. It was another thing he would have realized days ago if he'd been smarter. He didn't know who had sent the German, but there was something obvious that his victims had in common: Lou Martini and Sid Bigler had both gone in search of Bertie Jones' past. The German had killed one of them, and he could have killed the other. But he didn't.

The rest of the day was, by any objective standards, wonderful. Sid showered when he got home, picked up Amy, and they had what both agreed were the best tacos ever at Jimboy's. Over dinner, he told her the cheerful version of the day's events—the one where the women cried happy tears and everyone agreed to keep their secret. He had to tell Amy. She knew anyway.

After dinner they walked hand in hand by the pond in Land Park. They stopped and watched as a beautiful young family fed scraps of bread to the ducks, and had a sense that they were seeing their own future. The goodnight kiss in the car lasted fifteen minutes, and on several occasions Amy giggled and told her fiancé to behave himself.

Sid drove home, still tasting Amy's lip gloss and savoring what had been a perfect evening. He flipped on the radio, found Steve Miller singing *'Jungle Love,'* and cranked it up. It had been a day of highs and lows, but it was ending well.

And yet something wasn't right. It was in the background, like a white noise you can sometimes tune out, but it's always there. He thought again about Bertie and her mother, and wondered what they must be feeling at the end of this day. He thought about Lou Martini and Tom Trager and Dieter Hoffman. Some big pieces of the puzzle had begun to come together this afternoon as he ran along the levee, Sid was sure of it. So what was wrong?

'We live in a world of illusion,' sang Steve Miller, *'where everything's peaches and cream…'*

Here's the thing about a puzzle that's only partially completed: Every new piece that fits into place is exciting. With each piece, you see more of the big picture. But sometimes, the more pieces you fit together, the more obvious it becomes that some of the pieces are missing. And that's what was bothering Sid. He knew something was missing. He didn't know what it was, but it was huge.

Chapter 51

Another Monday at Sid's Deli, another twelve dozen Brown Sugar Cinnamon Rolls. One hundred forty-four heart attacks waiting to happen. As much as Sid appreciated the increased sales and the fantastic smell, he hadn't actually eaten one of the things since he was a kid.

During the summer in the sixties, Big Sid would occasionally bring his son to the deli with him. The boy didn't like the work much, but his dad paid him five dollars for the day, and Joe's cooking was considerably better than his mother's. Monday's were his favorite day to go, because kids have an almost endless capacity to eat garbage. Almost. One Monday in 1965, twelve-year-old Sid ate four Brown Sugar Cinnamon Rolls, barfed his guts up, and swore he'd never eat another one.

The promise lasted exactly twenty years. Sid got into work the morning after the dramatic meeting in Mary Jones' living room, smelled the butter and the yeast and the sugar, and found it irresistible. Four people stood in line on the sidewalk at 6:52 a.m. waiting for the deli to open as Sid sat down at his desk in the back room with a big glass of milk and his first Brown Sugar Cinnamon Roll in two decades. By the time the doors opened at seven o'clock, the line had grown to nine people and Sid was halfway through cinnamon roll number two. Awesome.

The place was packed from the opening bell and Sid was stuck at the register nonstop for three hours. He did okay for a while, but long before lunchtime he started having vivid 1965 cinnamon roll flashbacks, sweating and feeling queasy. Rose finally arrived to help about eleven o'clock, and Sid returned to the back room, proud of himself for not throwing up. He splashed some water on his face, then leaned over the deep sink and watched big drops fall from the tip of his nose and go thunk on the stainless steel. He was somewhere between seasick and hung over, and like a drunk swearing off the booze, he promised God that, if he lived, he'd never touch another Brown Sugar Cinnamon Roll again for the rest of his life.

Eventually he stood himself up, a little wobbly, but vertical, and something caught his eye. On his desk sat the folder with the name 'Bertie Jones' written on it. When was the last time he had opened it? He'd brought it back from the trip to Miami more than a week ago, and it had been collecting dust ever since. Once he'd learned Bertie's secret, the case was closed.

Sid wiped his face with an apron, slowly walked to the desk and flipped open the folder. The top page was blank except for one sentence at the top. He'd written it on the plane the afternoon he flew to Florida. *'Who would want to hurt Bertie?'* He was asking different questions then. It was a different time. A time when Gloria was worried that her friend might have been an intentional target the night that Trager was shot. No one seemed to be worried about that now. Why? What was different now? Maybe it was a question worth asking again.

Sid sat down, picked up a pen, and said out loud. "Who would want to hurt Bertie?" He ran through the names that had occupied his mind during his run yesterday afternoon.

Lou Martini? No. He might have been investigating Bertie's past, but he had no reason to hurt her. Not his style at all.

Donny Kakavetsis? No. No known connection there. Nothing made sense.

The German? No again. Sid couldn't think of any logical scenario that involved Dieter Hoffman. And besides, if someone had hired the German to kill Bertie, she'd be dead.

Tom Trager? Yeah. It was the same conclusion he'd reached running down the levee trail yesterday. If Trager was the one paying Martini to check Bertie out, surely it wasn't out of concern for her well-being. Sid wrote Tom Trager's name down on the sheet of paper. And as he did it, he heard once again that white noise from last night, the background drone that said something wasn't right.

Sid put down the pen and rubbed his temples. He still felt a little queasy, and playing detective was making his head hurt. The feeling that he was missing something grew heavier. He put his head down on the desk, closed his eyes and waited to feel better.

A phone was ringing somewhere. Sid opened his eyes and tried to figure out why he was sitting at his desk in the back of the deli. He could hear the sounds of a busy lunch through the open doorway, and the clock on the wall said 12:45.

"You gonna answer that?"

Joe had stuck his head into the room, and Sid finally figured out that it was the payphone on the wall by the back door that was ringing.

"Yeah. Yeah, I got it."

As he got up from the desk, he caught sight of the empty plate that had a few smears of greasy cinnamon goo on it and his stomach did a flip-flop. He reached for the phone and leaned against the wall.

"Hello."

"Sid, it's Woody."

"Hey, what's going on?"

"Things were a little slow, so I've been working on that project you gave me."

"Project?"

"Yeah," a hint of irritation in his voice. "You asked me to go through Porky Powell's criminal history, remember? Pull up court records, spend countless hours of my valuable time. Does any of that ring a bell?"

Oops. Sid had forgotten completely.

"Yes. Of course it does." Sid was still half asleep, but doing his best to sound sharp. "I just figured that once you guys closed the Trager case, you would've stopped looking into Porky's records."

"Uh-huh. Well, I promised my buddy I'd do this for him, and I did."

"Sorry if I wasted your time."

There was a very brief pause, and then Woody said, "Maybe it wasn't a waste of time, Sid."

That woke him up. Woody was doing his stoic cop act, but Sid knew him well. He had something big, and he was going to milk it.

"It was just like Martinez said at that meeting the other

day," Woody continued. "The guy was convicted on drug charges four times. Always possession with intent to sell. I looked those cases over pretty good, and there was nothing out of the ordinary and no names you'd recognize."

"Okay," said Sid. Not a very exciting report so far, but he knew something was coming.

"Well, it turns out he had two other cases that went to trial. One in '83 and another one earlier this year. Got off both times. One not guilty and one dismissed on a technicality."

"Lucky guy."

"Lucky my ass. Guess what name shows up in the records of both cases."

"Do I get any hints?"

"Think about it Sid. It's a lawyer. Porky got himself a new lawyer the last two times he got busted."

At some level, Sid probably already knew. There's some place in the subconscious where terrible, uncomfortable facts can hang out for days—maybe years—before walking out on the stage for everyone to see. It's like a Green Room for the truth. Mary Jones was able to lie to herself and keep her terrible truth there for decades. But not forever. And now the big piece of the puzzle that had eluded Sid last night was about to be handed to him.

"Take a shot," the cop prodded him again. "Who do you think Porky's lawyer was?"

"Bertie Jones," said Sid.

"Bingo," said Woody.

Sid sat at his desk a few minutes later, making a little to-do list. He was pretty sure he knew how it all happened, and now it was time to break the promise he'd made to the women yesterday afternoon. What he knew simply could not remain a secret.

He wrote *'Call Stokes'* and *'Call Gloria.'* Then, *'Somebody has to tell Mary Jones.'* It was a short list, but that was all Sid could think of so he set the pen down. There was no good reason to put it off, but he sat there a little longer, enjoying the calm, knowing that once he picked up the phone, he'd be dramatically changing the lives of people he cared about.

And then he thought of someone else to call. It wasn't essential, really. It was just a call he wanted to make, and for some reason it felt right to call him first. The guy deserved to know the truth after all these years.

Chapter 52

The Dade County Recorder answered on the first ring.

"This is Vic Meyers."

"Mr. Meyers, this is Sid Bigler."

"Young Mr. Bigler," he sounded happy to hear Sid's voice. "How are you?"

"I'm okay. Have you got a minute?"

"I do."

In fact, Sid and Vic Meyers ended up talking for nearly an hour. Sid had never fully explained the reason for his interest in Bertie Jones when he was in Miami, so he had to start from the very beginning. It was good for him to tell the whole story from start to finish. It was clarifying. It helped him better understand everything that had happened. Meyers asked a few questions along the way, but mostly listened, fascinated by the tale.

"Well, I'll be damned," the old man said when Sid finished. "I'm so sorry things ended up this way for that little girl. Beautiful little thing. Never met her myself, but I saw the pictures in the paper back then. Just beautiful."

"Yes, sir."

And then Vic Meyers said something so completely unexpected that it blew up everything Sid thought he knew about Bertie Jones and what had happened over thirty years ago. Something that would forever change the ending to the story.

"You know," said the voice on the phone, "that was 1953. There weren't a lot of Cubans in Miami back then."

Huh? At first Sid wasn't sure if he'd heard the man correctly. Had he said something about Cubans? Neither of them spoke for a few seconds, and the background hiss of the long distance connection seemed to grow louder. So did that white noise in Sid's head.

"I'm sorry, Mr. Meyers. What did you just say?"

"Oh, it was much later in the fifties when all the Cubans came here to Miami. That was when Castro took over. But back in '53 there weren't so many. I think that's why I remember that little girl so well."

A shiver went down Sid's spine.

"What did the little girl look like, Mr. Meyers?"

"Oh, she was beautiful. Black hair, and the biggest brown eyes I've ever seen. I'll never forget. Just beautiful."

Chapter 53

"I'll be back in time to close up," Sid said as he brushed past Joe at the grill. Rose Bigler felt her son give her a quick kiss on the cheek before he headed out the front door.

Capitol Park, a forty-acre garden that surrounds the beautiful white-domed seat of California's government, was only a block away. Sid crossed L Street and began walking quickly down the sidewalk that circled the park. He would have run, but the blue jeans and denim work shirt were all wrong. So he walked—rapidly, angrily—and he tried to grasp what he'd just heard.

It had only been a couple of minutes since he'd hung up the payphone in the back of the deli. The whole thing was like something from the *Twilight Zone*. It reminded him very much of a conversation with Gloria from five years ago, when out of the clear blue she called to tell him that their father was dead. He couldn't grasp it. The meaning of the words was unambiguous, but he simply couldn't take it in. It was like that now. Someone had just told him something that couldn't be true. And yet he knew that it was.

"Oh, she was beautiful. Black hair, and the biggest brown eyes I've ever seen. I'll never forget. Just beautiful."

An hour earlier he was so sure he had everything figured out, and now he was more confused than he'd been at any time since Porky Powell walked into the Ancient Moose and, with eight shots from a shiny, nine millimeter Beretta, started the chain reaction that had led him to this place.

A sheen of perspiration covered his face and he was breathing surprisingly hard. He'd gradually begun walking even faster, his body keeping pace with his mind as it raced, trying to catch up with the truth.

What if Meyers was wrong? That was certainly a possibility. After all, it had been thirty-two years. For god's sake, Mary Jones had already admitted to stealing the child, and her daughter, Bertie, was clearly not Hispanic. Shirley Temple looked more like a Cuban than Bertie Jones. Yes, it could all be a mistake. But something about Vic Meyers and his military efficiency told him otherwise. And something in his gut told him the same thing, too. He might have to find some photos of the little girl to be certain. But Meyers wasn't wrong.

Okay. If Meyers wasn't wrong, then what happened back in 1953? Maybe the story that Mary and Robert Jones told at the time was true. Their foster-child—the precious little Cuban girl named Anna—was really the one who died. They buried the girl and, heartbroken, left with their beautiful, blonde, biological daughter. That explanation solved the riddle, except…

Except, if it was true, then Mary Jones was lying today, right? She had sat in her living room a week ago and confessed to Sid and Gloria that she had stolen the foster child after her own daughter died. Why would Mary lie about something like that? It didn't make any sense. But Sid could think of no other explanation that worked for now.

The walking and the sweating and the thinking weren't mixing well with the cinnamon rolls. Sid cut across the grass and headed for a bench by some camellia bushes. No one was around, so he laid down on the bench and rested.

He could feel his pulse thumping on the side of his neck. His chest rose and fell with each breath. But as the seconds passed by his body grew quieter. He let go of his thoughts and relaxed, even thought he might doze for a little while. Lunch hour life went on all around him. Cars honked and birds sang, and somewhere in the Capitol, legislators were selling their votes to the highest bidder. But for Sid the world had become perfectly still.

And that's when it hit him.

His eyes popped open and in his head he heard the words of Nathan Bomke. It was the last thing the lawyer said, standing by their table at the Sutter Club, full of shit and indignation: *"In this world, all that matters is where you end up. Nobody needs to know what happens along the way."*

Sid jumped up and started jogging back toward the deli. Hopefully his mother could cover for him tomorrow morning. It was time to play another hunch. Time to book another flight.

Chapter 54

Sid's plane lifted off the runway of Sacramento Metropolitan Airport Tuesday morning at 7:22. The sun had risen on a cool, cloudless day, and he watched through the window as a mosaic of roads, rivers and rice fields grew smaller and smaller. The valley gave way to the Sierra Nevada mountains, and the mountains gave way to the desert. The flight was less than two hours, but the minutes crawled by and Sid found his confidence ebbing and flowing. If this was a cartoon, there would've been a little angel on one shoulder and a little devil on the other:

'You're a genius, Sid. How did you ever figure this out?'

'You're a dope, Sid. This whole trip is a waste of time.'

He did what he could to distract himself from the head games. He read the in-flight magazine cover to cover. Twice. He doodled on an air sickness bag, producing a remarkable likeness of Mr. Bill from Saturday Night Live and beating himself three times at tic-tac-toe. When the plane finally touched down, he skipped the baggage carousel and grabbed a cab for the twenty minute ride downtown.

And that's how Sid Bigler came to be waiting at the front doors when the central branch of the Phoenix Public Library opened at ten a.m.

A very nice librarian who looked like an older Shirley Partridge guided him to the microfiche viewers, then showed him where he could find the films for old copies of The Arizona Republic. The newspaper had been around for

373

nearly a century, but Sid only needed to go back thirty-two years.

'It was June of 1953 when Mr. or Mrs. Jones called the hospital to report that the foster child, Anna, had died suddenly.'

That's what Vic Meyers had told him the day they'd met in his office in Miami. Sid pulled open a huge filing drawer and began thumbing through the folders of microfiche, digging through history, trying to understand something that must have happened during the summer of the year he was born.

'We drove for almost four months... We didn't want to stay in one place too long because we didn't know if people were looking for us.'

That's what Mary Jones had said the night she'd confessed her sins in her living room. Sid found the files he was looking for, closed the drawer and sat down in front of a viewer. It was just ten minutes after ten o'clock, and it felt like he was the only person in the building.

He placed the first film in the viewer. The thing looked like a small x-ray from the doctor's office, except it was covered with little dark rectangles the size of Chiclets. A negative of a bingo card. With the flip of a switch the screen jumped to life, and as he turned the knobs, long forgotten pages of The Arizona Republic began to flash by. March. April. May. He stopped at June 1, 1953, and began reading.

By the time he reached the end of the first month, he'd gotten into a pretty good rhythm. He figured that what he was looking for would most likely be front page news, so he very carefully scanned page A1 of each edition. After that, he'd skim the rest of the front section, then take a look at

Metro before moving on. It only took him about a minute to eliminate one day's newspaper and get to the next one.

At that pace, it took a little over an hour to get through the first two months. July was just as fruitless as June. He moved on to August, 1953, and saw that nearly record heat was the subject of almost every headline the first week. *"City Scorches: 118 Degrees"* The second week was all about the monsoon rains, with extensive flooding in the *"Central Corridor,"* whatever that was. As August went by, Sid's nagging doubts began to gain the upper hand. This was a wild goose chase.

And then the front page of The Arizona Republic for August 24th, 1953 filled the screen. The headline read: *"Phoenix Girl Kidnapped!"*

He stared at the three words for several seconds, half afraid that they'd vanish. That he'd simply wished them into existence. But the headline was real. Sid closed his eyes, felt a satisfying rush of excitement to have perhaps solved a mystery more than three decades old. Then, almost immediately, he felt a pang of guilt, and the thrill gave way to a deep sadness. He tried to grasp the unimaginable loss. He thought of Niece Nelly and Niece Nicki, and wondered how Gloria and her husband could have survived if one of those precious girls had disappeared, trying each day to not assume the worst, never knowing what happened. Never.

"In this world, all that matters is where you end up. Nobody needs to know what happens along the way."

Nathan Bomke said it again in Sid's head. He opened his eyes and quickly scanned the article. No surprises. He made a note of the number on the slide so he could get a print of the article, then began to carefully read the rest of the newspaper—page by page—for August 24, 1953.

Because there was one more story to be told. There had to be.

But it wasn't there. Not in the front section, not anywhere else. He even took a quick look at the Sports section and the classified ads just to be sure. But there was nothing. His pulse quickened as he twisted the knob to jump to the next day. Tuesday, August 25th. The kidnapping still dominated the front page—no witnesses, no ransom note, hopeful parents, cops going door-to-door and people gathering in churches to pray. But again, nothing in the newspaper about the other story. He couldn't be wrong about this, could he? Sid turned the knob again to reveal the next day's newspaper.

And then he found it—two days after the initial kidnapping headlines—a surprisingly brief article on the second page of the Metro section. Right hand margin, close to the bottom. The words on the screen, written by a long-forgotten reporter in The Arizona Republic newsroom more than thirty years earlier, traveled through time to silence any lingering doubts that may have remained.

Sid Bigler sat in front of the microfiche viewer for another hour, reliving the summer of 1953. Day after day went by. The cops never figured out what happened to the kidnapped little girl. No sightings, no body, no clues at all.

And there wasn't another word about the other story. The one about the other little girl.

"Hello?"

"Hey, Gloria, it's me."

"What's up Little Brother?"

"I need you to do something for me."

"Why don't I like the sound of this?"

"I need to talk to Mary Jones. Tonight. Can you call her and ask her to come to your place? Maybe seven o'clock? And have Marty take the girls to a movie or something. The house needs to be empty."

"I don't understand. Is something wrong?"

"I can't explain right now. I've got another call to make, and they're just starting to board my plane."

"Plane? Sid where are you?"

"I'll tell you when I get there. Just call Mrs. Jones, and tell her to come alone. Can you do that?"

"Yes."

"Good. And there's one more thing I need you to do before I get there…"

Sid gave one final instruction to his sister, and then he made one more call before hurrying down the boarding ramp and onto the plane. He called the Sacramento Police Department.

Chapter 55

The engine was doing that stupid hiccup thing as Sid approached downtown on I-5, making the hula girl on the dash put on quite a show. His plane had landed seven minutes ahead of schedule, and he was more than halfway to Gloria's house when the damn Duster started sputtering and slowing down all on its own. He'd been carefully rehearsing what he was going to say to Mary Jones for the last couple of hours, but now his attention was focused on surviving the drive to his sister's home.

The problem was nothing new. Three or four times in the last year the car had done this, and each time it had miraculously healed itself before Sid could get it to a mechanic. But for the moment, keeping the car moving forward required turning the engine off while rolling down the road whenever it started to sputter, coasting for a few seconds, then re-starting the engine and picking the speed back up until it sputtered again. Eventually, the lime green Dodge turned onto Gloria's street and coasted—engine off— to a stop at the curb in front of her house. He was eight minutes late.

For better or worse, the car troubles had taken Sid's mind off the conversation that was just about to take place. But now, as he started up the path to Gloria's front door, he saw Mary's Continental parked in the driveway and he remembered what he was about to do. He pushed the doorbell button and tried to recall his talking points as he waited.

The moment the door opened, Gloria's face told him something was wrong. Siblings know the look. It was the one that said, *"Dad found out about the speeding ticket."* Sid stepped into the living room, felt the tension in the air, and discovered the reason for his sister's pained expression.

"Look, Sid. Mrs. Jones brought Bertie with her."

Sure enough. Bertie was still wearing her work clothes. Grey suit and lavender blouse. Blonde hair fell at her shoulders in big curls. She looked good.

"Yes," said Bertie. "I stopped by to see my mom on the way home from the office, and she said Gloria had asked her to come by tonight and talk with you about something." She gave him a shallow, empty smile. "So I thought I'd just tag along."

Sid noticed Mary Jones sitting on the end of the sofa, her eyes cast down, looking like a kid waiting outside the principal's office. Surely Gloria had told her to come by herself. But Bertie had shown up and now things were complicated.

"So what's going on, Sid?" asked Bertie. "We asked your sister what this is about, but she wouldn't tell us."

"That's because Gloria doesn't know," he said. It was a night for the truth.

"Doesn't know *what*?"

The question hung in the air. He really had intended to have this conversation with Mary Jones alone—there were still a few blanks to fill in. But what the hell. The moment was here, and Sid couldn't think of a reason to not see it through. The journey that began twenty-six days ago when shots rang out in the bar was about to end. Time to finally answer the question.

Gloria was still standing near the front door, arms crossed with one hand at her mouth, absent-mindedly chewing a fingernail. Bertie's mom glanced up from the sofa and risked eye contact with Sid. She looked afraid.

"I'm going to tell you a story." Sid said it to the room, but he kept his eyes fixed on Mary for the moment. "Stop me if I get something wrong."

Then he turned to Bertie and Gloria, and began.

"It's 1953. Miami, Florida. Robert and Mary Jones have two beautiful three-year-old girls in their home and life is pretty good. Bob drinks too much sometimes. Gets a little violent sometimes. But that's the way it goes, right? It's just life in the fifties.

"Then their daughter dies. Their *biological* daughter, Roberta, dies from meningitis. It happens so suddenly. Bob doesn't handle it well. He drinks, the violence escalates. Mary gets beat up pretty badly for the first time. And deep down Mary thinks she deserved it, because the girls were her responsibility."

Out of the corner of his eye, Sid saw Mary's hands clutch at her stomach, and he wondered if the pain she was remembering was physical or emotional. Or both.

"The other little girl isn't really theirs. Anna is their foster child. But they love her, and they can't stand the thought of losing both girls, so they run. Just a few days after the death of their real daughter, they pack up the station wagon and they run. They go from city to city, slowly making their way across the country, telling the little girl that she has a new name."

"Mom told me all this last weekend," Bertie interrupted. "I know all this."

Sid reached into his coat pocket and pulled out a folded piece of paper—a photocopy of one of the articles he'd found at the library that morning. He handed it to Mary Jones.

"I'm sure you're right, Bertie. I think you do know all this."

Sid looked at the stunning green eyes of Bertie Jones as he listened to Mary unfold the paper. A few seconds passed, and then he heard Mary begin to softly cry. He hated what he was doing, but he couldn't think of any other way.

"Your mom's an amazing woman, Bertie. Starting The WAVE, doing everything she can so that other women have a chance to escape the life that she couldn't. In some ways, it's like she's trying to atone for the sins of her husband all those years ago, don't you think?"

Mary began to sob now, like she had that afternoon with her face buried in Taffy the cat, only louder. The piece of paper slipped from her hand and fell to the floor. Sid bent to pick it up, then stood and faced Bertie again.

"I got to thinking about those trips your mother has been making to Phoenix," he said. "Starting another women's shelter there. The hours and hours of work she's done. Like maybe there was another debt to pay, you know? And then I thought about that drive across the country in 1953, running away from the past with a little girl that she'd stolen."

Sid handed the paper to Bertie. She trembled as she took it, maybe from fear, maybe from anger. Gloria walked over and stood by her childhood friend, and the two of them quietly read the copy of the faded newsprint as Mary Jones wept.

'Child Murdered in Van Buren'

'Phoenix Police responded yesterday afternoon to a call from the AutoLodge Motel on the 800 block of East Van Buren Street. Housekeeping staff reportedly discovered the body of a child upon entering the room to clean it around 1 p.m. The child, a Hispanic female, was reported to be approximately three years old. Police believe the cause of death to be a combination of shaking and blunt force trauma. A Caucasian couple in their 30s had checked into the room more than a week ago, but the motel management claimed to have never seen the child prior to the discovery of her body. A 'Do Not Disturb' sign had been hung on the motel room door, and police estimate the child had been dead for 36 to 48 hours before being discovered. Anyone with information regarding this crime is encouraged to contact the Phoenix Police Department.'

The room had fallen silent. Mary had managed to stop sobbing and was watching her daughter and Gloria read what was written on the page. Waiting. Sid noticed a Barbie Dream House in the corner of the room and smiled. Five or six Barbie outfits lay strewn around it, and at least a dozen tiny plastic high heeled shoes. He heard the toenails of Larry the German Shepherd click across the linoleum of the kitchen floor.

"Anna thought it was a game." Mary Jones spoke for the first time that evening, softly. "She was so smart and funny. We'd been on the road for two months, calling her by her new name every day, but she just thought it was a game. We'd call her Bertie, and she'd say, 'No, that's sissy's name!' And then she'd laugh.

"Bob was good to us while we were driving across the country. Hardly any drinking. He was sweet to Anna. He got frustrated sometimes when she wouldn't let us call her Bertie, but he never hurt her. Sometimes at night, after she was asleep, he got mad at me. But he never hurt the girl."

Mary was still just sitting on the couch. Her eyes were hollow. Distant. Her arms were folded gently across her chest, almost like she was holding a child. Sid and the two other women remained standing, helpless, waiting for the rest of the story.

"That afternoon in Phoenix he was drunk. First time he'd been really drunk since we left Florida. He'd gone out in the morning saying he was going to look for work, but he was back in the afternoon and I could tell it was going to be bad. He said he was sick of Arizona and that it was time to get moving. Told me to pack our things and get Bertie and take her to the car. The little girl ran to him and said, '*I'm not Bertie, I'm Anna.*' And Bob hit her. Not like you hit a child. With his fist. He hit her hard, one time. She landed on the floor, and she didn't move."

Bertie, with tears streaming down her face, started to take a step toward her mother, but Gloria reached out and stopped her, half hugging and half restraining her friend.

"Bob told the little girl to get up, but she didn't. So he picked her up and started shaking her. He was yelling her name and shaking her and shaking her. But she didn't wake up. Then he put her on the bed, and he left."

"Momma!" Bertie pulled away and hurried the few steps to where Mary was sitting. She dropped to her knees and buried her head in Mary's lap. Mary reached down and caressed the blonde hair, but kept looking at Sid and Gloria.

"I laid down on the bed and held her little body close to me, trying to keep her warm. But I couldn't. I was alone in the motel room with her for hours. It got dark, and Anna grew colder and colder while I held her there in the bed. Then I heard the key in the door, and Bob flipped the light on and began gathering up our stuff. He made two trips out to the car, and then he said, *'C'mon. We're leaving.'*

"I got up, still holding the little girl in my arms. Bob took her from me, kissed her on the forehead, and put her gently back on the bed. Then he took my hand and we walked to the car. And when I got in…"

Mary Jones looked down at her daughter, still running her fingers through the beautiful, golden hair. Then she took Bertie's face in her hands and raised it up until the green eyes met her own.

"And when I got in, there you were, Bertie. There you were."

Chapter 56

Sid heard his sister whisper, "Oh, my God," and felt her hand as she placed it on his shoulder. The two of them could only stand and watch as Mary and Bertie Jones confronted the very wicked truth about the moment they first met.

"I'm so sorry, Momma," Bertie said through her tears.

Mary pulled her daughter's face to her own, pressing their cheeks together hard, and said, "No, no, no, no. It wasn't ever your fault, honey. You've got to know that. Nothing was ever your fault." Mother and daughter clutched at one another and cried together for a long time, and Mary quietly said it again and again. "It was never your fault."

There was a terrible beauty about the moment. A tragedy as profound as any that Sid could imagine had brought these two together more than thirty years ago. The secret had somehow stayed hidden for so long, but now it was out in the open, and Mary and Bertie could face it together. For a moment, Sid let himself feel good about what he'd done. He desperately wished that he and Gloria could just quietly walk out the door and leave them alone to console and forgive—and to forget. But that wasn't going to happen. A happy ending wasn't in the cards.

"Bob developed liver cancer a couple of years after we got here."

Mary Jones must have felt the need to finish her story. Her eyes were glassed over and her fingers continued to run absent-mindedly through her daughter's hair.

"He didn't last long, and he continued to drink right 'til the end. And then he died, and I didn't know what to do. I almost called the police in Phoenix. I thought about it every day. But I couldn't. They would have taken Bertie away. Bob was gone, and I'd have been all alone."

A poignant silence filled the room. Mary had devoted her life to helping other women find relief from something that was tragically common—a cycle of violence at the hands of men that they love. But even after her husband's death, the cycle continued in her own life. Robert Jones had passed away in 1956, but it was like he was still there. Still finding a way to hurt her. Sid allowed another few moments to pass before stealing away her future.

"Something happened earlier this year."

His voice broke the silence, louder than he intended it to be. And as Mary and Bertie each came back from whatever place their thoughts had taken them, he finally saw the family resemblance he'd looked for in the past. It wasn't biological, of course. It couldn't be. But it was there in the way they looked at him. The way they faced the prospect of pain. It was the same look of fear that they shared, and the same way they tried to hide it.

"Somebody learned your secret, didn't they?"

"No," said the mother.

A few seconds passed.

"Yes," said the daughter. "Yes."

Bertie reached up and gently brushed her mother's cheek with the back of her hand, then stood and pushed her hair away from her face. Sid noticed for the millionth time in his life that she was beautiful.

"Six months ago, Tom Trager came to my office. I was surprised to see him. We didn't like each other and we seldom agreed on matters that came before the council. He told me he wanted me to change a couple of my votes, and I told him to go to hell. Then he said that he'd hired a private investigator and he knew all about my past." She looked very purposefully at Sid. "I assume you've figured all that out somehow."

Sid shrugged.

"When Trager started talking, it was like a door opened in my head, one I'd kept closed on purpose. I knew he was telling the truth. I was just six when daddy died. I think I only really remember what he looked like because his pictures are still around the house."

As she spoke, she walked to the big window that looked out at the park across the street from Gloria's house, her back to the others in the room. Empty playground equipment was just visible in the light of the streetlamps.

"I've always known that something awful had happened to me. Somewhere, deep inside, I've always known. And I knew my father had done it. When Trager came to my office that day, it all came back. Like finding out that the monster sleeping under your bed when you were a kid has been real all along."

A whimper came from Mary Jones as she sat at the sofa, but Bertie sounded strong and calm.

"So, when did you call Peter Powell?" Sid asked. "When did you arrange to have Trager killed?"

"There's no evidence that ever happened. You'll never

prove it."

"But that's what happened, right?"

No response. Sid's sister started to take a step toward her friend, but Sid raised a hand and she stopped. He waited for a moment, and then he took his best shot. If Bertie Jones had a weak spot, this would be it.

"I think I can connect you to all the players, Bertie. The only question is, was your mother in on it, too?

Sid watched his torpedo hit its mark. Bertie's head snapped toward him. The green eyes narrowed and the nostrils flared.

"That's why I wanted to meet her here at Gloria's house without you around," Sid said. "To see if she was involved in the killings."

The beautiful mask was completely transformed by rage now, and a furious Bertie Jones crossed way too far into his personal space, raising a finger to his face.

"Don't you dare drag her into this! If there's an innocent person in this world, it's my mother. My father was a son of a bitch. I can remember laying in bed at night and hearing him yelling at her." Her voice was loud, equal parts anger and fear. "Did your dad ever beat up your mother, Sid? Did Rose ever have to cover her bruises with make-up so she could drive you to school in the morning? Can you imagine what that's like? Can you?"

Bertie was yelling by the time she asked the question, and when she paused she was breathing hard. Seconds ticked by. He felt her breath on his face, and realized that this was the closest they'd been since they fell to the ground in each other's arms almost four weeks ago, the sound of gunshots ringing in their ears.

"I did it for her!"

She shouted it, loud enough for anyone in the house to hear. It was said more in anger than in self defense. An accidental confession, perhaps. But a confession.

They were still only inches apart. He studied her face. Saw her realize what she'd said. She opened her mouth to say something more, but no sound came out. Then she turned, walked to the sofa, and sat down next to her mother. Her hair brushed his face as she went by.

Bertie took Mary's hand, but the older woman looked like she'd completely checked out. Reliving the story was hard enough. To find out that your daughter was guilty of murder, that must have been too much.

"I just want to understand what happened, Bertie. That's all. I don't want your mother to suffer anymore, and God knows I've never wanted anything bad to happen to you. Tell me what happened and I'll keep my mouth shut. Otherwise, I'm calling the cops right now."

Bertie didn't move. Didn't appear to have even heard what he said. He picked up the telephone on the end table and began to press the buttons.

"Don't."

Sid looked up. Bertie's eyes were closed and her voice was flat.

"Please don't," she said.

He put the phone back in its cradle and waited.

"You said that if I tell you what happened, you won't talk."

"That's right."

"Not to the police. Not to anyone."

"You have my word. I swear to you."

Bertie took a few deep breaths, then opened her eyes and found Gloria.

"What about you, my friend? Can you keep a secret?"

Gloria's sense of right and wrong had always been much more refined than Sid's. For her, this was a bigger dilemma. Sid watched her struggle with the questions that her very healthy conscience was already raising in her mind, and he began to fear that the opportunity was going to pass by.

"Gloria," he said, "would you be willing to act as Bertie's attorney in all this?"

"What?"

"She's your friend. Will you be her attorney if any of this comes to light?"

His sister didn't see where this was going, and didn't answer him.

"Just say 'yes,' Sis. Trust me. Say you'll do it."

"Okay," said Gloria, still confused. "Yes."

"There." Sid turned back to Bertie. "Attorney-client privilege. Gloria can't say a word to anyone about this."

"Clever," said Bertie, and she smiled.

"Thank you," said Sid.

The smile faded. Bertie chewed the side of her lip for a couple of seconds. When she started talking, it was very matter-of-fact.

"If Tom Trager was just trying to ruin my life, I probably would've let him. But he had proof that my mother had kidnapped a child and taken her across state lines. Twice. Not to mention witnessing the murder of one of those children and remaining silent about it for thirty years. He was going to destroy my mother's life."

"So you called Peter Powell," said Sid.

"Yes. I'd represented him in a couple of *pro bono* drug cases. You probably found that out, too. I offered him five thousand dollars and told him where he'd be able to find Tom Trager."

"What about that shot he fired at us? Was that planned?"

"Perfectly, until you screwed it up. I was to stand up and try to warn Trager, just to make it look good in case someone got suspicious. He was supposed to miss me, of course."

"I pushed you into the bullet."

"You were quite the hero, Sid."

"So Porky runs away, but you can't have a junkie know your secret, right? You needed somebody to take care of that loose end. Plus, there was one other person that could tie you to the murder of Tom Trager—the private eye that dug up your past, Lou Martini. Did you have the German kill both of them?

"Yes"

"Where'd you find a guy like Dieter Hoffman?"

"A client referred him to me."

"Who?"

"Someone I've been very helpful to."

"Donny Kakavetsis?"

"Sorry. Attorney-client privilege."

"Of course. And then I started digging into your past, too. You were afraid I'd find the same things that Lou

Martini did, so you called the German again."

"Yes, but I told him to only scare you off because you're my best friend's little brother. That turned out to be a mistake. I should have just had him kill you like the others."

Bertie was still perfectly calm. She said it with no emotion, the same way you'd say, *"I should have ordered the meatloaf instead."* Ouch. It wasn't the kind of thing a guy wants to hear from the woman of his dreams. Sid did a quick, personal inventory and was pleased to discover that her words hadn't hurt him too badly. Then he took another moment and tried to think of any unanswered questions, but he couldn't. A senseless, heartbreaking story that began in Miami in 1953 was coming to a close 32 years later in his sister's living room on the other side of the country. His sister's face conveyed mostly shock, and who could blame her? It was so much to take in.

"So here we are," said Sid. "All the loose ends tied up. I promised I wouldn't tell the cops, and I won't. Gloria is legally bound to keep your secret. Unless your mom wants to turn you in, maybe you got away with it."

At that, Mary Jones stirred for the first time in several minutes. It was like she'd been sleeping with her eyes open, and suddenly awoke. She turned and looked at her daughter with the oddest expression. It was hard to read. She looked sad and tired, of course, but Sid had seen that in her eyes for as long as he could remember. Now there was something more. Something different. He saw a curious blend of compassion and contempt. She was both a mother who loved her child and a woman who hated violence and injustice, and she was struggling to reconcile the two.

Bertie saw it, too, and her calm façade began to slip a little.

"Momma?"

Mrs. Jones let go of her daughter's hand and looked at her for a long time while her competing emotions fought for the upper hand. "Is all of this true?"

Bertie made no effort to reply. There was, after all, nothing to say. Everyone knew it was the truth, so she sat and waited, her veneer beginning to crack. The child returned. Her chin began to quiver and her eyes filled once again.

Eventually, compassion triumphed over contempt and Mary held out her arms. Bertie curled into her mother's embrace, and Mary began to rock her gently as she must have done that first night in the car in Phoenix long ago.

"What are we going to do, honey?" Mary said. "What are we going to do?"

Sid heard Larry the German Shepherd's toenails click across the kitchen floor again, and looked up to see the dog round the corner and walk into the dining room. Mary and Bertie were in their own world, and didn't notice the dog, or the strange man who had walked into the room with him. But Sid and Gloria saw him. Blonde hair and moustache, and a bad corduroy suit.

"Bertie, this is Lieutenant Stokes," said Sid. "My sister left the back door unlocked for him. I think he's been listening in the kitchen for a while."

Chapter 57

Saturday afternoon. Exactly four weeks 'til the wedding. He sat at the curb, both hands on the steering wheel, looking straight ahead and still trying to think of what he was going to say. He'd been there for almost half an hour.

It didn't feel like November. It had to be eighty degrees out, and kids in the neighborhood ran around in shorts and t-shirts. An ice cream truck had stopped a few doors down and was doing a brisk business. In November.

"I'm very proud of you," Amy had said as she dropped him off at the airport that morning. She had offered to come with him, and now he was wishing he'd said yes. She was more than six hundred miles away.

The neighborhood had handled the years gracefully. Beautiful homes—mostly Spanish style with red clay roofs— lined the street on both sides. Mature palm trees stood sentry in every yard. This particular house was plainer than most. Tidy and friendly looking, but there was nothing remarkable about it. Under different circumstances, he would have driven right by, unaware that this was the place where the world had changed. According to the phone book, they still lived in the same house after all these years.

The Deli Detective closed the car door behind him and walked up the path to the front door. A wooden sign read, "The Andersons." Sid stood and looked at it for a long time before knocking. He wasn't sure why, but he thought it was one of the saddest things he'd ever seen. Finally his hand reached out and rapped three times on the door, and then he waited. He tried one last time in these final seconds to think of what to say. But the words for a moment like this didn't exist.

Then the door opened.

Later, as they sat talking around the kitchen table, Sid would notice the few remaining streaks of yellow that wove their way through her silver hair. He would see something familiar in the curve of her neck, the way she moved her hands. She would cry and she would laugh, and he would occasionally catch a glimpse of the beauty that once had been hers. Those were all things that he would see later.

But for the moment, standing at the front door of a house in Phoenix on a Saturday afternoon, all he saw was the tiny cleft in her chin. And the green eyes.

Paul Robins

ACKNOWLEDGMENTS

I am so thankful for the people in my life that give me the encouragement and freedom to spend a year writing a book. They are present on every page, though any errors or offenses are entirely my responsibility.

My first novel was dedicated to my wife. All of them would be, but I assume there's some rule against that, so Bridget gets top billing in "Acknowledgments." I adore her.

Ian Cornell was, once again, my indispensable sounding board and confidante. I couldn't do it without him. Ian and my friend, Sheila Auth, read the book several times and managed to catch every misteak except the one in this sentence. Joe Cipov gets credit again for sharing his cop wisdom, and my attorney pal Ken Rosenfeld was wonderfully helpful. For medical questions, I turn to Doc Stewart, master of both the stethoscope and the saxophone. And my source of all dental knowledge is the generous and affable Dr. Jerry Martin, who makes cavities fun. Thanks, too, to Rich Hanna (who runs faster than Sid) and Connie Neal, whose insights are astute and encouraging.

One of the joys of writing is finding new friends who can help you understand their unique and interesting professions. That's how I came to spend time with real life private investigator Doug Moutinho and martial arts wizard Dave Kovar—great guys not to be trifled with.

A special thank-you to Anne Rudin, Sacramento's former mayor and one of the most gracious ladies I've ever had the pleasure to meet. She has put up with my impertinence more than once. Our lunch discussing city government in the 80's was a delight.

Finally, there's a splendid organization in Sacramento called WEAVE that should not be confused with the fictional group in this novel. I admire WEAVE very much, and it's my hope that anything written in these pages would only reflect well on them and their fearless Executive Director, Beth Hassett. She has helped me understand a world that I grew up blissfully ignorant of.

ABOUT THE AUTHOR

Paul Robins is a successful broadcaster, an avid reader, a slow but devoted runner, and a writer of mystery novels. His morning radio resume includes brief stops in Detroit & Dallas, and a wonderfully long one in Sacramento, California. In TV-land, Paul appeared for several years on The Discovery Channel as one of "The Answer Guys" and is currently seen on PBS's "America's Heartland." He can also be found anchoring the news weekday mornings on KTXL FOX40 in Sacramento.

Paul has been married to Bridget Robins for 37 priceless years. His daughters, their husbands, and all the grandsons call him "Pops."

51149462R00226

Made in the USA
San Bernardino, CA
14 July 2017